Book one of The ABC Chronicles

DREW HALFPENNY

First published in Great Britain in 2022 by Gunmetal & Gilt Publishing.

Copyright © Drew Halfpenny, 2022

The moral right of the author is hereby asserted.

This is a work of fiction.
*All characters, events and places in this publication,
other than those clearly in the public domain,
are fictitious and any resemblance to actual persons,
living or dead, is purely coincidental.*
All rights reserved.

No part of this publication may be reproduced, stored in a retrieval system, or transmitted, in any form or by any means, electronic, mechanical, photocopying, recording or otherwise, without the prior written consent of the publisher, nor be otherwise circulated in any form of binding or cover other than that in which it is published and without a similar condition being imposed on the subsequent purchaser.

A CIP catalogue record for this book is available from the British Library.

1 3 5 7 9 10 8 6 4 2

ISBN: 978-1-7396970-0-6

To Sharon, Danny and Charlie

Thanks for all the love, support and similes all along the way.

For Sue

Thank you for your
Friendship and Support

ONE

The Cut

GILBERT SHRUGGED. THE RAIN-SOAKED autumn of 1891 had turned the bottom of the Cut into a quagmire. Banished by gangmaster Grubb to work alone in the foul, weed-choked sluices in the shadow of the lock, six hours of working ankle-deep in the icy, black, fetid water had made his feet numb and his resolve steel. The vile stench of rotting vegetation and dead insects made him want to vomit, but he refused to give Grubb that pleasure.

In the Cut, meks did the heavy, dirty work. Their durable synthetic bodies never tired, their clockwork mechanisms never faltered, neither foul air nor freezing temperatures could stop them, and, of course, they never, ever complained.

He was being punished, but worse, he was being humiliated. Grubb knew. His gang knew. And he knew. Enough was enough. His mind was made up. *If Grubb reports me to engineer Wainwright, I'll tell him where to stick the job. I couldn't care less*, he thought.

Only a few months earlier, it had been so different. An advertisement pasted onto his local bakery wall had announced in big, bold letters –

Wanted!
The Manchester Ship Canal Company needs strong young fellows to labour on the engineering marvel of the age.
Good wages.
Join us and become part of history!

His heart had leapt. This job was the opportunity of a lifetime. But as a local lad, he had struggled to fit in with Grubb's gang of Irish navvies, and after weeks of taunts from the flame-haired Flanagan brothers, he had finally snapped at the food cart.

Now, head pounding, blood rushing to his cheeks, he strangled the roar from deep within through gritted teeth. If only he had controlled his temper.

But no one would have heard his scream. The sudden, deafening drone of a dirigible overhead echoed off the lock's black brickwork. Normally, he would have watched in awe as the pilot banked the triple-bagger into the prevailing northerly wind, swooping low over the Cut and wheeling towards the aerodrome, but this was not a typical day. He bowed his head.

Bloody Flanagans!

Chill, dank air swirled around him. Hands stuffed into his pockets, shivering, alone in the shadows, shunned by his fellow workers, he awaited his fate. He tilted his head back, sucking in another lungful of the noxious stench, coughed, and a single tear squeezed from the corner of his stinging, screwed-up eyes.

Mercifully, his working day was coming to its end. At six o'clock, the whistle would blow, ending his ten-hour shift. Perhaps Grubb hadn't reported him. Maybe he would not get the sack. His sigh tasted of sluice filth. He pressed his lips together and swallowed hard to keep down the bile rising in his throat. He pulled out his pocket watch. It was nearly clocking off time, and tomorrow was payday.

Two minutes to the end of the shift.

A lot could happen in two minutes.

With every tick of the second hand, the closing whistle drew nearer, and work on the Cut wound down. NR-G meks and nippers, gathering discarded tools, skittered across the mud in all directions, like ants. To many, meks were the lowest of the low, but their menial efforts enabled the navvies to graft and the bosses to strut around in their tall hats and fancy clothes.

A gentle tug on his coat made him look down. Big, watery brown eyes looked up at him. The poor nipper was trying not to retch, pinching his nose between a grubby thumb and forefinger. Without a word, the lad pressed a small, dirty beige envelope into Gilbert's palm, turned on his heel and hurried away. *Tiny for a fourteen-year-old*, he thought. *He probably lied about his age to get the job.*

A loud burst of laughter from the shadows on the far side of the Cut, startled him. Grubb and his cronies were sharing a joke, and all eyes were on Gilbert. Although the lickspittle navvies around the gangmaster were laughing, Grubb stared daggers at him; his mouth bent into a sneer that could strip paint. Puffed-out barrel chest, hands on his hips, he was a double-handled chamber pot of boiling piss.

Gilbert returned the glare, crumpling the envelope in his tightening fist.

After another deep breath of rank air, he lowered his stinging eyes. 'Mr G Sparks,' was scrawled in child-like handwriting on the front, while the seal on the back was still wet with Grubb's slobber. He didn't need to open it. The contents were apparent, but he peeled the flap, reflecting on how he had never liked the job and reaffirming that they could stick it for all he cared.

His shoulders slumped. He had been summoned to engineer Wainwright's office after work to 'explain the incident at the food cart.' He ran his fingers over the grazed knuckles on his right fist and winced. *I don't care. It was worth it.*

Mud squelched under his boots as he stumbled on numb feet out of the sluices, jeers and laughter ringing in his ears. He trudged to the makeshift steps which led up and out of the partially completed lock, slipping as he stepped out of the muck, arms flailing in a crazy dance to regain his balance.

The six o'clock whistle interrupted another burst of raucous jeering across the Cut. He grasped the handrails and hauled his aching body up the stairs. Each reluctant step, leaving a muddy imprint, took him closer to his fate.

At the top, he surveyed the evening landscape. Weeks of persistent rain had finally stopped midafternoon, and the sun hung low above the southwestern horizon. Its golden rays danced like flames along the edges of the metal superstructures of the dirigibles gently swaying on their moorings at the aerodrome a quarter of a mile to the north-west.

The metronomic pounding of the pile drivers to the west slowed as their steam engines powered down. He closed his eyes. The warm sunlight made his cheeks tingle. Somewhere, a solitary blackbird sang a shrill eventide refrain. Was his song celebrating the sunset or announcing his presence to potential mates or rivals? Perhaps he was protesting the devastation of his habitat? Gilbert couldn't care less.

Come on, Bertie, chin up. There's always a bright side. The memory of his late mother's soft voice gave him much-needed strength. He straightened his back and stepped off the slick, wet brickwork onto the muddy path to the assistant engineer's office, his head held high.

After all, he was Gilbert Sparks, and he could do whatever his heart desired.

The sweet smell of damp soil was a welcome respite from the sluice stench. Wary of the slippery ground, he stepped carefully, his boots squelching in the thick mud. Up ahead, Gilbert recognised the wiry old night watchman searching for wood to fill his brazier for the night's vigil.

Stan Miller straightened and smiled. "Ayup, Gilbert. I hear you've been a naughty boy."

"Cut gossip travels fast." Gilbert shook his head. "I don't know, Stan. It's like being back at school. Here I am, just got the key-of-the-door, and I feel like they've sent me to the headmaster for six of the best. The bloody Flanagans are the problem, not me. If Wainwright sacks me, I'll tell him where he can stick the job."

"That's *Mister* Wainwright to you, lad."

"Aye, I know. I'll see you when I come out."

"Remember to take off your cap. Show him some respect, mind. He's got an 'orrible temper. 'Orrible."

Gilbert flicked a left-handed salute, and Stan waved him away with a smile and went back to gathering twigs and branches for his brazier.

Weeks of heavy rainfall had soaked everything, reducing work to a crawl. Cloying mud sapped energy and strength, morale was at rock bottom, the project was behind schedule, and the engineers were tetchy. Gangmasters struggled to keep discipline amongst the seventy thousand navvies stretched over the thirty-six miles of the big dig.

Delays cost money.

They needed a spell of dry weather to get back on track and lift their spirits.

Gilbert approached the assistant engineer's office, wiping the remaining mud off his boots on the scraper at the doorstep. Salteye Brook burbled behind the hut. Sunlight sparkled on the tips of the waves like silver dancers. He removed his cap and knocked on the door.

Silence.

He took his courage in both hands, turned the handle and stepped inside. Pungent pipe smoke leaked through the open door, stinging his nose. Trying not to cough, he squinted through the thick, smoky layer hanging at head height at Emmett Wainwright sitting behind his desk, drawing on a long-stemmed clay pipe. A stout, ruddy-faced man, Wainwright was a life-sized toby jug without the tricorn hat. The top of his desk was buried beneath a chaotic mass of papers and plans.

"Were you born in a barn, lad? Put th'wood in th'hole. You're letting all th'warmth out," he said, without lifting his head.

Quietly shutting the door, Gilbert stood in silence, gripping his cap with both hands for what seemed like an eternity. A blackened, pot-bellied stove in the corner blasting out a fiercesome heat, caused beads of sweat to roll down his face and neck. His shirt clung to his sweat-drenched body.

Wainwright leaned back in his chair and drew on his clay pipe, sending more thick clouds of grey smoke billowing towards the wooden ceiling.

"Now then, Sparks, what's going on? You must have done summat really bad for Mister Grubb to see fit to send you to me. He knows I'm busy, so it must be serious. What've you been up to?"

"It were nowt, Mister Wainwright."

"That's not what I've been told, lad. He says you started a fight. Is that right?"

Gilbert felt the blood rush to his cheeks. "The Flanagan brothers provoked me. They've been picking on me for weeks, so I did something about it. I decked Fergus, and if Grubb hadn't got between us, I would have given them both a good hiding."

Wainwright shook his head. "And what did this Fergus do that made you take a swing at him? It must have been summat bad."

"He called me Bertie." It sounded trivial, but he didn't care—it was important to him.

Wainwright's brow wrinkled as he raised his eyebrows. "And?"

"No one calls me Bertie. No one." Gilbert spoke through gritted teeth and tightened the grip on his cap. *He doesn't understand; nobody does.*

"Well, think before you pick a fight, lad. The Flanagans are ex-servicemen, you know. Navy, they tell me. They could have taken you apart, I reckon. Can't you take a bit o' banter?"

"It won't happen again, Mister Wainwright."

Wainwright slapped his hands on the desk as he pushed himself to his feet. "No, *Mister* Sparks, it won't happen again!"

Gilbert straightened his back, raising himself to his full height. "Are you going to sack me? 'Cos I don't think—"

"No, Mister Sparks. There lies the problem. You don't think, do you?" He paused for a few seconds, weighing up Gilbert, his eyes moving from head to toe and back again. "Mister Grubb wants me to sack you. And I probably should…"

"Well, you can—"

Wainwright raised a hand. "But I've got a better idea."

"I don't understand."

"No, I dare say you don't." Wainwright eased himself back into his chair. "You see, lad, it's my job to know what's going on around here, and one of my little birds tells me you're a good worker, a problem solver, and a quick learner. I like that in a young fellow."

Gilbert frowned, narrowing his eyes. Grubb had sent him to Wainwright's office to be disciplined. *Who's been watching me?*

"Hear me out, lad. I've built up a reputation as a man who always gets things done. When a project involves water, canals, aqueducts, bridges, piers and the like, the big wigs look to old Emmett Wainwright to do the job right and on time.

"I've worked with the greatest engineers this country has produced." It took a gargantuan effort for Gilbert not to roll his eyes. He had heard about Wainwright's boasts of past glories. "Isambard, Eugenius, you name 'em, I've worked with 'em."

Gilbert shrugged. "What's that got to do with me?"

"I have a crew that I use on all my projects. Grafters who are loyal to me. Men that I can count on to follow my orders to the letter, if you get my drift. My lads do the job proper. Chief engineers trust me, so they keep giving me contracts. That, in turn, guarantees work for my gang. Understand?"

Gilbert nodded. The heat was unbearable; sweat was pouring off him in rivulets.

"I like the cut of your jib, Sparks." He looked Gilbert up and down again. "So, are you interested?"

"Interested in what?"

"In joining the team, lad, in joining the team." Wainwright didn't hide his irritation.

Gilbert lowered his eyes and shuffled his feet. Wainwright's intense stare burned holes in his head as an icy realisation washed over him. Like a lost stranger at a fork in the road in a horror story, there was a right and a wrong direction to turn. The sweat on his back froze. He shuddered.

"Aye, Mister Wainwright, I'd like that very much."

Wainwright looked from under his bushy eyebrows and wagged his finger at him. "I figured you for a smart kid. I've already given instructions for you to join Horace Hastings's gang. They're working further up the Cut, well away from your friends, the Flanagans. Report to him in the morning, eight o'clock sharp."

"I won't let you down."

Wainwright tapped his pipe on the side of the table. "Just do as you're told and keep in mind, you're my man now."

"I don't suppose there'll be any more money in it for me? I'm earning four pennies, one farthing an hour. A bit extra wouldn't go amiss."

"Aye, I dare say it wouldn't. But you suppose right, no more money. Prove yourself to be someone I can rely on, and I'll look after you. Loyalty cuts both ways. Now, get off home."

Gilbert pulled on his cap and tugged the peak. His face tingled as he stepped out of the stifling office, the sweat chilled by the light evening breeze. Invigorated by a huge gulp of smoke-free air, he set off to the bike shed with a skip in his step. Stan must have been collecting kindling for his brazier as he was nowhere to be seen.

He shook his head, still trying to understand what just happened. Before he spoke with Wainwright, he was certain he was going to be sacked. Now, striding away from the engineer's hut with a secure job and a spring in his step, the future was rosy. He had always been skilled with his hands but never expected to get noticed by the bosses so soon.

The opportunity of a career in civil engineering, learning from the likes of Emmett Wainwright, was a dream come true. He couldn't wait to tell his father. Mum would have been proud, too. *Good for you, Bertie. Well done.*

When he reached the bike shelter, he stopped dead in his tracks. Lips pressed tightly together, balling his fists, he stared at his deflated bicycle tyres.

Bloody Flanagans!

Wainwright was wrong. He could take them. They were only flyboys. Rumour had it the Navy had discharged them from the First Air Battalion for disobeying orders. *They're not proper soldiers.*

He picked up his bike and set off on the mile and a-half journey home, with the setting sun at his back and wind in his sails

Back in the engineer's office, Emmett Wainwright sat back in his chair and pressed a clump of Ansties Extra Fine Shag into the bowl of his pipe. His meeting with Sparks had gone as planned.

Of course, there was always a risk when bringing in new blood, but the crew needed freshening up, and he was a big, strapping fellow, good with his hands by all accounts and eager to learn.

He chuckled as he thought of the big lad stood in his thick brown overcoat, green work trousers and filthy knee-length boots, twiddling with his cap and, judging by his lank black hair, sweating like a canary in a coal mine.

He walked over to the pot-bellied stove, using a spill to relight his pipe before closing the side vents with a poker. Starved of air, the blazing fire would die within the hour.

Soon he would make his way home, where his beloved Rosie would have his supper ready. *Ah*, he thought, *Thursday is kedgeree night*. He and the kids loved the exotic flavours from the East.

The sun was just above the horizon when he left his office to inspect the day's work. Daylight would soon surrender to the darkness; the evening autumn air was already acquiring its icy bite.

He closed the door and walked past the hut where the night watchman was busy trying to ignite the fruits of his scavenging. Nights turned bitterly cold at this time of year in the north of England.

"Evenin,' gaffer." Stanley touched the peak of his cap in deference.

"Looks like it might be a foggy one tonight, Stanley. Mist already rising out of the Cut, and the sun's not even set yet."

"Aye, that damned rain hasn't helped none. It'll be a real pea-souper later, I reckon. 'Orrible!"

Wainwright nodded and walked on. Reaching the edge of the lock, he peered into the newly built black brick chasm. Fifty feet below, he could just make out the brickwork at the bottom, shrouded in shadow and mist. Here at the easternmost end of the lock, he could look up the Cut towards the aqueduct which carried the Bridgewater Canal over the River Irwell. So ornate was the aqueduct's stonework that locals called it The Castle in the Air.

The setting sun bathed the scene in a golden light reminiscent of a Turner painting his friend Isambard had once shown him. Grey vapours wreathed stone piers, writhing, grasping for the aqueduct voussoirs, ghosts scaling the stones hewn by long-dead masons.

The aqueduct had stood for a hundred and fifty years because of the ingenuity of eighteenth-century engineers. What must it have been like back in those olden golden days? No steam engines, no diggers, no trains, just skill and raw, pure manpower. *Simple people in a simpler time.* He shook his head and sighed.

Nowadays, plans and modifications have to pass through committee after committee, each with its own agenda. Then there were the Connickle laws, the bane of free-thinking men. He cleared his throat and spat into the lock, causing eddies to form in the swirling mist.

Closing his eyes, he shuddered. The meagre warmth of the setting sun was dwindling. *Stanley will be glad of the heat from his brazier.*

A chill slid over his neck as a shadow passed across the sun. He turned to find the silhouette of an enormous figure standing a few feet away from him. Startled, he tried to peer around the man, looking for Stanley. How had the stranger got past the old man? He squinted up at the shadowed face, but even screwing up his eyes, he could not make out his features.

"Mister Wainwright? Mister Emmett Wainwright?" The man's soft and deliberate words were clouds of condensed breath backlit by the setting sun.

"Yes, who—"

"These are for you." The stranger thrust a wad of papers at his chest.

Wainwright looked down, grasping at the papers with both hands. Through narrowed eyes, he struggled to read in the shadow. He raised his eyebrows, "But these are my—".

The monstrous silhouette took a step forward, grabbing Wainwright's coat lapels in a vice-like grip and heaved him off his feet. Two more steps, then he launched the engineer off the lock.

He cartwheeled, limbs flailing, papers scattering in the chill breeze.

Wainwright smashed into the brickwork below with a sickening crack.

The stranger watched as papers fluttered in the evening sky like confetti, gently landing on the wet ground by the engineer's broken, grotesquely contorted corpse. He peered down into the dank darkness as Wainwright's dead eyes stared up at him, slowly disappearing under the ghostly mantle of mist eddies forming a cold, grey shroud around the body.

Satisfied he had completed his grim task, he spat over the side of the lock, turned and strode away without a thought of looking back. Only the night watchman stood between him and the safety of the road beyond.

Coat collar pulled up against the biting chill, his unblinking gaze focussed on the muddy path a few feet ahead. His metronomic pace didn't slow as the elderly man came bustling out of his hut, arms stretching to warm his hands at the brazier.

The night watchman caught his breath as the dark figure loomed out of the gathering mist. His old heart must have missed a beat, given his fearful expression illuminated in the light from the brazier's flickering flames.

Wainwright's killer strode on, heat from fire warming his cheeks as he neared the hut.

Their eyes met.

A moment of recognition preceded an exchange of nods, a grim accord of ruthless resignation.

The stranger walked on without breaking stride, disappearing into the inky blackness of a moonless night, leaving Stanley Miller to the bone-chilling fog.

TWO

New Dawn

THE JOURNEY HOME HAD been miserable. Flat tyres dragging on the paving stones, Gilbert pushed his wounded bicycle along the pavement for the last few yards, weary from such a lengthy walk. The sun had long since set, and the thickening fog had taken on the greenish hue of the streetlights as darkness descended. The army of lamplighters must have started early, anticipating another pea-souper.

Black smoke belched from chimneys atop rows and rows of terraced homes built for families of workers who toiled in the factories and mills, filling the freezing, foggy night air with the familiar smell of coal fires.

Fog muffling his footsteps and those of half seen passers-by, a thoroughly chilled-to-the-bone Gilbert trudged down Mayfield Street. The red-leaded doorsteps and fine lace curtains of the large, terraced houses announced industrious artisans lived there, a step above the less fortunate working-class families and a storey from the slums and hovels of the destitute. Home, for Gilbert, was halfway along the street.

Stomach grumbling, he opened the front door to the mouth-watering aroma of hotpot.

"That you, Gil bach?" His father shouted from the back of the house. "You're late, son. Been working overtime, have you?"

"There were a bit of trouble at work. I had to see old Wainwright." Gilbert walked through to the kitchen, where his father had set the table for the evening meal.

"Flanagan brothers, was it?"

"Aye. I shouldn't have reacted, but I'd had enough."

"That temper of yours will get you into proper trouble one day." He reached up and ruffled Gilbert's hair, winked, and smiled. "I hope you gave the annoying squirts a good hiding. It was about your mam again, wasn't it?"

Of course, it was. Gilbert was desperate to preserve his memories of his mother. She had called him 'my little Bertie,' and since her tragic death, he let no one call him Bertie, not even his father. Anyone using that name diluted the memory of her gentle, caring voice. The Flanagan brothers knew how to get under Gilbert's skin and revelled when they succeeded.

This was a discussion about his mother he didn't want to have tonight. "It won't happen again, anyway. Wainwright's moved me into the gang he takes on all his projects. It's a big step up for me."

"That's great, Gil bach. Proper proud of yourself, you should be."

"I join them tomorrow, so there'll be no more trouble from the bloody Flanagans."

"Language, Gil." His father disapproved of swearing.

His father started ladling the hotpot into two dishes resting on his mother's treasured floral tablecloth. He always tried to make mealtimes as they had been before the accident.

"Mam would be very proud of you, too. Although I'm not so sure she would've approved of this ship canal project. Very keen on nature and little furry animals, she was. Lots of natural habitat being destroyed because of the Cut. Your mam—"

"Mum would be happy that I've settled into a job I love and that they've rewarded my hard work. She'd understand. It's called progress, Dad."

"Whoa, bach. No need for raised voices at the tea table. I think about your mam every day, too, you know. When you're not here, I talk to her. We have some proper lively conversations, like when she was… anyway, I miss her every bit as much as you do.

"All I was saying—" he lifted his hand to stop his son interrupting again, "was just that your mam thought things were going a bit too quick, like. Railways, mills, and factories were ruining the countryside, and all the smoke from chimneys was making the weather worse. She said the fogs were thicker now than when she was a girl."

Gilbert sat in silence eating his hotpot, reflecting on how his father would never understand how the Industrial Revolution had changed everything for the good. There was no going back. *The world is a better place now than it was a hundred years ago.*

Even though his father's skills as a watchmaker were needed, with clockwork being the major power for rural machinery, trams, and small contraptions, steam was powering the Industrial Revolution.

Father advocated the old ways while Gilbert embraced the new. The construction of the ship canal would take years longer without the huge steam-powered tunnellers, diggers, and pile drivers, which justified their use in Gilbert's eyes. After all, the canal would provide a quicker, cleaner way of transporting goods in and out of Manchester, would it not?

Because he was feeling positive about the future, he chose not to argue, refusing to let anything spoil his mood.

"All me and your mam wanted for you, Gil, was for you to get a good job, settle down and start a family. It looks like you've found your dream job with Wainwright. Now, if we can just find you a nice young lady…" Dafydd Sparks smiled across the tea table, firelight twinkling in his eyes.

"Aye." Gilbert relaxed his shoulders and returned the smile. "Let me get my feet under Wainwright's table first."

As always, his father had done his mother's Lancashire hotpot recipe proud, and soon they were mopping up the last few drops with big wedges of crusty bread.

His father picked up the empty dishes and walked over to the Belfast sink. "I'll make us a brew."

Gilbert leaned back, stretching his arms over his head as his father spooned leaf tea into the teapot. He watched, counted, and smiled. *One per person and one for the pot,* his mother used to say. He thought about her every day, his guilt over her death never diminishing, wishing with all his heart that she was still here.

Since her death, he had found relationships difficult, both at work and outside. As soon as he got close to someone, he would do something stupid, causing the friendship to end in bitterness and rancour. His father reckoned he couldn't bring himself to love anyone because of the fear of losing them, but Gilbert knew better. No one would ever match his mother. He was perfectly fine on his own, and he would solve his own problems without anyone's help.

Father and son carried their cups of tea into the parlour and settled down in the easy chairs. The room had the musty, undusted odour found only in seldom-used rooms. The chair where his mother sat seemed especially lonely tonight.

Gilbert coughed.

"That's quite a bark you've got there, bach," his father said.

"Probably coming down with a chill. I've been standing in freezing cold water all afternoon." Gilbert wiped his nose on his sleeve.

"It's not the cough that carries you off…" His father waited for him to finish the saying that he had heard a million times.

Smiling, Gilbert cocked his head to one side, raising his eyebrow while remaining silent, trying not to roll his eyes.

"You know, Gil, you've got to stop blaming yourself for your mam's death. There was nothing you could do. It wasn't your fault."

"We wouldn't have been there if I hadn't mithered her to see the trains." Gilbert lowered his eyes.

"And she wouldn't have taken you if she hadn't wanted to…"

Gilbert raised his hands. "We've been over this a hundred times, Dad. You won't change my mind, and I don't want to talk about it tonight." He closed his eyes, resting his head on the back of his chair, and pictured his late mother's smile.

Memories of happy days flooded his mind. Going for walks, piggybacks home from his mother when his legs were tired, feeling so safe on her shoulders. He wished those long sunny days had never ended.

"Gil bach?" His father's gentle voice awakened him. "Time for bed. Early start for you in the morning. You don't want to be late for your new boss, now do you?"

Gilbert yawned, slowly pushing himself up from the comfortable chair, arms and legs still aching from the day's labour. While his father busied himself turning off the gas mantles, he checked and locked the front and back doors before making his way upstairs to bed.

Tomorrow was the first day of an exciting new start.

Gilbert woke early from a deep sleep, and after breakfast, with the prospect of a dry, sunny day, both he and his father left their bicycles at home; Gilbert chose to walk to work whilst his father took the tram. Although they set off together, they went their separate ways at the end of the street.

His father turned left towards the new tram terminus in the town centre. The recent extension of the Tick Tock Tram line into Eccles was a real boon for businesses but also for well-heeled locals who wanted to sample the sometimes dubious but always interesting delights of Manchester's pubs, taverns, music halls and less salubrious haunts.

Dafydd Sparks was a repairman at Aurelius Badger, the esteemed clockwork manufacturer. Their premises in Manchester were a short walk from Central Station, the hub for local trams and a principal station on the HyBrid train network, which crisscrossed the country. Although there had been strong public opposition to the expensive, trilateral HB2 line connecting Manchester to Leeds and both cities to Birmingham and London, many northern businesses, including Aurelius Badger, had benefitted from the fast, environmentally friendly service.

Gilbert's right turn onto Liverpool Road took him through Patricroft and Peel Green towards Barton. He acknowledged the cheery wave of one of the hardy men who worked at each end of the day in all weather— knocker-uppers in the morning and lamplighters in the evening—hazy sunshine lighting up his breath as the moisture condensed in the freezing air. *I wonder if that makes the fog worse*, he mused. He couldn't remember the last time he had such a frivolous thought.

Treetops rustled in the light breeze as he walked past the schoolhouse. He ran his fingers along the frosty edges of its black iron railings and smiled as the sunlight sparkled off the ice melting on his skin.

The distinctive clockwork tick-tock of a green and black tram echoed off the buildings on the main road as it rocked and rumbled along the rails. With his work bag over his shoulder, Gilbert felt so alive striding across the humpbacked span over the Bridgewater Canal and past the Patricroft Tavern, which still reeked of stale smoke and booze from the previous night's revelries.

Steam-powered tunnelling machines, diggers and pile drivers were starting up in the distance, shattering the early morning birdsong, but he was accustomed to working with their deep pulsating rhythm, and his steps soon fell in time with the heavy, steady beat.

Two hundred yards from Barton lock, the engines slowed and fell silent. Puzzled, he walked on, quickening his pace. A cart careened past him at speed, steel-rimmed wheels clattering along the cobbled streets, the driver cracking his whip at the galloping horse, trying to get every ounce of effort from the poor beast.

Rounding a small copse at the side of the road, he turned towards the canal workings. A pang of fear jolted through his body. Something terrible had happened. Navvies were running to the lock, many in the Cut, others along the banks.

Only once before had he seen this reaction, so he knew that someone must have been seriously injured, or worse.

His walk quickened into a run and soon became a dead sprint as he joined the hordes converging on the lock, where Stanley Miller, gaunt and grey, stood on top of the black brickwork with a shorter, younger man. Gilbert reached them and bent over, hands on his knees, gasping for breath.

"What's happened, Stan?" he said between gulps of air.

"It's 'orrible." Stan nodded towards the floor of the lock. "It's Wainwright. He must've been there all night, poor bugger. Horace, here, found him. 'Orrible."

Gilbert looked over the edge but stepped back in horror. Wainwright's body lay broken on the brickwork, surrounded by sheets of paper and a stunned, silent workforce.

"We've sent for the coroner and the police. It looks like an accident, but the men have been told to touch nowt in case there were foul play," Horace said.

"'Orrible to think I was sitting just over there outside my hut with Wainwright lying dead a few yards away. Poor bugger must have slipped."

"Don't go blaming yourself, Stan. No one thinks it's your fault."

"Fog was so thick, Horace, you couldn't hear nowt. I thought he'd gone home, poor bugger."

Gilbert's mouth was dry, panic rising in his chest as the enormity of Wainwright's death washed over him. "Why was he out on't lock in the fog?"

"I don't know, lad. I don't know."

A dirigible's motors sputtered to life at the aerodrome. Gilbert watched the airship gracefully rise from its mooring, banking to head in their direction. "Mister Wainwright was going to move me to his team. I was due to start today. I don't know what to do."

"That's my crew, lad. I'm Horace Hastings, Mister Wainwright's gangmaster. Or at least, I was until this morning."

They fell silent as the drone of the dirigible, that would have drowned their words, passed overhead and turned west, following the Cut towards Liverpool. Gilbert watched the dark crimson airship as it swung gracefully away. He could not drag his gaze from the intricate detailing on the dark red gondola. "So, what will happen to you and your crew now?"

"Your guess is as good as mine. S'pose they'll bring in a new engineer to take over this part of the project, but will they use my gang? They need us, but they know we were Wainwright's men, so I don't know if they will keep us on." He turned his head, hawking up phlegm that spattered into the mud.

"Here comes the coroner." Stan nodded at the police wagon turning off the main road and heading towards them.

Ice-cold realisation washed over Gilbert. Not only had his hopes for the future disappeared, but since he was probably the last person to see Emmett Wainwright alive, the police might want to ask him a few questions.

The grey, grim-faced man emerged from the vehicle, wearing one of the tallest top hats he had ever seen. His long, black, ankle-length coat was unbuttoned, flapping behind him as he walked. Reaching into his waistcoat, he pulled out his pocket watch, sunlight glinting off the finely engraved gold case.

A police officer appeared from the other side of the wagon, patting the police horse before joining the coroner. The two men strode over to the lock, and Horace Hastings was first to speak. "He's at the bottom of the lock." He pointed at the body. "Stairs are over here." The coroner nodded and made his way to examine the corpse.

"Now, gentlemen. What has occurred here?" The police officer tipped his helmet as he addressed the three men.

"I'm the night watchman, Stanley Miller. Me and Horace Hastings, here, work for Wainwright and found his body this morning."

The officer turned towards Gilbert. "And who might you be, young man?"

"Gilbert Sparks, sir. I saw Mister Wainwright last night before I set off home."

"We think he must have slipped off the lock in the fog. Poor bugger," Stanley chimed in.

"Do you, now? Well, let's see what Mister Shillington, the coroner, has to say, shall we?" The police officer eyed each of the three men. Gilbert looked away, lowering his eyes.

They stood in silence for what seemed like a lifetime, watching Mister Shillington making notes in his little red book as he examined the body and surroundings.

"Any chance of a cuppa?" The officer glanced around hopefully.

Stanley nodded, scurrying off to his hut. By the time he returned with a tin cup of steaming hot tea, the coroner had arranged for a stretcher to be brought to remove the body and was making his way back up the stairs to the top of the lock.

Mister Shillington tucked his notebook into his breast pocket as he approached the policeman. "No signs of a struggle. In my professional opinion, he slipped in the dark and fell to his death. Broke his neck and died instantly."

"Poor bugger," Stan said.

"You heard nothing, Mister—" the police officer checked his notes, "Miller?"

"Nowt. It was a proper pea-souper last night. I heard nowt."

"Next of kin?" The officer licked the tip of his pencil.

"He had a wife and kids. I'll get his address for you." Horace turned and made his way through the mud to Wainwright's hut.

"Get yourself off home, Mister Miller. You've had a long night and a bit of a shock this morning." The police officer said.

"Aye, poor bugger."

"And you, Mister—"

"Sparks, Gilbert Sparks, sir."

"Yes, Mister Sparks, go about your business. No point hanging around this grim place."

"Yes, sir. I'll see if Mister Hastings needs any help."

In Wainwright's hut, Hastings was rummaging through Wainwright's desk, cursing under his breath. Gilbert spread his arms. "I don't know what to do, Mister Hastings. If I can't join your crew, where do I go?" *Grubb won't want me, and I don't want to work near the Flanagans again.*

"Go back to your old gang, put in a shift, and collect your wages. That's what I'm going to do when I find this damned address. Stupid old fool. What was he doing on the lock? In the fog. In the dark. It makes no sense to me."

"I can't believe it either."

"Ha! Got it." Hastings held up an envelope in triumph. "Get yourself off to work, lad. Now, where has that police officer gone?" He hurried out of the office, looking left and right.

Gilbert followed and started along the north bank. Although there were still several men lingering in the lock, the steam engines were starting up again. *Just another tragic death on the Cut, and the job must go on.* But to Gilbert, a return to his old gang meant the end of hope and re-joining battle with the dreaded Flanagan brothers.

Although it only contained his lunch, his work bag had never felt heavier as he trudged away from a hopeful future back into an uncomfortable present.

That evening, watery light from the feeble horns of the waxing crescent moon gave little illumination as the nightly fog rose. Gilbert had collected his wages, knowing he had earned every farthing of the twenty-one shillings and threepence, toiling for six days of ten-hour shifts. But he couldn't bring himself to go home and tell his father what had happened to Wainwright. That would have to wait. He needed a beer.

The Patricroft Tavern was the nearest public house. Although he knew it would be full of navvies with money burning holes in their pockets and eager to drink themselves senseless, he needed something, anything, to lift his broken spirits.

He pushed through the tavern's double doors into a smoke-filled, heaving mass of male testosterone, laughing, shouting, singing and brawling. This was Gilbert's second time in a public house and the first time without his father.

Four almost identical RT-series mekamanikins behind the bar were working furiously to keep the beer flowing and the patrons happy. Gilbert fought his way through the bodies, boots scuffing the spittle-spattered sawdust, and waved a coin at the nearest barman.

"Now, young fellow-me-lad," it said in a flat, vaguely metallic tone, "you do not appear to be old enough to be visiting this hostelry. If you are not twenty-one, then *this 'kin* must—"

"I'll vouch for him." Stanley Miller, leaning on the bar, interrupted.

"Thanks, Stan." He turned back to the mek. "Pint of porter, please."

"That will be nine pence." The barman pulled a pint of the dark liquid into a pewter pot.

"You not working tonight, Stan?" He gave the mek a shilling and waited for the change.

"They told me not to work tonight, and I can't say I'm sorry. Bit of a shock this morning, old Wainwright lying dead in the lock all night yards away from me, poor bugger."

"I still can't figure what he was doing."

"There's some that say it weren't an accident." Horace Hastings put his hand on Gilbert's shoulder and his mouth next to his ear. "Perhaps he was murdered."

"Murdered? Wainwright? Who'd want to kill him?" Gilbert found it difficult to imagine the old engineer had any enemies set on killing him.

Hastings looked all around him, then leaned forward as Gilbert and Stan edged closer. "There's a rumour that there's a group of anarchists who are hell bent on stopping the canal being dug. Nasty bunch by all accounts."

"Anarchists?" Gilbert nearly dropped his beer. "But why kill old Wainwright?"

"Old? Show some respect, lad. Poor bugger," Stanley said.

"Because he was a famous engineer, an easy target, and they could make it look like an accident." Hastings straightened and banged his empty pot on the bar.

"Same again?" The attentive mek scooped up the pewter tankard and pulled another pint of porter into it. "That will be nine pence."

"Hard to get drunk at these prices," Hastings pressed each coin into the mek's outstretched hand.

"I can't see it," Stan said. "Coroner said there were no sign of a struggle and, anyway, the bricks was slippery because of the rain—"

"Easy to push an old man off, though, eh, Stan?" Hastings interrupted. "Why was he carrying his plans and reports onto the lock in the dark and in the fog? Some are saying the scattered papers was a statement by these bloody anarchists. There's some that think that it were one of them that pushed him off."

"I still can't see it." Stanley was stroking his stubbly white beard. "Who are these bloody anarchists, anyway? I've heard nowt about them."

"Of course, you haven't, Stan. They're a secret organisation. They don't want folk to know about them. That's why they make everything look like an accident.

"Do you remember when that boiler blew on the digger over at the new docks? Killed a dozen men, that did. I'll bet that were them, too."

Gilbert had been listening intently to Hastings's theory. Wainwright's death certainly posed a few questions, although the coroner and police said it was an accident. *Maybe they're wrong. Is it possible that he was murdered? Have the authorities covered up the truth to ensure nothing stopped work on the canal?*

Pointing his finger at Stan, Hastings wandered off into the melee of bodies muttering, "Mark my words…"

Gilbert signalled the mek, who dutifully refilled his pot.

"What do you reckon, Stan? Are anarchists attacking the Cut?"

Deep in thought, Stan was still stroking his chin. "No, lad, I can't see it. I'd have heard or seen the killer, wouldn't I? How could they get past my eagle eyes? I might be old, but I do my job. You've been reading too many penny dreadfuls."

Out of the corner of his eye, Gilbert caught sight of the Flanagan brothers pushing through the knots of revellers and heading in his direction. They were full of liquid courage and clearly spoiling for a fight. He turned to face them, fists clenched, ready to oblige.

Stan grabbed him by his arm and pulled him back. "Get off home! They're not worth the trouble. You don't want to be fighting them both, not on their terms anyway. You're a good lad, Gilbert. Take it from an old warrior. Choose which fights are worth the scars and fight on your terms, not theirs. Now, bugger off home!"

Draining the last dregs from his pot, Gilbert headed for the exit. As he stepped out into the darkness, behind him he heard Stan offering to buy the Flanagans a drink.

After only two pints, the freezing air hit him like a hammer. *How can anyone sup six pints of that every night?*

The main road into Eccles was the direct road home, but he chose the longer route along the side of the Bridgewater Canal. If the Flanagans came after him, surely, they would think he would take the quicker way.

Ha, he thought, *stupid Flanagans.*

THREE

Fight and Flight

THE BRIDGEWATER CANAL FLOWED under the humpbacked bridge, which carried the main road between Eccles and Barton, then turned in a broad sweep to the right towards the town centre. Longboats and barges bobbed gently on their moorings beside him. His stomach rumbling from the delicious smell of cooking wafting up from the watercraft reminded Gilbert he hadn't eaten since lunchtime. The meagre light of the moon, augmented by the boats' oil lamps, guided him along the towpath. Stones crunched under his boots as he kept a decent pace.

Having not walked this way in a while, the number of folks still living on the water surprised him. Laughter and arguments, passion and frustration, giggles and groans. All the moments of life were at home here.

Up ahead, the disused railway line connecting Manchester to Liverpool crossed the canal. Gilbert was thankful for the stone steps at the side of the old bridge leading up to the tracks, without which scrambling up the slippery embankment would have been impossible.

With the top step easily thirty feet above the water, his stomach churned as he peeked over the bridge wall. Instinctively, he looked both ways along the tracks, even though he knew trains had not travelled them for several years, before setting off towards the town centre. Ahead, pale moonlight glinted here and there off the mostly rusted rails as they disappeared into the shadow of the warehouses towering upward on the right side of the tracks. Some were so close that it may have been possible for earlier occupants of the buildings to touch the carriages as they trundled past. To the left, the steep embarkment fell away into the darkness

A shock ran through his soul. He recognised that these were the rails from which the locomotive had leapt and killed his mother. She had pushed him to safety, but the engine had crushed her fragile body. If only he hadn't persuaded her to take him to see the trains that day. If only.

Movement in the shadows fifty yards ahead made him stop dead in his tracks. He crouched and edged closer. The sounds of a fight echoed between the buildings. A dark, hooded figure pinned a taller man against a warehouse wall with his forearm, punching him in the side with his other fist. The victim was crying out in pain.

Light glinted off a blade. The hooded figure's arm rose and fell repeatedly.

Gilbert was ten yards away when he took off at a sprint, slamming his shoulder into the assailant. Caught off balance, the attacker landed heavily on the stone ballast between the rails. Gilbert kicked him hard in the ribs. The hooded man howled; the wind whooshed from his lungs.

The victim was sitting clutching his stomach, having slid to the floor, leaving a glistening dark stain on the soot-blackened warehouse wall. Around him, a pool of dark liquid was spreading across the ground.

Dazed, the attacker staggered to his feet, blade still in hand. Gilbert didn't hesitate and, stepping forward, he launched himself, boots first, into the man's chest, landing hard on his back on the railway sleepers. He rolled onto his hands and knees to find the assailant had disappeared.

He crawled to the edge of the embankment and peered into the darkness. It was impossible to see in the pitch black, but he could hear the attacker's attempts to scramble back up the steep, slick grass and mud. For once, he was grateful for the Manchester weather.

The injured man groaned, and Gilbert dashed to his side. A tall top hat lying in a puddle next to him told Gilbert he was a toff. In the dim light, he guessed the man was in his sixties or seventies, and there was no doubt he was dying. The stricken man motioned him to come closer, and Gilbert knelt by his side.

"Please... you must..." He was struggling to breathe, blood gurgling in his lungs. Every breath must have been agony. "Take the bag to Algy." His voice was a hoarse whisper. A satchel was lying in the dirt, its strap wrapped firmly around the toff's arm.

"Algy? Who's Algy?"

"Take...bag...Algy...Praetorian...Manchester." Bloody spittle lanced from his lips with every breath, every word.

Gilbert stood upright. "I want no part of this, mister. I don't know what happened here."

The man grabbed his leg. "Please...must...take...bag...tonight...important...no time."

A noise behind him made him glance over his shoulder at the embankment. The attacker must be very determined and stronger than he looked. Time was short. He unwrapped the satchel's strap from the dying man's arm.

After one last look at the old man, Gilbert knew he would never forget his anguished face for as long as he lived. Amid the pain and the knowledge of his imminent demise, there was a final glint in his gaze as the light left the old toff's eyes.

Lucid memories of his mother's death filled Gilbert's mind. He stood up, shaking, his heart pounding. Moonlight glinted off something blue and silver lying on a wooden sleeper. *The old man must have dropped it during the struggle.* He snatched the ornate walking stick off the ground, tucked it under his arm, and set off running for his life in the dark.

Weed-strewn tracks made a gradual descent into Eccles, but when the embankment was ten feet above street level, Gilbert stopped, listened, and turned, peering back into the darkness to see if the murderer was close. With no sign of movement and no sound of running on the gravel ballast, he stepped off the tracks.

He slid, half on his backside, using his heels to reduce his speed, down the wet grass to the pavement. Occasionally stopping to listen for his pursuer, he weaved through the dark back alleys between the terraced houses only a few streets away from Mayfield Street and home. *Dad would know what to do.* He always did.

Up ahead was Liverpool Road, the major thoroughfare into Eccles. It was the quickest way home *and* to the Triple T terminus.

A Tick Tock Tram filled with passengers rumbled across the end of the street as he reached the main road and turned towards the town centre.

Gilbert paused under a streetlight to examine the walking stick more closely. Its blue-lacquered shaft had a fine silver filigree inlay, but it was the handle which caught his attention. Heavy metal encased in rubber moulded into the perfect shape for a right hand.

Oddly, even for an ostentatious walking aid such as this, an ornate, silver, bowl-shaped ferrule covered the handle. Its overall diameter comfortably enveloped Gilbert's fist as he studied the vulcanised grip. He lifted the handle closer to his face to examine a pronounced knobbly protuberance inside the bowl.

Hard running steps sounded behind him. He half turned a fraction of a second too late. The sprinting man smashed him to the ground. Gilbert curled himself into a foetal position, clutching the satchel and cane as kicks and punches rained down on him. Eyes scrunched tightly shut, he instinctively kicked where he felt the attacks coming from and connected with a leg. A loud cry of pain erupted, and the attack briefly abated.

He struggled to his feet, gasping for breath as his attacker advanced on him, pulling a blade from a scabbard belted across his chest. Gilbert stumbled backwards into a streetlight, gripping the bag in one hand and raising the sturdy walking stick to ward off the assailant with the other.

Now the two men faced each other. Gilbert, heart pounding, gasping for air; his attacker calm, crouching, calculating. At that moment, Gilbert knew the man was a cold-blooded killer.

Although they were about equal height, his opponent was more muscular, heavier, and a skilled fighter. He was overmatched, and he had brought a stick to a knife fight.

His attacker's hood had slipped from his head, revealing a simple black leather mask covering his face; holes cut for eyes, nostrils and mouth. Gilbert stared into bright, iridescent, diamond irises surrounding pupils of polished obsidian—cruel, unforgiving, deep, and unfathomable. Beneath a finely groomed light brown moustache, thin lips stretched over gritted teeth into a smirk.

He lifted the satchel, shaking it wildly. "Take it, if this is what you're after!" Gilbert's defiant, trembling voice betrayed his fear.

"Oh, I don't want the bag, Prince Valiant. I want you. Dead." Calm and dripping with menace, the man did not speak like a ruffian.

"This is nothing to do with me. I—"

"Just want to go home to your mummy and daddy? They'll never see you alive again." This was not a threat; it was a statement of fact.

"But—" Trying to catch his attacker off guard, Gilbert swung the heavy walking stick with every ounce of his strength, striking something hard.

Stunned by the blow, his adversary staggered sideways but regained his balance as Gilbert's second swing narrowly missed its target.

"You'll pay for that." He dragged off the leather mask, blood trickling from an ugly, straight gash above his ear, staining his long blond hair.

Beneath the streetlight, Gilbert could see his attacker's features clearly. Circling to Gilbert's left, away from the walking stick, he must have been confident of victory to uncover his face. Gilbert mirrored his movements, back pressed firmly against the lamppost.

He was mid step when the man feigned right and pounced, pinning him with an arm across his chest while grasping his right arm. Gilbert dropped the satchel, catching his assailant's wrist as he thrust the blade at Gilbert's neck, stopping the point fractions of an inch from his throat.

Gilbert was flailing with the stick, finding a target, but with no leverage, his soft blows had little effect. It was taking every ounce of his strength to prevent the knife from biting into his neck as his attacker used his weight advantage, straining to drive the knife home.

To get a better purchase, Gilbert shifted his grip on the handle of the walking stick, his thumb brushing the gnarled bump in the filigree bowl. *Click!* The knob depressed, and the blue-lacquered casing sprung from the ferrule, revealing a two-foot-long, double-edged blade glinting in the gaslight.

He hacked at his attacker's knife arm with renewed vigour. Now, even with little leverage, the razor-sharp steel made quick work of both leather sleeve and muscle.

His attacker did not cry out in pain, but with each slash, strength ebbed from his arm, weakening his grip on the knife. Gilbert pressed his advantage and shoved hard. The injured thug reeled backwards, his shredded flesh spattering blood across the cobbles.

"Athos!" He stumbled, grabbing at his ruined arm. "Athos!"

Gilbert never saw what hit him, but it was massive, powerful, and pissed off.

Every bone in his body hurt as he lay on his back, winded, bloodied, his eyes squeezed tight, face contorted in pain.

A giant hand smashed into his chest, grabbing a fist full of material and lifting him upright.

"Athos! Leave him!"

Gilbert's feet were off the ground; he was suspended by a single fistful of coat. He squinted through the blood and sweat. His nose was inches from a snarling, sweating face, spittle dripping from an unkempt beard. Wide brown eyes filled with rage stared wildly under bristly eyebrows and long, straggly black hair.

"Drop him, Athos! Now!"

"No, Ray. I kill this blackguard." Spit lanced onto Gilbert's cheek, the giant's baritone voice making him wince.

"No! Help me… Help me, now…"

The monster's glare wavered, glancing at where his injured friend lay. He took one last snarling look into Gilbert's eyes and, with the flick of his wrist, flung him across the street. Cartwheeling through the air, he crashed onto the cobbles. His heartbeat pounding in his head, he watched through screwed-up eyes as the giant bent his enormous frame to pick up his comrade's limp, maimed body.

Despite the attacker's best efforts to staunch the flow, blood spurted from his ruined arm.

"Don't think this is finished." The wounded man spoke in a low, menacing voice, a half smile curled across his bloodied face. "You are a dead man. I will kill you and everyone you love."

The giant aimed one last glare at Gilbert, growled, and set off at a steady pace, cradling his cargo like a baby.

Gilbert rolled onto his back, wracked with pain. Beyond the streetlights, a horse-drawn carriage sped into the night. He remained still until the galloping hooves faded into the distance.

He wasn't sure how long it was before he felt able to regain his feet. The satchel and short sword lay at his feet; the blue-lacquered shaft was a few yards away. He picked them up, wiping the blood on his trousers before sheathing the blade back into the casing, which closed with a loud *click*. *The toff must have been expecting trouble. What's in the bloody bag that's so important?*

Whatever it was, it had cost him his life and almost Gilbert's. The old man had entrusted him to deliver it to Algy at the Praetorian, and it had to be tonight.

Reluctantly, he swung the strap over his shoulder, clasping the satchel to his chest with both arms. With every muscle aching, he limped towards the Eccles Triple T stop, glancing ruefully at the Mayfield Street sign as he passed, knowing his father would be waiting for him, but determined to fulfil his promise to the dying man. He would hand the parcel to Algy, then get home. *He won't believe what's happened.*

Gilbert wasn't sure he believed it, either.

Flickering light from the gas mantles on the walls of the Eccles Triple T terminus cast dancing shadows on the faces of the passengers as they awaited the clockwork mechanism's rewinding. This process took twenty minutes, and they waited patiently in silence for the conductor to beckon them forward.

Gilbert stayed out of sight at one end of the platform as the conductor invited the four waiting fares to board. Smudges from sticky, bloody fingers on the face and casing of his pocket watch made reading difficult in the halflight. The tram was due to leave in three minutes. He lingered a little longer.

He tucked the walking stick under his arm and squinted at the satchel. The old brown bag had seen better days; its worn leather and scratched brass buckles showed its age. Underneath its sturdy handle, a black enamelled plate bore the letters POP in gold. Were these the toff's initials? Gilbert's chin dropped to his chest; he just wanted this nightmare to end, to fulfil his promise to the dying man and go home. *Come along, Bertie; it'll soon be over.*

Precisely a minute before the scheduled departure, he stepped out of the shadows and limped to the double-decker green and black tram.

Legs aching after the evening's exertions, he stumbled on board, choosing a seat at the back to have an unobstructed view of the entrance and exit. The mek conductor stepped forward, its yellow gaze flicking back and forth across his dishevelled, blood-spattered clothing.

"Are you all right, sir? Do you need a doctor?"

Nosy passengers turned to stare, frowning, shaking their heads.

"No, thank you. I'm fine." Gilbert looked down at his trembling hands and, wiping the front of his coat, only succeeded in spreading the gore over a larger area. "Manchester Central, please."

"That will be tuppence."

He fumbled in his pockets for change and handed over two sticky pennies. The ticket machine, embedded in the conductor's forearm, clicked, whirred and clanked printing the small ticket, which Gilbert tore from the serrated slot.

Two passengers jumped onto the tram as it jerked into motion. They stared at Gilbert before sitting with their backs to him. The hair on Gilbert's neck stood up, panic rising in his throat. With an overwhelming urge to run, he looked left and right for an escape route.

"Oldfield Road, mek." One man thrust two fingers at the conductor, and they nudged each other, giggling like schoolboys. The conductor took the fares and issued the tickets without comment.

Satisfied he was safe for now, Gilbert turned his mind to his attackers. Who were they? 'Ray' spoke like a toff but fought like a hoodlum. He guessed the big lummox 'Athos' must have been his guard dog. Why did Ray attack him and the old man when Athos would have made quick work of it? *The thrill of the chase? The triumph of the kill? The delight in the power over life and death?*

He closed his eyes, shuddering at the memory of Ray's confident sneer and cruel, steel-blue stare.

And who is 'Algy'? *Algernon? Probably another toff.*

During the brief, uneventful journey into Manchester, passengers boarded and alighted at various stops. The mek driver rang his bell to clear the tracks ahead only occasionally. Trams ran to a tight schedule but were rarely late. Horse-drawn carriages, gigs and carts used the roads during daylight hours, but traffic was mainly hansoms after dark.

Gilbert was one of nine remaining passengers when the tram pulled into Manchester Central Hub. He waited until he was the last to step off the tram.

He marched along the platform, head down, glancing occasionally into the faces of curious passers-by as a HyBrid, an HB2 from Leeds, trundled to a halt ten yards to his right. Choking soot and cinders clouded the air as its three chuffing smokestacks coughed smoke high into the arched roof. Behind the coal tenders, unused dynamotive charge in its huge accumulators hummed as steam from the drive cylinders roared across the platform.

Satisfied he was not being followed, he hurried away from the bright lights into the welcoming shadows of the city streets. He gathered his bearings, remembering that the Praetorian public house was on Great Bridgewater Street, and it wasn't long before he picked out its gas-lit sign through the thickening mist.

Head bowed, he hurried across the road towards the brightly lit building, clutching the satchel firmly to his chest.

The tinkling strains of piano playing grew louder as he approached. Indistinct shapes moved behind the Praetorian's opaque, frosted glass windows. Though they were designed to block underage eyes, they only fuelled the curiosity of youngsters who wondered at what forbidden, grown-up pleasures took place within.

Gilbert wiped blood from his nose on his sleeve, wrapped his arms around the satchel, clutching it hard against his chest, and shouldered open the double doors.

FOUR

The Praetorian

Greeted by a raucous blend of laughter and music, Gilbert stood in the doorway, eyes adjusting from the hazy gas streetlights to the pipe and cigar smoke-diffused lamplight inside the Praetorian. No one was listening to the player piano belting out an up-tempo tune. Patrons in its vicinity shouted to be heard over the racket.

He tightened his grip on the satchel that had caused one death and almost his own, and lowering his eyes, made a beeline for the bar. Drinkers edged away to avoid contamination from his filthy, bloodied clothes. A mek barman trundled over to him, its expressionless yellow eyes lingering for more than a second on the bloody bag.

"Now, young fellow-me-lad," it said. "You do not appear to be old enough to be visiting this hostelry. If you are not twenty-one, then *this 'kin*," it pressed its splayed-fingered hand on its chest and nodded solemnly, "must escort you from the building."

"I am twenty-one, sir." A drunk at the bar sniggered. Gilbert flushed and leaning closer to the mek lowered his voice. "I'm looking for Algy. Do you know where I can find him? I need to give him this case."

"*This 'kin...* will get Algy for you. Please take a seat over there." Eyebrow raised, it pointed over Gilbert's shoulder.

Next to the player piano was the only unoccupied seat in the room. POP inscribed in black and gold letters on the wooden chairback told him it belonged to the satchel owner and explained why it was empty.

He sat bolt upright, conscious that folk around him had lowered their voices. Many had stopped talking, and several glared at him. He closed his eyes, bending forward, still clutching the bag tightly to his chest.

Without sight, his other senses were amplified. The acrid smell of tobacco smoke, snippets of conversations heard despite the piano's blare; "Percival's chair!" "Shame!" "Disgraceful!" "Algy will sort him out." Gilbert felt the dead toff's tacky, bloody mess between his fingers. Behind his tightly shut eyelids, the old man's face, burned into his memory, came into sharp focus.

What am I doing here? He was rocking back and forth.

"I understand you are looking for Algy." A lilting female voice with an unfamiliar accent spoke gently to him.

He opened his tired eyes to a pair of shiny, bright blue long-heeled shoes. His gaze moved slowly upwards along ebony legs, which disappeared into the deep spilt-front skirt of a cobalt satin dress trimmed with yellow ruffles.

Hands pressed against her knees, she leaned over him. His gape lingered a little too long on what seemed to be never-ending cleavage bubbling out of her plunging neckline. When their eyes finally met, her dusky, stunningly beautiful, heavily made-up face took him aback. She wore her jet-black hair in an intricate bun, and her soft skin shimmered in the lamplight.

"Didn't your momma tell you it's rude to stare?" she said. "And you might want to close that pretty little mouth of yours."

"Sorry, miss. I'm not looking for business. I'm waiting for Algy. The barman was going to find him."

The woman's moist lips continued to smile, but her eyes told a different story. "Business? You think I'm a working girl?"

"Oh, sorry, er, ma'am. I thought—"

"I see you have a case which belongs to a dear friend of mine. Perhaps you can tell me how you came by it?"

The din in the bar had subsided to murmurs and whispers. The player piano was silent.

"Beggin' your pardon, ma'am, I was told to return this satchel to Algy. I must hand him the bag and go home."

Still leaning forward, she spread her arms. "I am Algeria Rebekah Darling, but my closest friends call me Algy. *This* is my establishment, and I believe you, and I need to talk in pri—."

Crack! The sound of the drunkard's slap on Algeria's Rubenesque backside broke the silence in the bar. Startled, she sprang bolt upright but in a single motion, pivoted to her left, grabbed the man's right shoulder with her left hand and gripped between his legs with her right. Fragile, tender parts compressed hard.

The drunk's leering expression instantly turned to pain and horror, eyes wide, sweat beading and running down his dirty face.

Time stood still. There was a sharp intake of breath from those close enough to see how she was controlling her assailant.

"Please… Please."

"Please forgive me? Is that what you are trying to say, dearie?" Inches from the terrified man, her expression was the ice-cold personification of power. She delivered the mocking question with a slight tilt of her head.

"I... I... I..."

"I am so sorry for attacking you in such a despicable manner?"

The drunk nodded vigorously, flinging sweat from his hair onto Algeria's dress.

"Now, dearie, if you were truly filled with remorse, you would have removed your lecherous hands from *my* hips."

The words struck him like a jolt from a dynamotive battery. Filthy hands sprang from her body and hovered inches from her dress, stiff fingers splayed, shaking. Algeria's hand twisted and squeezed harder as he tried to pull away from her vice-like grip. He straightened, gasping for air.

"Now, I believe I have your full attention."

The sweating man nodded nervously.

"Please allow me to explain the errors of your ways. My choice of clothing does not give you the right to lay your hands on me or disrespect me. It matters not if your decision to slap my behind was because of your inability to hold your drink, or because your two giggling friends at the bar egged you on. You have crossed a line.

"So, how do you think we should make sure you do not make such a foolish choice in the future?"

Without warning, she brought her knee sharply into the back of her right hand with such force it lifted the man off his feet, and he crumpled to the floor, moaning in pain, cupping both hands between his legs.

Narrowing her eyes, she beckoned his friends from the bar with a crooked forefinger, and they weaved across the room to stand unsteadily in front of her.

Playfully leaning towards them, smiling, she placed a hand on each of their shoulders and whispered. "Pick up this worthless piece of shit and remove it, and yourselves, from my establishment. Oh, and if I, or any of my staff, see you in here again, you will be very sorry."

The two drunks struggled to lift their friend, but eventually, all three stumbled out through the main doors.

She turned to Gilbert.

"Now, young man, we have business that requires privacy." She motioned him to stand, firmly linked his arm with hers, and together they strolled towards the door at the side of the bar.

There were a few wolf whistles and jeers from the far side of the room but shushes from drinkers who had been closer to the crushing action soon drowned them out.

Algeria nodded to the barman, and some of the garishly dressed ladies at the bar stepped away to mingle amongst the patrons. Conversations resumed, and the player piano belted out 'Ta-ra-ra Boom-de-ay' as she opened the door to the rooms at the rear.

Heart pounding, Gilbert stepped through the doorway and into the unknown.

Gilbert entered the dimly lit hallway, followed closely by Algeria.

"Keep going forward to the end of the corridor," she said, pointing the way.

The passage had three doors on each side before opening into a large room. Had it not been for the dozens of chairs and the long table, he would have thought it was a ballroom.

Tightly gripping his arm, she spun him to his left and marched him towards a white door painted with red roses shaped into an ornate letter *A*. Beneath this hung a sign which read 'Private - Strictly No Admittance'. Stepping into the doorway, she made an arch with her arm, forcing him to squeeze past her ample body. Her sweet perfume made him light-headed as he edged into the room.

"To be clear, this is *my* suite, shugah," she said. "No one enters unless at my invitation. No one. Do you understand? You are safe here." She motioned him to sit.

This was obviously Algeria's boudoir. Surrounded by walls decorated in red, black, and gold stripes, an oversized four-poster bed with mauve satin sheets and more cushions than Gilbert had ever seen, dominated the room. At the foot of the bed, a chaise longue draped with the same opulent mauve satin sat between two plain white cane chairs. A third chair faced the flawless mirror on her golden dressing table. To avoid looking at the reflection of his battered face, he chose a seat at the side of the chaise longue.

Algeria unpinned her bun, letting her hair cascade onto her shoulders, and picking up the chair from the dresser, she plonked it a few feet in front of him, the chair's open back facing him. The split in her skirt enabled her to swing her leg over the chair, and she sat resting her chin on her folded arms on the chair back, her bosom hovering alluringly over that dark place at the top of the split in her dress.

Gilbert's quickening heartbeat pounded in his ears. Beads of sweat trickled down his face as he fought not to stare.

She was revelling in his discomfort, running the tip of her tongue slowly between her red lips, moist lipstick glistening enticingly in the lamplight.

"Now, we are alone. Tell me. What I am supposed to think? You stroll into my bar, carrying my dear friend's satchel covered in blood.

"For all I know, you've killed him and come looking for a reward. So, who are you? And how did you get that bag?"

"You're not going to hurt me, are you, miss?"

"I have no intention of hurting you, shugah, but you *will* tell me everything that happened tonight."

Gilbert tried to shake himself out of his stupor. He looked at the satchel still clutched to his chest. The knuckles on his left hand were white as his fist clenched the shaft of the blue cane. His mouth was dry, and Algeria's sickly-sweet perfume consumed him, pervading every sense. It was so powerful; he could taste the sound of her voice echoing in his head. The room receded, her smiling moist lips begging him for the truth.

He had to tell her… everything.

His feverish account of the night's events included every minute detail, from avoiding the Flanagan brothers and stumbling on the murder to Ray's attack and fighting a giant. Sweat poured off him as Algeria's body shimmered with an ethereal glow. Light from the gas mantle gleamed off her glistening, dark, undraped limbs. Gilbert couldn't wrench his eyes away from her gently rising and falling bosom as she calmly listened to his tale. When he finally fell silent, he was panting, heart racing, head spinning, his clothes drenched.

Algeria leaned forward and patted his trembling thigh. "There, there, Bertie, dear. You're safe here."

He stared at her long, elegant legs. "Please don't call me that, miss. Gil, or Gilbert, is fine, but not Bertie." Physically and emotionally spent, he felt overwhelmed by the night's events. He was covered in cuts and bruises, blood and dirt staining his skin and clothes, yet looking up into the warm, inviting eyes of this angel, this sparkling beauty, he fought an uncontrollable urge to hold her and kiss her and…

Self-control lost, he leapt from his seat, trembling hands reaching, yearning, lusting.

"Gilbert!" Algeria's brutal slap knocked him back, almost toppling the chair onto the floor.

"First, I am certainly old enough to be your mother." The words landed as painfully as any punch. "Second, don't call me *miss*. And finally," she paused and lowered her voice, "I have a confession to make."

"Wh-what?" He reeled backwards, rubbing his stinging cheek, shaking his head. He opened his eyes to Algeria wafting a small vial of green liquid under his nose. Pungent fumes stung his nostrils, making his eyes water.

"I'm sorry, but I had to know the truth. So, I gave you something to loosen that pretty little tongue of yours." She licked her lips again.

"You drugged me?" Gilbert's voice was a squeak accompanied by raised eyebrows and a deeply furrowed forehead.

"Please understand. You walk into *my* place, carrying *my* friend's case and cane and covered in *his* blood for all I know. I had to learn what happened and quickly. So, I splashed a special little perfume on my dress. It acts as a truth drug, but my gals use it to lower inhibitions." Her eyes narrowed, and she smiled as she glanced below his waist. "*That's* why I had to give you the antidote."

Gilbert flushed, dropped the satchel, and cupped his hands in front of his groin to hide his embarrassment.

"My gals mix the drug in their perfume to, well, let's say, speed things up a mite." She put her head back, and her laughter sent gentle tremors rippling along her soft, glistening breast.

"But it doesn't affect you?"

"Oh yes, shugah, it has the same effect on me, but I can control the urges because I know what's happening."

"Do you use it often?"

She stiffened and frowned. "I do not!"

"So, you're not... I mean, you don't..."

"No, mister, I am a respectable businesswoman." She tossed her hair back with a flourish.

"Sorry, miss."

"No, Gilbert." Algeria's shoulders slumped. "I regret having to put you through that, but it was necessary considering the gravity of the situation. Sometimes we have to take drastic measures. And please, call me Algeria."

"There's so much I don't understand. I have so many questions."

"I'm sure you have. But first, kindly fulfil my friend's last wishes."

Gilbert picked up the satchel and passed it to her. Still feeling the effects of the drug, he caught his breath as her warm fingers brushed lightly against his.

"We need to clean up your cuts and bruises." She walked over to the four-poster and pulled a cord by the bedhead. Seconds later, there was a knock on the door, and a young woman, wearing a thin cotton dress and little else, stepped into the room. He looked away, fearing any more embarrassing reactions.

"Hot water, flannels, soap and towels, please, honey, and linen for dressings. Please ask Eli to bring us something to drink. Any preference, Gilbert?"

"A nice cuppa would go down a treat, miss."

The young woman acknowledged Algeria's nod, turned on a sixpence and skipped through the door, closing it gently behind her.

Algeria walked over to the chaise and sat demurely, hands clasped in her lap.

"The case and cane belong to Percival Obediah Pale-Chevalier, Mother rest his soul. He was a dear, dear friend of mine. I've known him for twenty years or more. Many will sorely miss him," she said. "I need you to tell me his exact whereabouts so we can recover his remains."

"Was he married?"

"His wife passed a while back. They didn't have any children, and he lived alone."

"Why was he attacked, and what's in his bag?"

"I don't—"

A knock on the door interrupted her answer. Without waiting for a response, the young woman entered, bearing a bowl of steaming water. The mek who had spoken with Gilbert at the bar earlier followed closely behind, carrying a silver tray with a teapot, cups, saucers, milk and a pot of sugar cubes, towels draped over his arm. They carefully placed everything on the dresser.

"Thank you, my dears."

The young woman flashed a coy smile at Gilbert as she left. The mek arranged the teacups and picked up the milk jug.

"It's all right, Eli, we'll pour. Any more trouble in the bar?"

"There have been no further problems." The mek glanced at Gilbert.

"Then, I won't keep you from your duties any longer." Dismissed by Algeria's casual wave, Eli glided across the floor and closed the door behind him.

"Does the young lady work here?" Gilbert asked.

"If by *work* you mean in the rooms outside, no, she doesn't. She assists in the kitchens with her mother. How do you like your tea?" She walked to the dresser and poured milk into the cups.

"Hot and sweet, as I like my women." He winced as soon as the words left his mouth. *Why did I say that?*

"I think you need another whiff of antidote, shugah."

Gilbert lowered his eyes.

"So, the working girls are meks?"

"Certainly not. We tried XT-Cs a few years ago, but the gents around here didn't take kindly to them. Soft leather, lubrication and brass were too unyielding for my discerning clientele."

Gilbert flushed.

Hands on her hips, she towered over him. "Right, shugah, off with your coat, waistcoat, and shirt. Let's see what they did to you."

He grimaced as he undressed the upper half of his body. Every twist and turn found another ache or pain. Algeria took his clothes and laid them neatly on the chaise longue. Sweat glistened on his toned torso, but other than some angry purple and brown bruises on his front and back and abrasions to his arms, hands and face, there were no serious injuries.

Algeria sat him by the dresser, and pulling up a chair, she perched facing him, wetting the flannels and dabbing at his injuries to remove as much dirt as possible.

"What's in the satchel, miss?"

She flashed a look of mock anger at him. "Don't know, Bertie."

"Sorry, mi… Algeria. I don't understand what's happening. Why can't I just go home? My father will be worried about me."

"Not tonight, shugah. You must stay here."

"In here… In your room?"

"Yes, *alone*. Until I examine the contents of the bag, I can't let you leave. It's for your own safety."

"But—"

"I won't argue with you, Gilbert," she said, a hint of weariness in her raised voice.

"Can we please open the bag?"

"For the last time, no. You are such a mitherer. I will open the satchel, alone, when I am good and ready."

Gilbert did not have the strength to fight back. Maybe it was the effects of the drug, but he just wanted to sleep. The events of the evening were catching up with him.

Algeria grabbed the strap and swept the bag from the dresser. "There is a jerry under the bed if you need it, shugah. I can't have you wandering around looking for the gentlemen's toilet in the darkness, and you'll have clean water in the morning so you can do your ablutions. Good night, shugah." She blew him a kiss and strode to the door amid the swishing of her skirts.

Gilbert heard the key turn in the lock. He was here for the night, whether he liked it or not.

Sat alone in the relative calm of the meeting room, Algeria watched shadows cast by the flickering gas mantles dance on the walls to the distant rhythms of the player piano, still belting out music hall favourites. The raucous laughter was subsiding as Eli's staff ushered recalcitrant patrons off the premises. She glanced at the clock. Eli must have called last orders forty minutes ago.

Algeria had spread the contents of Pop's bag across the table. She bowed her head and stretched out her arms, trembling hands pressing on the scattered documents. *The Founding Fathers established the Order for this very moment*, she thought.

After the Great Enlightenment of 1776, a groundswell of self-awareness and conservationism spread around the world. Scores of altruists gathered like-minded free thinkers into groups and societies that preached and practised the protection of the environment. The Venerable Antediluvian Order of the Custodians of Magna Mater was one such secret society formed by well-meaning academics and philanthropists in the northwest of England. There had been eight leaders of the Order since its inception. They called themselves High Fathers.

The ninth leader adopted the title of High Mother.

Algeria wondered how any of the previous eight High Fathers would deal with this crisis. *Poorly*, she thought. She admired her painted fingernails before running her hands over her cinched waist and shapely hips. *I am perfectly equipped for the task*. Her wry smile reflected her pride at her achievement but also acknowledged her personal sacrifice and more than a hint of bravado. *Who am I trying to kid? Me?*

She sighed and stuffed the papers and notebooks back into the bag. She slumped in the chair, looking up at the ceiling, tears trickling from the corners of her eyes. "Oh, Pop, why, oh why? What on earth have you stumbled upon?" The empty room did not reply.

The documents were alarming.

Knowing that Pop had died protecting the satchel, she had been hesitant to open it. When she had finally emptied the bag onto the table, she gasped at each new revelation in his carefully compiled compendium of notes of his clandestine investigations. They made for difficult reading. *Has he discovered an organisation which was the very antithesis of the Order?* If his conclusions were correct, and she had no reason to doubt her old friend and mentor, this was the gravest threat they had ever faced.

Muffled metallic clunks from the main bar announced Eli was bolting the outer doors. It was fifteen minutes more before the mek bustled into the meeting room. He came to a halt a few feet from Algeria's table and cocked his head to one side, a single eyebrow raised.

She wiped her face dry with her fingertips.

"Gather the Order for an emergency meeting," she said.

"Certainly, Algeria. When will this meeting be held?"

"Here, tomorrow, at two o'clock. Only invite members who can make it. We daren't wait any longer."

"*This 'kin* will locate as many as possible," he said. Everyone was aware of the mek communication network; few knew how it worked, and most had no interest in finding out. It was efficient and quick. That was all she needed right now. "Will there be anything else this evening?"

"I won't be sleeping in my boudoir tonight. Do we have any unoccupied guest rooms?" she said, nodding towards the stairs.

"Room four is clean and available. Do you require a bath?"

"Yes, it's been a long day."

Eli bowed and scurried away.

Algeria reached behind her back to undo the bow that held taut the laces of her corset and, unconstrained, exhaled in comfort. Tomorrow's meeting was going to be pivotal. The worst fears of the Founding Fathers were fomenting on her watch. The Order must go to war against a fearless foe, a dedicated and relentless enemy determined to achieve its goal with no thought of self-preservation. Somehow, she must convey the size of the threat and rouse her cohort to action without creating panic.

Gilbert was the key. He would need to be handled carefully. She needed to recruit him into the ranks.

For the first time in her life, Algeria was fearful for the future, not just her own but also that of Mother Earth and every living soul on the planet.

FIVE

Meeting

VOICES?

Voices.

He heard voices. Whispers from another life, another time, another world.

No sensation. Numb. No, not numb. Nothing. He felt nothing.

Detached. Incorporeal. A disembodied spirit. Still. Expanding.

He was everything; he was everywhere.

He was nothing; he was nowhere.

Alone.

Adrift in the everlasting emptiness of inner space.

Infinite, yet infinitesimally small. The liminal space between worlds, between thoughts, between words.

Free.

Floating. But tethered to the physical world by the whispering voices.

"Do you think he will die?" Uncaring. Cold.

"Maybe." An audible shrug.

"Oh, well. Heir today…"

That voice…

"Gone tomorrow." Latent malevolence. Laughter.

Father? Ray's ethereal inner voice evanesced into the enveloping void as his consciousness tumbled into diabolic desolation.

Sometime midmorning, Gilbert stirred from a fitful sleep, awakened by the tumblers clicking into place as the key turned in the boudoir lock. Eli popped his head around the door, checking whether Gilbert was awake, before silently sweeping into the room. He clapped his hands twice, and two of Algeria's girls bustled in carrying food, tea, hot water, fresh towels, and new clothes, placing them on the dresser where his old, ruined clothing had been.

Eli shooed the young women out of the room, following close behind. The key turned in the lock again, and Gilbert threw back the sheets, swinging his legs over the side of the bed too vigorously as his bruised, aching body reminded him of the previous night.

He attacked his breakfast, like a hyena on a warm carcass, before washing and dressing in the fresh clothes.

Five minutes before noon, Algeria entered the room wearing a demure green dress buttoned up the front to her throat, the style in sharp contrast to her ensemble of the previous evening.

Gilbert leapt to his feet. "When can I—"

Algeria raised her hand. "I've opened the bag, shugah. You're not going anywhere."

"I don't understand. You can't hold me here!" Gilbert's heart was racing. Could he force his way past her to the unlocked door?

"Gilbert!" She took a half-step sideways, positioning herself directly between him and the doorway. "You won't make it, dearie. Even if you got past me, they won't let you walk out of this building without my permission. I want you to attend a meeting."

"Meeting? No, I need to see my dad. He'll be sick with worry." He took a sideways step, but Algeria mirrored his move.

"Don't!"

"You can't keep me here!" Gilbert crouched; every muscle tensed like an overwound watch.

Before he could react, she stepped forward, slapping him hard. "You need to grow up."

Gilbert staggered backwards, angry and embarrassed rather than hurt. Under different circumstances, if she had been a man, his retaliation would have been swift and brutal. But she was a woman, maybe twice his age.

"You didn't have to do that, miss." He rubbed the sting from his reddened cheek. "I wouldn't have hurt you."

She grabbed him by the shoulders. "Listen. I really need you to be at the meeting this afternoon. You must understand what we are up against. All right?"

Gilbert nodded, cheek still stinging.

Without another word, she turned her back on him and left the room.

Alone again, he sat on the bed, head in his hands. *Why can't I keep my big nose out of things that don't concern me? Too hasty, too often.*

Dad said it would get me into trouble, and he was right. He was always right.

During the next few hours, a steadily growing hubbub accompanied the muffled sound of chairs and tables being moved.

A few minutes before two o'clock, the noise subsided, the boudoir door opened, and Algeria beckoned him forward. There were over forty people in the large room beyond: some sitting, some standing, all facing the long table. She guided him to a seat next to hers.

He sat, head bowed, while she remained standing, waiting for silence. "I'm sure you have heard the sad news about our fallen brother. Please be upstanding for a minute of silent remembrance for Percival Obediah Pale-Chevalier, who died last night in the Order's service."

Chair legs shrieked in resistance as the assembled stood, hands clasped, eyes lowered. The silence was deafening. Gilbert peeked at the faces, many twisted in grief, anger or both.

"Thank you, brothers and sisters." Algeria looked around the room. "Before we begin, I want to say a few words about Pop. Everyone who knew him respected him. Despite his advanced years, his dogged determination to root out wrongdoers was matched only by his love of the Order.

"His peers will remember him as a loyal and trusted compatriot: a friend who, only when asked, offered sound advice. He recruited most of our younger members. Looking at your faces today, it's clear he was an excellent judge of character.

"Pop understood the gravity of our work and the damage unregulated industrialisation does to the Mother. He died in our service, and we must not let his death be in vain."

All eyes were on Algeria as she raised her arms wide, turning her palms upward as if lifting a heavy load. As she had done countless times before, she tilted her head back and began the Exhortation:

> "The Earth is our Mother and our Mistress.
> She is kind; she is cruel. She gives, and she takes.
> Praise be to Mother Nature for birthing all life.
> Every animal, every species. Every plant, every genus.
> Woven into a wondrous tapestry of life.
> Together, we are whole.
> Our hearts and minds united, we pledge our fealty to Mother Earth.
> We are the custodians of Magna Mater.
> We are the curators of her tapestry, keepers of her garden, tenders of her flora, and protectors of her fauna.
> This above all else."

"This above all else." The adjuration echoed around the room. Those with chairs sat, but Algeria remained on her feet. She took a deep breath.

"I declare this emergency meeting of The Venerable Antediluvian Order of the Custodians of Magna Mater open." She paused and gazed at the panorama of worried and curious expressions. "I see Eli and his 'kin have located a great number of us."

A heavyset gentleman, considerably older than Algeria, holding a very tall, silver top hat, used his cane to raise his corpulent body upright.

"Point of order, High Mother." His voice was deep and gravelly, ruined by decades of expensive cigars and crusted port.

Algeria acknowledged Thaddeus Oswald Lisney and motioned him to speak.

"High Mother, I look forward to hearing your explanation

for calling us here today, but I believe I speak for everyone here in asking, who in the name of the Mother is that?" He pointed his cane at Gilbert. "He's sitting at the top table! What gives you the right to bring an outsider into this sacred place?" He glowered at Algeria, his ruddy cheeks framed by his resplendent white mutton chops. Then, raising his bushy eyebrows, he looked around the room, seemingly for support. "I hope this meeting won't last too long. I have a filly running in the four-thirty at New Barns." He flopped back into his chair to a chorus of sighs and giggles.

Gilbert flushed, squirming in his seat.

Algeria spread her arms wide. "Ozzie, indeed, all of you, may question my judgement in bringing a stranger into this hallowed hall. But you will understand why when you hear the extraordinary events which have brought us here today.

"This young man, Gilbert Sparks, risked his life trying to save Pop. Then, he bravely fulfilled our fallen brother's dying wish when walking away would have been easier." She placed her hand on Gilbert's shoulder and looked into his eyes.

I wish I had run away. He returned her smile.

Algeria summarised the events of the previous night to gasps and exclamations of anger. Gilbert hardly recognised her dramatisation. He didn't believe he acted heroically. In fact, he considered his actions to be reckless to the point of stupidity.

"Which brings us to the contents of Pop's bag." Algeria held aloft the battered satchel to another chorus of gasps and exclamations. She eased open the bloodied buckles and pulled out dozens of sheets of paper and a small black book. She raised the documents over her head, shaking them vigorously.

"Pop died for these. Gilbert risked his life to get these to us. Pop uncovered a plot so evil that I believe Magna Mater is facing her greatest peril. I believe our forefathers founded the Order for this very moment. We must rise and face this threat head on!"

A tidal wave of noise erupted as the faithful leapt to their feet shouting, arms waving, fists clenched.

Gilbert remained seated, adrift on the wild stallions of pandemonium.

Algeria placed the papers on the table and raised both hands, beseeching silence. The gathered lowered their voices to a general murmur punctuated by requests for quiet from the older members.

"Pop documented each anarchic act, every so-called accident over the last decade, from minor derailments to the chemical plant explosion at Pomona. He found a pattern and dug deeper." She paused as the level of conversation rose, waiting for it to subside.

"But it was his discovery of this notebook," she held up a small black book for everyone to see. "Which confirmed his worst fears. A cabal of evildoers committed the atrocities. Each planned and documented. A demented cult, the self-styled… Anthropocene."

The room exploded with noise again. Algeria waited for the commotion to die down before she recommenced.

"Written on the last page is a manifesto of hatred, the scrawled notes of a madman. He opposes the sacred theories of Arthur Buckingham Connickle." Everyone present except Gilbert bowed their heads.

"Their goal is to speed up industrialisation in the guise of a fight against oppression. They are working to have the Connickle laws repealed, advocating that a free society benefits all and empowers science to find solutions to repair the damage caused by their unfettered progress.

"The manifesto is a lie."

Algeria placed the book carefully on the table, reached into her pocket, and unfolded a page torn from the notebook. It was covered in the same spidery writing.

"There is bile and hatred here. Make no mistake, the author of this abomination has no love for his fellow man or Magna Mater. The real purpose is the collapse of society into every-man-for-himself: individual freedom without personal responsibility. If his plan succeeds, he may set in motion a train of events that could cause irreversible damage to the environment."

Stunned silence.

Gilbert picked up the notebook and turned the pages feverishly.

"How do we stop them, High Mother?" A young, bearded black man dressed in aviator overalls shouted from the back of the hall.

"How do we find them? Who are they?" A shrill voice cut through the rising cacophony.

"That's why my brave friend is sitting here, Lady Marsh." She patted Gilbert on the shoulder as he continued to thumb through the pages. "I believe the signature on the manifesto belongs to the leader of this cult. This self-styled prophet calls himself... Raven."

Gilbert froze; his jaw dropped. He stared at Algeria.

"Yes, Gilbert. The man called Ray who murdered Pop and tried to kill you is the depraved mind behind this evil."

Gilbert's stomach churned. He had been lucky to survive the attack by this Raven killer. Only the chance discovery of Pop's hidden blade had saved him from certain death.

"Gilbert Sparks. You are the only one amongst us who has seen his face. Only you can identify this monster." The words struck him like cold steel. He held his head in his hands. He didn't want this. He wished he had run from the scuffle on the embankment.

He looked at the notebook through tear-blurred eyes. A spasm jolted his body when he saw, written at the top of a scruffily scribbled page, a date that would be etched in his brain until his last breath. He slowly rose to his feet, unfolding as if pulled by the strings of some unseen puppeteer, shaking, his heart pounding, tears flowing.

"Gilbert? What's wrong?" Algeria grabbed his arm.

"He killed my mum!"

"What?" She prised the book from Gilbert's shaking hand and read to the assembly. "Third of August 1881. Disabled points, first line, Eccles junction. Derailed 11.20 Liverpool train out of Manchester. Result - Success. Track inoperable for two days. Death of innocents an unexpected bonus. Public outcry. Derailment classified as an accident." Algeria closed the notebook and put her arm around his shoulders as he sobbed. The room was hushed.

"I'm so sorry, shugah."

She eased him back into his seat. "I was going to ask you to join our cause and help us find this Raven. I was going to ask the gathered members to accept you into our sacred society." She looked up at the stunned faces in the hall, eyebrows raised, a silent question. Every head nodded. "But I believe I know the answer."

"I'll kill the bastard!" Gilbert sprung to his feet. "He took my mum from me!" Years of self-recrimination were melting away. His mother's death wasn't his fault. It was Raven's, and he would make the rogue pay for his suffering.

If the only way he could wreak his vengeance was to join this secret society, the Order, or whatever it called itself, then so be it.

"Ace." Algeria beckoned the black aviator from the back of the hall and asked him to escort Gilbert to her boudoir. Heads turned to watch him, still sobbing, trudge across the room.

Ace closed the door behind him and sat Gilbert at the dresser.

"I *will* kill him," Gilbert said.

"And we will help you." Ace placed his hand on Gilbert's shoulder, meeting his steely stare.

SIX
Decisions

His head pounded and floods of searing pain flowed through his body as he regained consciousness from the laudanum-induced sleep. Ever-changing light patterns danced on his closed eyelids from the sunlight streaming through the gently swaying branches outside his bedroom. The familiar odour of his pillow confirmed he was home.

The gentle waft of petrichor from the garden chilled his cheeks. It must have rained while he slept. Every tick of his bedside clock was a hammer striking the anvil of his eardrum. His laudanum-enhanced senses were all-encompassing.

There were other sounds in the room.

He was not alone.

A million needles of dazzling sunlight stabbing into his brain rewarded his gargantuan effort to prise open his eyelids. They snapped shut, returning dilated pupils to the sanctity of darkness.

"Curtains, Athos!" Ray instinctively knew his acolyte was close. He was always there; loyal, unquestioning, obedient. The troublesome patterns dimmed.

With the unpleasant metallic taste of blood in his dry mouth, memories came flooding back. He had lost a fight and, being unaccustomed to losing, someone was going to pay for his injuries.

"Raynard, dear boy, you've returned to the land of the living." His father sat to the left of his bedside on the hard-backed chair. "What on earth happened to you?"

Ray grimaced as he tried to move. "Oh, I'm sure Athos has told you about last night's events. A terminally stupid fool interfered in my business."

His father snorted, unwelcome glee in his voice. "Well, he certainly made a mess of your arm. You've lost an awful lot of claret. I thought your loyal guard dog's sole purpose was to protect you. Maybe you feed him too much."

Athos growled under his breath.

"It was an underestimation, nothing more. I won't make the same mistake next time."

"Next time, dear boy?" Unable to contain himself any longer, his father chuckled. "You won't be going anywhere for some considerable time. Isn't that so, doctor?"

Ray hadn't noticed the tall, dapper gentleman stood quietly by the window. "I'm afraid the injuries to your biceps are quite extensive, Mister De'Ath. It is going to be months before you regain complete control of your arm, and you won't achieve anything approaching full strength for a year. You see, the nerves and musc—".

"Doctor Penfold-Mewling," Ray spoke calmly. "I will be out of this room within the week. I'm sure my father will pay for a prosthesis."

"Prosthesis?" The doctor's surprised reaction did not ring true.

"Yes, Doctor. I want a mechanical sleeve to support and protect my arm."

"Sir! I know what prostheses are." The doctor did not hide his displeasure at the inference. "I am not convinced *you* understand the ramifications of their usage."

"Really? Then pray, tell me your concerns, so I can make a more informed decision."

"Yes, Doctor. I would love to hear why you believe fitting my son with prosthetics would be a bad idea." His father's supportive posture was unconvincing.

Ray glimpsed his father's meaningful stare at the doctor. *They have discussed this possibility and have decided without consulting me.*

"There are several things you must consider…"

"Go on, Doctor." Ray stared at his father.

The doctor cleared his throat. "First, mechanical arms are heavy and uncomfortable. They are a recuperative tool to enable bedridden patients to gain some movement in their limbs. I cannot recommend their use to anyone who can move around freely. The pressure placed on back and chest muscles, sinews and bones would be detrimental."

"I see," he said, "please continue, Doctor."

"Second, we attach the sleeve to the torso with thick leather straps. We anchor it at the shoulder and elbow to protect the injured biceps. One achieves movement by amplification of infinitesimal movements of the forearm and hand.

"As the tissue heals, the mechanics in the sleeve will become difficult to control. There comes a time when one arrives at the point of diminishing returns; prolonged usage of the prosthesis inhibits muscle growth as the body becomes accustomed to the mechanical assistance."

"In your valued opinion, Doctor, in my case, how long before I reach that point?"

"Four to six months."

"Pray, continue."

"Continued use beyond this would cause total dependence."

Ray narrowed his eyes, addressing the doctor directly. "Just so I understand. Prolonged usage of a prosthesis, once I am mobile, will damage my back because the extra weight would make my body to be lopsided. Further use beyond, say, four months will hinder my return to full fitness. That is the absolute extent of your concerns, Doctor?"

Ray's father nodded at the doctor. Ray watched a single bead of sweat form and trickle down the doctor's face.

"Then I have the perfect solution to allay your fears, Doctor."

"Really?" His father feigned boredom. "Enlighten us, dear boy. I'm sure you are far better informed than our esteemed doctor."

"Fit me with prostheses to both arms to balance the weight, and I use them for only three months. An elegant solution to a simple problem."

"I don't think you understand how the sleeve works, sir." The doctor's words almost tripped over each other in his eagerness to refute Ray's argument. "The mechanics do not replace muscle strength; they enhance it. They amplify.

"A prosthesis attached to a normal functioning arm, particularly with your muscle mass, why, it would increase your power tenfold. You would not be able to control the power. The human body is a complex network of nerves and tissue operated by thought and reflex.

"You could, inadvertently, of course… kill someone." The doctor glanced nervously at Ray's father, who sat unmoved.

"Come, come, Doctor. Let's not over-egg the pudding."

"The cost is prohibitive." The doctor was floundering for excuses. "And it's just unnecessary. You don't need it."

Ray had won the argument.

He shifted his weight, one side of his mouth curling upwards. Athos recognised the change and took a step forward. Ray lifted his right hand off the bed, his forefinger raised. Athos stopped.

"Let me explain something, Doctor. You can't tell me what I *need*, because I *need* nothing. When I was a child, I *needed* things—a mother, friends, love. To be in need is to be subservient to others." Ray waited for an interjection from his father. The silence was deafening.

"Being denied those things, I learned how to live without. Now, I *need* nothing. But I do *want* things, and I *want* some things very much. Right now, I *want* two prosthetic arms. A yoke, indeed, as powerful as the ones worn by the accursed navvies working on that infernal ditch.

"We will pay you well for your services. I'm sure my dear father will testify that there would be severe consequences for anyone preventing me from getting what I want. Do you understand, Doctor?" Ray spoke calmly. The doctor watched his raised finger, eyes unblinking, his face glistening with sweat.

"I understand perfectly, Mister De'Ath," he said.

Ray slowly lowered his finger. Athos stepped back into the shadows.

"Then it's decided." Ray turned to his father; his face wreathed in a triumphant, mirthless smile. "Ensure the good doctor has the funds to buy my equipment."

His father closed his half-open mouth, sighed, and nodded.

"Now, if you don't mind, I believe I want a drop or two of laudanum to help me sleep awhile. Athos, please go with

Doctor Penfold-Mewling to make sure he gives me the correct dosage."

Athos growled.

Ray lowered himself into the welcoming womb of his bed as they filed out of the room, the doctor glancing nervously over his shoulder as the giant breathed noisily on the back of his neck.

When the door clicked shut, he allowed himself to wince. The pain in his arm was becoming intolerable as his last dose of laudanum ceased to be effective. The next few days were going to test his resolve, but soon his injury would not impair him; he would be stronger, and nothing, no one, would stop his righteous crusade.

But first, the blackguard who shredded my arm will pay a terrible price.

In Algeria's boudoir, Gilbert soon discovered that Aquilla Ulysses Sixsmith loved the sound of his own deep baritone voice and needed no excuse to talk about his favourite topic—himself. So, Ace talked, and he listened. It was a welcome distraction from his dark thoughts.

As the only son of a major cotton importer who owned three large warehouses in the centre of Manchester or Cottonopolis, as many called it, Ace's parents had sent him to boarding school when he was seven. Being the only black student in his year, he struggled to settle, but having developed a passion for the Classics, particularly Latin, his housemaster suggested a career in the clergy or the law. He chose the latter and gained his law degree from Cambridge University.

After a brief tenure in chambers in London, he became so disillusioned with the legal profession that he returned north. After months of fudgelling around in his father's properties, he met Pop, who recruited him into the Order.

Of course, his passion for conservation put him at loggerheads with his industrialist father, who accused him of wasting his academic achievements and the opportunities afforded to a privileged few. But like so many children born to newly rich entrepreneurs suckling at the teat of the Industrial Revolution, he lacked the ambition and motivation of earlier generations.

After agreeing to leave the family business, he negotiated a comfortable monthly allowance, many times what Gilbert would earn in a year, and his father purchased him a small airship to keep him out of his hair. The airship was Ace's pride and joy.

Gilbert cherished the pocket watch his father had given him for his twenty-first birthday.

A few minutes after three o'clock, Algeria opened the door and beckoned four more members of the Order into the boudoir. She walked straight to Gilbert and put her arms around him. "Are you all right, shugah?" she whispered.

He nodded. *Of course, I'm not all right.*

She turned towards the newcomers. "Allow me to introduce Connie, Rory, Issy and the handsome young man at the back, Lemmy."

Gilbert acknowledged each with a nod.

"Ahh, *amicis meis.*" Ace strode over to them, arms spread and hugged his friends.

"Take no notice of him," Issy said. "He has this annoying habit of speaking in dead languages, mostly Latin. We rarely have a clue what he's saying, but we've picked up the odd word." She shook Gilbert's offered hand warmly.

Connie was next to step forward. At six feet, she was as tall as him and, judging by her handshake, Gilbert decided he would not want to gamble his life on whether he was stronger than her. Worn with no adornment, her wavy black hair cascaded onto her shoulders.

"We call ourselves the Stormriders, and we are at the disposal of the Order. Between the five of us, we own two dirigibles moored at Barton," she said, and beaming at her sister, who was slightly taller, "This is my twin, Rory."

Slim and elegant, dressed in a black suit over a crisp white shirt and tie, Rory strode forward, hand outstretched. "Good to make your acquaintance. Please excuse the formal attire, but I had planned an evening at The Gaiety." Rory's handshake was firm and vigorous. Musky pomade smelling of wet soil and mint was plastered on her short black hair, which gleamed like a wet skull cap. She wore it parted on the left and fixed into small kiss-curls on her forehead and in front of her ears, framing her intense dark eyes.

Lemmy was last to step forward. "Pleased to meet you, old bean." He said and hurriedly stepped back behind his friends.

"The Order has resolved that you need to be kept safe, but, of course, I can't keep you locked up in my bedroom forever." Algeria frowned at Lemmy's smirk. "So, the Stormriders will take you to Abel Throgmorton at Pendle Hill. I want you out of harm's way. He will look after you, and he might pass on some of his fighting skills.

"It appears the Anthropocene is a much larger organisation than the Order. Pop's investigation suggests they have tendrils everywhere, even in the Palace of Westminster."

"In Parliament?" Ace said, "To influence government policy? That's outrageous!"

"So it seems."

"We have to stop this madness before this blackguard, Raven, becomes too powerful," Ace replied.

"But first, we need to get Gilbert to Abel's as soon as possible. Can you fly him up there today?" Algeria said.

"*Freyja's Grimalkin* is yours to command, High Mother." Ace, Lemmy and Issy put their hands to their hearts.

"You can count on the *Dragonfly*, too," Rory said, winking at Connie, who returned her smile.

"Thank you, all." Algeria turned to Gilbert, placing her hands on his shoulders. "I know these last two days have been an ordeal, but it's my duty to keep you safe. I'll get a message to your father telling him you are working at the other end of the ship canal and not to expect you home for a while. Hopefully, you can stop worrying about him."

"Thanks, miss." He picked up his new overcoat and followed the Stormriders as they filed out of the door.

"Be careful, shugah, and say hello to Abel for me."

Gilbert nodded as he dragged on his cap and turned up the collar on his coat. He would avenge his mother if it was the last thing he did.

The soot-blackened Italian-styled facade of the Athenaeum belied the opulence of the gentlemen-only rooms, which were unrivalled throughout the city.

Thaddeus Osgood Lisney had made the short walk from the Praetorian in a matter of minutes. He checked in his topper and cane before strolling into the bar where his friend Ignatius was sitting in a sumptuous armchair by the window overlooking Princess Street.

"You're late, Ozzie, old chap. We've only just got time for a snifter before we need to get a growler to New Barns," Ignatius said.

"It will have to be a quick one, Iggy. Mustn't miss the four-thirty." Ozzie called over a waiter. "Whisky and water. Make it a double, boy. Chop, chop!" He clapped his hands as the mek hurried away.

"So why the holdup? I was about to leave without you."

"Bit of a problem over at Algy's place. You remember Algy, don't you?"

"Oh, yes." He cleared his throat and winked. "Formidable woman. Once found myself at the wrong end of a tongue lashing for calling her a tuppenny whore. Not been near the Praetorian ever since."

"Have a care, old chap. That tuppenny whore happens to be a very good friend of mine."

Both men guffawed, but Ozzie knew she was not a woman who suffered fools gladly. He leaned forward and lowered his voice. "Well, apparently, some blighter murdered Percival Pale-Chevalier and attacked a young lad."

"Percy's dead? Murdered, you say? Why would anyone kill him? The old boy was eccentric, but he didn't have a nasty bone in his body."

"No idea. It doesn't seem to be a robbery, though. Nothing stolen, apparently."

The waiter returned with Ozzie's drink, and the two men fell silent until the mek trundled away.

"What about the other chap that was attacked. Young lad, you say?"

"Sparks. Gilbert Sparks. I think that was his name. Just an oik that works on that infernal canal. He says he fought off the attacker and injured him badly. Algy wants to protect him for some blasted reason and talked about sending him to Pendle to a friend of hers to keep him safe. It all seems excessive to me." Ozzie leaned in closer and tapped his nose. "Hush, hush, old man. Mustn't tell anyone."

"Mum's the word, old chap." Iggy tapped the side of his nose. "I've forgotten everything already."

Both men laughed as they eased back in their chairs.

Iggy called the waiter. "Call us a hansom." He turned to Ozzie. "You should have finished your drink in the time it takes that mek to get us a cab."

The two men chatted about horses until a cab driver appeared at the door.

"Hansom for Earl Ignatius Death!"

Iggy sighed, as he had countless times before. *They always say it wrong. De'Ath, not Death.* He slowly raised his hand. "Come on, Ozzie. Our carriage awaits."

SEVEN

Scales and Feathers

Two shiny onyx landaus picked up speed as they left the confines of the city. Ace had urged the drivers to make haste, and the horses responded to their whips and exhortations. Connie and Rory were in the vanguard while Gilbert rode with Ace, Issy, and Lemmy close behind. His breath clouded the window as they sped by buildings blackened with soot, wheels rattling over the well-worn cobbles. Dirty street urchins in ragged clothes scurried away from the horses' iron-shod hooves.

TThoughts spun around his head. The guilt he had suffered for too many years had become rage. Raven would pay the ultimate price for what he had done.

Gilbert looked across the carriage at Issy and Lemmy in their finery. They were giddy at the prospect of another adventure. *What am I doing here?*

"Penny for your thoughts?" Ace appeared concerned.

"Everything is happening so fast."

"Algeria says you're the key to finding this knave, Raven. You know what he looks like. Surely you want to help us?"

"I just want to avenge my mum. Your stupid crusade doesn't interest me. I'm going to kill Raven. That's all."

"I understand."

"No, you don't. How can you understand what I'm going through?" Gilbert's heart was pounding, his face flushed, tears welled and spilled down his cheeks. "I'm a working-class lad, a navvie on the ship canal. My dad's a watchmaker. I don't belong here with you toffs, playing your silly games in your secret society. I want this done with so I can go home and get on with my life!"

The carriage fell silent. Gilbert sat sobbing, head bowed, unable to meet the gaze of his companions. Tears squeezed from tightly scrunched eyes splashed on his trousers.

Issy leaned forward and whispered. "We know this is difficult for you, dear. But we need each other. You need us as much as we need you. The Order will keep you safe so that we can work together to find and stop Raven."

"We can beat this jumped-up bully-boy," Lemmy chimed in. "It'll be fun." Issy and Ace flashed angry glances at him.

"Take no notice of him," Issy said. "We're on the same side here. We have the same aim, just different reasons for stopping him."

Gilbert slumped in his seat sobbing, his fists clenched. The clippety-clop of horses' hooves and the rumbling of wheels on the cobblestones cut through the uneasy silence. They passed a group of girls skipping with a rope and two young lads with a hoop and stick, and children's laughter filled the carriage. He thought of happier days with his mother, and his shoulders relaxed.

"I need time to think. It's all too much…"

"We'll look after you, won't we?" Issy said.

"Of course, we will." Ace put his arm around Gilbert. "We'll make sure we keep you out of harm's way. You'll have your shot at Raven. You'll avenge your mother's murder."

Gilbert wiped his face and nodded. What choice did he have? He would use these self-styled Stormriders to get to Raven, then leave them to their stupid secret society.

The rest of the journey passed without another word being spoken.

On arrival at Barton Aerodrome, Connie and Rory joined Gilbert and the others as they walked past the flapping airsock at the perimeter and across the grass airfield to where the dirigibles bobbed on their moorings.

Gilbert had never been this close to airships. Although he had seen hundreds of them in the sky high overhead, standing in the shadow of these flying miracles made him realise just how enormous they were.

There were scores of them moored at the aerodrome. The majority were triple-baggers, but there were a few massive four-baggers and a gaggle of tiny two-bag air yachts.

They approached a gunmetal and golden gondola suspended beneath twin sleek, feline, black envelopes, rounded at the front but tapering to a point at the rear. Each envelope, containing two LTA airbags covered in a grab-net and rigging, was attached to the superstructure and bulwarks.

Ace turned and walked backwards with his arms spread wide, a huge grin on his face. "Welcome to *Freyja's Grimalkin!*" He had to raise his voice over the drone of the idling engines. "That grizzled lump stood by the scales is Jonah, our engineer and pilot."

Hands on his hips, Gilbert gazed up at the colossal airship and whistled. She had four stub-nosed motors, two on the outside of each envelope. Their black casings had ornate golden swirls. At the rear of the gondola, fancy gold script announced the name of the impressive craft on the huge black rudder.

Jonah Wyvern stood and waved at the approaching group. "Are we off on a trip?" He was a short, stocky man in his midforties dressed in aviator's coveralls. A leather cap covered his mostly bald head, and his bushy brown beard didn't quite hide his cheery smile.

Countless straps, belts and buckles crisscrossed his moss green overalls and standing with his hands on his hips, he cut a formidable figure.

"Only a couple of hours to sunset. Hope it's not a long journey. I don't want to be trying to land this beast in the dark... again," he said.

"Just a short flight to Pendle and back, Jonah. With your impeccable flying skills, we'll be home well before nightfall." Ace turned and winked at Issy.

"Aye, we can make it comfortably if we don't dally. Are we going to see Abel?"

"We are indeed. Our good friend here, Gilbert Sparks, needs a ride." Ace motioned Gilbert forward, and Jonah strode over, hand extended in greeting.

"Pleased to meet you, young man." Jonah's handshake was energetic. "Can you step over here for me, lad? I need to find out how much ballast to drop to compensate for the extra baggage." Jonah almost dragged Gilbert to the scales.

"Fourteen and a half stone. That's two hundred and three pounds. Strapping lad, ain't he?" Jonah winked at Issy, who looked up at the heavens.

"Come on, Jonah," she said. "Let's get moving. Abel isn't expecting visitors, and I don't want to arrive late and ask him to put us up for the night as well."

"Where's Connie and Rory?" Gilbert asked.

Ace narrowed his eyes as he surveyed a cluster of air yachts. "Over there. Three ships across. The green and tangerine two-bagger. *Dragonfly* may be small, but she's fast and agile."

Air yachts were recreational dirigibles built for speed with a single, smooth canvas envelope stretched over a light aluminium frame containing two massive LTA bags. The superstructure above the gondola was minimal. *Dragonfly*'s envelope, superstructure and gondola were painted in a dark green and tangerine livery.

Gilbert could make out three figures clambering up the rope ladder to the gondola. "Who's the other young lady with Connie and Rory? Can the air yacht carry three people?"

"I hope you are not commenting on the ladies' weight, young Gilbert," Lemmy said.

"No! I just meant—"

Lemmy slapped Gilbert's back and laughed. "Tabby is the *Dragonfly* pilot, and she's a damn fine engineer, too."

Ace and Issy had boarded *Freyja's Grimalkin*, and they beckoned Lemmy and Gilbert to climb up as Jonah released ballast into the aerodrome's storage tanks.

The interior of the gondola was open to the elements, although, because of the size of the twin envelopes, rain would only drench the deck in the strongest of gales. Jonah kept a constant eye on the weather to ensure the safety of the airship. In gale-force winds, even the most powerful of dirigibles were at the mercy of nature's power.

Brass tubing, gauges and flying controls covered the inside of the prow, while the rest of the interior comprised seating and storage areas. Weight distribution was a major consideration in dirigible design; the smaller the airship, the more sensitive it was to load changes and placement. Even in larger dirigibles like *Freyja's Grimalkin*, pilots preferred not to overload either side and distributed passengers and cargo evenly from front to back. A balanced ship was an efficient ship.

In the gondola's prow, a pale purple mek covered in black 'tattoos' sat motionless. Gilbert had never seen a mek so still.

"What's up with him?"

Jonah twisted his neck to look. "Queequeg? He's an old MT-21. Shares piloting duties with me. Looks like he's sleeping, don't he? As far as I can tell, they don't need sleep, but not moving for a while gives their self-winding mechanisms the chance to catch up.

"Every now and again, he takes a power pellet, or whatever they're called, and lies there, eyelids twitching. But don't make the mistake of thinking he's unconscious. He's listening."

"Power pellets? I thought meks were just gears, pulleys and fancy clockwork. Never heard of them needing pellets." Gilbert stared at the mek. "Do you give them to him?"

"No, lad. His supply gets topped up when he gets his annual check-up. They're stored in a little box in his arm. He pops a pellet when he feels the need. Summat to do with his Babbage engine, they tell me, not his mechanics. I've no idea how they work, but old Queequeg here seems to run better after a break."

"Ha! I've learned something new today." Gilbert walked over to the mek and ran his fingers over his 'skin'. "Unusual paint job…"

"Unique name, too, don't you think?" Ace put his hand on Gilbert's shoulder.

"Aye, I suppose so. What does it mean?"

"Father's idea of a joke."

"I don't get it."

"Private thing between me and him." Ace turned away abruptly. "All clear for takeoff, Jonah?"

Jonah gave the thumbs up.

"Detach from docking. Let's go!"

Jonah flipped the switch to disengage the powerful electromagnet that held the foremost point of the envelope to the iron mooring post. The big dirigible rose majestically, spiralling slowly to starboard as the old pilot gently feathered the rudder in the still afternoon air. Four hundred feet above the airfield, he pointed the airship westward and gunned the motors.

The deck lurched and trembled beneath Gilbert's boots. He looked through the glass windshields that surrounded the gondola as the ground continued to recede. His stomach churned.

Jonah banked northward towards the heart of Lancashire. Gilbert lost his balance, crashing onto a seat attached to the side of the hull. By the time he had recovered, they had risen to six hundred feet in the air. He cautiously raised his head above the bulwark.

Below, a patchwork of olive green and golden fields gleamed in the autumn sunshine. From this height, he could see the huge steam diggers, augers and pile drivers dotted along the seventy-yard-wide cut gouged through the countryside. The River Mersey and the canal workings snaked westward towards Liverpool, and the coast was visible in the distance. Farmhouses and small villages looked like children's toys.

Gilbert's head was spinning. He keeled over onto the deck, his stomach turning somersaults. A sudden cold sweat stuck his clothes to his trembling body. He sat up, pressing his back against the hull, vomit rising in his throat with every movement of the airship.

"It seems our guest is afraid of heights. You should have told us, Gilbert." Issy put her arms around him. "Get a bucket,

Lemmy. We don't want to be swabbing the decks all the way to Pendle."

Gilbert saw no more of the landscape from the air. Huddled on his seat, arms wrapped tightly around his legs pulled up to his chest, he spent the journey fighting his terrors, barely holding down his last meal.

Only when he heard the low hum of *Freyja's Grimalkin's* electromagnet attaching the airship to the mooring mast did he uncoil himself. His legs felt like jelly as he scrambled down the rope ladder and planted his feet resolutely on terra firma.

I will never go up in one of those bloody contraptions again, he thought as his stomach finally lost the battle, convulsed, and sprayed vomit onto the damp grass.

"Someone is having sweet dreams." Letitia Lovegrove, Ray's flirtatious QT mek, whispered in his ear. "Is my dear, sweet Raven dreaming of his Letitia?"

Many years ago, a governess with a long-forgotten name had shortened his given name, Raynard Vincent, to Ray-Vin and despite his father absolutely forbidding its use, upon reaching his teenage years, Ray insisted everyone should address him as Raven.

"Always, my dear, always." He eased open his eyes to find her face inches above him, her bright yellow eyes staring into his. "Raven is in pain, Letitia dear. Can you get me a glass of water?"

Without a word, she leapt into action and scampered out of the room, returning with an empty glass and a jug on a silver tray. Raven edged himself up into a sitting position. He hadn't mastered the metal exoskeletons yet, but he would. Pulleys and gears splayed across his back and stretched the full length of each arm. He groaned with the effort as every attempt to move caused searing pain in his mutilated muscles. But he would persevere.

"Poor dear, sweet, Raven." Letitia stroked his hair.

"How's my favourite son?" His father tapped on the door with the ivory handle of his cane.

"Your *only* son, Father, and I am fine. Definitely on the mend."

Ignatius De'Ath bristled. "Get that damned mek out of here. We need to talk."

Letitia pouted and fluttered her eyelashes.

"Please leave us, Letitia. We'll spend time together later."

Letitia sped out of the room, brushing past his father and slamming the door behind her.

"Did you see that? It barged into me on purpose."

"If she touched you, it was because you were in the way. You can't attribute human emotions to a machine."

"Yet you address the infernal mek as 'she'. Curious…"

Raven sighed. "I call her *she* because *she* has lived with me at the Lodge for twenty-four of my twenty-eight years. Her programming has been updated every year to ensure her care has been appropriate for my age. *She* has been my constant companion as I grew from child to man, hidden from the world to save your shame. *She* was here, caring for me, while you lorded it up in the Hall—the salacious ninth Earl of Wraithmere, famous for lavish balls and unrivalled hospitality, whilst your son languished here, far from accusing eyes. What would you have me call *her*?"

"I didn't walk all the way over here to bandy words with you about that ghastly piece of junk."

"You bought her…" Raven winced in pain as he shrugged.

"Yes, I did. Second biggest mistake I ever made."

His cage rattled, Raven's feathers ruffled behind his half smile.

"So, what brings you to my humble abode? Have you come to inspect your latest investment?" He spread his new arms wide, leather straps straining against his body, the yoke anchors digging into his shoulders as pain knifed from his slashed biceps.

Ignatius sniffed. "Most impressive, Raynard." The words did not match his expression. "No, I have information about the pugnacious oik who bettered you and caused this great expense.

"I'm not sure what's worse, the immense cost or having to listen to you bemoan your ignominious defeat."

"Information?" Raven was all ears.

"Just his name and his whereabouts…"

EIGHT

Fugue

Colour was returning to Gilbert's face when he joined his companions walking from the moored dirigible.

Jonah stayed behind to add two hundred and three pounds of ballast from the storage tanks. Gilbert and the others walked down the slope along the treeline to a house nestled in the woodland on the side of the hill.

Dragonfly circled in the skies above, keeping a close watch, ensuring no one had followed them. Although he had no reason to believe the Anthropocene knew of their plans, Gilbert was grateful they were taking care.

Abel Throgmorton and his daughter must have spotted *Freyja's Grimalkin* and walked out to greet the travellers. A sturdy, heavyset man a little under six feet tall with black hair and a waxed, curly moustache, Abel wore a blacksmith's thick leather apron. His bare arms and bulging biceps reminded

Gilbert of the strongman in the travelling circus his mother had taken him to every Mayday. A pang of sadness surged through him, remembering her giggles.

Abel's daughter, walking a few steps behind him, had her father's pale green eyes, which were stunning against her darker skin. She wore a plain white dress over her lithe, muscular body. Welder's goggles wrapped around the crown of her short topper, which covered most of her dark hair. Gilbert bobbed from side to side, craning his neck to catch glimpses of her as they approached the property.

"Abel!" Ace shouted. "Good to see you, old chap!"

"Aye, you too, Ace. It's been a while. Is that a new face?"

"Yes, indeed. That's why we're here." The Stormriders reached Abel, and there were handshakes all around. "This is Gilbert Sparks. Algy wants you to look after him for a few days."

"How do you do?" Gilbert offered his hand.

Abel took it and looked quizzically at him. "Anything for the High Mother, but you must be damned important for Algeria to send you here."

Ace handed Abel a small brown envelope. "Gilbert needs to lie low. Some bad people want to do him harm. And… we bring terrible news." Ace put his hand on Abel's shoulder. "Percival has been killed."

"Pop? Murdered?"

"I'm afraid so. Be on your guard."

Lemmy checked his pocket watch and turned to Ace. "We should be leaving."

"You're in safe hands," Ace said, thumping Gilbert on the back, then nodded to Lemmy. "Let's get back to Jonah, as he'll be getting worried about the light."

Gilbert said his farewells to the Stormriders before turning to Abel.

"Dottie will show you to our guest quarters and help you make up your room. We've had the odd guest here over the years."

"Follow me," Dottie muttered as she marched past the house to a large, dark building on the edge of the woods, leaving her father to watch *Dragonfly* wheel away back southward.

The sun dipped behind Pendle Hill, adding a sudden chill to the air, mirroring the coolness between Gilbert and Dottie as they entered the silent building. It took a few seconds for Gilbert's eyes to adjust as he stepped out of the golden evening sunlight.

The air was thick with the distinctive stench of coal dust and molten metal. An old iron forge with enormous bellows, a huge black anvil and a slack tub dominated the dark workshop. Rows of pincers, hammers and tongs hung from hooks on soot-stained walls above workbenches and an industrial vice.

On a small table, light from a dim oil lamp sparkled off tiny splashes of gunmetal, pewter, bronze, silver and gold on ceramic crucibles. *This is no ordinary smithy.*

"Your father's a blacksmith?"

"How on earth did you guess?" Dottie didn't hide the venom behind her surprised expression.

"I don't see any horseshoes or cartwheels."

"There's no call for that 'round here."

"So, he's a specialist, then? Does he make things for the Order?"

"You ask a lot of questions."

This is like drawing blood from a stone. "He makes weapons, doesn't he?"

"Are you a member of the Order?"

"No, but—"

"Then I'll leave it to my dad to decide what he tells you. If he trusts you, he'll tell you what we do."

A blackened staircase at the back of the smithy led to a discreet, partially hidden doorway. At the top of the stairs, Dottie unlocked the door to a plain room with basic furniture and a small bedstead with a thin mattress. Acrid smoke from the forge below stung Gilbert's nostrils.

"We haven't needed to open this for a while. If we'd known you were coming—"

"You'd have baked a cake?" A hopeful smile accompanied Gilbert's interruption.

"I would have aired the room and made the bed," she said flatly. "There are extra blankets and sheets in the wardrobe."

She opened the windows and helped him with the bed linens. "Are those the only clothes you have?"

"There wasn't time to pack."

"Best put the eiderdown on, then. It gets cold at night up here."

She had to stand on tiptoes to reach up to the top shelf of the wardrobe to get the thick cover, her taut calf muscles visible below her simple cotton dress.

Gilbert stepped forward. "Let me. I can easily rea—"

"I don't need your help." She pulled the heavy blanket down, almost losing her balance.

He backed away, hands raised.

"There's a privy downstairs out back and a water pump in the forge. You'll find bowls and towels in yon dresser." She pointed to a small cupboard by the bed. "Supper in the house in an hour— nothing fancy, mind. Use the back door. We eat in the kitchen."

With that, she spun on her heel and, quietly closing the door behind her, she stepped down the creaky staircase. Gilbert dashed to the window and watched her stroll to the stable at the rear of the farmhouse, kicking casually at stones on the dirt path. He figured she was roughly his age and clearly knew how to handle herself.

The light breeze blowing through the room was laden with aromas from the countryside; some pleasant, others less so.

He turned from the window and let his aching body flop backwards onto the eiderdown. Hands behind his head, he interlaced his fingers and studied the old cobwebs that hung from the ceiling. They would have to go if he was going to be here for a while.

Total silence apart from the evening birdsong filled his ears. *Blackbird*, he thought and sighed. *I'll just have forty winks.*

Raven closed his eyes and waited, smiling.

Gears whirring, Letitia had arrived outside his bedroom seconds before the gentle tap. As expected, the door flew open, and she flounced into the room, striped white and gold long-sleeved dress swinging freely on her mechanical hips. Her attempts to surprise him never failed to amuse.

"Letitia, you startled me."

She giggled like a naughty child caught with a hand in the sweetmeats jar and cocked her head to one side. "Did you miss your sweet little Letitia?"

"Of course, sweetling, but what brings you here so early in the evening?"

"Dear, sweet Raven. What are you proposing?" Her eyelashes quivered suggestively. "There is someone called Bertram Gunn here to see you. He says you are expecting him. Do you like Letitia's dress? Letitia chose it especially for Raven."

"Very fetching, my dear. Please show Captain Gunn in?"

"Letitia will get him at once." She pirouetted through the door, slamming it behind her.

Raven sighed. He enjoyed her playfulness, but why could she not do anything quietly? The new prostheses were proving difficult to control, and his injured arm hurt like hell, but he continued to wean himself off the laudanum during the day, only taking one or two drops each night to help him sleep. Slowly, his mental acuity was returning, and soon he would be stronger than ever.

Another telltale whirring, a gentle tap, and the door crashed open. But this time, Letitia was not alone.

"Ahh, Captain Gunn. Good of you to come at such short notice."

"Are you all right, sir? There's been rumours…"

"I'm fine, Bertram, and as you can see, I have some improvements." Raven spread his arms and clenched his fists, feeling the power surge through the prostheses.

"So strong, so handsome." Letitia glided across the room to look out of the window.

"I want you to do me a favour." He trusted Gunn. He was a good soldier. "There are two brothers working at Barton lock on that accursed ship canal who are perfect for a job I have planned. Recruit them to our cause."

"Consider it done, sir."

"Thank you," Raven said. "Is there something you need?"

Bertram shuffled his feet, his unseemly stare unwavering as sunlight streamed through Letitia's flimsy dress, revealing her hourglass-like mechanical figure. He took a sharp intake of breath as she slowly turned to face him, cocking her head and fluttering her eyelashes.

He snapped his gaze to the floor. "No, sir. I want for nothing. You kindly take care of all my needs."

"Then I will bid you farewell. Report to me when you have

the Flanagan brothers." Then, speaking directly to Letitia, he winked, and making a discrete hand gesture as Bertram turned away, he said, "Please escort the captain off the premises."

She giggled and glided across the floor, linking arms with Bertram. "Goodness!" she said, "What big muscles you have, Captain Gunn. Do you like Letitia's dress?"

"Call me, um, Bertram." The door slammed behind them.

Raven's pale face and blond hair were dappled by the sun's rays streaming through the gently swaying trees. The sweet scent of late-blooming roses wafted in on the breeze from the gardens.

His plans were coming together nicely. With his head resting on the back of the armchair and his heavy prostheses on its padded arms, he closed his eyes, listening to the ambient sounds drifting through the open window: Athos grumbling as he pottered around the garden; magpies chattering when he got too close to their nest; Letitia giggling.

If everything went well, he would kill two birds with one stone. The next attack would deal a massive blow against the Connickle clowns and exterminate that vermin Sparks.

The roses' aroma suddenly smelt even sweeter.

For three long, boring, rainy days, Gilbert only ventured out of his room for meals with Abel and Dottie. Conversation had been cordial, but he felt he was intruding on his reluctant hosts.

On the third night, the rain stopped. He needed to get out of his room before he went mad. So, he lit an oil lamp and wandered into the woodland behind the forge. The sweet scent of wet grass reminded him of the long autumn walks with his mother along the River Irwell.

As he ventured further under the canopy of trees, dry

leaves and twigs crackled and snapped under his feet. The delicate breeze brushed the tops of the tall spruces, a rustling accompaniment to his steady stride.

He was grateful for the lamplight, as the pale, horned crescent moon glimpsed through the branches did little to illuminate the interior of the woods. Holding the light high above his head, purple shadows cast by its yellow flame danced with his every step.

Wet leaves glistened, flickering like tiny flames. Overgrown bushes and low-hanging boughs made this seldom-walked path difficult to follow, but he strode on, glancing back towards Throgmorton's Forge occasionally for fear of getting lost.

As the wood thinned, a huge dark shape rose in a small clearing; the blackened husk of a long-dead yew, its burnt black shards of broken bark thrust into the night sky, crooked fingers grasping for the moon. Many years had passed since lightning had devastated this ancient tree, but there was evidence of new life around the base, where ferns, mosses and fungi blanketed the root boles.

At the far side of the clearing stood a large rectangular stone, its edges worn smooth by weather and years of usage.

Gilbert followed the old path as it skirted the trees, kicking at the overgrown foliage barring his way. He placed the lamp on a short tree stump and sat on the pale-yellow slab, gazing at the ancient yew. The cold rock sucked the warmth from his bones. Somewhere close, an owl screeched, and a startled small animal scurried behind him in the undergrowth.

Pipistrelles silently crisscrossed the sky: darting, wheeling effortlessly through the darkness, catching and devouring their insect prey. In the deathly silence, overwhelming despair descended on him. Pangs of dread coursed through his listless body.

The hair rose on the back of his neck.

He was not alone.

In the woods, an unseen primordial evil prowled, hidden in the dark. Eyes unblinking, it watched and waited. Treetops rustled, and an ill wind whispered, plotting a snaking path through the dark. Gilbert's eyes flicked left and right, the only movement possible from his terror-frozen body. Every second held an unknown terror preparing to strike.

A dank, wet stench rose from the undergrowth, filling his nostrils. Mist ghosts swirled through the trees, forming a grey, impenetrable shroud. The deathly chill of the stone consumed his body. Petrified, unable to move, he was merging with the rock. He would never leave this place.

Dark thoughts spiralled through his mind, endlessly deepening, out of control. Mired in mental torment, he willingly surrendered to the inevitability of death.

A high-pitched squeal behind him broke his fugue. The small rodent had not been fast enough. Owlets would eat well tonight. Heavy-limbed, he dragged himself to his feet, shaking his head and staggering wildly. Grasping for the lamp, he sprinted blindly away from the evil, across the clearing to the path that had brought him to this place. Twigs whipped his face as he hurtled through the woods, the track barely visible in front of him.

He didn't look back, fearful of what he might see. Only when the forge was in clear sight was he able to slow his pace and catch his breath. His pounding heart and laboured breathing filled his consciousness.

Finally reaching his room, he barred the door and buried himself beneath the covers, trembling.

NINE
ECHOES

LAUDANUM, BITTERSWEET LAUDANUM.
Raven mixed a couple of drops of the prepared tincture in sweet water and virtually threw the liquid to the back of his throat. He shuddered as the sugar failed to completely mask the bitter bite of the drug on his tongue. Then, pulling the eiderdown up to his chin, he settled into the warmth of his bed. It was early afternoon, but why should that matter? What if he wanted to while away a few hours in splendid euphoria? Who could stop him? Athos? Father? He snorted. *Let them try…*

The strength was returning to his arm by the day. His recovery had been going well despite his struggle to ween himself off the pain-killing opiate. Laudanum eased the agony, but the deadening of his mental acuity was frustrating. Concentration was difficult, decision making almost impossible. Soon he would free himself from the powerful drug. *But not yet...*

A welcome soporific haze infused his brain as the poison coursed through his veins, numbing, slowing his breathing and unlocking memories. He closed his eyes, heightening his senses. Sounds and scents filled the room, inciting long-forgotten echoes of his past.

Breeze-rustled leaves became the crisp, swishing crinolines of guests arriving at a lavish ball glimpsed from between spindles on the gallery's balustrade. Ambrosial autumn jasmine evoked the scent of his precious Temperance's hair.

Vivid memories washed over him in waves, drifting on a sea of consciousness, crests and troughs in an emotive maelstrom.

One moment, he was a child again, happily playing with Nanny. Then, as a young man walking hand in hand with dear, innocent Temperance, the sun shining through her delicate blonde ringlets, never doubting he would spend the rest of his life in her arms and losing himself in her lustrous eyes.

Giggling as Father chastised him for sticking Nanny with a pin, again.

A pimply, gawky teenager, he relived skinny dipping in the freezing waters of the lake on the estate at midnight with local girls bought by his father and the exhilaration of each urgent thrust when he lost his virginity with a girl he never saw again.

His face stinging from his beloved Temperance's slap as she stormed out of the Lodge, leaving him bewildered and confused, while Father smirked in the shadows.

Every fibre of his being felt the humiliation as his twelve-year-old self soiled his pants while standing in a corner, punished by a cruel governess.

The exhilaration of each urgent thrust as he plunged the knife into her again and again, feeling her life ebb away in his arms, the light fading from her questioning eyes. Father cuffing him around the head, angry at having to clean up his bloody mess.

Raven's lips stretched into a wide smile.

Click! A door closed. Someone had entered his bedroom, and, motionless, barely breathing, he waited. Amplified senses strained to catch the smallest clue.

The intruder was familiar with the room as they avoided the squeaky floorboard a few steps from the doorway. Twin pungent stenches of body odour and stale tobacco invaded the sweet aroma of jasmine, bespoiling his reveries. *How does such a big man move so silently?*

"Athos, my friend." Mumbled words from a distant, deep internal place spilled from his arid mouth.

"I am sorry. I have woken you."

"I wasn't asleep; just resting my eyes before Letitia brings my afternoon tea."

"It's late."

"Uh?" Raven half-opened his eyes to find the room undulating in darkness. Lit only by the faint moonlight from the open window seen through his drug-blurred vision, lapis lazuli tree shadows slow-waltzed around his bedroom walls. *Damned laudanum!*

"I spoke with Gunn. He wanted you to know that the men you asked for have joined our cause."

"The Flanagans?"

"Gunn didn't tell me their names. Sorry…"

"No matter." The slurred voice sounded annoyed. "If there's nothing else…"

Athos stepped into the moonlight from the window, casting a black shadow across the bed as he fumbled in his pockets. He hovered next to the bed and, finally finding a neatly folded note, he pressed it into Raven's limp, clammy hand. "Gunn asked me to give you this."

"What is it?"

"Details of the Runcorn job. He said you'd need it for your journal."

"I can't read it now… place it in the book, and I will write it up tomorrow."

Athos took the note and opened the top drawer of the tallboy. He rummaged through the contents, carefully at first, but his movements grew more frantic.

"What's wrong?"

"The book isn't here."

"Of course it is."

"No. It is not."

"Try the next drawer."

Athos closed the drawer and opened the one below it. After a few seconds of poking around, he closed it and faced the bed. "It is not there."

"We'll find it in the morning when we have light." Raven's voice was distant. He was losing the battle, trying to prevent his heavy eyelids from slamming shut.

The bedroom door clicked.

Alone again, he succumbed to the opiate. Its exquisite embrace welcomed him back to a world without pain and suffering, a rapture of ephemeral memories, a kaleidoscope of vivid colours, the like of which he had never seen.

Impossibly distant echoes of whirring gears, a faint click, familiar aromas and a crinkling of crinoline.

Letitia?

After a restless sleep, Gilbert's mind was in turmoil when he walked into the kitchen. Were the fast-fading memories of last night real, or just nightmares?

Dottie was waiting for him in a beige shirt and trousers with dark brown knee-length boots and, of course, her trademark topper and goggles. "Dad wants to see you in the smithy after breakfast."

Gilbert shrugged and pulled up a chair. "I've got nothing better to do." He picked up his drink and slurped the hot beverage noisily.

She slammed her mug onto the table. "You know, from what he tells me, we're taking a massive risk looking after you. Show some gratitude!"

"Gratitude? Stuck in the middle of nowhere with you two while Raven plans his next killing? I should be hunting him down, not here, sitting on my hands."

"I'm sure you'll have your chance to play the hero."

"I'll make the bastard who killed my mum pay. I couldn't care less what you or anybody else thinks about me."

"Good! Because you aren't making any friends here. There are bigger forces at play. This isn't all about you!"

"The Order needs me to stop Raven, and I want him dead. Although we both want the same thing, they need me, but I don't need them. So, I'm just wasting time here."

"You might be the only person who knows what he looks like, but he's seen your face, too, stupid. The High Mother ordered us to keep you safe while she finds out more about his plans.

"To be honest, I'll be happy to see the back of you so we can return to normal." She stormed out of the back door, slamming it so hard it almost came off its hinges.

She doesn't know what I'm going through. No one does. He finished his breakfast, left his plate on the table, and headed over to the smithy.

Thankful that Dottie was nowhere to be seen, he popped his head around the entrance of the forge.

Abel was working the bellows. Stripped bare to the waist, his massive, muscular body glistened with a mixture of sweat and coal dust. This immense man would be a fearful opponent. Gilbert stepped closer. Beads of perspiration formed and rolled down his face as the intense heat hit him. The acrid stench was choking and so overwhelming he could taste it.

"You wanted to see me?" He raised his voice to be heard over the noise inside the smithy.

"Aye." Abel looked up and chuckled. "You look warm, lad. There's a couple of benches out front. Get a bit of fresh air, and I'll be out in a minute."

Gilbert stepped outside and inhaled deeply. The sweet, cold air made him cough and chilled the sweat beading on his flushed cheeks. He wiped his face and neck with his handkerchief before sitting on the seat. Under his feet, the grass sparkled, wet from the dawn mist that was gradually lifting.

Rhythmic hammering from the forge shattered the early morning pastoral peace, and it was three-quarters of an hour before Abel wandered out, drying his slick torso with a dirty towel.

He sat on the bench opposite Gilbert, body reeking from the muck sweat of his labour. "Algy wants me to tell you about the Order to help you understand the peril of the Anthropocene. She's faced a few problems during her time as High Mother, but she thinks this new threat will be the sternest."

"I don't care what they are trying to do, Abel. I just want to stop Raven. Nowt else."

"Aye, lad, I know you're hungry for revenge, but I don't think you realise what you're up against. I am sure about one thing, though."

"And what's that?" Gilbert felt a lecture coming on.

"You can't tackle Raven and this Anthropocene crowd alone. You'll need all the help you can get."

"Kill the bastard, problem solved." He brushed his hands together, wiping off unseen filth.

"If only it were that simple. There's a bigger picture to consider, and Algy will not have you running around like a loose cannon. The Order has been Algy's life, her passion, since she was a girl. Although her father was only a foot soldier for them, she believes in our cause with every fibre of her being.

"She's a formidable woman, Gilbert. You must never underestimate the lengths she will go to for the cause. She's done things no ordinary person would do. So, make no mistake, the Order means everything to her, and she won't let you act alone if she thinks you might get in the way.

"When she became High Mother, she took over from High Father Cuthbert Pilkington-Green, who—"

"Sir Cuthbert Pilkington-Green?" Gilbert sat up straight.

"Aye, lad. Now, being a Member of Parliament meant he wasn't up to snuff making decisions at the local level up here. He rarely came to meetings, but he got important laws passed. With help from him and a few other members of the Order, we got the Connickle legislation through. You learned about Arthur Connickle in school, eh?"

"Well, I know a bit about him…" Gilbert flushed, having heard of him only a few nights earlier at the fateful meeting in the Praetorian. School was not a pleasant memory for him.

"Ha! So, you didn't learn your ABCs." Abel slapped his leg and laughed. "Arthur Buckingham Connickle was a toff, never worked a day in his life, but after his parents put him through university, he travelled far and wide, studying other cultures. There wasn't one corner of the British Empire he didn't visit.

"To most folk, he was a historian and scientist, but he was much more than that. He was a brilliant thinker, a philosopher. He made the connection between how folk live and where they live. He noticed the closer to the North and South Poles or the equator people live, the more of their days they spend trying to survive. But in the two bands in-between, where food and water are plentiful, living is easier.

"Folks who live in these areas don't need to worry about foraging or hunting for survival, so they have time for more, shall we say, noble pursuits? In his view, all the great art, poetry, inventions, exploration and scientific discoveries come from cultures based in these fertile zones.

"Now, some folk dismiss his conclusions as a lack of understanding of tribal societies on his part. But he wasn't commenting on intelligence or inferiority; only about opportunity, you understand?"

"I'm pretty sure them that live in Angel Meadows spend all their lives trying to survive. I doubt any of them have written any great poetry."

Abel smiled and leaned forward. "He was explaining the effects of geography on cultures, not politics on people."

"What has any of this got to do with Algy and the Order?"

"I'm getting to that." Abel was rocking on his seat, hands clasped, speaking with intensity. "It was when he expanded on the ground-breaking experiments carried out by Eunice Foote connecting industrialisation and climate that he sent a shock wave across the so-called civilised world.

"He examined historical data going back hundreds of years and found that since the start of the Industrial Revolution at the beginning of the century, the polar and the equatorial regions have been getting warmer; not by much, but measurably. Frozen areas at the poles are shrinking, while the uninhabitable areas around the equator are expanding.

"Something had to be done to slow the pace of industrialisation. In his view, doing nothing would lead to a climate catastrophe. The privileged habitants of the fertile zones were responsible for slowly poisoning Mother Earth for everyone.

"This is the Connickle conundrum. We all want the benefits of scientific discovery—steam-powered machinery, gas street lighting, mills and factories churning out cheaper clothing—but at what cost?

"No one wants to stifle invention and discovery, but what if the next brilliant idea made life much easier but poisoned Mother Earth more quickly? It's human nature, lad. Most people couldn't care less about the effects on the planet in the future, as long as there is something in it for them now.

"So, the Order and other like-minded groups pressed the government to pass laws to slow down scientists and engineers. The Patent Office vets new discoveries and inventions before they are registered. They control the railways, waterways, roads, iron and steel production.

"Although even now, there are those in the Order who believe the Industrial Revolution is still moving too fast.

"The High Mother believes the Anthropocene plans threaten the future of the planet, and we must stop them at all costs. Getting rid of this Raven fellow may be the first step, but from what Algy said in her note, it won't be easy. They're everywhere."

"So… I'll play my part and kill Raven, with the help of the Order, of course, and leave them to get on with disbanding his followers," Gilbert said.

"Aye, well, if that's what you choose to do. But she wants you to join the Order, and remember, Algy always gets what she wants."

Gilbert understood the implication. "At the moment, I don't know. Ask me again after I've killed Raven."

"Confident lad, aren't you?" Abel smiled. "Killed lots of men, have you?"

"No, but I will kill this bastard if it's the last thing I do!"

"There's no need to raise your voice, lad. I'm not doubting your intentions. I understand your hatred. He killed your mum, after all."

"Aye, and Wainwright and Percival. Don't forget them."

"Pop was a good friend. He was just as dedicated to the cause as Algy." Abel lowered his voice. "Are you sure you can take a life? It's not as easy as you think. Hatred will drive you, but it will cloud your judgement. From what you say, this Raven is a stone-cold killer with no regard for human life.

"Killing comes easy to him because it serves his purpose. To him, anyone who gets in his way must be removed. Man, woman or child; it makes no difference to him. I've known men like this." Abel gathered his thoughts. "Algy has asked me to do three things."

Gilbert raised his eyebrows. "Keeping me out of the way was one, I guess."

"To keep you out of danger, to make sure she doesn't lose the only person who can identify Raven, was the first thing, yes. She also wants me to teach you a few fighting skills."

Gilbert snorted.

Abel looked around to see if Dottie was in earshot, leaned forward, and lowered his voice. "Unlike you, lad, I have killed—for country and for the cause. It's not as easy as you think, and I'm not proud of it."

Killed for the cause? "And what else does she want you to do?"

Abel sat back and folded his arms across his barrel chest. "Here at Throgmorton's Forge, we make the finest blades, swords, knives and axes in the Empire."

"They're not much use against a gun," Gilbert said with a smirk.

"A pistol has a single shot, but blades last forever. Oh, and you wouldn't be sitting here today had it not been for Pop's cane-sword."

"You made that?"

Abel nodded.

"Algy has asked me to tailor a weapon to fit your skills, but first, I need to find out your fighting style."

"What type of weapon?"

"That depends on how you fight."

Gilbert had not had many fights in his young life, but every one of them resulted from a loss of temper or a lack of judgement.

"We'll start tomorrow afternoon." Abel weighed Gilbert up. "We don't want you spoiling your new clothes, so I'll get Dottie to ride into the village to rustle up some trousers and a shirt for you. Have you seen her this morning?"

"Aye, at breakfast."

"She'll be around somewhere. If you bump into her, send her over to the forge, will you?"

"If I see her, I will."

Abel stood up and stretched his back. "No rest for the wicked," he said, turning on his heel and stumping off towards the smithy.

Gilbert had no intention of looking for Dottie after the morning's altercation. He felt more than a little guilty that she had been on the wrong end of his foul mood. He walked to the forge and peeped round at the stables. A two-wheeled gig sheltered under an awning at the side of the building told him either she had taken the horse for a ride or she was still skulking around the farm.

He turned to wander up the hill to where *Freyja's Grimalkin* had moored a few days ago. Wary of being out in the open after his chat with Abel, he stayed close to the treeline leading up the gentle slope.

Halfway to the mooring pole, he heard the familiar steady drone of approaching engines. Although the airship sounded high in the sky, he didn't want to risk being seen, so he ducked into the trees, crouching behind a bush, waiting for the airship to appear over the summit of the hill. A few seconds later, a green and orange two-bagger cruised into view, rocking as the side wind buffeted the light craft.

Dragonfly! Relieved, he puffed out his cheeks as the air yacht sailed overhead towards the buildings. Tabby turned the dirigible sharply over the smithy without losing speed, the gondola swinging at forty-five degrees to the envelope.

As he watched, Abel stepped outside and waved to Connie and Rory, who were leaning over the edge of the hull. *Tabby must be a heck of a pilot.*

As quickly as it arrived, the air yacht was heading back to Barton. Gilbert wondered if they had been visiting regularly to check on his safety.

Was Algy over-reacting to the Anthropocene threat? Was his life in danger? He wasn't sure, but she was worried enough to send *Dragonfly* out patrolling the skies.

He clambered up to the top of the hill and, leaning against the mooring post, he surveyed the surrounding countryside. The sun was high in the sky, and a fresh breeze was shaking the trees. Smoke rose from the chimneys of the farmhouses dotted around the hills and valleys.

Gilbert shielded his eyes from the sunlight and scanned the skies to the south. *Dragonfly* was flying as straight and true as an arrow. As he peered across the heavens, he was surprised by how many airships he could see from this perfect vantage point. He counted nineteen.

He stretched out on the grass and gazed up at the cloudless sky, but the clippety-clop of a cantering horse interrupted his reverie. Dottie had returned to the forge. Gilbert hoped she had forgotten his mood earlier in the day, but it was still twenty minutes before he ventured back to the farmhouse.

An English rose, poise, elegance, and timeless beauty: all were attributes Lucinda Portia Theodosia Marsh indisputably possessed. But she was so much more.

Unfortunately for her mother, Lady Patience Marsh, the suitors' descriptions of her ill-tempered, self-adoring, brattish daughter were equally true. Seated opposite her in the carriage, Lucinda ferociously beat the air with her fan.

"Are we almost there, Mama? Two hours in this stuffy carriage is simply too much." The journey from Bacup had been slow and arduous.

"For the umpteenth time, Lucy, we will arrive when we arrive and not a second earlier. Indeed, if the road was any shorter, we would not reach our destination!" A glance at Lucinda's expression confirmed the attempt at humour had missed the target.

"I promise you, Mama, if this earl is a fat warthog with bad breath and hairy ears... I can't, and I won't."

Lady Patience sighed. *It's going to be a long day.*

Cobblestone-clattering wheels quietened to a low rumble on the pulverised stone carriageway leading to Weepingbrook Hall. "At last!" Lucinda said as they trundled through the ornamental gardens that flanked the approach to the dark, gothic building. The sweet scent of jasmine and honeysuckle filled the carriage, but Lucinda held her handkerchief to her mouth and wrinkled her nose, seemingly determined to turn sour even the most favourable event.

"Best behaviour, Lucy dear."

Lucinda rolled her eyes.

The coachman pulled up in front of the imposing vaulted portico of the Gothic country pile and helped each lady alight. As they climbed the steps, the huge wooden doors creaked open, and an old MT-series mek glided forward.

"Good afternoon, Lady Marsh. *This 'kin*," the mek bowed its head, "is Silas. The earl has asked *this 'kin* to show you directly into the music room. Please follow."

Silas turned and disappeared into the house. Lady Marsh bustled up the steps, trying to keep up with him, with Lucinda skulking reluctantly behind.

As expected from the dark exterior, the grand foyer was bleak and imposing. Double staircases curved up to a first-floor gallery overlooking the main doors, and a huge black chandelier suspended from the vaulted ceiling two storeys above dominated the room. Silas opened a door in the dark wooden panelling under the gallery and stepped aside, allowing the ladies to enter.

Lady Marsh took a deep breath, straightened her back, and marched through the doorway, followed by Lucinda several steps behind, her eyes fixed firmly on the floor. They were barely across the threshold when the door closed with a loud clunk.

Windows stretched along one side of the music room with French doors at the far end leading into the orangery. A mercifully silent, upright player piano stood against the opposite wall.

"What a creepy mek. He gave me the collywobbles." Lucinda shuddered. "So, how old is this earl?"

"He is a sprightly fifty-five."

"Ugh. You must be joking."

"Now, you listen to me, young—"

The door swung open, and Ignatius Balthazar Cyrus De'Ath, the ninth Earl of Wraithmere, strode into the room. Dapper and clean-shaven, the middle-aged gentleman with long, grey hair had a confident gait.

"Ahh, Lady Marsh, so good to see you again." He stepped forward, grasped her by the shoulders, and brushed his lips on each rouged cheek. "And this must be Lucinda. A rare beauty." He bowed to take her hand and kissed the back. While looking up into her impassive, cold blue eyes, he smiled, motioning them to sit. "Please make yourselves comfortable. I've asked Silas to bring tea."

"Thank you, Ignatius. A hot drink would be most welcome." Lady Marsh sat next to Lucinda.

"So, Patience, how's Bartholomew? Still trying to eke out a living at Irwell Mill?"

"He is very well. Thank you for asking."

"How old is he, now? Seventy?"

"He's sixty-six. Business is steady, but, of course, it will improve when we can use the new canal."

"He believes he can send products along the river to the docks at Salford. Ha! Good luck with that."

"I don't think—" Patience paused, hearing a faint knock when Silas entered carrying the tea.

"On the table, Silas." The mek placed the tray down and picked up the teapot to pour. "Leave it!" Ignatius snapped. Silas nodded and left, closing the door behind him. "Infernal meks. I can't stand the blighters."

"We have something in common, my lord." Lucinda said, "Silas is singularly creepy."

"Please, my dear, call me Ignatius."

"Mama tells me you are looking for a wife to give you a son and heir."

"That's a little forward, young lady. But essentially, you are correct. In providing me with an heir, you will carry on the Marsh and De'Ath bloodlines, and our son will become the tenth Earl of Wraithmere, eventually inheriting the estate."

"What's in this for Mama?"

"Lucinda, I—" Lady Marsh blushed at the inference that there was a pecuniary interest in this transaction for her.

Ignatius raised his hand. "It's all right, Patience. I'm sure your daughter doesn't mean to imply any impropriety. To make things crystal clear, as your husband, I would be happy to help your mother and father financially should the need arise. But the continuance of our bloodlines is my chief concern."

"*Your* bloodline, my lord, is not *my* concern."

Lady Marsh leaned closer to Lucinda and whispered. "You are my only daughter, and I only desire what's best for you, my dear. You are young and have your entire life ahead of you, and this is a genuine opportunity to acquire a title in your own right, as well as secure the future of our family. I'm sure Ignatius will make sure that you will want for nothing."

"I can only echo your mother's sentiments, Lucinda. Should you agree to walk out with me, I will satisfy your every need." He poured a splash of milk into each china teacup and topped up each from the teapot. "Sugar?"

"One teaspoon for me; two for Lucy, please."

Lucinda was deep in thought as they sipped their Darjeeling, and when she spoke, she chose her words with care. "If I agree to a formal courtship with you, Ignatius, I insist a chaperone is present until I am comfortable meeting you alone."

"Perfectly reasonable, my dear. I am happy for your mother to accompany us. I assure you that my intentions are honourable. Will you be able to grace us with your presence during our romantic liaisons, Patience?"

Lady Marsh had been listening open-mouthed to the exchange, concerned that the future of her family hung in the balance.

Unbeknown to Lucinda, her husband's business was in a precarious financial position, with the bank threatening to foreclose on borrowings and repossess the spinning mill unless substantial investment was forthcoming. Although they had chosen not to reveal the extent of the problems to Lucinda, judging by her daughter's change in attitude towards the old earl, perhaps she understood more than they realised. *Clever girl.*

"I am happy to chaperone my beautiful daughter, although I sincerely doubt there would be any unbecoming behaviour."

Ignatius's sly smile did not go unnoticed. "Please permit me to show you both around by humble family pile."

"It's certainly unusual." Lucinda flicked open her fan and began agitating the surrounding air.

"They completed the principal part of the building in 1349 during the reign of Edward III. I believe those dark times influenced the beautiful gothic design. Bubonic Plague was ravishing the country during its construction, resulting in many examples of religious symbolism in the architecture…" Ignatius paused as Lucinda stifled a yawn. "Maybe we should finish the history lesson another time. Would you like to see our ornamental gardens before you make your way back to Bacup? They are the finest in Cheshire."

"Yes, that would be delightful." Lady Marsh relished the change of topic. The Plague was not a suitable subject of conversation for ladies of delicate disposition.

"I will have Silas prepare a picnic for your journey. I am sure there must be a scenic place to rest and enjoy your repast."

"Very thoughtful, thank you."

Ignatius pulled the bell cord by the player piano to summon Silas, who appeared at the door within a matter of seconds.

"Prepare a selection of sandwiches, sweetmeats and cordials in a picnic basket for our guests."

"Certainly, sir." Silas left for the kitchen as silently as he had arrived.

"Creepy," Lucinda repeated her initial assessment of the mek.

"Please…" He offered his hand, but Lucinda swished past him, ignoring his approach.

Unflustered, he guided them through the orangery and into the formal terraces, proudly describing the plants and flowers. Rhododendrons, roses and jasmine flourished in raised beds bounded by small walls. Winter and Japanese honeysuckles climbed trellises, providing distinctive fragrance throughout the year.

Lucinda wrinkled her nose and again covered her nose and mouth with her handkerchief as she hurried past their overpowering aromas. Lady Marsh recognised her daughter's disdain. *Yes, dear*, she thought, *I'm sure these abominations will be the first to be culled once you are the lady of the house.*

The horses had taken on sufficient water from the trough by the stables to sustain them for the return trip, and the coachman was walking them to the front of the hall when Silas appeared from a side door with the picnic hamper. Ignatius placed it in the carriage and inquired when he might see them again.

"They have invited us to cut the ribbon at the opening of the new Triple T Terminus at Oldham next Saturday. Perhaps we can meet you afterwards? Say two o'clock if that's agreeable?"

Lucinda nodded at her mother's suggestion.

"Most agreeable. I will wait with bated breath for the day to dawn." Ignatius bowed and grasped Lucinda's hand before she could pull it away. He looked up into her eyes as his lips barely brushed the back. Was her demure smile a tacit promise for the future? It mattered not. This coupling was a business arrangement in which they were both willing parties, to varying degrees.

Nicely done, Lucy. Lady Marsh smiled in approval at her daughter and rapped on the inside of the carriage. The coachman encouraged the horses onward, and she took a last look at the Hall as they pulled away.

The dark building was certainly impressive. As they turned towards the main road, she glimpsed movement in the stables. Was that a gigantic figure in the shadows? She craned her neck, twisting her body to get a better view. If it was a man, he must have been over seven feet tall.

"Mama?"

"Nothing, dear, just a trick of the light, I'm sure?" But Lady Marsh's puzzled expression belied her true feelings.

TEN

INSIGHT

HIGH ON THE HILL above the Forge, in an earthy grove strewn with pine needles, Gilbert sat on one of nine felled tree trunks arranged in a circle. Threatening dark clouds overhead matched Gilbert's mood.

He was early, rigorously scratching the skin under the coarse brown canvas shirt and trousers Dottie had bought him. When he tried them on, they had hung so loosely on his body that he had to use a series of belts to stop him from walking out of them.

Why did he still feel annoyed by Dottie? Last night's evening meal and breakfast had been cordial. She joined in conversations only occasionally and avoided eye contact with Gilbert.

Upon returning from the village, she had left his clothes on his bed, giving him no chance to apologise. *I'll never understand women*, he thought.

As a child, he remembered overhearing his mother telling a young friend that the secret of a long-lasting relationship was never to go to bed after a row without making up. *That must be for married folk*, he thought.

He was still prickly when Abel strolled into the clearing, carrying a large sack. He was wearing plain blue, heavy-duty twill overalls and an aviator's skull cap held in place with a chin strap.

"Here, put these on." He reached into the sack and tossed some protective padding across to Gilbert.

"Where's your padding, old man?"

"Don't need any." Abel's smile had disappeared.

Oops, I think I've poked the bear.

He slipped the torso padding on, fastening it like a waistcoat, but putting on the arm and head protection proved more difficult. By the time he had buckled his chin strap, Abel was arranging a series of wooden sticks and paddles with carved handles.

"Looks as if they've seen some use." Gilbert examined the array laid out on the log.

"Aye, lad. We've had a few folks pass this way, some for training, others to weigh up for weapons. It's important to tailor the weapon to each fighter's style. Size is one consideration, but there are others, such as, and not least, concealment. Walking through town with a broadsword might draw unwanted attention."

"So, the wooden sticks represent different blades?"

"Aye. The handle, guard and cheek mimic the original weapon in weight and balance, but these training tools are not lethal."

"So why do I need this padding?"

Abel picked up a short knife and thrust it into Gilbert's stomach before he could move. Doubled up in pain, Gilbert fell backwards and sat in the dirt, clutching his belly.

"Without the padding, you'd be holding in your entrails. Even a wooden stick can do some damage." Abel said, chuckling. Gilbert didn't see the funny side of the sudden attack but was glad the padding had taken the brunt of the thrust.

Abel offered his hand and hauled Gilbert to his feet. He dusted himself down, trying desperately to look unhurt.

"Choose your weapon."

Gilbert stepped forward, and after a few moments to consider his options, he picked a small knife with a curved blade.

"Bold choice. That's a karambit from Malaysia and the Philippines. It's a slashing weapon used for both attack and defence. Let's see if you have the skill to master it."

Abel picked up an identical wooden stick, and they walked to the centre of the circle. Abel stood square on to Gilbert. "Whenever you are ready."

Gilbert circled to his right and, holding the karambit high, lunged at Abel, who deftly parried the attack and hooked Gilbert's wrist with the inside of the blade, knocking him off balance and drawing the wooden blade across his throat. Had the blades been real, he would have been bleeding from two major arteries and facing certain death. Abel pulled Gilbert to his feet. "Try again."

Gilbert thrust at Abel's chest with the point of the curved blade, but Abel stepped sideways and forward, allowing the blade to pass between his chest and arm, trapping Gilbert's forearm before drawing his own blade across Gilbert's throat.

"Well, judging by your first two attacks, the karambit is not for you. You would need years of tuition, and we don't have time for that. Pick something straighter."

"You choose," Gilbert said. Blood rushed to his cheeks, eyes flashing.

"We're only sparring, lad. You need to control that temper of yours." Abel squeezed Gilbert's shoulder. "The British army uses stilettos for close combat. Let's give that a try." He picked up two thin wooden blades with very pronounced guards. "Keep your thoughts free of emotion. If that's possible…"

He's mocking me! I'll show him. As Abel offered him the knife handle first, Gilbert grabbed it and lunged at Abel's ribs with all his might, only to find Abel had stepped sideways, the wooden blade stabbing harmlessly into thin air, throwing him off balance. Two sharp stiletto thrusts punched into Gilbert's side, knocking the wind from his lungs and leaving him on his knees, gasping.

"And don't let your opponent manipulate you into doing what he wants you to do." Abel shook his head and sighed. "We have much work to do if you are going to stand any chance against this Raven."

"I've beaten him once."

"By luck, not skill." Abel offered his hand and pulled Gilbert to his feet.

Abel was right, of course.

"I'm messing with you, lad, but understand, fighting Raven won't be easy. I can help you with weapons and teach you basic skills, but you're going to need courage, cunning, and a cool, clear mind, as well as controlling that fiery temper of yours.

"A fight is just as much a battle of wits as skill and strength. I've seen strong warriors beaten by a devious tongue."

Gilbert stood, shoulders slumped, crestfallen at how easily Abel had embarrassed him, but in an actual fight, that would have been the least of his problems. Dead men don't blush. *I'm going to need all the help I can get.* He straightened his back and nodded.

"That's the spirit." Abel slapped him on the shoulder, a little too vigorously for Gilbert's comfort. "Now, pick up the knife, and I'll show you how to switch grip from normal to ice-pick, a few attacking and defensive styles, then we'll see what Dottie's rustled up for us to eat."

Gilbert took a deep breath and picked up the wooden stiletto.

Freyja's Grimalkin's flight across the Pennines had been blissfully serene, and as they walked away from the safely tethered airship, Jonah spread his arms wide, sucking in a lungful of fresh South Riding air. "Dad used to call it 'God's own country'. There's nowt like it anywhere else in the world."

By his side, Lemmy nodded his tacit approval without raising his eyes. Issy and Ace were a few paces in front, taking short, wary steps down the steep, grassy incline overlooking Wigtwizzle with its impressive Elizabethan mansion. The surrounding rolling hills and meadows were dotted with sheep and partitioned into irregular shapes by dry-stone walls.

In the distance, a faint rainbow hovering over Whitwell Moor appeared brighter against the backdrop of ominous dark clouds gathering in the northeastern sky.

They had entrusted Queequeg with the airship, which was moored out of sight on the other side of the hill from the village. Jonah was enjoying this rare excursion. Too often, he would be left to guard the airship while the intrepid Stormriders took off on an adventure, but in this remote location, Ace had ceremoniously invited him along to 'join the fun'.

Ace looked back over his shoulder. "Magnificent, indeed, but unless that impressive rainbow is a permanent feature, the northern landscape cannot match the Arcadian topography of the Cambridgeshire countryside.

"This bleak terrain lacks the bucolic charm of the lush green pastures, trees and bushes clinging to the banks of the Great Ouse and the River Cam."

"Nah. It's too flat down south. You can't top these moors. Look at the little villages nestling between the hills. Blessed perfection."

"That's enough, you two." Issy dug Ace in the ribs with her elbow, then lowered her voice. "You should know better than to bait a Yorkshire man about his beloved county. And remember, he's got to fly us home later, so it's probably not a good idea to wind him up like a clockwork soldier."

Rumours of unusual goings-on had prompted Algeria to dispatch them to Wigtwizzle Hall as a possible site of the Anthropocene headquarters. This remote place on the reaches of the southern Pennines was sparsely populated, but reports filtering across the hills of unusual activity around the ancient hall warranted further investigation.

Ace doubted the probability of the hypothesis because of its limited accessibility, but Lemmy's infectious enthusiasm, supported by Issy, had won the day and Jonah, as always, was keen to visit the county of his birth.

"What do you suppose those are?" Lemmy pointed at six progressively larger circles of charred ground.

"Campfires?" Ace said.

"Maybe… but why would anyone stay out here when there's a lovely pub in yonder village?" Jonah nodded at the small group of buildings along the road from the old hall.

"What makes you think there'll be a pub in the village?"

"This is Yorkshire. Every village has a grocer, a church and a pub."

"And how do you know it's lovely?"

"Have you not been paying attention, old chap? This is Yorkshire. Everything here is better than everywhere else." Lemmy said with a smile and a wink.

"Aye, you may poke fun at me, but you know I'm right." Jonah set his jaw.

"At least we'll have somewhere to stay that's warm and dry." Issy pulled her coat together and folded her arms.

The slope was levelling off as the four companions approached the place where a wide dirt track traversed the hill. They turned onto the pathway leading towards the old mansion and the small village beyond. Lemmy was grateful to be on flat ground, striding confidently along the wheel-worn trail. "Fresh tracks," he said.

"Aye, carrying summat heavy, an' all." Jonah narrowed his eyes and pointed behind them. "Looks like it left the track back there a-ways, either coming from or heading to the field where we saw the black circles."

"Keep your wits about you. We may be walking into a den of Anthropocene." Ace put his arm around Issy, and the four strode on towards the hall.

The dirt track became a narrow, crushed stone road which crossed a gently flowing stream via a humpbacked bridge. A hundred yards further on, a driveway to the left led up to Wigtwizzle Hall. They each cast casual glances at the old building as they passed in silence. There were no signs of life, and though it was an unusually chilly late autumn evening, smokeless chimneys indicated there were no fires in the grates.

"We'll see if they have rooms available in the village pub that Jonah has confidently predicted, then return under cover of darkness." Ace turned to Jonah. "You do the talking. Locals will be less suspicious of a stranger speaking like them."

"I should've known you wanted me along for a reason. You'd better hope my North Yorkshire accent doesn't spook them."

"Perhaps you could give a few lessons in the local vernacular, old chap." Lemmy slapped him on the back. "I'm darned good with foreign languages, don't-cha-know."

Issy rolled her eyes before linking Ace and setting off towards the village.

The 'lovely pub' was a large coaching tavern called The Wagon and Horses. Ace and Jonah shared the large room, while Issy and Lemmy took each of the remaining two rooms.

The landlord had insisted on payment up front, and although he eyed them with suspicion, his icy stare thawed when Jonah told him they were going to the hall later that evening. Behind him, his three companions exchanged knowing glances. On leaving the bar with keys to their accommodation, they gathered in Ace's room.

"Looks promising, don't it?" Jonah was licking his lips.

"The landlord's change of attitude was interesting. If he thinks we're involved with the hall's occupants, was his newfound friendliness out of fear or respect?" Ace stroked his beard.

"I'm starving. When do we eat?" Lemmy asked with pleading, puppy dog eyes.

"When we get back. Let's reconvene here at seven o'clock." They checked their pocket watches before Issy and Jonah went to their own rooms.

Just after 7.00 p.m., they strode through the busy taproom. More than a few heads turned to stare at them, and Lemmy thought he detected malice on the faces of a few. The barman exchanged unsmiling nods with Ace as he dried a pewter mug with a small hand towel. Outside, their breath billowed in the chilly air.

"Friendly bunch," Lemmy said. "Did you notice anything unusual?" He raised an eyebrow at the puzzled expressions of his companions. "No meks. Just the landlord and a couple of barmaids serving drinks."

"This is Yorkshire. We—" His friends' peel of laughter cut Jonah's explanation short.

They arrived at Wigtwizzle Hall after a few minutes' brisk walk along the road and down the driveway, illuminated only by moonlight. Darkness shrouded the building, its black and white half-timbered architecture barely visible in the shadow of ancient trees in long-unkempt gardens. Within, cold rooms were absent of lamplight.

"Has anybody got a lucifer?" Issy asked.

Jonah struck a match and held it up to the dirty window.

"*Semper paratus.*" Ace patted his back.

"Perhaps there's a back door." Lemmy stuck his hand out for some lucifers, then crunched through the gravel towards the back of the building. At the rear, a large empty stable stunk of horse dung, and there were wheel tracks like those on the dirt track crisscrossing the muddy yard. He returned to the front of the building to find himself alone.

"Over here." Issy's hoarse whisper came from the other side of the property. Lemmy walked blindly towards the voice, tripping over the open hatch of the entrance to the cellar and landing on its open wooden door.

"I say! What luck! I could easily have fallen down that hole."

"Shh, I'll help you down the ladder." She grabbed his arm and guided him onto the rungs."

"No need for shushes, old girl. The place is deserted." He struck a match. "Barrels? I was expecting wine racks, not beer!"

"They're empty." Issy banged her fist on the nearest of a dozen barrels, sending a hollow rumble around the stone walls. "And judging by the scrape marks on the cellar floor, there were many more stored here."

Footsteps across the floor above dislodged flecks of dust to float, glittering in the lucifer's light. Issy pointed upwards and beckoned Lemmy to go with her upstairs to join the others. The stairs lead to an empty pantry on the ground floor, and they followed the glow from Jonah's match into a large room.

"There's lots of evidence of recent occupancy." Ace was examining documents scattered on a table. "But it seems they have moved on, never to return. Sadly, we can't find any proof Raven was here."

"So, it's been a wasted journey?" Lemmy kicked at a length of brass tubing on the parquet floor, sending it spinning across the room.

"Hardly." Ace threw a handful of papers onto the table.

Lemmy puffed out his cheeks, flicking through page after page of typed anti-Connickle rhetoric, bursting with invective. "Somebody dislikes our inspirer. This has to be Anthropocene, doesn't it?"

Ace nodded. "We've seen enough. Let's head back to the Wagon."

They hurried along the road, arriving at the public house dusty and dishevelled, turning the heads of the patrons once again, their lively conversations falling to a murmur.

"Did you get what you wanted, officers?" The landlord turned to his regulars sat at the bar. "Looks like they've been scrambling around in an empty building to me."

"What's that you say? You think we are members of the constabulary?" Ace's voice boomed across the room as he strode up to the bar, pressing his palms on the counter.

The barman took a step back as Ace leaned closer to him. "You stand out like a sore thumb. What else could you be?

Snooping about in the dead of night. Those folks at the hall never gave us any trouble. We never saw 'em most of the time."

"Now, see here, my good fellow. I assure you and your customers here that we are not police officers. We were looking for a friend. Perchance you have met him? Tallish chap, blond hair goes by the name of Ray, although his friends call him Raven, and his partner, never leaves his side, giant of a man, called Athos."

The landlord and patrons shook their heads, looking around at each other. Either they were actors worthy of treading the boards at The Old Vic, or they had genuinely never seen Raven or Athos.

"When did they leave the hall?" Issy eased Ace away from the bar.

"Their carriages and wagons passed through the village the day before yesterday, miss. These toffs were friends of yours, were they?"

"Toffs?" Issy said.

"Aye. Most of the gents had toppers, and the ladies wore fancy clothes. But you'd know that if you really were friends of theirs, now, wouldn't you?" The barman looked Issy up and down but turned away when his eyes met her icy glare.

"Had they been at the hall long?" she asked.

"About two years, weren't it, Seth?"

The bearded old man nursing his drink at the bar nodded. "Closer on three, I'd say."

"We've had quite enough of this nonsense. Our business here is our own and, frankly, has nothing to do with you. Now, we should be very grateful if you would serve us drinks and food before one of our party expires from lack of sustenance." Ace put his arm around Issy's shoulders.

Lemmy saw an opportunity. "Tell me, landlord, you are an experienced, licenced victualler, are you not?"

"Aye, that I am. I've been serving the good folk of Wigtwizzle for nigh on fourteen years."

"Seems closer on twenty, I'd say." Seth slurped a mouthful of beer as his friends laughed.

"Then, let me ask you a question… What is a firkin?"

"That's easy. It's a small seventy-two-pint barrel."

"Wrong," Lemmy said, "A firkin is a British standard measure of excess usually found in units of two."

"Huh?" The landlord scratched his head.

"Allow me to give you examples." Lemmy took two one-pound notes from his wallet and placed them in the palm of his hand. Extending his arm, he began a slow turn, starting at the forty-something barmaids who watched him with suspicion, arms folded, their lips pursed.

"These ladies, here, are too firkin' lovely for this hostelry. It's too firkin' cold outside, and these good folk appear to be too firkin' thirsty to be bothered about us.

"So, here's two firkin' pounds!" He completed his 360-degree turn by slapping the pound notes on the bar. "A round of drinks for everyone in the house on me!"

Cheers and laughter erupted around the room as he stepped nimbly to the side to avoid the onrushing locals eager to get their free drinks and followed his friends to an empty table in the corner.

"That'll cost you a bob or two. These 'good folk' will order more than one drink out of your purse. We're in Yorkshire, you know." With a wink and a grin, Jonah chided Lemmy.

"I counted sixteen drinkers, so two pounds should cover at least two drinks each."

"Nicely done, old chap," Ace said, "It was becoming somewhat tense."

"Are we heading back tomorrow?" Issy asked.

"Yes, but now we know Wigtwizzle Hall is unoccupied, we can have a quick search in the daylight before we leave. Jonah, be a splendid fellow and order our usual refreshments. Oh, and ask the landlord what food they can rustle up for us. We have plenty to discuss."

Gilbert had prepared lunch for Dottie and Abel. He flopped into a chair, every muscle, sinew, bruise, and cut hurting like hell, his body aching in places he didn't know he had.

For each of the last three afternoons, training had become progressively tougher, with Abel showing his imperious prowess in armed and unarmed combat. He had lost count of the number of times Abel had knocked him down and picked him up.

No matter how hard he trained, he doubted he would ever be skilled enough to defeat Raven. But each night, he went to bed thinking of his mother, and each dawn, he recited the names of those who had died at Raven's hand. Resolve refreshed, his hunger for vengeance hardened, he made a vow to work harder.

Every day, Abel worked hard in the smithy before breaking for lunch. This morning, Dottie had been working with him and was first to appear at the kitchen door, wearing olive green dungarees and little else. Welding goggles rested on the dark blue topper skewed at a jaunty angle atop her head. Her arms glistened with sweat, and her face was smeared with dirt. *Looks like you've been using those goggles, judging by the clean rings around your eyes.*

"I'm going to freshen up," she said. "Dad will be here in a few minutes."

Gilbert nodded.

"No training today. Dad wants to talk to you after lunch."

"What about?"

"Dunno. Probably just giving you a break. After all, it can't be much fun getting beaten up every day."

"Hah, hah. Very funny. He tells me I'm a quick learner."

"Really?"

"Yes, really."

Dottie snorted. She walked over to the sink, filled a bowl with water, and took it outside to wash.

Why does she wind me up so, and why should I care what she thinks? Gilbert banged his fist on the table.

"You pissed off at something, lad?" Abel strode in bare-chested, dragging a dirty towel across his body.

"Just getting frustrated. I don't understand why I'm here. I won't find Raven and his mob by hiding, and I'll never have your fighting skills. What's the point?"

Abel sat at the table and started picking at his food. "You're a good lad, Gilbert, but you need to learn patience. You're too hot-headed. To give yourself a chance in a fight against an experienced opponent, you must have ice in your veins." Abel ruffled Gilbert's hair. "Listen, we'll go to the clearing after we've eaten. No sparring today, just talk, all right?"

Gilbert nodded. "Can I ask you a question?"

"As long as you're not asking for money."

"Dottie never talks about her mum. Is she still alive?"

Abel stiffened. "I'd keep off that subject if I were you. She doesn't like to talk about her... and neither do I."

"But—"

"If you don't want your head chewed off, steer well clear of it, understand?"

I've hit a nerve. "I didn't mean to pry."

"Leave it, son. I'll see you in the clearing in ten minutes." Abel leapt to his feet, chair legs screeching on the stone floor, and stomped out of the kitchen, leaving Gilbert alone, bewildered.

What on earth was that about? He shook his head and leaned back in his chair. Dottie was drying herself and staring at him through the open kitchen door. *If looks could kill…*

He finished his food, gulped some water, and headed outside. She brushed past him without saying a word.

Gilbert looked up at the angry shreds of black clouds looming against the slate grey sky. *Even the weather's turned against me.* At that moment, if he had known how to get home, he would have walked there barefoot. He had not felt so alone since the day his mother died. Memories of her death began washing over him in waves once again. Sniffing back the tears as he sat on the bench outside the smithy, he buried his head in his hands.

"Come on, lad." Abel came out of the forge, carrying a canvas bag, and put his arm around Gilbert's shoulder. "Let's go."

They walked up the shallow slope to the clearing in the trees and faced each other, straddling one of the tree trunks.

Abel leaned forwards, hands clasped together. "I've been pushing you hard, and you've stood up to the physical challenge, but you must change your temperament to have a chance against this Raven fellow. Emotion clouds judgement and you're too quick to anger, too impetuous. You'll lose the fight before you start. I know you need to avenge your mum's death, but you mustn't let your rage blind you. Do you understand?"

"How can I control my temper when every time I close my eyes, I see his snarling face?"

"Observe and analyse, slow your breathing, look for weakness, ignore everything that isn't relevant. If you're outmatched physically, use deception. Don't pity yourself if things aren't going your way. React, adapt and never give up."

Easier said than done when my blood's boiling. Gilbert nodded.

"Before I show you what's in the bag, just one more piece of advice. If you are over-matched, don't be afraid to turn and run. There's an old saying about discretion being the better part of valour. There's a fine line between bravery and foolhardiness."

Thinking before acting did not come naturally to Gilbert.

Abel picked up the canvas bag. "I have something for you." Reaching into the bag, he pulled out two short swords and scabbards. Similar to a short cutlass, the wider, slightly curved, double-edged blades were only a little over twelve inches long. "Strap 'em on. See how they feel."

Gilbert's eyes widened, a broad grin spreading across his face. The blades slid smoothly into the scabbards, and he buckled them to his thighs. Strangely comforting, cold steel chilled his flesh through his thick trousers. The buckles on the leather straps fastened at the front just above the knee and at the top of his thigh, blades curving backwards. He patted the hilts. "Thanks, Abel. They are… gorgeous."

"I've designed the hilts so you can easily switch your grip between regular and ice-pick during a fight, and I've even made them look like tools."

Gilbert crossed his arms and drew the swords from the scabbards, swishing the beautifully balanced blades, forming figure eights in the air as he rotated his wrists.

"There'll be plenty of time to practise with them. The High Mother isn't in any rush to have you back."

"I've got to find Raven."

"Aye, lad," Abel said. "Listen… Algeria wants me to tell you about the Order. If she knew what I'm about to say, she wouldn't be best pleased, I dare say, but you need to know the truth.

"The Order is not only a bunch of well-meaning conservationists. Many of the higher ranks are fanatics with a deep-running belief that, as members of The Venerable Antediluvian Order of the Custodians of Magna Mater, they have a mystical connection with Mother Earth.

"I'm just a foot soldier, Gilbert, but some would do *anything* for the Order. In their eyes, you share their goals, or you are part of the problem. Choose your friends carefully."

"I don't have any interest in the Order. Once I've done what I need to do, they can continue their crusade without me."

"You think they'll let you leave just like that?"

Gilbert stiffened. *They can't stop me, can they?* "Then maybe I'll join. I'm not thinking past killing Raven…."

"It's a lifetime commitment if you enlist."

The sound of an approaching dirigible distracted him, and Abel pulled out his pocket watch and frowned. "That's odd… Rory and Connie are early today." He stood up, twisted and stretched.

Gilbert squinted skyward, trying to glimpse the air yacht as the roar of engines grew louder, echoing between the trees.

"Always remember, Gilbert, when—"

Whoosh! A crossbow bolt missed Gilbert's head by inches, smashing through the side of Abel's skull.

Gilbert spun around to see who fired the shot as a low-flying four-bagger, heading towards them, climbed to rise above the wood that surrounded the clearing.

"Abel!" Gilbert leapt behind the log to where his mentor had fallen, but his anguished cry would forever remain unanswered.

DREW HALFPENNY

ELEVEN

Smoke

Losing sight of the airship, Gilbert scanned the skies as he sprinted through the trees, whipped by branches, and hurtled down the hill, screaming as loud as his labouring lungs would let him. "DOTTIE! DOTTIE!"

She stepped out of the stables and, seeing Gilbert's anguished expression, ran to meet him.

"What's wrong? Where's Dad? What have you done?" Fear turned to anger, and she tried to brush Gilbert aside. He grabbed her by the waist, pulling her close.

"He's gone... They've killed him... There's an airship." He was gasping for air, scanning the skies over the woods. "There!" The dark red dirigible was turning towards the Forge. "We must go. Now!"

"No!" The steel in Dottie's calm voice took him by surprise.

"You don't understand—"

"We have time before they moor. Gather what you can, and I'll meet you back here." She shoved him towards the smithy and sprinted away to the house.

Gilbert didn't argue. He dashed through the smithy, up the stairs to his room and, scooping up his meagre belongings, raced downstairs. Dottie ran in as he was putting a few tools in a bag. She grasped his arm and dragged him outside towards the woods.

"Now, we run!" She took off at speed into the trees, with Gilbert in hot pursuit.

The path looked different in the daylight, but soon he realised it was the track he had once ventured along. Dread constricted his chest, pangs of fear weakening his legs.

When she reached the edge of the clearing, she stopped, spreading her arms to prevent him from passing. "Be careful. Follow me. Keep to the stones. Don't disturb the leaves and bushes."

"What?" Gilbert frowned.

"No time for questions, just do as I do." She turned and tiptoed deftly on the flat yellow stones dotted around the ruined yew. When she reached the blackened trunk, she squeezed inside a split, which started a few feet from the ground, widening as it rose. Jagged edges pulled at her clothes, but she was careful not to leave any trace. Disappearing into the empty husk, she thrust out a hand to beckon Gilbert forward.

As a child, he had been useless at hopscotch, but he leapt across the stones nimbly without brushing the foliage.

To squeeze through the crack, he had to climb until he found a place wide enough. Once inside, he gasped at the size of the cavity and retched at the stink of decaying vegetation. Eight or nine adults could have stood comfortably in the hollow trunk.

Dottie was up to her knees in wet, stinking foliage, scrabbling around the floor with one hand, holding on to the side of the rotting husk with the other. "Don't just stand there, help me," she said.

"What are we looking for?" He bent down and started running his hands through the noxious mixture of mulched leaves and dead insects.

"A big iron ring." She plunged her other hand into the morass of filth. The rancid mulch was inches from her face, and then, trying not to retch, she was pulling at something with all her strength. "Move!" she shouted. Gilbert jumped to the side.

"Let me try." Easing her out of the way, he knelt and thrust his arms into the ooze. The ring was so slimy that he needed both hands to grasp it. Heaving with all his might, the wooden hatch came free with a loud creak. Dottie helped to push once it had broken the surface of the muck. Dead insects and rotting vegetation tumbled into the newly uncovered opening.

She reached into her bag and produced a paraffin lantern, struck a match and lit the wick. "Watch your step. The stairs are slippery."

Gilbert peeped into the hole. The lamplight showed a tight spiral of stone-hewn steps.

She handed him the lamp. "You first. I'll cover our tracks."

Too wide at the shoulder to negotiate the staircase without contorting his large frame, he squeezed himself down the tight spiral as quickly as he was able. The bare room at the bottom had stone seating on each wall. The low ceiling made it impossible for him to stand without stooping, so he sat on a slab. At the top of the steps, Dottie slammed the hatch shut.

Unlike Gilbert, she had no problem negotiating the stairs. "Lower the wick. We need to save fuel," she said as she stepped off the stairs. He dimmed the light from the lantern as Dottie strode purposely across the underground chamber. Small holes bored in a line on one side of the ceiling appeared in the shadows.

"What did you bring?" She snatched the bag off him and rummaged through the contents. She caught her breath when she saw her father's poker. Extending a trembling hand, she ran her fingers over the handle last held by her father's powerful hand. Silent tears trickled down her cheeks. Taking it up, she prodded at the holes. Small amounts of detritus cascaded into the room as she unblocked them, one by one, enabling thin shafts of light from the world above to illuminate the chamber.

"Air, light and sound. We're safe for now, but we need to keep quiet." Her voice was a hoarse whisper as she sat still holding the poker, peering up at a tiny speck of sky visible through each vent.

Gilbert nodded.

"I covered the entrance as much as I could, but I don't think they'll come near this forbidden place." Her shoulders slumped; her voice cracked with emotion.

"What is this place? Where are we?"

She leaned closer and lowered her voice to a whisper. "This yew tree was sacred for a coven of witches a couple of hundred years ago. It was their bolt hole in times of trouble, too. No one, not even the locals, knows who dug this chamber or when. Dad always thought someone made it many generations before the coven discovered it.

"When we found it, Dad replaced the rotten hatch and cleaned out this room. Ever since I was a child, he told me to run and hide here if anything happened to him." She took a deep breath, and her lip trembled.

Gilbert rose from his seat, but the sound of footsteps in the undergrowth above their heads stopped him in his tracks. Dottie put a finger to her lips as, one by one, the light from each air vent went out as figures approached the stricken tree. Gilbert held up three fingers; Dottie nodded. Both listened intently, waiting for the thud of boots landing on top of the hatch, their only escape route.

"This place gives me the fuckin' creeps. Are you sure they came this way, Bertram?" Gilbert caught his breath, clamping both hands over his mouth in horror. The accent was unmistakable.

"Aye, big lad and a young flibbertigibbet of a lass. They definitely ran this way."

Dottie frowned, both at the slight on her character and Gilbert's stifled exclamation.

"Doesn't look as if they've trampled through here. They must have turned off the path back there and gone to ground."

A second Irish accent confirmed his fears. "There's something not right about this place, Gussy. I'm getting the collywobbles. Let's get out of here."

Gilbert and Dottie sat in total silence as the three men trudged out of the clearing, one of them kicking angrily at the leaves. After waiting a few long minutes, satisfied they were safe, they relaxed. "The bloody Flanagans are Anthropocene. I knew there was something not right with them."

Trembling with grief and relief, Dottie crept across the room, stooping to avoid the low ceiling. "What happened to Dad, Gilbert? I don't understand. Why did they kill him? Why?"

He stood and put his arms around her shaking shoulders. "They fired a crossbow bolt from the airship. I think they might have been trying to get me but killed your dad by accident."

Dottie's body stiffened. "The High Mother should never have sent you here."

"I wish she hadn't, too." Gilbert squeezed harder as sobs wracked her body. They held each other until the drone of engines passed overhead.

"I can't leave him there without seeing him," she said.

"Let's get out of here."

They climbed from the chamber, out of the hollowed tree, into the clearing, and tiptoed across to the path. "Why do we have to stand on the stones?"

"Dad thinks the witches spread a potion containing a drug that makes you terrified and disoriented. Scuffing the leaves releases the vapours. The more time you spend in it, the deeper you fall under its spell and the harder to escape its influence."

"Even after hundreds of years, it still works?"

"Perhaps there was more to the witches' skills than we know."

Gilbert nodded in agreement, having experienced firsthand the effects of the coven's craft.

The smell of burning was getting stronger as they neared the forge and farmhouse. Dottie broke into a flat sprint as she saw the buildings in flames. Black smoke billowed high into the sky. There was nothing they could do. "The stables!" Dottie could see the blaze engulfing the building. The distinctive sickly stench of burning flesh told her that her beloved horse had perished in the fire. "Why? Why have they done this?"

"I don't know." Gilbert was pacing. He felt helpless. "We'll bury your dad, then get away before they come back." He struggled to contain his emotions. Dottie had lost everything. She was in shock. What they would do next, he did not know. But he knew he was going to kill Raven and the Flanagans for what they had done today.

He would put an end to this once and for all. With or without the Order.

"*Pulchra dies.* What a day to be soaring above the clouds." With both hands firmly gripping the port side railing of *Freyja's Grimalkin*, Ace closed his eyes and took a deep breath as the warm air caressed his face.

Small puffs of cumulus were forming below them as thermals rose and condensed. The dirigible rode the heated airwaves over the foothills to the east of the South Pennines as Queequeg added a feather of power to the engines, tilting the nose upwards.

Rocked lightly by the gentle crosswind, the gondola cradled its passengers over the hills as the powerful airship effortlessly gained height to avoid clear air turbulence from the undulating landscape.

Queequeg deftly trimmed the gondola's attitude as they reached the zenith of the shallow climb and levelled above Dovestone Rocks. Behind them, Wigtwizzle was barely visible in the haze, receding into the distance.

Ace marvelled at the spectacular views of the valleys and gorges.

Jonah doffed his hat to the heavily tattooed mek. "Not too shabby for an old MT-21," he said with a smile and a nod at Queequeg, who returned the nod without taking his yellow eyes off the prow and the horizon beyond. "Looks like we're going to get rain from them clouds later."

They maintained their height as the ground fell away on the western side of the hills. At over a four thousand feet, on a clear day, they would have been able to see the west coast from North Wales to the bay of Morecambe, but haze limited their view to a few dozen miles.

Lemmy and Issy sat astern, riding the gondola's gentle rocking-horse-like pitching and swaying. "Ace, old chap, do you think we ought to lose some height? It's getting chilly, and poor Issy has goosebumps on her goosebumps!" Lemmy said, gently rubbing her arms. The temperature had dropped noticeably after crossing into Lancashire. Jonah chuckled.

"Yes, *amicus carissimus*, I believe you have a point." He turned to Queequeg. "*Fiat*, Queequeg." The mek acknowledged the instruction with a nod and pushed the nose of the airship into a shallow dive.

Lemmy guffawed. "Ace, old bean, we are indeed fortunate that our clever mek understands your Latin gibberish. Oftentimes, the rest of us don't have a clue what you're saying."

"I've picked up a few words. I think it's quite jolly." Issy and Ace shared a smile.

Jonah sat on the starboard side of *Freyja's Grimalkin*, casually surveying the landscape and watching for other dirigibles to avoid close aerial encounters. He had settled his head on his folded arms, resting on the bulwark, when something caught his eye, and he sat bolt upright, staring into the distance, hand above his eyes shielding the bright sunlight.

Ace noticed his sudden movement. "Problem, Jonah?".

"If I'm not mistaken, there's a fire in the hills around Pendle close to where we dropped off that Gilbert what's-his-name."

Issy turned to stare from her seat in the stern. "I think you're right. We should take a closer look, Ace. There may be trouble."

"Let's go, Ace. We might get some action." Lemmy was rubbing his hands together with glee, much to everybody's consternation.

"Queequeg, head for Pendle and lose more height. We need to have our wits about us. Until we know everyone's safe, assume the worst."

The big airship turned sharply to starboard, and Queequeg made a steep dive, doubling their speed in a matter of seconds. The manoeuvre was uncomfortable to all but the mek, who remained implacable as the others held on, trying to keep their last meal down.

"Sometimes, I wish I had giros and gears like our purple friend." Lemmy's complaint fell on deaf ears as everyone clutched their stomachs.

They levelled at twelve hundred feet and sped towards Pendle Hill. Flying at speed at this height was foolhardy, even suicidal, as dirigibles and hot air balloons cruised between six and fifteen hundred feet. At this breakneck pace, even the mek's superior reactions would not save them if they encountered any airships.

They hurtled directly at the clouds of black smoke billowing from blazing buildings, hoping the fire wasn't at the Forge. As they approached, all eyes were on their burning destination, and their worst fear was confirmed.

Throgmorton's home and smithy were engulfed in flames.

As they passed the inferno, without instruction, Queequeg turned sharply, lifted the nose to reduce speed and brought *Freyja's Grimalkin* to a hover a few hundred yards from the well-established blaze. They watched in horror as paraffin canisters exploded, sending convulsing clouds of fire into the air. The gondola was lurching to starboard as everyone moved to get a better look.

"No sign of life! I can't see Abel and Dottie!" Issy shouted above the crackling and popping sounds from the flames.

Ace gripped the bulwark, knuckles white, rage burning in his chest. *How? How has this happened? Is this the Anthropocene?*

The port side of the stern exploded, wooden shards and splinters tearing through the gondola. Grapeshot from a four-bagger swooping in from high above the woods had blasted into them. Only one projectile had smashed into the hull. The rest missed their target, harmlessly pummelling into the hillside.

The envelope containing the LTA bags was undamaged, but two large splinters had careened into Lemmy's thigh, slicing through bone and muscle alike. The ferocity of the impact had knocked him off his feet, and he lay unconscious on the deck.

Freyja's Grimalkin wheeled to starboard from the thunderous jolt. "Jonah! Take the controls! Get us out of this spin! Queequeg check superstructure and rudder! Issy, keep your eyes on that red blackguard!" Ace barked out orders like a Gatling gun.

Jonah increased power to the engines and spun the wheel to counter the spin.

"Superstructure and envelope are undamaged. Hull damage is superficial, gondola integrity intact." Queequeg's monotone voice was an oasis of calm amongst the chaos.

"Next time, we won't be so lucky," Jonah said.

"They're coming around again!" Issy shouted, pointing at the dark dirigible accelerating towards them.

"Full power, Jonah!" Ace bellowed. "Hard a-port!"

The engines roared in protest as Jonah applied maximum power, and the airship lurched forward and to port in the nick of time as a second grapeshot volley screamed past the hull. Their attackers wheeled away at speed.

In the seconds before a third volley would doubtless bring down his beloved ship, Ace's mind whirred frantically.

With only hand weapons on board, they were helpless against the other ship's cannons. *Their pilot is skilled. Ex-military*, he thought. *Come on, Ace, think!*

Issy was tending to Lemmy's horrific injuries, Jonah was trying to put distance between them and their attacker, and Queequeg was astern, watching the dark dirigible inexorably gaining on them. "They will be in range within ninety seconds," Queequeg stated in his matter-of-fact tone, which, for once, Ace did not find calming.

He surveyed the interior of the gondola. Eyes flicking left and right. Amongst the blood and carnage, he spied a solution.

"Jonah! Reduce speed to slow-ahead and zigzag to prevent them from getting a clean shot. I want them to think we are a sitting duck." He winked at Jonah, who met his wicked smile with wide eyes and open-mouthed silence.

"They'll blow us to pieces!"

"They've missed twice. They'll only fire when they are sure of the kill-shot. When they are lining up the shot to blow us out of the sky, that's when we'll pounce." He patted Jonah on the shoulder.

Ace had never let them down in a crisis before, so Jonah followed his instructions. He reduced power, and *Freyja's Grimalkin* fluttered like a butterfly, gently bobbing and zigzagging in the breeze.

Ace made his way to the stern. He tapped Queequeg. "Be a splendid fellow and move to the prow. I'm sure Jonah would appreciate your help in trimming the airship." Queequeg glided gracefully forward, avoiding the debris on the deck. Ace ducked below the aft bulwark and shouted. "Queequeg, tell me when they are a hundred yards behind us! Jonah, when I give you the signal, I want you to turn 180 degrees to starboard, then gun those engines!"

Ace crouched, nerves shredded. "Queequeg?" The mek remained silent. "What are they doing?"

"They appear to be preparing to shoot, but Jonah is making it very hard for them to get a bead on us…"

A few more seconds elapsed. "Queequeg?"

"They are *almost* a hundred yards behind us."

"Close enough! Jonah! Time to fight back!"

Jonah made a slow turn to starboard. There was a moment when their adversary had a shot at the broadside of the hull or envelope, but they missed their opportunity. Jonah turned on the power and sped straight at their attacker.

Within seconds *Freyja's Grimalkin* was alongside them, and Ace raised himself above the bulwark, struggling with the airship's huge harpoon. He took aim and, in one movement, launched a long steel barb streaking towards their envelope.

The grapple snared the thin aluminium skin, and Ace wedged the heavy brass gun barrel against the hull to take the strain. The steel cable screeched across the top of the bulwark as the two airships powered in opposite directions.

As the cable pulled taut, the grapple barbs gouged a jagged rip over half the length of the enemy's envelope, damaging the outermost LTA bags and sending plumes of purple gas gushing from the mortal wound.

Badly damaged, the red airship lost height, and Ace released the cable before the stricken ship pulled *Freyja's Grimalkin* down with them.

Their buoyancy comprised, the crew of the ruined dirigible had no choice but to jettison ballast, but even that was insufficient for them to stay airborne, and they continued to drop nose-first. Their forward-facing cannon pulled them earthward, and it did not surprise Ace when the heavy gun and munitions plummeted over the side.

He turned his attention to the inside of *Freyja's Grimalkin*, motioning Queequeg to take the controls. A jubilant Jonah strode over to Ace and slapped him on the back. *Too hard.*

"*Lupus non timet canem latrantem.*"

"That's a new one…" Jonah looked perplexed.

"*Per angusta ad augusta.*"

"I give up."

"Ace… We need to get Lemmy to hospital." Issy was holding his limp, unconscious body. Blood matted her hair and soaked her clothes. Most of it was Lemmy's, but wooden splinters that had been spinning through the gondola had lacerated her arms, too. They huddled together in a pool of congealing blood.

For once, Ace was speechless. His heart sunk. *Why Lemmy?*

"Full speed, Queequeg," Jonah spoke calmly to the mek. "Find us a mooring as close as possible to the nearest hospital."

Jonah knelt with Issy and helped her tend to Lemmy's catastrophic wounds. Ace watched on in horror as the life of his best friend slowly oozed onto the deck of his airship. There were no words.

"Ace! Ahoy, Ace!" Connie's frantic voice pierced the silence. He looked over to starboard. The gondola of *Dragonfly* was alongside, bobbing along in the vortices from *Freyja's Grimalkin*'s airscrews. "What's happened!" Her lined face was a picture of anguish.

"Ace! Pull yourself together!" Issy shouted.

"It's Lemmy. He's injured. We're taking him to hospital. They attacked us…" Ace's voice trailed off.

"What can we do to help?"

"There's nothing you can do…"

"We have to get to Abel's place. He'll be expecting us."

Ace paused. *How do I tell them that Abel, Dottie, and Gilbert are dead?*

TWELVE

Family Values

LUNGS BURSTING, HEART RACING, sweat pumping from every pore, Gilbert was losing ground behind Dottie, who showed no sign of slowing as she powered through the woods. Where does she get the energy?

Burying her father in a shallow grave had been a harrowing ordeal for her, but she refused words of comfort from Gilbert. Head bowed, she had knelt for a while by his makeshift resting place.

"A prayer?" he asked.

"A promise." She wiped a glistening cheek with the back of her hand.

The argument over their next move had been lively. Finally, she reluctantly agreed they should make their way to the Praetorian. Twilight had fallen by the time they left the Forge.

She set a furious pace, and after two hours of unrelenting speed over rough terrain, their path was lit only by pale moonlight flickering through the swaying treetops in the wood. During their flight, hardly a word had passed between them.

"Dottie!" Gilbert barely had the breath to call out. "We need to stop for a rest."

Hands on hips, she slowed to a walk and turned around, her eyes red. "Just a short break; they will be searching for us."

Gilbert folded onto the wet ground, panting. Twisting onto his back to look up at the night sky, he tried to drag air into his burning lungs.

"The road is a couple of miles away, but we're still a long way from the nearest Triple T station." Dottie sniffed back tears as she paced like an anxious sentry.

"Sit down. You need to rest, too." He raised his torso, supporting his weight on an elbow, shuddering against the chill night air. "Let's light a fire and settle down here until morning. Even if we were to reach a Triple T tonight, we will have missed the last—"

"No! Not here," she said. "We must keep moving. What if they are right behind us?"

"How? They won't risk flying in the dark, and we haven't heard or seen any sign that they've been tracking us on foot. Please, Dottie, let's stop and rest until daybreak and make a fresh start in the morning."

Dottie's shoulders slumped, and she walked over to where Gilbert lay. She put her head back, and tears squeezed from her screwed-up eyes.

"We need to find shelter. This is too open to the elements." She turned and squinted into the darkness to the south. "There's an old drift mine in the hillside half a mile over there."

Across the fields, he could barely make out the dark hills silhouetted against the sky.

Gilbert stood up, every muscle aching, and he followed her to the edge of the woodlands. At the open pasture, they broke into a steady jog, reaching the foot of the hill in a matter of minutes.

With no visible path up the incline, they scrambled up thirty feet of loose shale to a wooden walkway running laterally across the hillside that led to the boarded-up mine entrance.

"No one's used this place in a long time." Gilbert pulled at the rotting, splintered planks partly covering the opening, making a gap wide enough for them to squeeze through.

Dottie found an oil lamp hanging on the wall. It took her a few seconds to light the dry wick, revealing a dirty grey interior with a few dust-covered rusty tools strewn across the floor.

Gilbert gathered wood, rags, and anything that would burn, and they soon had a small, crackling fire that cast crazy, dancing shadows on the long-abandoned walls.

They hadn't eaten since early afternoon, and Gilbert's belly grumbled a loud complaint of neglect. "My stomach thinks my throat's been cut."

Dottie didn't return the smile. "What? Sorry, Bertie, my mind was elsewhere."

Gilbert bristled. A strangled grunt, his choked-off, fiery response was a second too late. *'Bertie' reflex as sensitive as ever... idiot!*

"What? What have I said? You've done nothing but whine and complain since I buried my dad. Or have you forgotten already?"

"Sorry, Dottie. It's just... Mum used to call me Bertie, and every time someone uses that name, it's harder to remember her voice. Memories are all I have of her... The Flanagan brothers called me that, knowing how I would react, and it's because of them we're sitting here now." He bowed his head.

"No, it's *your* fault we're here. You need to grow up. I know your memories of your mum are precious, but you can't live the rest of your life snapping at everyone who calls you Bertie. And, yes, I said it again."

"What was your mum like?"

"No, Gilbert, don't. I won't talk about her when I've just lost my dad."

"You and your dad must have really hated her."

"Stop it, Gilbert."

"Don't tell me to grow up when you react just as angrily whenever anyone mentions *your* mum."

Dottie stared at him, open-mouthed. "Enough, Gilbert. You know nothing about her. You don't understand how hard it was for me and my dad.

"He raised me single-handedly since I was a young girl. He showed me more love than you can ever imagine. While she… she stomped off to… ugh." She sprung to her feet and marched away from the fire, disappearing into the darkness of the mine.

Too tired to chase after her, he sat by the fire, fuming. When she had not returned for almost half an hour, he grabbed the lamp and walked, crouching, further into the excavations. He found Dottie sitting in the darkness, shivering, arms folded around her knees.

"Sorry," he said.

"Are you, Gilbert? Are you, really?"

"Yes, but why should you believe me?"

"You're so wrapped up in your own feelings and need for revenge, you don't care about anyone else. But don't worry, I'll get you back to the Order. Perhaps they can help you fulfil your destiny, while I will fulfil mine, alone."

"Come back to the warm." He helped her up, and they retraced their steps.

Sat on opposite sides of the fire, they could not look at each other. Gilbert broke the silence. "I *am* sorry. I didn't mean to upset you. You've just lost your dad, and I shouldn't have brought up your mum."

Dottie stared into the flames.

"To be honest, he told me never to mention her to you. I should've listened. I won't do it again, I promise."

She nodded without looking up.

He wanted to reach out and wrap his arms around her, tell her everything was going to be all right, but he couldn't because it would have been a lie.

"Get some sleep. Early start in the morning."

Wrapped up in their coats, they lay as close to the fire as they could, resting their heads on their bags.

The oil lamp had expired long ago. Cold stone walls sucked the heat from the flames that were slowly dying until only the light from its glowing embers lit Dottie's face. This was the first time he had really looked at her without being forced to look away by an angry glare.

Strands of black hair had fallen across her face. Maybe her nose was a little too small and her mouth a little too wide, but that didn't matter. Her fragile beauty belied her strength, but even as she slept, a veil of sadness shrouded her face.

When he arrived at the Forge a lifetime ago, he saw the happiness in her sparkling green eyes. She was devoted to her father, feisty and confident. Now, he was dead and her home, her life, destroyed.

It was his fault. He may as well have fired the fatal shot. If only he had minded his own business; if only he hadn't seen Raven's face; if only he had not taken the bag to Algeria, if only he had not found out the truth about his mother's death. If only...

Now, Bertie. If ifs and ands were pots and pans…

He sighed. He could not change the past, but the events of the last few weeks that had brought them to this dark place, would decide their future.

As the light from the embers grew faint, it became impossible to make out her features. He closed his eyes, resigning to do whatever was necessary to help her regain her happiness, even if that meant not being part of her life.

But first, they had to get back to Algeria. The Order needed to know what happened at the Forge.

Algeria will know what to do, and Dottie will be safe.

Ace and Issy sat in the prow, silent, staring astern. He put his arm around her shaking shoulders as she sobbed. "Goodbyes are never easy," he said.

Doctors and nurses had done everything in their power to save Lemmy, but they were not optimistic he would recover from his injuries. Catastrophic trauma and loss of blood had left him weak and fighting for his life.

Ace had dragged Issy, weeping, from Lemmy's bedside. She desperately wanted to stay, but he convinced her that there was nothing more she could do for their fallen friend, and they had to get back to Barton before dark.

Jonah tilted the nose of *Freyja's Grimalkin* upwards once it detached from the mooring mast. The hospital receded into the distance as the airship gained height, and after a slow, graceful, rising arc, they headed south. Few words passed between the solemn passengers until they approached their destination.

"Are Lemmy's parents in London?" Ace knew they had to be told of his injuries.

"I think so. Parliament doesn't go into recess for another month, and his father wanted to vote on something important. We must get word to them somehow," Issy said.

Lemmy's father was the Honourable Jeremiah Nathaniel Amory Philpott, who represented Manchester East at the Palace of Westminster. He was also a high-ranking member of the Order, and, as an ardent advocate of the Connickle laws, he was a leading light in pushing their agenda through Parliament.

"He's a fighter. Don't give up on him."

"Never."

"Aye. If anyone can pull through, Lemmy can," Jonah said. "He might be a bit of a joker, but underneath, he's as tough as old boots."

"Will Algy send an airship to bring his mother?" Issy said.

Ace nodded.

"The Anthropocene is getting too big for their britches. First, they attack the Forge, then us. They're coming out of the shadows. I think they're planning something big." Jonah was often Job's comforter, but Ace hoped he was wrong this time.

"For once, you may well be right, *mi amice*. That's why we need to get this old bird fixed and ready to fight. The Mother was on our side today, but next time we might not be so lucky. Let's give her claws to defend her honour."

Jonah vented a little LTA and dipped the nose as they reached the tree-lined northern perimeter of the aerodrome. They descended steadily as he reduced the power to the airscrews, steering towards the docking berths.

"*Dragonfly*'s here!" Issy pointed at the green and tangerine livery as Jonah caressed the airship into position and attached it to the mooring post next to the tiny air yacht.

"The ship's yours." Jonah patted Queequeg's shoulder. "Take good care of her." He followed Ace and Issy clambering down the ladder and let out a long, low whistle when he saw the damage to the stern. "We were very lucky."

"Lemmy would have a different opinion." Issy looked at the blood still soaked into her clothes.

"Had we not dashed to starboard, I fear the grapeshot would have destroyed the rudder, and we would have been sitting ducks. They could have blown us out of the sky. *Felix culpa.*" Ace tried to find something positive about the traumatic events.

"We can patch her until we get her properly repaired." Jonah looked up, stroking his chin.

"When will she be fully operational?" Ace didn't relish the idea of being grounded for very long.

Jonah took a sharp intake of breath, making the sound every engineer makes before quoting how much the work will cost. "Hard to say. If the weather holds up, we'll have her flying in a week or two."

"I want her tickety-boo in three days." *I can't have her out of commission for any longer. Algy needs us.*

Jonah shook his head. "I'll do my best, Ace."

As this was the first time both Stormrider crews had met since the ambush of *Freyja's Grimalkin*, Rory, Connie and Tabby were eager to learn more of the events at the Forge. They listened in silence as Issy described the burning buildings and how the Anthropocene dirigible had almost blown them out of the sky.

"Wonder what happened to the ship you slashed?" Rory asked.

"Fucking sky-pirates." Tabby flushed as everyone stared at her. "If you'll pardon my French."

"Last I saw, they were dropping fast with little left to jettison," Ace replied.

"We'll scoot around to see if we can find the blackguards."

Rory looked over at Connie, who nodded her approval.

"Too late in the day. The sun will set soon. There aren't many repair shops that can accommodate a ship that size. If we keep our ears to the ground, it'll turn up."

"Algy needs to be told," Issy said. "She'll be devastated."

Everyone bowed their heads, apart from Ace, who was deep in thought.

He was replaying the scene at the Forge over and over. *The fire must have been raging for at least an hour. I'm missing something. Why were they still there? Surely, they should have been miles away? Did they want to be found, or was there another reason?*

"Come on, Ace, let's get moving. We're all dreading seeing Algy, but it's getting late." Issy said.

Ace shook his head. "Yes, indeed. *Tempus fugit.*"

Amaranthine traces of dawn tinged the eastern sky as Gilbert and Dottie climbed out of the mine, stretching after their uncomfortable night on the hard ground.

Gilbert looked north towards Pendle. Beneath him, a low-lying morning mist shrouded the fields, forcing the wood's leafless treetops into jagged fingers grasping for light. Further in the distance, black wheels atop unnumbered colliery pitheads spread across the vast Lancashire coalfield poked through the grey vapours.

"I reckon we're fifteen miles from Bury Triple T. Walking will take us most of the day if we have to keep off the roads." Dottie's words condensed in the chill air as she spoke.

"We can't walk that distance without something to eat." Gilbert's stomach growled an exclamation point. "I'd kill for a proper breakfast."

"We'll head for Green Booth and get a bite there."

"Never heard of it. How far is it?"

"It's a mill town five or six miles away in the valley below the woods."

"We'd better get moving. This fog will give us cover, and the sooner we start, the sooner we get back to the Praetorian."

They stuffed their belongings into their bags and patted off as much dried filth as they could from their clothes before scrambling down the hillside.

The mist had burned off by late morning. Gilbert was conscious they were visible from the air and spent most of the time scanning for airships, ears straining. As they marched along the hedgerows, picking at the blackberry bushes and scrumping apples, every sound had them scurrying for safety.

Whether it was a tractor in a nearby field, horses' hooves on the road ahead, the distant drone of engines or even a sudden chattering of magpies, they dove for cover first and considered the source after. The journey would be long and nerve-shredding at this fitful pace.

"We must take a chance and try the nearest farm. Surely, they'll have something proper to eat," Gilbert said.

"That's risky. We don't know whether any of the folk 'round here are Anthropocene."

"But I have these." He patted the handles of his blades.

"Really? They're farmers. They'll have guns." Dottie dismissed his attempt at reassurance. "But you're right, we need to eat. We'll try the next farm we see."

Five minutes further along the road, through a gap in the hedgerow, they spotted a white building with a pale grey thatch and scrambled through the brambles into the fallow field beyond. The buildings appeared and disappeared as they crossed the undulating meadow.

Giddy laughter of children playing accompanied the telltale ticking of a tractor working the fields as they neared the farmhouse. The drone of a passing dirigible made them quicken their step.

Young children, who had been chasing hens in the farmyard, stopped and watched open-mouthed as Gilbert opened the five-bar gate into the farm. Probably reacting to the sudden silence, a short, buxom woman with long blonde hair tied in a bun bustled out of her kitchen, drying her hands on her flowery pinny.

"Goodness, gracious," she said. "What on earth happened to you, dearies? Are you hurt?"

Gilbert and Dottie looked at each other. Dust from the mine and filth from inside the hollowed tree caked their clothes and faces. *No wonder the kids stopped playing.*

"No, we're fine. We were on our way to Bury, but the horses bolted with our cart, and we've been travelling through the night. We've not eaten since yesterday. Is there any chance we might buy some food? Bread and cheese, maybe? We've got money…" Dottie scrabbled in her bag.

"No need for that, my dears. When Godfrey gets back from the fields, I'll be preparing food for this rabble. You are welcome to join us, and I won't hear a word against it." She put her hands on her hips. "But you're not coming into my kitchen in that state. You'll find a hand pump and trough at the side of the barn. Get yourselves cleaned up, then I might let you in."

"Thanks, missus." Gilbert touched the peak of his cap. The starving companions had no intention of refusing the offer of a meal.

"And I'll not have any of that, my lad. Call me Mabel. Missus, indeed." Turning nimbly, she scuttled back into the house, mumbling.

They hurried across the farmyard, followed by a gaggle of giggling kids. The younger of the children were nearly as muddy as the two bedraggled strangers, but a rap on the kitchen window from a wooden spoon stopped them in their tracks, and the youngsters returned to their hen chasing.

They brushed as much of the dirt from their clothes as they could, hung their hats on pegs in the barn, then took turns pumping water for each other to wash the filth from their hands, arms, faces, and hair.

A young man, who Gilbert assumed was the eldest, brought them each a towel to dry themselves, and they sat on the edge of the trough, waiting for Godfrey's return and Mabel's inspection of their cleanliness.

"How many kids do you reckon they have?" Dottie asked.

"Well, we've seen five so far. But there's a big age gap between the young man and the toddlers. There could be six or seven more."

"Really?" she said.

"You know what country folk are like."

Dottie dug her elbow into Gilbert's ribs.

The ticking grew louder as Godfrey's tractor approached. Hens and chickens scattered as the rusty machine, which had seen better days, trundled into the farmyard. It may have been old, but the clockwork mechanism purred like a moggy full of monkfish.

Godfrey steered into the barn, stopped the motor, and strode over to them. Godfrey was a tall, wiry man with a cheery smile. "Well, now. Who do we have here?"

Gilbert opened his mouth, but Dottie jumped in before he could speak. "I'm Dorothea, but most folks call me Dolly, and this is my cousin Albert, but he prefers to be called Bertie." Gilbert almost lost his balance and slid into the water.

"Bertie, eh? That's a proper royal name." *Crack*! Godfrey

slapped him a little too hard on the shoulder.

Gilbert tried to smile through the stinging pain.

Godfrey bowed with an exaggerated flourish. "Godfrey Ollerenshaw at your service. You look as if you've been dragged through a hedge backwards." His loud, bellowing laugh echoed around the farmyard.

"You should have seen them before they scrubbed up." Mabel appeared at the kitchen door and beckoned the two hungry travellers. "Let's have a look at you."

They sploshed through the mud and stood to attention, awaiting Mabel's approval as she examined their hair, hands, and fingernails.

"You'll do, but you'll have to take off those boots before you come into my kitchen. And you can unstrap them tools, if you want?"

"I'll keep my tool belt on, missus, er, Mabel, if that's all right?"

She cocked an eyebrow at him, then winked at Dottie as Gilbert bent to unbuckle his boots.

"I understand, dearie. An artisan never likes to be separated from his tools." Mabel furrowed her brow as she scrutinised the leather sheaths strapped to his thighs.

The kitchen was filled with the mouth-watering aromas of freshly baked bread and home cooking. *Just like Dad's hotpot*, Gilbert thought.

A large table dominated the kitchen. Gilbert counted twelve chairs and gave Dottie an 'I-told-you-so' nudge. Mabel ushered them to sit, then stepped back to the door and clattered her ladle against the pan hanging by the entrance. Within seconds, children filled the remaining places, except one; Mabel returned to her stove.

"Soup, cheese, and bread. Give me a hand dishing up,

Alouette."

The eldest girl stood and skipped to her mother. Apart from their obvious age difference and a few pounds, they were like two peas in a pod. *I bet that's how Mabel looked at her age.*

Gilbert smiled, guessing the young woman was nineteen or twenty, maybe three years younger than the eldest son. He reckoned the ages of the eight children spanned sixteen or seventeen years.

Mabel made sure everyone had soup before taking her seat next to Godfrey at the head of the table.

"So, my dears, what do folks call you?" she said.

Godfrey pointed at each of them with his spoon. "Well, princess, that young lady is Dolly, and the strapping young chap is her cousin, Bertie."

"I might have known you'd know their names before me, pokin' your nose into everyone's business." Mabel's stern expression made the children giggle.

"Thank you for letting us share your food. We are very grateful," Dottie said.

"Very grateful," Gilbert repeated without lifting his nose from the bowl as he slurped the steaming soup. The younger children watched Gilbert open-mouthed as the soup disappeared noisily in double quick time.

After they had mopped up the last few drops, everyone tucked into the bread, cheese, and conserves piled high on the table. Gilbert had more than his fair share of the food, much to the disapproval of Dottie, who kicked his shins twice to no effect.

"Godfrey?" Mabel winked at Dottie.

"Yes, princess?"

"Have you finished your work in the fields?"

"Indeed, I have, princess."

Mabel cleared her throat and put on her poshest accent. "I have been meaning to go to Bury market, and it's such a splendid day for a ride. I wonder if you might be so kind as to take me this h-afternoon?"

"Of course, dearest, it would be my pleasure."

"Dolly, Bertie." She nodded to each. "We would be 'onoured if you accompanied us." The children were all smiles and giggles. This was not the first time their parents had mimicked toffs at the kitchen table.

Dottie put her hand on Gilbert's arm. "Why, Mrs Ollerenshaw, Bertie and I would be delighted to accompany you. We thank you most kindly for your generous offer."

The entire table erupted in laughter. It was the first time he had seen Dottie laugh. As the chuckles subsided, he noticed Mabel was staring at him again.

"Can I be excused from the table, Mrs Ollerenshaw? I must get our hats from the barn," he said.

"It's Mabel." She looked to the heavens. "And of course, you can, dearie."

He headed to the barn while Godfrey hitched the horse to the buggy. Dottie joined him by the trough when Mabel went to change into her posh clothes.

"Cousin?" Gilbert raised his eyebrows. "Was that the best you could do?"

"I had to think quick. They're good people. I don't want them mixed up in this mess. A careless word to the wrong person…"

"And Bertie? You did that on purpose, didn't you?"

Dottie's silence spoke volumes.

"What do you make of Mabel?" he asked.

"Judging by her kids, she's a doting mum. There was much

love in that kitchen." She looked at her feet, took a deep breath, then raised her head. "But I bet she wears the trousers in the family. Sharp as a tack, she is."

Gilbert handed over her topper and goggles. "You do the talking, Dottie. I can't think as quick as you."

Godfrey walked the horse and buggy around, and they waited for Mabel to come out in her finery. When she finally stepped out of the kitchen barking orders at her children, she was resplendent in a crimson coat with a snow-white linen bonnet tied with a wide red ribbon. A matching ivory parasol and handbag completed her outfit. Head held high, she strode to the buggy, and Gilbert offered his hand to help her up into the back seat with Dottie before climbing into the front with Godfrey. With a slap of the reins, they set off in the afternoon sunshine.

Autumn scents from the passing Lancashire countryside filled the open carriage. Gilbert and Godfrey chatted about engineering, farming, how Mabel had bought the farm with her inheritance from a rich relative, and how lucky he had been that she had fallen head over heels in love with him. Their whirlwind courtship had swept him off his feet.

Gilbert tried to divide his attention between Godfrey and the lively conversation behind him, but the horses' hooves and metal-shod wheels prevented him from catching most of it.

The forty-five-minute journey passed in no time, and soon they were pulling up outside Bury Triple T terminus. Dottie hugged Mabel, and Gilbert shook Godfrey's hand warmly.

"I can't thank you enough." Dottie was holding Mabel's hands.

"Aww, it were nowt, Dolly. We had to come to market, so dropping you at the Trip was the neighbourly thing to do."

As Gilbert jumped from the buggy, Mabel grabbed his

arm, stood on her tiptoes, and pressed the side of her face to his. "Some advice, Bertie, dear. Let go of whatever's holding you back. Sometimes, you must leave something behind to move forward. Take a chance. Tell her how you really feel. What have you got to lose?"

She pulled away from him, and a fleeting glimpse of a lifetime of fathomless regret in her dark eyes was shaken away with a blink as she turned to Godfrey.

Clearing her throat, she raised her voice. "Come along, my dear. We have shopping to do!"

Mabel leaned out of the carriage and gently fluttered her handkerchief at Gilbert and Dottie as the buggy headed into the town centre.

"What did she say?" Dottie asked.

"She knew we were lying."

"She knew *you* were lying."

The tram was ready to leave as they took their seat, and once they were underway, Gilbert paid the conductor.

Throughout the journey, Dottie's high spirits evaporated, distilling into a condensed, impenetrable melancholy. Progressively more silent, she pushed away all of Gilbert's attempts at consolation. He wanted to hold her so much, tell her how sorry he was, but she would not countenance his efforts.

By the time they pulled into the Manchester Central Hub, very few seats remained empty. Chattering passengers hurried off the tram, leaving them, heads bowed, sat in silence.

"Come on, we need to go." Gilbert tucked strands of unruly hair under Dottie's topper before they stepped onto the platform. Deep in thought, she hardly acknowledged him. He grabbed her hand and had to drag her across the road to the Praetorian, each step more reluctant than the last.

Meks scurried around the bar, preparing for the day's

onslaught of thirsty customers. Eli stood at the entrance, having just unbolted the doors as the clock ticked past opening time. Gilbert's nodded greeting met an unblinking stare.

"We need to see Miss Algeria right away," he said. Dottie's gaze had not left the floor.

"*This 'kin* will tell her you are here." Eli scuttled across the barroom at speed and returned seconds later, beckoning them forward.

Even though Gilbert knew the way, Eli escorted them to Algeria's boudoir, where she was sitting bolt upright at her dresser, hands in her lap, back to the door.

"Miss Algeria, I've brought Dottie Throgmorton and some terrible news…" Gilbert said, halting when he saw her tear-stained reflection in the dresser's mirror.

Algeria spoke without turning. "Hello, shugah… and it's been a long time, Dolly."

Gilbert flashed a surprised look at Dottie. *Dolly?*

Dottie glared at Algeria and spat her reply through clenched teeth. "Hello, Mama."

THIRTEEN

Secrets

Spittle flew from Raven's snarling lips, his mechanically enhanced hands shaking, balled into tight knots as he yelled, "Get up!"

Sprawled on the carpet in his shadow, Bertram Gunn raised himself onto an elbow and wiped the blood from his mouth with the back of his hand.

"Get up!"

Clambering to his feet, Gunn staggered backwards, still dazed from the blow. Raven grabbed him by his lapels before he fell. "Tell me exactly what happened. Who took the shot?" he said. Each word was spoken quietly and deliberately.

"What?"

"Who fired the bolt that missed Sparks?"

"I did."

"And which genius decided to torch everything?"

"We lost him and the girl, so we burned the buildings in case they were hiding in 'em."

"Why did you attack the airship? You *do* remember the airship? The one that gutted *The Bloody Harpy*?"

"We thought they were..." Gunn's voice trailed off when Raven released his grip and walked away.

"At this time, our crusade depends on secrecy. The campaign to discredit government policy by disabling infrastructure through 'tragic accidents' can only be successful if we stay in the shadows.

"Why do you think I sent you to dispose of Sparks? Because he knows my face, and if they discover my identity, the plan will fail. Do you understand?"

Gunn nodded. "Yes, but—"

"Listen," Raven interrupted, his raised hand demanded silence. "Not only did you fail, but you also compounded your failure, announcing our existence to the world by burning buildings and attacking an airship.

"Then, not satisfied with that, you set a new level of incompetence, losing an aerial skirmish and almost destroying *The Bloody Harpy*. Give me one good reason I should let you leave this room alive?"

Gunn bowed his head. "Because I can serve."

"I didn't hear you."

"I can still be useful to the cause, and you need me." Gunn's voice rose steadily in pitch and speed.

Raven turned to stare out of the window, glancing at Athos, standing silently in the corner, hands clasped together, watching.

"It's really quite annoying that so many people seem to know what I need. No, Captain, I don't need you, but I do demand your fealty.

"If I let you continue to serve, make no mistake, you'll give me absolute obedience and unerring loyalty. Do you understand?"

"I won't fail you again."

Raven turned back to face Gunn. "No, you'll never fail me or the cause again." Athos took a single step forward; a shake of Raven's head, and he returned to the shadows. "Your next failure *will* be your last."

Gunn released the breath he had been holding with a loud sigh.

"Now get out of my sight and make sure *The Bloody Harpy* is operational in forty-eight hours. I want you and the Flanagans ready for action."

Without a word, Gunn hurried out of the Lodge as fast as his feet could carry him, shutting the door quietly behind him.

Raven sat back in the wingback leather chair and winced. "If only all my disciples were as loyal as you, my friend."

"Can I get you anything, Ray?" Genuine concern coloured his voice.

"No. I am trying to wean myself off laudanum. I can endure the discomfort during the day, but I take a drop to help me sleep through the night."

There was a light tap on the door, and it flew open. Letitia flounced in, wearing a garish primrose and periwinkle hooped dress spattered with scarlet poppies.

"Dearest, sweet, Raven. The ninth Earl of Wraithmere is here to see his bastard son." Letitia's programming did not include diplomacy.

Ignatius strode into the Lodge, taking off his top hat and gloves. He looked around for someone to take them from him. Neither Letitia nor Athos offered, so he placed them on a small table by the door and leant his ebony and silver walking stick against the wall.

Raven sighed. "I wish you wouldn't talk to Letitia that way, Father. I know what you think of me, so it really isn't necessary to get her to trumpet your disdain whenever you pay a rare visit."

"It amuses me, dear boy. Can't you take a joke?"

"Oh, we both know your jibes and insults aren't jokes."

"Tell your mek to make tea, and you can explain how my dirigible got damaged almost beyond repair."

"Letitia, please bring us a pot of Darjeeling for two, cream and sugar."

"Letitia will do anything for her dear, sweet Raven." Her eyelashes fluttered, clicking almost inaudibly.

"Athos, please go with Letitia and take the rest of the day off. Thank you for helping earlier."

Athos, who had watched the earl like a hawk from the moment he stepped through the doorway, nodded without moving his intense stare.

Letitia floated serenely out of the room, accompanied closely by the long-striding giant.

"So, dear boy, what happened to *My Crimson Princess*?"

"First, the airship belongs to me, and you know full well she's *The Bloody Harpy* now. Yes, she had a minor accident over Pendle Hill, but it's just a scratch, and she'll be fine in no time."

"Just a scratch? I heard they virtually eviscerated the old girl, and Gunn's mission to dispose of Sparks failed, too."

"Who's told you that?" The vein on Raven's temple bulged, his fists clenched, expression fixed in a half smile.

"Oh, I have my sources, dear boy, but as I don't want any of them to suffer a mysterious accident, they shall remain unnamed."

"You're spying on me? Really, Father, is that any way to treat your only son?"

"Just looking after my interests. But, in all seriousness, once you've killed this chap, Sparks, it's time to give up this

Anthropocene nonsense. Our good name must not be linked to this humbuggery."

"Why is the De'Ath name so precious to you and Grandmomma? Grandfather wasn't exactly a paragon of virtue, was he? How many bastards did that old bull sire? Four? Five? Before drinking himself to death and leaving Grandmomma to raise you alone."

"Now, you listen to me!" Ignatius strode forward, straightened his back and, looking down his nose, prodded his forefinger sharply into Raven's chest. "I've fought hard to shed the stigma of my father. Now De'Ath is a respected name in society circles!"

"Is it really, Father? Yet you're no better than him, are you? Getting a fourteen-year-old scullery maid pregnant and confining the poor girl to live here in the Lodge? Thank God she died in childbirth. Her life would have been misery with you."

"That's enough! You will not speak of your mother in this manner! I thought the world of her."

"Would you have married her?"

Too many seconds of silence removed any doubt. "I, I would have looked after her…"

"Don't treat me like a fool! You would have left her here in the Lodge to look after me, hidden from your precious high society sycophants, visiting only to satisfy your carnal urges.

"I am, and always will be, your most embarrassing mistake."

"Yet here we are."

"Yes, in *my* home. Even now, my very existence remains your dirty little secret. For twenty-eight years, you have been ashamed of me for what I represent; your inability to control your lust."

A gentle knock, a door flung open, a blur of colour, and Letitia glided around the furniture, placing the silver tea tray on the table.

"Leave us!" Ignatius said, dismissing her with a wave of the hand, but she ignored the instruction, her gaze fixed on Raven.

"Thank you, Letitia. We can pour. Please return to the kitchen."

She flashed a glance at Ignatius as she slalomed back to the door, slamming it behind her.

The earl's voice dripped with venom. "And what of you, dear, sweet Raven? What about your secrets? Have I not kept you from the hangman's noose? How many innocents have you killed? My misdemeanours pale into insignificance compared to your crimes. You should be on your knees thanking me for what I've done for you."

"You made me who I am. So, you are responsible for everything I have done and everything I will do. I am a product of both your lust and your neglect. Every death is on your hands, and the only reason you protect me is to keep your precious reputation," Raven said, pouring the tea into two cups. Anger coursed through his veins, but he spoke calmly. "Now, you will drink your tea and leave me at peace. One lump or two?"

In the dimly lit meeting room at the Praetorian, a large moth flittered around the only oil lamp. Wings bounced noisily off its glass chimney, casting silvery shadows dancing across the walls.

Two weary figures sat in silence, heads bowed, staring at the pale reflections from their beer-stained table. The stench of stale tobacco smoke hung in the air as raucous laughter and music drifted along the corridor each time the bar door opened.

Eli placed two full pewter tankards between Gilbert and Dottie and glided away to tend to his paying patrons.

"When were you going to tell me?" Gilbert broke the uneasy silence.

"It's none of your business." She took a large swig of the dark brown porter.

"Now I understand why you and your dad wouldn't talk about your mum."

"You understand nothing! You know nothing about my life!"

"Then tell me."

"Ask her." She jabbed a thumb towards Algeria, who had appeared in the doorway, her silhouette haloed by the boudoir's ethereal light enflaming the edges of her hair and shimmering through her diaphanous gown.

"All that matters to me is that you are both alive. Ace thought you were dead, killed at the Forge. It's such a relief," Algeria said.

"See, Gilbert? It always has to be about her. The pair of you should be the best of friends. You're kindred spirits." She downed more gulps of porter.

"Dolly, I understand how you must feel. You've lost your dad, your home, and everything, but we need to talk. I want to make amends." Algeria walked over to the table and sat next to her.

"You really don't get it, do you? You sent us away just so you could fulfil your dream of leading the Order. Then you send *him* to the Forge, and now Dad's gone." She glared at Gilbert, squirming in his seat. "It's because of both of you that I've lost everything."

I don't want to be in the middle of this. The chair legs screeched across the floor as he sprang to his feet. "Do you want me to leave? I—"

"Sit down!" Dottie and Algeria spoke in unison, casting an embarrassed glance at each other.

Algeria began, "Before you were born, times were different. Because of the colour of my skin, most people shunned us, and some were openly hostile. But the Order welcomed us into their fold. They accepted us for who we were, for our beliefs, not how we looked. We were so much in love and, when you came along, so blessed.

"As I became more and more involved with the cause and rose through the ranks, it was your dad who wanted to take you somewhere safe, not me. He was worried enemies would target you to destroy me. That's why he set up the Forge in Pendle but continued to work for the cause he believed in so much. More importantly, you were out of harm's way. We both gave up so much."

"Then why send *him* to us?"

"Because I thought he would be as safe as you had been up there for fifteen years, and I had no reason to believe the Anthropocene was even looking for him. To be honest, I hoped Abel would convince him to join the Order and teach him some fighting skills while we searched for Raven.

"I regret that decision with all my heart, shugah. I've lost my beloved Abel, and I almost lost you."

"I can't do this... I just can't..." Dottie said, tears welling and overflowing onto her cheeks.

"It's been a long day, Miss Algeria. Can't you two talk things through another time?" Gilbert reached for Dottie's hand.

"I didn't want to have this conversation tonight either, shugah, and there's something else we need to discuss."

Gilbert sat up straight. "You've found Raven?" His eyes widened.

"No. Ace and Issy discovered something troubling."

Gilbert's shoulders slumped. *I don't care about anything else. I want him.*

"While searching for Raven, they stumbled upon what appears to be a recently vacated Anthropocene base in a little village in the South Riding of Yorkshire. There was no sign of Raven but there was evidence it had been a place where chemists, alchemists, biologists, geologists, and Mother knows whoever else, had been working towards some devilish plan."

"But what? It could be anything, bombs, poisons. They could blow up anything or befoul our water supplies." Gilbert tried to sound interested.

"We don't know, but he's planning something… and soon. He is ramping up attacks on public transport; railways, trains and trams are easy targets and make big headlines. But with thousands of miles of tracks and hundreds of stations, we can't cover everywhere. We are vulnerable, shugah, and I don't like it one bit."

"What are your plans, Mama?" Dottie said, her lip curled. "How are you going to save the planet this time?"

Algeria did not take the bait. "We'll keep searching until we get that snippet of information that exposes him."

"Raven and that big lummox Athos can't be that hard to find," Gilbert said.

"Someone is hiding him, but I'm also concerned about how they found you at the Forge."

"Perhaps they followed *Dragonfly* on one of her daily visits? We found out about them; maybe they found out about us." Gilbert studied Algeria as she considered the possibility that the Anthropocene had discovered the Order.

Even a casual observer would see that the two women sat side by side were mother and daughter. Although Dottie had her father's bright green eyes, she had her mother's intense, almost hypnotic gaze, sensual lips, and exasperating pig-headedness.

"If they were aware of the Order and the Praetorian, they'd have attacked by now, shugah. But they must have found you somehow. Now it's even more important to keep both of you safe."

"This is hopeless. I shouldn't be hiding. I need to be out there hunting the bastard. You can't lock me away."

"In the Mother's name, Gilbert." Dottie banged her fists on the table, spilling porter on the already stained surface. "It's not about you. We must stop them to save lives. When are you going to wake up to what's happening?" She covered her face with her hands and sobbed.

Algeria reached for her but pulled her hand back. "It's late," she said. "Eli has prepared a couple of rooms upstairs. Let's get some rest."

Gilbert put his arm around Dottie and helped her stand. *The last few days have been too much for her.*

He turned to Algeria, but she had disappeared into her boudoir. Dottie was still sobbing. He gently kissed the top of her head and guided her to the stairs.

"Sorry. So much has happened so quickly." Her voice shook as she squeezed out the words between sobs.

"Things will be better after a good night's sleep. New day, new hope, eh?"

Dottie's nod was not convincing.

No way of finding Raven. No chance of stopping the Anthropocene. *Where do we go from here?*

The voice in his head had no answer.

At Barton Aerodrome, the constant pounding of steam engines, pile drivers and diggers working along the ship canal shattered the peaceful scene of airships gently bobbing on their moorings, while pilots and engineers tinkered on their craft. Work on the canal had started earlier than usual. *Making hay while the sun shines,* Tabby thought, as droning airships overhead made her look skyward.

Sunlight had scarcely peeked above the hills on the eastern horizon, but dozens of dirigibles of all colours and sizes crisscrossed the skies. She cocked her head and held her hand above her eyes to shield the morning glare, peering up at them as they traversed the heavens.

Many of the older three-baggers belched smoke from labouring engines as they bobbed around beneath the fluffy clouds, ducks in white water, the slightest zephyr rocking their old, ugly gondolas.

Newer, streamlined airships cruised gracefully towards destinations unknown at steady speeds, engines purring, powering through the air, the sun's rays sparkling across their sleek envelopes.

Tiny, darting air yachts flitted at lower altitudes, pilots showing off their aerobatic skills to passengers, many of whom would regret their choice to fly so soon after breakfast.

Tabby smiled. The aerial pageant gladdened her heart. So many aeronauts were going about their business or simply enjoying the promise of a glorious day.

Hard to believe we are at war.

She returned to tinkering with *Dragonfly's* port engine, which she had in pieces at the side of the airship. Its tone had been 'off' on their last few flights, and she had promised herself to investigate at the first opportunity. With Connie and Rory not due back until later in the afternoon, she jumped at the chance to detach the motor from the superstructure and delve beneath the cowling.

Rory had called her a *bona fide* artist with engines and all things mechanical. She wasn't used to compliments, and her heart swelled that her talents were so appreciated.

If only she admired her in other ways.

Tabby was a country girl raised by loving parents. Although she was one of four siblings, her brothers would eventually run the family farm, as she had no interest in crops and livestock. As a youngster, she dismantled their mechanical toys to see how they worked. Sometimes she would even re-assemble them.

When she was older and stronger, her father let her loose on the farm machinery and found she had a genuine talent with both clockwork and steam-powered machines.

She attended a small church school in the village and hated it with a vengeance, not least because the other girls bullied her unmercifully because of her weight. Although her brothers defended her when they were able, they were not always around to support her.

Neglecting her studies, she left at twelve and resigned herself to staying at the farm for the rest of her life, working for her father and then her brothers.

A chance meeting with Connie and Rory had taken her on a different, more exciting path. A year and a half ago, a green and tangerine air yacht had coughed and spluttered overhead, landing heavily but safely in a nearby field.

Tabby had raced to see the brightly coloured craft. She had seen nothing so gorgeous as it rested, tilted to one side, the envelope still supporting most of the small gondola's weight.

Connie had shouted to her to fetch her father or anyone who could have a look at their troublesome port engine, the same one lying in pieces in front of her. It shocked the twin sisters when Tabby clambered on board and detached the faulty motor, and within an hour, *Dragonfly* was lifting into the air, engines humming in unison and Tabby's ears ringing with compliments, particularly from Rory, the tall, slim, black-haired, dark-eyed sultry goddess.

A few weeks later, *Dragonfly* had returned. Rory offered Tabby the job of engineer on the gorgeous air yacht with the opportunity to take over as pilot in time. She considered the offer for a full millisecond before accepting on the spot, much to the surprise of her brothers and the admiration of her parents.

Since then, she had proved herself to be a skilled engineer and natural pilot, taking over from Doris, or Dozy as Rory called her, the MT-18 mek whose flying skills were, at best, perfunctory.

Movement outside the vast hangar on the far side of the aerodrome caught her eye. This was the first time she had noticed any sign of life from that part of the sprawling airfield. Sunlight glinted off the silver and black building as its gigantic doors rumbled open.

Hand over her eyes, she squinted across the airfield. The low morning sun illuminated the frenetic activity inside.

"Jonah!" she shouted at *Freyja's Grimalkin* in the next berth.

"What's up, chuck," he said, popping his head up from behind the bulwark.

"Look!" She bounced up and down, pointing at the hangar. "The doors are closing. Can you see?"

"Aye, lass! Definitely a red airship in there. I can't be sure if it was the one that attacked us. My old eyes aren't what they used to be, but it could have been."

"Fuck me, if you'll pardon my French. How did it get here? It couldn't have limped all the way from Pendle. Whoever owns that fucker must have a few bob."

"Methinks Ace might be interested to know that, too."

And Connie and Rory, thought Tabby. "Let's see what they say when they get back. What time are they due?"

Jonah checked his pocket watch. "In four or five hours, I reckon. Ace will want to check how I'm getting on with the repairs. I'm sure he thinks I can work miracles."

"Ha. I'll give you a hand when I've put this squeaky little baby back together."

"I'm grateful for any help I can get."

"Be with you within the hour."

Tabby carefully cleaned and reassembled the motor, oiling gears and tightening nuts and bolts before replacing the cowling. She fixed it on the superstructure, fired it up and listened to it sing. *Problem solved*, she smiled and dusted off her hands extravagantly.

She shut off the engine and joined Jonah onboard *Freyja's Grimalkin*. "What can I do to help?"

He stood up and stretched his aching back. "Give me a hand fixing this new harpoon. Ace wrecked the old one."

"Aye, aye cap'n." Tabby put on her best pirate voice and saluted.

So engrossed were they in their work that the rest of the morning and afternoon passed quickly, and they didn't even hear Ace and his three companions arrive in his landau as the sun dipped close to the trees, casting long shadows across the rutted airfield.

"Ahoy, the ship!" Ace bellowed before putting his foot on the bottom rung of the rope ladder, making it taut for Issy to climb. Tabby leaned over the side and waved to Rory and Connie. "Over here! We have some news."

THE CONNICKLE CONUNDRUM

Everyone gathered around Tabby and Jonah on *Freyja's Grimalkin's* deck. Ace alternated between listening to the engineers and peeking over their shoulders at the mysterious building nestling in the trees, silhouetted by the crimson sunset.

"Has anybody seen any movement over there since this morning?" Issy asked.

Jonah and Tabby shook their heads. *We've been busy*, Tabby thought.

"What's the plan, Ace? Are we going to stroll over there for a peek?" Connie asked.

"We wait 'til dark. We'll know if anyone is still over there because they'll need light to work. So, we have time to kill. Any suggestions?"

"I'm so hungry I could eat a kid with a scabby head." Tabby rubbed her belly and licked her lips.

"That's settled, then. We will have an early dinner. Now, who knows the nearest hostelry that serves scabby heads *bien cuit*? If you'll pardon my French, I prefer mine well done." Everybody laughed. Tabby blushed.

They found a place to eat nearby. Although scabby heads were not on the menu, the food was delicious and the conversation lively. Ace told Tabby and Jonah that Algeria was going to send the *Brynhildr* to bring back Lemmy's mother. It was several hours later, with bellies full and thirst slaked, when they returned to the pitch-black airfield.

Tabby looked around. To the south, flames flickered from a brazier as a night watchman kept warm on his lonely vigil by Barton lock. Gas lamps dotted sparsely along the winding road running east to west provided some light, but heavy clouds blotted out the moonlight, swathing the aerodrome in darkness.

Ace nodded towards the far side of the airfield. "No lights, *ipso facto*, no one's at the hangar. It seems the birds have flown the coop."

"Unless they are working in the dark…" Issy said.

"Or sleeping there…" Jonah joined in with the speculation.

"For fuck's sake, if you'll pardon my French. I've been waiting all day for this."

"All right, all right." Ace raised his hands, feigning submission. "Watch your step across the airfield. There are deep ruts from carts and tractors."

"I'm too old to be running 'round ploughed fields in the dead of night. I'll stay and keep a lookout." Jonah said as he climbed into the carriage. "If there's any trouble, someone give a loud blast on a whistle, and I'll go for help."

The Stormriders looked at each other, arms spread.

"I've got one." Tabby pulled a police whistle out of one of her many pockets. "Mum and Dad gave it to me, you know, just in case."

"Well done, Tabby, always prepared," Rory said. Tabby was glad the darkness hid her blushes.

They picked their way carefully across the uneven ground. The hangar loomed out of the gloom as they approached, and they realised the enormity of the building. Finally, they reached the apron in front of the huge double doors, muddy boots leaving footprints on the concrete.

"Let's find a window," Issy said. "Connie, Rory, Tabby, you take that side. We'll take this."

The Stormriders split up and went their separate ways, left and right.

As she rounded the corner between the walls and the trees, Tabby kicked something lying in the uncut grass and bent to pick up the object. It was a small hurricane lamp. She shook it and heard the faint swishing of paraffin in the reservoir.

"Have you noticed how far back the building goes?" Connie said. "Why haven't we seen this from the air?"

"I don't know. Camouflage?" Rory shrugged in the darkness.

They scrambled on between the trees and side of the hangar, sometimes having to squeeze past overgrown bushes, until fifty yards along the featureless wall, they found a locked door and a partly open window. They spoke in whispers.

"Light the lamp," Connie said.

Tabby scrabbled in her pockets for a match, but Rory produced a box of lucifers before she could find one. They lit the wick and clustered together, peering inside. The darkness within devoured the light from the small lamp, but there, in the middle of the hangar, supported by stout wooden staves, a deep red dirigible with a gashed envelope emerged from the gloom.

Connie whistled. "Ace made a mess of it, didn't he?"

"There's some writing on the hull towards the front," Tabby said, squinting through the hazy darkness.

"Yes, it says—"

"Turn that bastard light out, Gussy. I'm tryin' to sleep!" An irate Irish voice boomed across the hangar.

"Fuck off, Finn! I don't have a light!"

The three companions froze. Tabby blew out the lamp. They stood in the dark, ears straining, eyes wide.

"There *was* a light, but now it's gone."

"You must have been dreaming, you eejit."

"Well, I'm wide awake now. I'll have a scout 'round."

Rory grabbed Tabby and Connie and pulled them away from the window, and they took off running back from where they came, clothes snagging on branches, stumbling in the darkness. When they reached the front of the hangar, they fell in a tangled heap, tripping on the concrete apron.

Ace and Issy rounded the other side of the building at a dead sprint, arms waving, urging the *Dragonfly* crew to get moving.

The five runners converged about a hundred yards from the building, panting, arms flailing, trying to stay upright on the sodden, uneven ground. From behind them, a loud rumble rent asunder the night air. The hangar doors were trundling open.

"Down!" Everyone hurled themselves headlong onto the ground as soon as the instruction left Ace's lips. All around Tabby, panting companions lay still in the muddy grass, gasping for breath. Her heartbeat thundered in her ears, terrified, knowing if she moved, their pursuers would see her silhouette against the streetlights in the distance.

Outside the hangar behind her, a faint voice shouted something about 'bloody kids,' and the gigantic door rumbled shut, locking with a clunk. She rolled onto her back and glanced at the hangar. No sign of movement. A wave of relief washed over her.

They lay on the airfield for a few minutes in silence, catching their breath. When they finally stood, Rory told Ace and Issy that they had seen the dirigible and confirmed it was their attacker.

"That was too close for comfort. Maybe we shouldn't have chanced it. We've learned nothing we didn't already know," Issy said.

"*Dulce periculum.*"

"Oh, I don't know. We learned one thing." Tabby strode ahead of them. "Its name."

"What?" Ace lengthened his stride to catch her up and, grabbing her shoulder, pulled her around to face him.

"*The Bloody Harpy*," she said triumphantly. "She's called *The Bloody Harpy*."

Raven's face tingled as he stepped out of the Lodge into the frosty evening air. Night-scented stock lining the path in neatly planted rows released an intensely sweet aroma as his coat brushed the flowers. He enjoyed a midnight stroll around the small country garden at the side of the Lodge. Floral perfumes caressed and calmed the fury raging in his heart, which grew stronger with every passing day.

He sucked a lungful of the delightful aromas through his nostrils and exhaled slowly from his mouth. Tonight, the pain in his arm was acute. *Maybe one drop of laudanum before bed*, he thought. *Just one…*

"Dear, sweet Raven, are you coming back inside? Your Letitia is lonely." She stood in the doorway, pouting and fluttering her eyelashes.

"I will come in presently, my dear. It's such a beautiful night."

"Is it beautiful, dear, sweet Raven? Is it as beautiful as your sweet Letitia?"

"No, my dear, nothing can match your beauty." Human ears would detect the condescension in his voice, but Letitia's aural sensors and programming heard only the words she had elicited.

"Letitia will wear something special for you tonight, dear, sweet Raven. Lace or satin?"

"Satin tonight. Now hurry along."

Letitia giggled, spun around, and disappeared into the Lodge. Raven sat on the wrought iron bench in the centre of the garden, took another long, satisfying breath, and closed his eyes as he exhaled. A tear rolled from the corner of his eye. *If only she was a real woman. If only she was Temperance.*

"Ray." The deep baritone voice was unmistakable.

"Athos, my friend. You're out late. Can't you sleep?"

"I need to speak with you."

For Athos to seek him out during his nighttime musing, it must be important. He motioned him to sit.

"There is something I must tell you. This is a hard thing for me." Athos leaned forward, hands clasped together, knuckles white, eyes focussed on the ground.

"What's wrong?" Raven felt the stirrings of anger in his belly. Rarely had he seen Athos so nervous.

"It concerns your father."

"Don't make me drag it out of you." Raven tried to control his rising rage, speaking slowly and deliberately as Athos was clearly on the horns of a dilemma. "Just tell me. Spit it out!"

"Your father is going to marry. He plans to sire a child, a legitimate son to—"

"I know what it means. How have you come by this revelation?"

Athos recounted the visit of Lady Patience Marsh and her daughter Lucinda. From what he had overheard and from questioning the earl's manservant, Silas, he had pieced together the purpose of the meeting. "I'm sorry, Ray, there can be no doubt. You are going to be usurped."

Raven's countenance was a picture of serenity. As a child, he had learned to control all outward expressions of emotion, even when overwhelmed by pain, rage, fear, embarrassment, jealousy, joy and ecstasy. He hid his feelings behind a mask of implacable indifference. Face cloaked in calmness, his mouth curled into a half smile.

Athos had seen this expression many times. Raven appeared calm before launching frenzied attacks against enemies. Had it not been for the rattling of his arm mechanics magnifying every tiny involuntary twitch into violent tremors, Raven appeared to be deep in thought, gazing into the night sky.

But beneath his serene expression, his mind was racing. To lose his inheritance was unthinkable as the Anthropocene needed him and his finances.

"Ray?" Athos had remained silent for several minutes, waiting for the arm convulsions to subside.

"I must learn to manage this reaction. Displaying emotion is a weakness that I will not show to any man." He took a deep breath and closed his eyes, gradually regaining control.

"What would you have me do?"

"Use our people to find out whatever you can about this Lucinda Marsh trollop and report back to me, but before you leave, help me remove these prostheses."

Raven noted Athos's apprehension as he edged forward. *Good*, he thought. *He feels my fury. He still fears me.*

Athos took the prosthetic yoke from him and stepped aside.

"Sleep well tonight. You have a busy day tomorrow."

Athos nodded and lumbered away as Raven strode back into the Lodge, rage burning in his heart.

Letitia was sitting demurely on his bed, biting her lip, wide eyes fixed on the area just below his belt buckle. "Dear, sweet Raven," she said. "You have been so long. Did you forget your dear, sweet Letitia?"

He gently took her hands and pulled her to her feet, her delicate pink satin underwear shimmering in the lamplight.

Pressing his cold hand on the side of her synthetic face, he gazed into her yellow eyes with the same salivating indifference a hungry man has for the cries of the dumb animal slaughtered to provide the rack of lamb on the silver platter before him.

She nestled her head into his palm and purred.

"Turn off your memory function," he said.

"But dear, sweet Raven. Letitia wants to remember every moment of our time together. Memories are precious to your Letitia."

His voice hardened. "Turn it off. I don't want you to remember tonight. Turn it off, now!"

"Dear, sweet Raven. You are scaring your Letitia."

For once, a tiny part of him was pleased the quivering mek gazing up at him was not his beloved Temperance.

FOURTEEN

Discovery

The clock struck eight as Gilbert sat in the meeting room yawning. The previous day's sunshine had surrendered to late autumn rain again, matching his grey mood. Breakfast had been a predictably tense affair, with Algeria and Dottie exchanging superficial pleasantries between glaring daggers behind each other's back.

Eli hovered around, busying himself cleaning tables and taking dirty crockery back to the kitchen. Opening time was still two hours away. Less salubrious establishments in the city opened earlier, but Algeria preferred to attract a better class of drunkard.

Gilbert needed to talk to his father. Was it one week or two since they last spoke? So much had happened.

"I'm going home to see my dad this morning," he said.

"Don't tell him anything, shugah. Even knowing about the Order will put him in mortal danger."

"My lips are sealed. He thinks I've been working at the Liverpool end of the Cut, doesn't he?"

"Yes. We told him you were doing long shifts and bunking with the rest of the navvies."

"I'm coming with you," Dottie said. "I need some fresh air."

"That's not a good idea, Doll. Gilbert wants to be alone with his dad, I'm sure."

"You don't mind if I come along, do you, Gilbert?"

Gilbert fixed his gaze firmly on the floor, trying to concoct a tactful answer. Thankfully, Algeria saved his embarrassment. "Then you'll both need new clothes. I can't have you meeting his father looking like that, Doll. And you, shugah. Your dad will think you can't look after yourself."

"You're right, Miss Algeria. We can't go to see my dad in this state."

"I'll pop to Beaty's on Deansgate. It's been a while since I ventured over there." An involuntary tremor shook Algeria's whole body. That part of the city was unpleasant in daylight but became a seething cauldron of sordid life after sundown where pickpockets, cutpurses and scuttlers preyed on unwary revellers, relieving them of coin intended for the gambling dens or brass houses. "I know your sizes, Gilbert, but I'll need yours, Doll."

She picked Fanny, one of Eli's QTs, to accompany her, leaving Gilbert and Dottie kicking their heels.

Eli opened on time, as always, and the early thirsty rabble streamed in. Lunchtime came and went before Algeria flounced through the door, followed closely by the shuffling mek weighed down with packages.

"I should have taken two helpers," she said. "The BU-T window displays captivated Fanny so, and she struggled with the boxes."

There were three complete outfits for Gilbert and eight for Dottie. "Just to put you on, Doll. Next time we'll have a proper shopping trip together?"

Dottie nodded, and they took their new clothes upstairs to change.

Gilbert chose the most basic outfit and strapped his tool belt and weapons to the brown woollen trousers. *Not half bad.* The reflection in the full-length mirror of a middle-class artisan staring open-mouthed from under a modest topper was a far cry from that of a lowly ship canal navvie.

Rushing downstairs to thank Algeria, he almost knocked Dottie off her feet in the rush. She had chosen function over fashion, too. An almond shirt with khaki trousers and knee-length brown boots beneath a long tawny brown greatcoat. The terracotta topper and her trademark welder's goggles grounded the aeronautical look.

"Aren't you the handsome couple?" Algeria stood, hands on her hips, beaming.

"Thanks, miss. Don't know how I'll ever repay you."

"Just take care of that daughter of mine." She smiled at Dottie, who grabbed Gilbert's hand and dragged him through the main bar and out into the rainy street.

"Whoa! What's this all about?"

"Let's get one thing clear. We are not a couple. There is no *we*."

"That was nowt to do with me. Speak with your mother."

"Good. As long as we both know where we stand." She adjusted Gilbert's short topper and fastened the top button on his shirt and smiled. "That's better. Right, let's go see your dad."

I really don't understand women, he thought.

Out of the corner of his eye, Gilbert saw the conductor beckon the passengers forward to a green and black tram. A glance at his pocket watch confirmed they had less than a minute to board before it was due to set off.

"Come on, Dottie!"

They dashed up the station approach and managed to jump onto the Eccles-bound tram just as it jerked into motion.

Twenty-five minutes later, they pulled into the Triple T terminus and took the short walk to Mayfield Street. A few yards from the front door, Gilbert demonstrably patted his pockets. "Damn. No keys. Can't remember when I last had 'em."

Dottie rolled her eyes.

"It won't be a problem. Dad will be home. Friday's his day off."

But when they reached the door, there was no reply despite knocking several times, each progressively louder.

"Ayup, Gilbert!" Mr Arbuthnot, the neighbour from two doors down, popped his head out of a window. "Forgot your keys, lad?"

"Aye. Have you seen my dad?"

"Not for a few days."

"When you see him, can you tell him I came home, and I'll see him as soon as I can?"

"Going back to your digs in Liverpool, are you?"

"Just popping back to Manchester. I'm not sure where I'll be working next."

"You've not been sacked, have you? Your dad won't be happy if you have!"

"No, no. Nowt like that. The engineers move us around, that's all. I might be working at this end of the Cut for a bit." He had to think fast and choose his words carefully because soon they would be on the lips of anyone who listened to the old gossip.

He linked arms with Dottie, waved a cheery farewell, and marched her away from the elderly man.

They strode on in silence, Gilbert deep in thought. Mr

Arbuthnot watched all the comings and goings on the road. Local folk said he hid behind the curtains, spying on everyone. *If he hasn't seen my dad for a few days, then he's not been home.*

A glance at Dottie caught her staring at him from under knitted eyebrows.

"I'm sure he will be all right," she said.

"I forgot you can read minds." He tried to sound cheery. "Aye, let's get back to Manchester."

He spent the journey churning over every imaginable reason for his father not being at home. The same explanation kept returning.

Raven!

Heavy raindrops pinged a discordant melody on the metal railings and treads as Ace trudged up the stairway wrapped around the outside of Barton Aerodrome's octagonal four-storey tower. The wrought iron stairs were the only way to reach the control room, and in this weather, they were treacherous. Half a flight behind him, Issy was pulling herself up with the cold, wet handrails.

He reached the viewing platform and stopped to catch his breath. Issy joined him a few seconds later, and before knocking on the door, they looked across the rain-sodden airfield at the silver and black hangar to the north. There were no visible signs of activity.

Ace knocked, and they entered the airy, glass-walled air traffic control room. The 360-degree outlook over the airfield and the surrounding countryside was impressive.

Working at their desks, the triumvirate of controllers did not even raise their heads.

He glanced at the three telltale bowler hats perched on the hat stand. These men were career artisans, several classes beneath him; bureaucrats, whose work was administration and management, they had little contact with aviators and did nothing to monitor or direct the movement of airships. As time-serving company men, they dutifully collected rent and ensured every berth was replete with fuel, LTA and ballast.

These fellows will bend over backwards to help me, he thought. He cleared his throat. "Good afternoon, gentlemen. I wonder if you can assist us."

"That depends." A thin, balding man sat in the closest chair, raised his head from his paperwork and squinted at Ace between his green sun visor and half-frame glasses.

"Well, my good fellow, we had a minor incident with a ship which we believe is in the silver and black hangar over yonder." He jabbed his thumb towards the hangar behind him without turning to look. "We thought we should write a brief note to the owner."

"I'm not your good fellow, and who the devil do you think you are, barging in with not so much as a by-your-leave? This isn't public property, you know."

Taken aback, Ace tipped his top hat. "I *do* apologise for the intrusion. I am Aquilla Ulysses Sixsmith, and this is—"

"I am Isadora Amaryllis Windlass," Issy said. Head held high, hands on hips, she flashed an angry glance at Ace.

He pointed at his beloved airship. "If you care to look, the black four-bagger over there, *Freyja's Grimalkin*, is ours."

The three men did not turn their heads.

"Check the ledger, Tom." The thin man leaned back in his chair and checked the elasticity of his braces with his thumbs as he eyed the two visitors.

"Everything is up to date. In fact, they've paid in advance to the end of the first quarter of next year."

Ace smiled at the man's eyeroll and loud sigh.

"I can't tell you who owns the hangar, 'cos it's none of your business. Why don't you just walk over there and speak to them yourselves?"

"Bit awkward, old chap. We had a scrape with their red airship, you know, *The Bloody Harpy*. Somehow, I doubt they would welcome us with open arms."

"*The Bloody Harpy*, you say?" Tom thumbed through the ledger feverishly. "Never heard of it."

"We're sure that's the name," Issy said.

"The only red airship around here is *My Crimson Princess*. There's no such airship as *The Bloody Harpy*. We'd know, wouldn't we, lads?" The thin man watched his fellow administrators nod in agreement.

"Then we will bid you farewell and thank you for your kind assistance." Ace looked down, raising his eyebrows. "Oh dear, my boot is undone. We can't have that, can we?" Straightening after fastening the rogue boot buckle, he put on his topper and, touching the brim, nodded to each of the three men in turn before opening the door for Issy.

"What a waste of time," she said as they stepped warily down the slippery stairway. "Odd they didn't know of *The Bloody Harpy*."

"Well, it was a waste…" He reached into his pocket and handed a docket to Issy. "Until I found this on the control room floor."

The bill read, 'To: Sir Horatio Marmaduke Wyndham-Welch MP. Black and Silver Aerodrome Services. Barton Aerodrome.'

"Got 'em," said Issy.

"Hold fast!" Ace stared at the vacant berth next to *Freyja's Grimalkin*. "Where's *Dragonfly*?" Turning to the north, he shielded his eyes from the rain. "The hangar doors are open! *The Bloody Harpy* has disappeared, too!"

The carriage ride from Bacup had taken a trice over an hour, and Lady Marsh had endured Lucinda's incessant complaints throughout the brief journey. Had they not been going to see Ignatius afterwards, she doubted her daughter would have accompanied her to the ceremony.

Oldham was a dirty, downtrodden mill town, and under any other circumstance, Lucinda would not be seen dead in such a place, but the Grand Opening had brought the local great and good to celebrate this new northernmost outpost of the Triple T line.

Rain had fallen steadily all day from a charcoal sky, subduing the celebratory atmosphere at the tram terminus. Appetising aromas from street vendors wafted across the bedraggled crowd who had gathered to watch the festivities. Drab lower classes huddling together stared up in awe at the dignitaries in their fancy clothes on the raised platform in front of the new station.

Gentlemen sporting stovepipe top hats and ladies beneath extravagant Gainsborough chapeaux exchanged pleasantries, trying to make themselves heard over the local colliery brass band playing rousing tunes to lift the spirits of the impatient throng in the dreadful weather.

Behind the podium, the wet, yellow and black livery of the new Northeastern Line tram sparkled as raindrops dappled its surface. The clockwork mechanism on the far side was not visible from the stage, but its slow, loud clicking beat a rhythm different from the brass band.

"How much longer is this going to take, Mama?" Lucinda sat pouting in a magnificent azure blue dress next to her mother, dressed in an equally stunning scarlet ensemble with layered crinoline underskirts. The temporary canopy had failed to keep the ceremonial group dry. "I don't want to look like a drowned rat by the time we get to Weepingbrook Hall. What will Ignatius think?"

"The ceremony is due to start in ten minutes. We'll be on the road to Wraithmere within the hour."

"Believe me, dear, I have no intention of staying long after the ribbon cutting in this frightful weather. As soon as the photographer has recorded this momentous event for posterity, we will say our farewells and set off for your tryst." Lady Marsh was inwardly happy at Lucinda's words. *Heavens, suddenly she cares what Ignatius thinks*, she thought, *that's a major step in the right direction.*

The band stopped playing, raindrops pitter-pattered against the canopy, and the unmistakable drone of dirigibles in the skies above lifted the expectations of the soaked multitude.

The Mayor of Oldham stepped to the lectern and raised his hands for silence. After a few moments, the general hubbub diminished to an indistinct murmur, and the ceremony began.

A seemingly unending procession of local business owners, town councillors and Triple T company executives expressed their gratitude to the workers whose efforts had contributed to the successful extension of the tram network. To a man, they were certain the 'good people' of Oldham would benefit.

After half an hour of speeches that no one listened to, the mayor called Lady Marsh and Lucinda to step forward and cut the ribbon. *Finally!*

Their coachman held a large black umbrella over their hats as they stepped from under the canopy.

The crowd gasped as a massive four-bagger roared by no more than a hundred feet above the crowd. So huge was the craft that raindrops momentarily stopped bouncing off the spectators in its lee. Fearful faces turned skyward, distracted by the dark crimson airship.

"That was too low." Lady Marsh said when her voice could finally be heard above the roar. Her heart was in her mouth. Dignitaries on the podium had a perfect view of the dirigible climbing away eastward, towards the foothills of the Pennines. The mayor stepped forward; his hands raised to calm the crowd.

"It's all right, everybody, nothing to worry about. Just one of those young rich kids showing off. Please settle down, and we'll finish the ceremonial part of today's festivities.

"The first tram is due to leave the station in twenty minutes." He tucked his pocket watch into his waistcoat. "Ladies…" He backed away from the lectern and sat down.

"Mr Mayor, ladies, gentlemen, and good people of Oldham!" Sporadic applause and cheers from the bedraggled hoi polloi ensued.

"Mama?" Lucinda tugged at her mother's sleeve.

Lady Marsh had seen the airship climb into the wind, turn, and head back towards them at a ferocious pace. But she continued. "It gives me great pleasure to declare this Tick Tock Tram Terminus…"

"Mama? Look!" Lucinda pointed at the dirigible as it began a rapid descent, vented purple gas streaming in its wake. Heads in the crowd turned to stare at the red and purple blur. At the outer edges, frenzied revellers stumbled as they tried to escape the impending horror.

"Open!" Lady Marsh, shouting above the roaring engines, cut the royal blue ribbon strung loosely across the stage, and the two ends fluttered to the ground.

Engines screaming, the airship was diving directly at the terminus. Lady Marsh pulled her daughter into a smothering embrace.

"Mama!" Lucinda put her arms around her mother, and they hugged tightly, staring at the nose of the airship as it accelerated towards them. Tears streaming, Lady Marsh covered Lucinda, turning her back to shield her from the plummeting terror.

From somewhere in the crowd, a gunshot, a futile attempt to end the madness, ignited the airship's venting gases, changing it into a shrieking fireball.

"For Raven! For freedom!" a single jubilant voice screamed from the frenzied grey masses.

Who on Earth is—? The airship smashed into the podium, ending Lady Marsh's final thought, the massive explosion incinerating everyone in attendance in the blink of an eye. Clouds of black, acrid smoke billowed into the slate sky.

The Bloody Harpy had shrieked her last.

Earlier that Saturday morning, Rory and Connie had watched as Issy and Ace climbed the iron steps up the aerodrome tower while Tabby cleaned and polished brass fittings on board *Dragonfly*.

On the far side of the airfield, the hangar doors rumbled open, and four burly ground crewmen dragged out *The Bloody Harpy* with tethers. Unable to attract the attention of their compatriots in the control tower, Rory ordered Tabby to take off, and they followed at a safe distance.

Flying low to avoid detection, they skimmed the trees, weaving from side to side across the countryside. Despite the purposely erratic movements, Connie kept her eyes firmly fixed on *The Bloody Harpy*.

"I don't think they've spotted us," she said. "They're flying straight and true."

"Look!" Rory pointed as another airship rose to join their target. "Three-bagger?"

"Yes, any ideas where we're heading, Tabby?" Connie stepped to the back of the tiny gondola where Tabby stood, one hand on the wheel, one on the controls. *Oh no, we have a problem.* "We have a tail."

Tabby looked over her shoulder. "Where did that come from?" Another black airship was rising rapidly astern.

"I don't know, but it's signalling to our friends up ahead."

As they watched, the airship escorting *The Bloody Harpy* turned to head directly towards them. *Dragonfly* was trapped between two menacing assailants, a rose between two thorns.

"We can outrun them. Get us out of here!" Connie gripped the port bulwark as Tabby whipped the ship into a sharp ninety-degree curve to the east. Both three-baggers matched *Dragonfly*'s course, removing any doubt of their intentions.

So, the hunter has become the hunted.

Connie's stomach turned as Tabby tried to shake off their closest pursuer, who mirrored every twist, turn, climb and dive. *Dragonfly* was nimble in tight corners, but her pursuers were more powerful. Now unable to track *The Bloody Harpy* and the route back home blocked, they were in a fight for survival.

"They'll be on us soon, Tabby. Head for the Ten Hills." Connie pointed to Winter Hill, the highest of the small group of highlands in the West Pennine Moors. They dove and wheeled to starboard. Turbulence buffeted the tiny craft as wind shear between the steep gradients increased. While Rory and Connie kept tabs on their pursuers, Tabby concentrated on keeping them from smashing into the rocks.

"They are nearly on us!" Rory shouted.

"Hold tight!" Tabby flung *Dragonfly* into an impossible spiral; the gondola swung horizontally to the ground as tremendous centripetal forces strained the superstructure to its limit. Then, reversing course in an instant, they just missed the Rivington Pike beacon by a whisker.

The closest dirigible, unable to match the air yacht's agility, overshot them by hundreds of yards but circled back in a wide arc. Their pursuers now joined together and barrelled down on them. Tabby applied maximum thrust to the motors, and they darted away, weaving through the valleys between the slopes.

The rocks to starboard erupted as grapeshot slammed into the hillside.

"We can't manoeuvre! We're sitting ducks down here!" Rory shouted as a second shot roared past them, slamming into the cliff face ahead. Tabby dropped ballast to take them into the clear air above the hilltops as a third round whistled under the gondola.

Like a flyweight dodging the lumbering blows of two cruiserweights, Tabby took evasive action. She flung *Dragonfly* through the torrential rain, deftly bobbing and weaving. But this was not a prizefight. It was a bareknuckle brawl; brutish thugs pouncing on an unprepared victim with murderous intent.

"Make sure those blackguards don't get a bead on us," Connie said. "I wish we had weapons! We can't run forever." Tabby's skilful piloting was buying precious seconds, but it was only a matter of time before *Dragonfly* would succumb to the remorseless attack.

Tabby's skin was slick with sweat from the physical and mental effort. Her sodden shirt clung to her as she twisted her body to throw the air yacht in all three dimensions.

Although their larger marauders could not match her agile movements, they only needed a single clean shot to bring the small craft crashing down. They chased and harried her relentlessly.

Connie and Rory exchanged a worried glance. The intense sororal empathy between the twins transcended the need for words; they returned their focus to their attackers. As Rory turned to Tabby, the gondola shook. One loud ping, followed by another, then another, as the rigging securing the LTA bags snapped under the strain. Tabby's frenetic efforts had resulted in vital cables rubbing against the unyielding superstructure, and, not designed for such violent aerobatics, they frayed and snapped like dry twigs. *Dragonfly* was increasingly sluggish and unable to manoeuvre, with Tabby having barely enough control to keep them airborne.

Tabby had to baby *Dragonfly*'s controls, terrified to try sudden changes in direction or height. Rory and Connie watched as the two black dirigibles closed in on them, lining up their forward cannons. Connie leapt across the deck and put her arms around her twin sister, who kept her steely stare on their approaching annihilation. She buried her head in Rory's neck and sobbed.

Time stood still as they waited for the inevitable.

Boom! A cannon shot discharged. Connie raised her face in time to glimpse a gunmetal and golden blur wheel away as two black dirigibles spiralled earthward like fluttering whirligigs, debris falling from their shattered rudders. *Freyja's Grimalkin* had smashed the sterns of both gondolas with a single blast, and wooden shards from the explosion had pierced their LTA bags.

Connie wiped her eyes, and still in each other's arms, the twins jumped around laughing in a deranged dance.

Tabby slumped across the controls, drained physically and emotionally. "Fuck, I need a drink, pardon my French."

Freyja's Grimalkin pulled alongside, mirroring *Dragonfly*'s crawl.

"Ahoy, *Dragonfly*!" Ace shouted. "Were those blackguards making unwelcome advances?"

"We were just playing with them," Rory replied.

Connie looked over the side as the two dirigibles, struggling to recover their rudderless spins, spiralled from view. "Thanks, Ace. We would be history if you hadn't intervened," she said.

"*Faber est suae quisque fortunae et sic semper tyrannis.* We were the instrument of their inevitable downfall."

Connie and Rory looked at each other, shrugged, and laughed. But the laughter soon subsided. Tabby stood transfixed, eyes wide, mouth open, pointing to the northeast, where a pall of smoke mushroomed high in the air.

Oh, no. Connie hung her head. "Our attackers accomplished their mission after all. *The Bloody Harpy* has struck. Mother, what have they done?"

FIFTEEN
Flowers

Raven woke with a start. His arm ached, and although he rarely slept during the day, the exertions of the previous evening combined with a heavy, two-drops-of-laudanum-induced sleep had left him exhausted and listless.

Letitia had been sent for reconstructive engineering.

Fingering the ripped edges of the ruined pink satin bodice at his side, he closed his eyes and smirked, remembering the previous night's fun and games, which had lasted long into the early hours of the morning.

Now, with Letitia indisposed and Athos busy carrying out his orders, there was little to occupy him, so he spent Saturday alone recuperating. The never-ending rain pitter-pattered against the windows all day, and by midafternoon, he had succumbed to its hypnotic rhythm.

His pocket watch showed almost a quarter to five. Athos should be back soon, and, as if on cue, there was a sharp rat-a-tat-tat on the door.

But it was not his giant friend who strode into the room.

"There you are, Ray. Where's that infernal mek of yours? It usually lets me in." The frown on his father's face made him smile.

"Athos has taken her to Isaac and Bogart for repairs and replacement parts. Are you all right, Father? You seem even more angry than usual."

"I hope they scrap the irritating little… ugh… But I didn't come here to talk about that pile of junk. Grandmomma and I have decided that this Anthropocene nonsense has gone far enough. You've had some fun, but now it's time you did something with your life."

"The cause means everything to me. We will re-shape the future of the world."

"You believe that, don't you? Are you really that arrogant?" His father's face flushed. The vein in his temple stood proud, throbbing.

"You mustn't get angry, Father. Do you have your heart tablets?"

"Who the hell do you think you are? You impudent—"

"Really, Father. Is that any way to speak to your only son and heir?" Raven's half smile concealed the rage surging through his body. He was thankful he was not wearing the yoke as his balled fists pushed deeper into his trouser pockets.

Through the window behind his father, a carriage was rumbling past the house towards the Lodge. The clip-clop of hooves grew louder as it approached and stopped outside, but there was no reaction from his father. *A little deaf are we, Father dear?*

Athos flung the door open and stomped into the room. Startled by the unexpected noise, his father lurched backwards.

"There's been a terrible accident." Athos spoke directly to Raven without acknowledging his father's presence.

Well played, Athos, perfect. He leaned forward in his armchair. "An accident, you say? Oh, dear. Where? Is anyone hurt?"

"A dirigible has crashed into Oldham Triple T terminus during the opening ceremony. Hundreds are dead."

The blood drained from his father's face as the horror hit like a sledgehammer. He grabbed the nearest chairback for support, wheezing as he gasped for breath.

"You've turned such a peculiar colour, Father. Are you well?" He wanted to howl. Every fibre of his being was screaming at him to grab his father, laugh in his face and tell him he knew about his plans to disinherit him. But outwardly, his calm expression didn't waver. "Athos, please get my father a whisky. Not the 12-year-old, the cheap one. It's purely medicinal, after all."

"This is your doing." His father's voice wavered as he slumped into the chair.

"Excuse me?" Raven raised his eyebrows.

"This has your filthy fingerprints all over it!"

"Really, Father. Do you believe I am responsible for every mishap?"

"If I find out—"

"You will do what, old man?" The edge in Raven's voice cut like a rapier. "I'll tell you precisely what you'll do. Nothing." He sprang from the chair and, taking the glass from Athos, considered flinging the whisky in his father's face before placing it gently into his trembling hand.

"As I see it, there are only two plausible explanations for the calamity at Oldham this afternoon. Perhaps this tragedy is an unfortunate accident, in which case you owe me an unreserved apology.

"Or maybe I commanded a loyal acolyte to sacrifice his life to kill hundreds of innocent people just to execute Lucinda Marsh, to thwart your pathetic attempt to sire a son and cheat me out of my rightful inheritance.

"If this were the case, I would have illustrated the lengths to which I will go to safeguard my birthright."

"How? How could you possibly…?"

"You can't hide your plans from me, and if you try to disinherit me again, you won't live to regret your stupidity."

His father downed the whisky in a single gulp.

"So, Father. You decide. Unfortunate mishap or execution?"

Head bowed, gripping the arms of the chair so tightly that his knuckles went white, Ignatius mumbled, "Mishap."

Raven turned his back and smirked at Athos. "I didn't hear you."

"Accident, God damn you!"

"You need to understand that we are everywhere. If you instruct your solicitor to change your last will and testament, or if you inform the police of our culpability for Oldham, I will know. In fact, if you do anything against us, I will know."

"You bastard! I should have smothered you at birth!"

"Yes, probably, but you didn't. So, you must live with the consequences of your lust *and* your cowardice.

"Poor, sweet, innocent Lucinda is dead because of you. I may have been the weapon, but you pulled the trigger."

The empty whisky glass narrowly missed Raven, crystal shattering against the wall.

"Athos, escort my father to his home. I don't want any harm coming to him on the long walk," he said, turning his back to face the window.

Behind him, the door clicked shut. Horses' hooves announced their departure as he poured himself three fingers of 12-year-old whisky and settled in his chair. A large mouthful of the sharp liquid slid down his throat. He savoured the flavour on his tongue and the warmth in his belly, raising his glass in a silent salute to Bertram Gunn, a faithful martyr to the cause.

Of course, Athos would have killed him had he not carried out his orders, but Gunn was not aware of that. Father blaming himself for the deaths of the Marsh bitch and her mother was perfect.

I will send flowers to Lord Marsh. After all, the poor man has lost his dear wife and beloved daughter. He chortled into the glass as he took another swig.

His arm still ached, and he missed Letitia. But today was a good day.

Tabby had worked for Connie and Rory for over eighteen months, but they had never invited her for a drink. They had often complimented her on her maintenance and piloting skills, but this felt different. This was acceptance. This was becoming part of the team.

She sat in the hansom, facing the twins who were in deep conversation about their father, clothes, how frightfully smelly the canal workings were, and lots of nonsense that did not interest her one bit.

But she could not care any less. She was riding into Manchester with the twins for a drink or two or more, and that made her deliriously happy.

Eyes closed, she relaxed, listening to her surroundings as the carriage rocked from side to side. Hooves clattering on the cobbles, children playing, and, in the distance, a church bell chiming. Inside the cab, the conversation had stopped. Sneaking a peep with one eye, she caught Connie nudging Rory as they watched her. They burst into fits of giggles.

The hansom pulled up outside a white public house in a part of Manchester not familiar to Tabby.

"Here you are, ladies." The driver jumped nimbly from the back of the cab and opened the door for his passengers to alight. Connie paid the fare and gave the driver a generous tip. "Thank you kindly, ma'am." He touched his topper in deference and stuffed the money into his waistcoat.

Tabby read the sign emblazoned across the front of the building. "Lee Ren-dez-vuss hotel."

"It's pronounced Le Ron-day-vu. It's French for the meeting place," Connie explained.

"Well, fuck me, if you'll pardon *my* French."

Laughing, they linked arms, Rory in the middle, pulling them towards the brightly lit entrance, narrowly avoiding two men stumbling out of the public house, arm in arm.

"What ho, Rory!" one reveller shouted from a few feet away. "Do you mind if we take your growler?" The cab driver winced and coughed into his sleeve.

"What ho, Archie!" Rory shouted back. "I doubt the driver has another fare, so I'm sure he will be agreeable to taking you wherever your hearts desire."

The driver rolled his eyes and sniffed, clearly reluctant to take the two tipsy toffs.

"Where to, er, gents?" he said.

The drunks laughed loudly at each other before clambering into the cab. Rory, Connie, and Tabby continued their march to the entrance. "Three gals out on the town. Watch out, world, here we come!"

The main bar was not what Tabby was expecting. She was not a regular visitor to these establishments, but every public house she had visited before had been raucous, brash, and full of men intent on getting as drunk as they could with whatever coin they had in their pockets. Witnessing a brawl or two was commonplace in her experience.

This place was different. The atmosphere was subdued with customers talking without shouting. Of course, there were small areas of merriment and laughter, but overall, the ambience was good-natured and refined.

Connie ordered drinks at the bar while Rory and Tabby found a table near the window overlooking the Rochdale Canal, which ran parallel with the appropriately named Canal Street, and flopped onto the high-backed chairs.

"Is Archie a friend of yours?"

"He's an associate of our father. We just frequent the same hostelries."

"He was a rum bugger, if you'll pardon my French."

Rory smiled. "He certainly likes a drink or six."

Connie returned from the bar with a tray of fancy cocktails. Tabby's eyes lit up at the array of coloured drinks in a variety of glasses. "I've never had a cocktail. Honestly, I can count on the fingers of one hand the number of times I've been in a pub, and that's a fact," she said.

"Well, it's certainly a day of 'firsts' for you." Connie counted on each finger. "First aerial skirmish, first trip to Le Rendezvous, and now your first cocktail. Perhaps there will be even more 'firsts' this evening."

Connie winked at Rory, who flushed, flashing a fleeting glare.

"So, Miss Connie, what is the clear one that has floating bits of leaf?" asked Tabby.

Rory answered before Connie, "Mint julep, made with real mint leaves. Very healthy, I'm sure. The green drink in the tall glass is a green fairy, and the brownish one is a new concoction from America called an old fashioned."

Tabby could hardly contain herself. Her heart swelled so much she thought it was going to burst. *Mum and Dad would be so proud of their little girl.*

They talked and drank for a while. Tabby was having the time of her life, and evening had turned into night when Connie abruptly stood.

"Well, my dears, it's time for me to wend my merry way home."

"Aw, can't you stay a bit longer?" Tabby pouted and fluttered her eyelashes at Connie, who, in return, gave Tabby a mischievous, extravagant wink before turning on her heel and breezing out of the bar, waving gaily over her shoulder.

"What's that about?" Tabby raised an eyebrow.

"Oh, nothing, sweetie." Rory ran her forefinger absentmindedly around the rim of her glass, then pulled her chair closer to Tabby. She slid her fingers tenderly underneath Tabby's, resting her other hand, palm up, on the table. "Can I ask you a personal question?"

"That sounds ominous." Tabby pretended to be nervous but covered Rory's open hand with hers.

"Is there someone special in your life?"

"Well, I have a handsome boy waiting for me back home—" Rory jerked her hands back, but Tabby's reactions were fast, and she grabbed them before they were out of reach. "He's a gorgeous ginger tom who loves to snuggle, and he's a very good mouser."

Rory's shoulders relaxed.

"Whatever's the matter? You're trembling." Tabby leaned closer and pressed her body against Rory's arm.

Rory lowered her gaze, her thumbs tracing circles on the back of Tabby's hands. "Ever since you joined us on the *Dragonfly*, I have been keeping an eye on you."

"In case I did something wrong?"

"No, of course not. We have total confidence in our gorgeous, talented engineer pilot. Actually, I think you are rather spiffing."

"Blimey! No one has called me gorgeous or spiffing." Tabby blushed.

Rory was smiling, staring intensely into Tabby's baby blue eyes. "You've been with us for almost eighteen months. I can't remember ever seeing you with a beau."

"Nah, I don't have time for lads. Them that can be bothered talking to me, are either immature or old enough to be my dad." Tabby wrinkled her nose and took a sip of her drink. "There was a young lad who worked on the farm who got a bit too handsy once and tried it on with me. I told him to leave me alone, but when he wouldn't stop, I slapped him so hard I left a red handprint on his face. Dad gave him what-for, too, and made him sling his hook.

"I've never really fancied any lads, and they don't care for me. I mean, why would anyone fancy this?" She looked down at her ample body, making an extravagant gesture with her hands.

"I do. You're lovely, kind, funny, intelligent, talented…"

"That's the demon drink talking, but please go on…"

"Not at all. I knew how I felt about you on the very first day we met." Rory was gazing at Tabby's petal-like lips.

They edged their chairs together, legs rubbing against each other, faces inches apart. Tabby tilted her head to one side, closed her eyes, and slightly parted her lips. Rory leaned forward and accepted the invitation. She brushed her lips gently across Tabby's, the tip of her tongue running along the inside of her upper lip. Tabby gasped and caught her breath, then pulled away, savouring Rory's sweet taste on her lips. "Why did you wait so long?" Eyes half-open, she focussed on Rory's moist, glistening mouth.

"I, I wasn't sure how you'd react. I didn't want to spoil our friendship. We're still friends, aren't we?"

Tabby gently squeezed her trembling hand. She had never seen her like this. Rory was usually the stronger, more confident of the twins. She looked at their entwined hands. "I'm not sure, chucky egg... I hope we are going to be more than friends."

Rory returned her smile. "I don't believe anyone has called me that before... I think I like it."

They reached for each other, mouths open, urgent tongues darting and probing, hands tenderly stroking faces, fingers running through each other's hair. Time stood still. No sounds, no distractions. Eyes closed, their hearts pounding, yearning, needing more.

When they reluctantly eased their lips apart, a tear was trickling down Rory's face. "Whatever is the matter, chuck?"

"I was scared you would reject me. I'm so happy you didn't."

"I wanted that kiss to last forever. I've never felt this way." Tabby's body tingled, her heart racing. She yearned for so much more. Through blurry eyes, she gazed at Rory's slim, elegant body, her every movement a rhapsody, and in her eyes, she saw her own feelings mirrored.

Rory's confident air was returning, her nervousness dissipating like steam from a kettle. "I think we need another drink," she said, easing her chair backwards, and she strode off towards the bar.

Tabby ran her tongue over her lips again. For several glorious minutes, she had been oblivious to her surroundings, but now her senses were returning. Conversations, laughter, a pungent whiff of tobacco, and she was back in the room, suddenly very much self-aware. She drained the last dregs from her glass and glanced around to see if anyone had watched their passionate embrace.

Most of the bar's patronage was male and, unsurprisingly, showed no interest in her. A handful of women sat at tables in pairs, and a group of four ladies flamboyantly dressed sat at the opposite end of the bar from Rory, who was in deep discussion with the barman.

One of the ladies, a heavily made-up platinum blonde, her buxom figure cinched tightly into her gold and green brocade bustier, raised her glass and, open-mouthed, winked theatrically in her direction. Tabby flushed and turned away, wishing for Rory's quick return.

When Rory finally returned with two gin and tonics 'to liven up the palette', Tabby told her about the wink from the woman at the bar, and Rory glanced over her shoulder.

"An old flame," she said, smiling, shaking her head. "I have no idea how she breathes in that corset. She means no harm, sweetie, just a cheery hello." They sipped their drinks, talking about nothing in particular, gazing into each other's eyes, when Tabby spied the barman gliding across the room towards their table.

Rory saw him and grasped Tabby's hand. "I have a surprise. I hope I'm not being too presumptive, sweetie."

The mek bowed his head. "*This 'kin* has prepared the top room according to your instructions."

"Champagne with two flutes?"

"Yes, Miss."

"A bathtub filled with bubbles?"

"Yes, Miss, and at the perfect temperature."

Tabby sat open-mouthed as Rory took her hand and smiled. "I think we need to get you out of those grubby clothes."

A tingle coursed through Tabby's body, and she trembled. *Anticipation? Trepidation? Excitement?*

"Fuck, yes! If you'll pardon my French." She put her arms around Rory and pressed her soft curves against her hard body. Then, hand in hand, they strolled towards the stairs leading to the upstairs rooms. As they walked past, Rory's old flame winked, flashing Tabby a wicked smile.

"The key is in the door?" Rory asked the barman, pressing a coin into his palm.

"Yes, thank you, Miss Marrable."

Rory kissed Tabby on the cheek. "This night will belong to us forever. Let's make the most of it, because we don't know what tomorrow will bring."

Issy heard the rattle of hooves on cobbles, muffled by the thick fog shrouding the city, long before she saw the horse and carriage. Ace had sent his landau to collect her, and while she enjoyed a walk, she was grateful for the ride in the inclement weather.

Thoroughly wrapped up in her heavy woollen coat, she closed the door to the warm home she shared with her parents and stepped into the dank, grey Manchester morning. The freezing air made her cheeks tingle, and she coughed as it hit her lungs. She pulled her coat tight and scurried along the frosty path to the carriage, the driver tipping his topper as she clambered on board.

Twenty-five minutes later, the landau was pulling up outside the Praetorian. With visibility reduced to a few yards, the two-mile journey had been ponderous, the driver barely able to see past the horse's ears, which bounced around as it alternated between a trot and a walk.

"Come along, Issy. Stop your lollygagging." Ace was beaming from ear to ear as he offered his hand to help her down the steps of the carriage.

"Someone's in a cheery mood," she said. *Hard to raise a smile in this freezing fog. What's tickled his fancy, I wonder?*

"Algy's waiting for us inside."

Ace tapped on the window; Eli opened the door. On Sundays, the Praetorian did not open to the public until noon, the previous night's hangovers keeping regular patrons from resuming their carousing.

They hurried through the main bar, along the corridor to the back room, Ace still smiling, unable to contain himself. Issy narrowed her eyes, adjusting to the lamplight.

"Dottie! Gilbert!" She skipped across the meeting room to embrace them, her arms stretched wide. "I thought… We thought you were dead."

"They killed my dad," Dottie said.

"Oh, I'm so sorry." *Words are never enough.* Issy crushed the breath from Dottie's body as she wrapped her arms around her in a bear-hug.

"They wanted to see you before they left," Algy said.

"We're going to my dad's house. We tried last Friday, but he wasn't there," Gilbert said.

Issy squeezed Gilbert's hand. "Be careful in the fog. It's not awfully pleasant out there."

"Come on, Dottie, let's get moving."

Issy helped Dottie to button up her coat and straightened her topper and goggles. "Wrap up, my dear. It's freezing out there."

Algy kissed her daughter on the forehead and waved the pair off as they disappeared down the corridor, through the main bar, and out into the cold.

"I wanted to talk to you both alone. They have enough to worry about."

Issy glanced at Ace. "Trouble?" she asked.

"I'm afraid so. The Anthropocene is getting bolder."

"What've they done?" Ace's sunny mood had soured.

Algy took a deep breath. "There have been a few minor attacks, but now they've destroyed Oldham Triple T station by crashing an airship into the opening ceremony. Hundreds of innocent lives snuffed out in the blink of an eye."

Ace smashed his fist into the table as Issy slumped into a chair. *It was The Bloody Harpy*, she thought, *murderous bastards*.

"Why? What do they have to gain by such a senseless act?" Issy threw her face into her hands.

"There's more terrible news, I'm afraid."

Issy raised her head to face Algy, her brow furrowed and mouth open in a silent question.

"Lady Marsh and her daughter were amongst the dignitaries at the ribbon cutting."

Ace sat next to Issy and put his arm around her.

"I don't understand. Why? Why are they doing this?" Issy's despair was turning to anger.

"We were expecting a major assault, but not at Oldham. We thought Manchester Central was going to be the target. A city-centre hub for HBs and Triple Ts was more likely. We'd heard whispers that an attack was imminent. But we guessed wrong. It seems they've changed their tactics from damaging infrastructure to murdering innocents.

"The blood of the fallen is on our hands. I've failed." She lowered her eyes.

Issy stood and put her arms around Algy. "No, High Mother. Something tells me we are only at the beginning. Shots may have been fired, but we have lost neither the battle nor the war."

They embraced for a few moments before Ace cleared his throat and spoke. *Poor Ace, he struggles with grief,* Issy thought.

"We have news, too," he said. "As you know, we've been indulging in a spot of clandestine snooping to see what we could learn about the airship that ambushed us."

Algy and Issy released their embrace. Algy's gentle smile told Issy she was probably thinking the same about Ace.

"Well, we found out that the dirigible that attacked the Forge is *The Bloody Harpy*, and until yesterday, it was hangared at Barton. The aerodrome chaps had no record of it, but we discovered the hangar is owned by Sir Horatio Marmaduke Wyndham-Welch, a Member of Parliament and, most likely, Anthropocene."

"And *The Bloody Harpy*?" asked Algy.

"Connie and Rory followed it from the aerodrome, but two airships ambushed them. It may well be the airship that carried out the strike at Oldham." Ace bowed his head.

Algy reached for Ace's arm. "Even if *Dragonfly* had pursued it to Oldham, they couldn't have prevented the attack, shugah. They caught us unawares."

He nodded but continued to stare at the floor.

"If only we—" Ace instinctively ducked as a deep rumble shook the building. The ground rocked violently. Dust and cobwebs floated gently from the ceiling, covering everything in a fine white coating. Ace lost his balance and fell into Algy's arms.

"What was that?" Issy shouted.

Ace pulled Algy to her feet. "Let's get out of here!"

They stumbled through the main bar and outside into a chaotic scene. The morning fog had dispersed into a thin mist. The sickly-sweet smell of cordite hung heavy in the air as a small, black mushroom cloud rose above the HyBrid tracks between Castlefield Viaduct and the blackened arch of Manchester Central.

Particles of charred debris fell like blossom petals on the bloodied victims running, staggering or crawling from the building.

Close to the station approach, a hansom lay on its side. Its injured horse, still tethered to the cab, kicked and thrashed, struggling to stand.

Issy stared open-mouthed at the horror. *They've derailed a train.*

The scarred boiler and the foremost crumpled smokestack of a HyBrid engine jutted through the glass and metal front elevation onto the station approach. Its other two smokestacks were inside the building, buried under the rubble. Steam roared from ruined flues and cracked cylinders.

The crushed wreckage of a green and black tram, caught in the path of the rampaging HyBrid, lay on its side, ticking furiously. The huge drive wheels churned at a runaway pace, now unrestrained by its destroyed flywheel.

Shrill police whistles reverberated everywhere. Issy put her hands over her ears to deaden the piercing sounds and peered through the mayhem and confusion. Almost every glass roof panel of the station was shattered, metal frames twisted into grotesque shapes.

On the approach, the wounded were being helped by people with less serious injuries. Issy's stomach turned. There would be fatalities.

Realisation washed over her like an ice-cold shower. Blind terror gripped her as she set off running to the stricken green and black tram, and she slammed into a seven-foot hulk running from her left. She crashed hard into the debris-littered road and twisted onto her back.

Dark, startled eyes glared down at her. For a moment, she thought he was going to stamp on her, but he grunted and loped away without offering a hand of assistance.

She clambered upright and sprinted towards the smouldering wreckage.

Deafened by the chuffing of the engine, disoriented by the accumulators' deep hum reverberating through her brain, she deduced that both steam and battery power had been active as the train left the rails.

Nothing would have stopped it ploughing through the platform like a knife through butter.

But the train should have been slowing down. Were the engineers Anthropocene?

A glance at the footplate told her they would never discover whether they were martyrs to, or victims of, the evil cult.

Behind the tender and the accumulators, carriages were strewn like toys around a child's untidy nursery, but Issy's immediate concern was the crumpled green and black.

She franticly scrambled over broken glass and brickwork, hoping for the best but fearing the worst.

Dottie and Gilbert must be somewhere in or under the mangled tram.

SIXTEEN

CHASTITY

ALTHOUGH INVITATIONS TO THE hall had been infrequent, the view from Weepingbrook's drawing room remained Raven's favourite. Ornamental gardens filled with plants provided colour and perfumes from spring to autumn. Behind the blooms gently swaying in the light breeze, the gentle flow of the Bridgewater Canal attracted elegant herons, darting kingfishers and colourful waterfowl.

But the industrial landscape a hundred yards beyond spoiled this tranquil scene. Huge pile drivers, augurs, and diggers towered above the trees, churning, thick smoke blackening the sky, the raucous clamour of vulgar navvies shattering the peace.

Even on a Sunday, will they not give us a moment's rest? He was not a pious man. Indeed, he despised all religions with equal ferocity, but surely even he deserved quietude.

He drained the last few drops of his father's finest Scotch from his father's Tiffany tumbler and raised the empty glass against the light. A kaleidoscope of colour sparkled through the finely cut crystal. Squinting at the etched pattern, he rolled his eyes. *Ugh! Cherubs and angels! Typical!*

He was about to pour another two fingers of the deliciously expensive tincture when his father strolled through the open doorway, surprising him.

"What the devil are you doing?" Stomping across the floor, he snatched the decanter from Raven's hand.

"Just having a celebratory drink, dear Father. Surely, you don't begrudge your son sampling your finest, do you?"

"You arrogant cockalorum. Get out of my home! Now!"

"Calm yourself, Father. Don't you want to hear about my momentous victory and bask in our glory?" Raven sat behind his father's huge Greenman oak desk, running his fingers casually over its black carvings.

"Leave me alone!" His father was short of breath.

"I'll tell you the news. We'll toast my success, then I'll leave you in peace."

His father clutched the back of a chair, face contorted and flushed, trying to gulp lungs full of air.

Raven did not so much ignore his father's discomfort as revel in it. He was going to enjoy this moment of triumph. "Earlier today, we successfully executed the next phase of our blueprint for the future." He allowed himself a moment's pause and a smile at the apt choice of words. "We derailed a HyBrid, smashing it into Manchester Central, disrupting the entire transportation network. It'll be weeks before the hub is fully operational, and the powers-that-be will have to divert precious resources from other projects to hasten the works.

"But we have more cause for celebration. Athos has assured me that our dear friend, Mister Sparks, was a victim of our actions. Oh, glorious serendipity! I launch a HyBrid into the station, and it lands on Sparks. Delicious. Two birds with one HyBrid."

Beads of sweat were rolling down his father's face. Teeth clenched, eyes wide, his white knuckles clamped around the high-backed chair.

"You are unusually silent, Father. No profane pearls of wisdom? No vicious barbs?"

No longer able to support his weight, his legs buckled, and the old earl slumped to his knees. "Pills." His voice was barely audible. "In the drinks cabinet… Please, Raynard!"

Raven took a half-step towards the cabinet but strode past to the door, locking it with a loud click, dropping the key into his breast pocket and patting it gently. "We don't want Silas interrupting our little heart-to-heart." *Ahh, the irony.* An insignificant part of him wanted to help his father, but he did not wish to waste this opportunity. "Is your black heart finally giving out?"

"Ray, don't do this…"

Back on the other side of the desk, Raven poured another drink and, turning his back, sipped from the glass, staring out of the window.

"I've always loved the ornamental gardens. So relaxing, don't you agree, Father?" He didn't wait for a response. "When I was a child, the only thing I ever wanted was your love. I tried everything to elicit even the smallest sign, the tiniest token of affection from you. But over time, I had to accept you didn't love me, and there was nothing I could do to change that.

"During your rare visits, I would see your eyes flash in annoyance if my laughing was too loud or if I spilled a drink or if Nanny had reason to chastise me. Finally, I accepted your anger as verification that my existence mattered."

"I gave you… everything. You… wanted… for… nothing."

"You hid me from the world, kept me prisoner. Ashamed of what you had done to my mother, you punished *me*. I was just an inconvenience of your lust, an anchor around your neck."

"We thought… you died… but… you lived."

"Oh, I've heard that story a million times. How Mother screamed and screamed for hours in labour. How the good doctor bravely battled to save us both. How he dragged me lifeless from the womb, severing the cord that tethered me to her dying body and breathed life into me. As my cries filled the bedroom, hers fell silent. Very dramatic."

"I wanted… her… and you… to live."

"You wished I'd died instead of her. I've known that all my life. You made sure of that."

"I loved… her."

"But not me? The fruit of your union?"

Sweat rolled off his father's contorted face. His eyes were wide and pleading, every breath a tortuous battle.

"And if she'd lived? Would you have married a lowly servant girl? Would you have presented us to an unsuspecting world, and would we have lived in the Hall? We both know that wouldn't have happened. If you had any intention of making an honest woman of her, you would've revealed her to the world long before my birth.

"No, you would have banished us to the Lodge, married for convenience, and visited only to satisfy your lust."

"Your mother… she wanted… you… to live. I… promised her."

"You have always resented that I lived, and she didn't, haven't you?" Raven spat out the words.

"I... covered up... for you... every... evil..."

"Evil, Father? Is that how you see your son?" Raven turned around to find his father lying on his side on the carpet, clutching his chest, grey-faced, lips turning blue.

"I must... tell you."

"What, Father? That you love me? Too late, old man."

"No... your mother..."

"My mother? Say her name, damn you!" Raven raised his hand.

"Mabel... her name... is Mabel..."

"Mabel was her name, Father... *was*."

"No... she's... alive, Ray... she... didn't... die..."

Silence.

Raven watched open-mouthed as his father squirmed on the carpet. Could this evil man, in cahoots with the doctor and a succession of carers, keep his mother's survival a secret for the last twenty-eight years? His father's laboured gasps convinced him of the truth.

"Nice try, Father."

"It's... true... Ray. Please, my... tablets. I can... tell you... how to... find ..."

If she had lived, why did he lie about her death? Why did he not let her take me away? Did she not love me enough?

"You're lying to save your skin."

"It's true, she... used... me. I... had to... pay... She... threat—"

"Liar!" Raven raised his hand to strike his prone father but stopped short of delivering the blow. "Why did you keep me alive, hidden in the Lodge? Why didn't you smother me? You wanted to, didn't you? Admit it, damn you!"

"I vowed... she made me... I... loved..."

"Love? You don't understand the meaning of the word." Raven knelt and listened to his father's wheezes, the gaps between breaths lengthening. Lowering his face to his father's ear, he spoke gently. "You know what they say, Father. Heir today… Earl tomorrow."

His father reached out, eyes narrowed, looking beyond his pointing finger. Strength ebbing, muscles failing, his limp arm dropped, and drawing a final sharp breath, lips moving, he exhaled his last.

Did he say Mabel?

Raven turned his head to see what his father's dying eyes had been staring at when Death stole the breath from his lungs. Was he reaching for his tablets in the drinks cabinet or something else?

On the wall next to the cabinet hung an unremarkable landscape of a quaint farmhouse with a grey thatched roof, surrounded by lush green fields and hedgerows. He shuddered at the vomit-inducing cloying pathos of pastoral life. *How fitting that was the last image he saw.*

The tenth Earl of Wraithmere placed the empty whisky tumbler in his father's dead fingers and crept out of the hall.

A veritable hat-trick of victories.

Father's pathetic pleas and desperate lies didn't save him from his deserved fate. Letitia would not be back for a few more days, so any celebration had to wait. Still, joy filled his heart.

Without a doubt, this must be the best day of my life.

Voices. Anxious, urgent, somewhere on the outer edge of consciousness. Distant words, barely audible beneath the thunderous, overwhelming ringing in his ears. His head was about to explode.

Where am I? Who am I? Why is everything dark, and who's driving that train through my brain?

The unmistakable reek of antiseptic. *Hospital.* The metallic taste of blood and pain wracking every bone in his body told him why he was there.

Now, if I can just figure out who I am...

"Gilbert?" The bandages across his face prevented him from opening his eyes to see the owner of the vaguely familiar voice. "Gilbert, shugah?"

Gilbert! Yes, that's me! "Miss Algeria?"

"Thank the Mother. We thought we'd lost you both."

Both? "Dottie! Where is she? Is she all right?" Panic rose in his chest. The mental fog was clearing as memories slowly came into focus. They were sitting on a tram, having just bought tickets. Dottie dropped a thrupenny bit and bent down to pick it up, loud rumbling, then nothing.

"I'm here." A warm, trembling hand wrapped around his. "Only a few cuts and bruises. I'm fine." *Is she crying?*

"Dottie? Is that you?"

Fingers tightened for a fleeting moment. *She's weeping.*

An unfamiliar stern voice startled him. "I can only let you stay a few more minutes, ladies. This young man needs to rest."

"He's going to be all right, isn't he, nurse?" Dottie's voice was cracking with emotion.

Do I look so terrible?

"His head has suffered a nasty knock. With this type of injury, there is a strong chance he has a concussion, so the doctor wants to keep him under observation."

Fading footsteps. The nurse must have gone to tend to patients in more urgent need of her care and attention.

"What happened? The last thing I remember is sitting on the tram." The enormity of the tragedy weighed heavier on Gilbert with each passing second as Dottie squeezed his hand tighter in the uneasy silence. "Something terrible has happened, hasn't it?"

"Shugah..." Algeria paused. "We don't want you worrying. You must concentrate on getting well."

"Tell me, Miss Algeria. I need to know." Heart racing, a jolt of fear compressing his chest, he gasped for breath.

"We believe they planted a small bomb just outside the station and derailed a HyBrid. The train left the tracks. Its momentum sent it slicing along the platform, through the buffers and the ticket offices into your green and black."

The horror of the atrocity was incomprehensible. Beneath the roaring in his brain, he lay motionless, trying to gulp air, panting in the crushing silence. "Were many... hurt?"

"The HyBrid drivers didn't survive, and dozens are injured. There will be more deaths, but we have no way of knowing how many." Algeria lowered her voice as if she was passing on a secret not to be overheard.

"We were lucky. The HyBrid smashed into the front of the tram's clockwork mechanism, which shielded us from the brunt of the collision, toppling the tram onto its side and spinning it around. The window must have smashed into your head and knocked you out cold, and you falling onto me stopped me being thrown around, so I just got a few bruises, nothing to worry about," Dottie said.

"Issy was sure you were both dead when she found you, unconscious, covered in blood, lying on top of Dottie in a tangle of wreckage." Algeria's voice shook. *They're both crying.*

Algeria cleared her throat and patted Gilbert's arm. "I'm going to leave you now, shugah. They've moved Lemmy here from Bury, and his mother arrived from London yesterday."

"Lemmy? How is he?" Gilbert jumped at the chance to change the subject.

"Oh, you know him. He never stops joking. See you later." She failed to disguise the sadness in her voice.

When the footsteps had receded, he searched for Dottie's hand, gripping it tightly. Dottie's sniffing back tears filled the silence.

"I can't carry on." Gilbert was glad he couldn't see her expression.

"You need to rest." Dottie gently stroked his arm.

"They're too strong, and there are too many of them. We can't stop them."

"You're not thinking clearly. Let's talk again when you're feeling better."

"They've killed my mum, your dad, Wainwright, Percival, Lady Marsh, and God knows how many today. I thought if I could just kill him…" Gilbert shook his head. Pain lanced through his skull. Shattered bone crunched inside his face. "What was I thinking? I know he has to die, but I don't have the energy."

"The Order needs you; Mam needs you, and I need you." Dottie's voice was trembling but had a hint of steel. "That is, *we* need you…to find Raven. The Anthropocene mustn't achieve its agenda. We can't let them win. The future of the planet may depend on it, and only you have seen his face."

The future of the planet? On me? Really? I want Raven dead for what he's done, not what he might do. "What keeps you going, Dottie? You've lost everything."

"How could I live with myself if I sat back and did nothing? Mam's right about this Raven. He is very dangerous. He—" she fell silent as someone entered the room, footsteps drawing closer.

"Is that you, *bach*?" The gentle Welsh lilt was unmistakable. Gilbert's heart leapt.

"Dad?" Gilbert tried and failed to sit upright. "Thank goodness you're all right."

"Thank goodness *I'm* all right? You're the one lying in a hospital bed covered in bloody bandages."

"How did you know…?"

"Your two friends here, Isadora and Aquilla, brought me. Turned up in a carriage, they did, proper fancy like. They told me what had happened, and I didn't even know you were back from Liverpool!"

Gilbert smiled. He hadn't heard Issy's and Ace's Sunday-best names for a while. "We were coming to see you. If we'd been in the tram shelter… well, we wouldn't be here to tell the tale."

"Hello, Mister Sparks. I'm Dottie. I was with Gilbert when…" He guessed she was shaking his father's hand. *Damn these bandages!*

"Very pleased to meet you. We passed the station on the way." He let out a low whistle. "You were lucky to get out of there alive. Who would do such a thing?"

"We think it was the An—"

"Anarchists, Mr Sparks," Ace interrupted Gilbert. "We don't know for certain, but there are rumours that a group of terrorists are behind it. The authorities will find out who's responsible and bring the evildoers to book."

"Well, they must be a proper bad lot to do such a thing. On a Sunday, an' all."

Thanks, Ace. The less Dad knows, the better. Will I ever learn to keep my big mouth shut? Maybe I'm not cut out for this secret society nonsense. I could get someone hurt.

"Goodness! We can't have all this fuss! This young man needs rest!" Words booming in his head like peels of thunder announced the return of the stern nurse. Dottie flinched with his involuntary squeeze of her hand, which he forgot he was still holding. "Come along, now. I need to check these wounds and change his dressings."

"How long will he be in hospital, nurse?" His father's voice was so tender, so caring, that Gilbert struggled to hold back his emotions.

"Well, that depends on how serious his concussion is. Doctor may keep him under observation for a few days. Now hurry along, please. There are scores of patients to look after, and crowd control isn't part of my job." The nurse's strict tone portrayed a tall woman with a severe countenance in a dark blue uniform with a crisp, clean white apron, shooing away his friends and family like a goose-wrangler.

"We'll bring your father to see you tomorrow, Gilbert. We're so pleased you're all right." Issy touched his arm.

"Take care, son. Get a good rest, now."

Dottie remained silent, squeezing his hand and stroking his fingers with her thumb. She slid her hand along his, maintaining contact right to the end of their fingertips as she joined the other visitors' shuffling footsteps, dutifully filing out of the room, leaving him alone in his darkness and despair.

The ringing in his ears had subsided a little, but the pain in his head was more intense. A torrent of consciousness flooded his brain. Unanswerable questions. An endless struggle to understand. Why was this happening to him? Why did everything depend on him? Why were so many people hurt? Why, why, why…

"Right, Mr Sparks." The nurse had returned. "Let's remove your dressings and clean your cuts. Then you can rest."

"Can I have something for the pain, please, Nurse?"

"Not tonight. We need to understand what's going on inside your head, and laudanum might do more harm than good."

Gilbert's groan turned into a cry of agony as the congealed blood surrounding his wounds was pulled away with the lint dressings. Jagged lines of pain seared across his face as she cleaned the lacerations to his brow and cheeks.

As soon as she had gently removed the encrusted clots around his eyes, he could finally prise open his eyelids, and an intensely bright, blurry scene gradually came into focus.

"I'm Nurse Chastity, dearie. Your wounds are clear of infection. Let's see if we can keep it that way." The voice belonged to the short, dumpy woman leaning over him. Her round, smiling face filled his field of vision.

He gasped as she leaned back. Blood spattered across her cap and apron showed the horrors she had encountered tending to the injured, more than any words could describe.

"Don't worry," she said, "the blood's not all yours."

Now he understood Dottie and Algy's distress and why his father had been subdued. The carnage in the wards must be horrific. Tears trickled from the corners of his eyes.

"Doctor says your fractures need support and protection. You're booked in for surgery tomorrow."

"Fractures? Surgery? I thought I just had a concussion."

"Something hit your head very hard. You're lucky you didn't lose your right eye. You have calvaria, parietal, temporal, sphenoid and zygomatic bone fractures."

"I have a friend who sometimes speaks a strange language. I don't understand him either." Gilbert tried to smile. In blinding agony, he stopped trying.

"Sorry, dearie, it's been a long day. Forehead, temple, eye socket, cheekbone, and skull just above your ear." Nurse Chastity pointed to each area. "Lots of minor breaks which could prove catastrophic if you suffered another blow to the head. Doctor is going to fit you with metal supports."

"Sounds expensive." *And terrifying.* He resisted the temptation the wipe away the warm blood trickling down his face.

"Your young lady's mother says she'll foot the bill, whatever it takes to get you back on your feet."

"I guess I'm precious to them…"

"Aw, that's lovely."

Precious, yes, but not in the way you're thinking.

"I'll just give you clean dressings, then leave you in peace."

Nurse Chastity gave Gilbert a sip of water. She placed pads over his eyes, and he lay still while she re-wrapped his wounds. Once again, deprivation of sight magnified sound and the sharp pain of every bone-crunching head movement a thousandfold.

After what seemed like hours, she finally finished. A gentle pat on his arm and the wheels of her trolley squeaked out of the ward.

I hope I've kept my good looks. Lessons not learned, he made the mistake of smiling at his own joke. After the searing pain subsided, the muffled sounds of everyday hospital life seeped through his bandages, but franticly wheeled gurneys, hurrying footsteps, raised voices and cries of anguish told him this was not an ordinary day. And days like this would be commonplace if the Order failed to thwart the Anthropocene.

Maybe Dottie and Algeria are right. Perhaps I can make a difference.

We must stop Raven. Whatever the cost.

SEVENTEEN

Consequences

For as long as he could remember, Raven had yearned for this day. Finally, his father lay six feet under, and he was going to realise his birthright.

Eight days had passed since the attack on Manchester Central. Letitia had returned, fully restored, and they had celebrated his good fortune in their customary manner.

Eight days had passed since the attack on Manchester Central. Letitia had returned, fully restored, and they had celebrated his good fortune in their customary manner.

Grandmomma taking charge of the funeral arrangements for her son had suited him perfectly.

Now, he stood at the back of the ostentatious meeting room of Postlethwaite, Dumfry and Dunn, solicitors to the nobility and executors of the last will and testament of Ignatius Balthazar Cyrus De'Ath, the ninth Earl of Wraithmere (deceased). The floor-to-ceiling rosewood panelling, leather upholstered chairs and large inlaid desk reeked of beeswax. He imagined the principals ensconced in those chairs each day and, eyes closed, he inhaled the sweet smell of their success. *So, this is how the leeches spend their ill-gotten fees.*

Only the sturdy wooden base of the hat stand prevented it from toppling under the sheer volume of head-furniture hanging precariously from its hooks and branches. Toppers of every fashionable height and hue decorated its length, but not a cap to be seen.

The ladies, of course, still wore their bonnets, cloches and Gainsboroughs, most of which were secured by stout hatpins holding them at just the right angle, making removal unthinkable.

He surveyed the gathered hopefuls, mildly surprised by how many had come along for the reading. Row after row of cushioned seats filled with the bony backsides of distantly related family, friends, servants, and other hangers-on waited for the appointed time. *There will be slim pickings for these vultures*, he thought. The less cautious amongst them turned to sneer at him and his giant associate, looking down their noses before whispering to their partners.

He had received similar stares at the funeral a few days earlier. His grandmomma, the dowager Countess Gertrude Eupheme De'Ath, was in her element accepting condolences and meaningless platitudes. Proud and straight, she had stood by his coffin despite her advanced years, a vision of black bombazine and camphor, a thick lace veil covering her tear-stained face.

Raven had remained detached from the mourners in the church to avoid the tiresome eulogising and feigned reverence. Even at the interment, he witnessed the obsequies from a distance, peering through the frosty morning mist at the grey faces around the grave. *So little emotion*, he had thought, so *typically De'Ath*.

He learned from his grandmomma before the funeral that she was the only family member who knew of his existence. *Soon, they will discover how Father's lust has dashed their hopes of a share in his fortune. Delicious!*

Behind the impressive desk, a suitably sombre Mr Dumfry sat in silence, waiting for the appointed hour of 11 o'clock. Raven mused if they had chosen old Dumfry to read the will because of his lugubrious, gaunt, almost deathly countenance. Peering over his pince-nez spectacles at his bejewelled gold pocket watch, he seemed to be barely breathing. As the clock chimed, he snapped shut the watchcase and tucked it into his waistcoat.

A gentle nod and his clerk dutifully locked the doors before turning to face the gathering, head bowed, hands clasped reverentially. The impatient attendees' attention switched to Dumfry, and the general hubbub gradually subsided as the hopeful focussed on the old fossil.

Dumfry cleared his throat. "At the instruction of the deceased, it is my solemn duty to read the last will and testament of Ignatius Balthazar Cyrus De'Ath, ninth Earl of Wraithmere, to all those he insisted be present at this anointed hour."

Father had a sense of humour, after all. Raven smiled. He wasn't interested in the legal mumbo-jumbo and waited patiently for the announcement of the inheritances to begin. He noted with glee that some of the gathered sat up straighter in their high-backed chairs, eager to learn of what treasures they were getting as the distribution of the estate began.

The paucity of the early bequests caused a stir amongst the assembly. Expected, even promised, large inheritances were inconsequential. Conversations in the room grew louder.

Accusations, laments and even doubts of the late earl's sanity bounced around the wood panelling.

The largest of the legacies was the establishment of a trust fund from the sale of investments for his great-nephew Wynton, which 'if invested wisely, should yield an annual stipend of five guineas'.

"Outrageous."

"Derisory."

"Had the old fool lost his marbles?"

Raven stood in silent triumph; joy concealed behind his half smile.

"Gentlemen! Ladies!" Dumfry was struggling to make himself heard above the clamour. "Just two more behests. Please, show respect for the late earl's last wishes."

"Respect? *Respect*? I've journeyed by carriage from Lancaster for this charade!" A middle-aged man stood up, pointing at Dumfry. "If I find out…"

The burly clerk, who had stepped silently from the door, firmly eased the barracker back into his seat.

Raven neither knew nor cared about the angry man, but he very much enjoyed his perceived injustice.

The noise died down to the indistinct murmur of the disgruntled.

"To my beloved mother, the Countess Gertrude Eupheme De'Ath, I bequeath a lifetime interest in Weepingbrook Hall and an annual income of fifteen hundred guineas. The Hall is her home, and there she shall remain for as long as she wishes or for the rest of her life." Raven saw his grandmomma's shoulders slump. *Relief? Disappointment?* He couldn't tell, and he didn't care.

"The Hall, grounds and buildings which make up the Weepingbrook Hall estate, together with the residue of my worldly goods, I leave to my son, Raynard Vincent De'Ath. As my heir, he is in remainder for the Earldom of Wraithmere, and I hereby instruct Postlethwaite, Dumfry and Dunn to carry out the requisite procedures to make sure the Earldom remains extant on my demise."

Gasps, exclamations and cries of incredulity rang around the room as, one by one, the seated malcontents turned to gape at the tall blond fellow with prosthetic arm enhancements and his giant companion standing implacably at the back of the chamber.

An irate, middle-aged gentlelady yelled, "Well, I never… he had a bastard!"

"Have a care, Mrs Hathersage! We will not tolerate that language in these chambers." Dumfry brought the reading to an abrupt conclusion after announcing the final few sentences and the details of the witnesses to the earl's signature.

Malcontents traipsed from the room, collecting their hats and glowering at the soon-to-be tenth Earl of Wraithmere. There were mutterings about contesting the will and even a suggestion of exhuming the newly deceased earl to seek evidence of foul play. *As if I would murder my beloved father.* No challenge would yield results for the discontented.

Raven and Athos were last to leave. Dumfry stood by the door and offered his hand to Raven.

"You will ensure swift distribution of the estate following the conclusion of probate proceedings, Dumfry?" Raven asked.

Dumfry withdrew the unaccepted offer of a handshake. "Yes, Raynard. We shall make the bequests according to your late father's wishes."

"Shouldn't you address me as lord?"

"You are Mister De'Ath until the ratification of the letters of patent. Indeed, you can thank the first Earl of Wraithmere for having sufficient forethought to not stipulate that only legitimate male heirs can succeed to the title."

"A legal nicety. Just do your job and send me the bill on completion of your obligations."

"That won't be necessary. Your late father paid in advance for the work."

"Then I will bid you good day."

Raven and Athos strode out of the rosewood-panelled room. *They can't stop me now.*

Finally well enough to leave his hospital bed, Gilbert popped his head around the doorway of the world-renowned prosthetics ward at Manchester Infirmary. It was a hive of activity, with the newly admitted victims of the Anthropocene atrocity stretching the resources of the small department to the limit. He suppressed a sneeze as the pungent mix of disinfectant and light machinery lubricant stung his nostrils, making his eyes water.

Unlike most wards in the infirmary, nurses encouraged patients to move around, and Lemmy was hobbling from bed to bed, passing the time of day with fellow patients. Spotting Gilbert, he waved cheerily and limped back to his bed, using a crutch for support.

Because Gilbert hadn't seen Lemmy since before the attack on *Freyja's Grimalkin*, the severity of the injuries shocked him. Doctors could not save his badly mutilated leg and had to amputate well above the knee. Lemmy now sported a permanent prosthetic implant attached to the stable part of his femur.

"What ho, Gilbert."

"Ayup, Lemmy. How's the new leg?"

Lemmy crossed his eyes and wrinkled his forehead. "I'm one of those half-man, half-machine creatures straight out of a penny dreadful."

"You'll be going home soon, the way you're skipping around."

"While there's still a chance of infection, they won't let me go until everything has completely healed." Lemmy leaned closer. "You couldn't smuggle in a shovel, could you, old bean? Maybe I can tunnel my way out."

"This is the third floor. It's wings you need." Gilbert smiled at Lemmy's infectious laugh. "How's your mum?"

"Beside herself with worry about her little boy, and, of course, Father is having a torrid time, too. He's a Member of Parliament, don't-cha-know, battling the self-styled Freedom Brigade who are trying to get the Connickle laws repealed. They're absolute bounders. He's even received threats of violence. Can you imagine? I don't know what the world's coming to when elected officials can't do their job without being threatened.

"So, I've told her I'll be fine and to return to London to support Father. The Order will watch out for old Lemmy. Algy has asked Connie and Rory to whizz her back to London. What about you, old chap? That's a handsome chunk of bronze on your face. Nice filigree work."

Gilbert automatically touched his protective mask, running his fingers across the intricate, ridged patterns scribed into the metal. Bronze covered most of the right side of his head above the jaw, completely encircling the angry purple bruises around his eye. Nestled in the puffy bruising was a pale brown iris floating in a bright red pool of burst blood vessels.

"I'm trying to decide if you're a Spartan warrior or going to a masked ball," Lemmy said, beaming.

"This big chunk of metal is temporary, but the doctor said I'll need permanent implants to support the splintered bones."

Lemmy slapped Gilbert's shoulder. "We're both lucky to be alive, old pal-o'-mine. Let's make the most of our second chance."

Gilbert turned down the corners of his mouth and nodded in stoic agreement.

"Algy's going to need both of us fighting fit if we have any hope of nullifying the Anthropocene threat. I understand you don't share our goals, but our motives to stop Raven are just as strong as yours, and Algy needs every resource available to her. You're a big part of her plans."

"Aye, I've lots of reasons to want him dead. But we can't stop him if we can't find him."

"He'll make a mistake. Remember, he has to be lucky every time he tries something; we have to be lucky only once."

"But how many will die before that happens?"

"None, if I can help it, shugah." Algeria strode in, followed by Dottie. "We're moving Heaven and Earth searching for him. It's only a matter of time."

"I hope you're right. This carnage has to stop."

Dottie put her arm around him. "Come on. Let's get you back to the Praetorian." She turned towards Lemmy and beamed. "You're looking well."

"I'll be out of here soon, all tickety-boo, ship-shape and Bristol fashion. You'll see."

"Ace and Issy will be pleased to have the old gang together again," Algeria said.

They said cheery goodbyes to Lemmy, but Gilbert couldn't help but feel sorry for him. *He's smiling, but his eyes are screaming, 'get me out of here.'*

As they stepped outside into the cool Manchester rain, he gulped a lung full of air. Even the stench of horse dung and the reek of tobacco smoke were a welcome relief from the unrelenting aseptic smell of disinfectant and carbolic.

"Your dad agrees it's best for you to stay at the Praetorian for a few days, so we can keep an eye on you while he goes to work without having to worry," Dottie said.

"And it keeps him out of danger, too," Algeria added.

The route back took them past the mangled wreckage that was once the ornate facade of Manchester Central. The HyBrid and tram had been removed. Deep scoring on the station approach was the only evidence remaining of the violent collision. Dozens of workers had been feverishly toiling to restore the formerly impressive frontage.

Blood drained from Gilbert's face. The building was in a sorry state. The heartbeat of the city's transportation network would be restored, but the lives lost could never be replaced. *What drives him to take life so indiscriminately?*

Dottie's stare was straight ahead, unable to look at the damage. She must have seen horrors when Issy and Ace dragged her from the tram. Horrors she would not soon forget.

"They got the HyBrids back on schedule within forty-eight hours, and most of the tram lines are now operating. So, their plan didn't work." Algeria's positive take on the attack fell on deaf ears.

"Disrupting the city's trams and trains wasn't his only reason for the derailment." Gilbert rounded on Algeria. "He wants to kill people. He's sending a message, and death and destruction are his calling cards.

"And stop saying it's the Anthropocene. They're just following orders. Raven enjoys taking life and he won't quit. That's why I have to find him. I must…" Gilbert's voice trailed off. Dottie was sobbing. He tried to put his arm around her, but she shrugged him aside.

"Stop it, Gilbert! Stop it! *We* have to find him. *We* have to stop him. This isn't about you! You're never going to understand!" She stormed away, back towards the hospital.

Gilbert turned to run after her, but Algeria grasped his arm. "Come along, shugah. She'll be all right. Let's get you back to the Praetorian. Eli will cobble together something for you to eat. You must be sick of hospital food."

Gilbert set his jaw and nodded.

What is wrong with them? Don't they understand! Raven killed my mother and Abel and Percival and Wainwright and countless others. He's evil, and I will get him with or without their help.

Battered by powerful gusts and torrential rain, *Dragonfly* was an angry nymph flittering around the dark sky above Barton. Although the return journey from London had taken considerably less time than the outbound flight, the strong tailwind had made it unpleasantly bumpy. Connie was thankful Tabby had replaced and strengthened the damaged cables before setting off on the errand.

They had set off for the capital midmorning in blustery conditions, and for the entire journey, Lemmy's mother had alternated vomiting over the side with complaining about the cramped interior of the tiny air yacht. She was more accustomed to the stability and comparative luxury of the commercial six-baggers, which handled lively weather with ease.

The decision to wear full aviator's kit kept Connie and Rory warm and dry. Tight-fitting overalls and caps had protected them from the brunt of the rain and wind. Lemmy's mother had not had the benefit of that choice and was dressed in wholly unsuitable street clothes with a flimsy bonnet, which was ripped from her head minutes after they detached from the mooring post.

At first, Connie had been sympathetic to the poor woman's sorry plight, but she had exhausted her supply of apologies and platitudes long before they offloaded her at their destination.

A quick turnaround and strong tailwinds had resulted in *Dragonfly*'s arrival at Barton Aerodrome before the sun dipped below the horizon, but after battling the elements for several hours, Tabby's whole body ached.

"Almost home, Tabby." Connie acknowledged the pugnacious pilot, sliding an arm around her shoulders. "You've earned a good night's sleep tonight." Out of the corner of her eye, she glimpsed Rory's wicked grin and the playful lick of her lips.

"I'll treat us to a meal at Le Rendezvous. It's been a long day," Rory said.

"I'm just looking forward to my bed." Tabby stifled a yawn.

"Me too." Rory raised an eyebrow. Connie rolled her eyes.

"Come on, girl. Get this bird in its nest, then we can relax."

Several minutes of intense struggle concluded with a successful mooring, and Tabby dropped the anchor to further secure the dirigible to terra firma.

"Fuck, that was tough, if you'll pardon my French." Beads of perspiration rolled off her glistening face as she flopped into the seat she had hardly used during the flight.

"We can excuse you for anything after that landing. Nicely done!" Connie slapped her on the back, unsure whether it was sweat or rain that sprayed from her sodden overalls. She needed to get into dry clothes before she caught a chill.

Startled by the sudden drone of powerful engines, Connie instinctively ducked as a three-bagger swooped over them, casting a long, dark shadow across the airfield.

"That was awfully close," she said, squinting through the torrents pouring off *Dragonfly*'s envelope.

The jet-black airship manoeuvred into a berth fifty yards away. The pilot made quick work of successfully connecting to the mooring post.

"That fucker looks familiar, if you'll pard—"

"Yes, it does." Rory pointed to the newly patched stern. "That's one of the bounders that attacked us."

She had hardly finished speaking when a second three-bagger descended through the rain, engines shrieking against the howling gale and deftly attached to a mooring post on the other side of *Dragonfly*.

Connie frowned at Rory. "Coincidence?"

"I think not."

"Fuck!"

They crouched behind the bulwarks. "If they followed us, why didn't they attack us while we were in the air?" Rory asked.

"They wouldn't chance a long shot in this wind. We were bobbing all over the sky, and they would've shown themselves," Tabby said.

Connie raised her head above the side of the air yacht, then ducked back into safety. "Four of them climbing down the ladders, two from each ship, carrying pistols. Any chance of taking off, Tabby? Tabby?"

Tabby was busy rummaging through her tool chest. Already, she had placed a large steel spanner, a sledgehammer and a long-handled, spiked maul hammer on the deck.

"Not in this gale. We'd be in the trees before you could say Jack Robinson. Mooring in this wind was hard enough but taking off from a standing start is a different bag of spanners. Ha! Found it." She emerged from the chest with a shiny, short-barrelled blunderbuss cradled in her arms like a newborn infant. "I knew this old dragon might come in handy one day."

Connie raised her head again. "They're almost on us." Before she could duck behind the bulwark, a shot exploded into the side of the gondola, sending splinters of wood narrowly missing her face.

Tabby's wet, trembling hands were struggling to load and charge the dragon. A grappling iron thudded onto the starboard bulwark close to Connie, burying its barbs into the wooden hull. She tried to prise it off but failed.

Another clanged against the brass railing on the port side, its flukes hooking onto and sliding along the slick metal towards Tabby.

Springing across the deck, Connie lunged for the maul hammer. "Get ready to pull up the anchor, Tabby!"

A hand grasped the rail. Bedraggled, wind-whipped hair and a toothless smirk followed. Eyes wild with blood lust widened as the maul cleaved the ruffian's skull like an overripe melon. Unable to dislodge the spike from the splintered head, Connie released her grip on the handle before the body's dead weight pulled her over the side.

A pistol appeared near the port grappling hook, waving from side to side as if seeking a target. Rory smashed the sledgehammer into the hand gripping the grapnel. Ruined fingers let go, sending the gunman toppling, his agonised scream cut short by unyielding concrete.

"Now, Tabby, the anchor!" Connie bellowed at the stern, but Tabby was still trying to load the dragon and reacted too late. A muscular thug had clambered aboard and clasped Rory in a bear-hug from behind.

Tabby threw her weight against the lever to raise the anchor, causing the gondola to lurch wildly. Now only secured to the mooring post by electromagnets, they were at the mercy of the wind, spinning, bobbing violently.

A fourth assailant was clinging onto the grappling rope, unable to climb up or down, tossed around by the gale. Attempting to dislodge the grapple, Connie leaned over the side and stared into the barrel of a pistol. The gunman pulled the trigger as the gondola bucked sideways. Hand slipping on the wet grip, his wayward shot ripped through her upper arm. She wheeled backwards from the force, her eyes squeezed tight from the searing pain.

On all fours, Connie fumbled around the deck, searching for Tabby's spanner, grimacing with pain, her hands sticky with warm blood trickling from the open wound. Fingers brushed cold steel, and she snatched at it.

Battling the searing pain, she stumbled blindly to the grapple and, using the spanner as a lever, dislodged it, sending wood splinters flying. The screaming man, still clasping to the sodden rope, plunged through the rain, hitting the ground with a loud grunt. She sat back on the deck, squeezing her arm to staunch the blood loss.

Rory was struggling to break free from her assailant. They slipped and crashed onto the deck, awash with blood and rainwater. The burly man was first to regain his feet and drew his pistol from his belt, taking dead aim at Rory.

"NO!" Connie screamed and hurled the spanner at him. He grinned and pulled back the hammer with his thumb. His head exploded in a mass of splintered bone, brain, and blood before he could pull the trigger. The recoil from Tabby's dragon launched her backwards, hitting the stern bulwark hard as the man's carcass toppled onto the deck like a side of beef.

"No one tries to kill my girl!" Tabby was panting, still holding the smoking blunderbuss tightly with both hands.

Connie looked over the starboard side. Two corpses lay on the muddy airfield. But an injured attacker was dragging himself through the mud towards the dirigible, his left leg bent at a grotesque angle.

"Drop anchor, Tabby." Connie grimaced with pain. "We can't let him escape."

Once the ship had stabilised, Rory clambered down the unfurled ladder and trudged across the sodden aerodrome, leaning into the gale, rain drenching her flying suit. She reached the crawling man and grabbed his collar. He spun around and threw a haymaker, but she was too quick and smashed him with a brutal right hook, his limp body flopping in the mud like a stunned slaughterhouse steer.

The wind behind her, she dragged him back to the air yacht where Tabby was waiting at the foot of the ladder, holding onto a rung, resting the sledgehammer on her shoulder.

"Ask him!" Connie raised her voice above the thunderous wind, leaning over the side of the gondola in blood-soaked overalls that would not have looked out of place in Water Street Meat Market.

Rain spattered the man's face as he regained consciousness. With Rory's boot pinning his unbroken leg, his eyes widened when he saw Tabby shouldering arms with the heavy hammer.

Rory bent over him.

"Good evening, friend. My name is Aurora Phoebe Marrable, and I'm the twin sister of Constantia Hortense Marrable, the woman you tried to murder.

"While I recognise you were doing another's bidding, and there was no personal malice in your action, I'm sure you must accept it's my sororal obligation to exact a terrible retribution for your crime. To that end, you and I will become better acquainted later.

"But first, you will give me the information I seek. So, my good man, tell me, where will we find your boss, your prophet, your leader, Raven?"

The man spat and laughed through gritted teeth. "You don't know what you're talkin' about, bitch! You'll get nowt from me!"

"A large part of me is so pleased you said that." Rory raised her eyebrows and nodded at Tabby, and the howling wind accompanied the man's screams in a barbaric duet, as daylight surrendered to the darkness.

EIGHTEEN
NEW HORIZONS

AS A STARLESS NIGHT fell on the city, Raven's carriage rumbled past the low life of Manchester as they shuffled along Deansgate in the freezing rain. Lit only by the diffused green light of the streetlights reflected on the sodden cobbles, the lost souls drifted between sleazy drinking dens. *The brass brothels will be busy tonight,* he thought, smiling at his passenger as she fluttered long eyelashes that clicked noisily across her yellow eyes.

Blazing gas lamps illuminated the florid signage of The Gaiety Theatre, luring slum-dwellers and stately homeowners alike. It was one of the very few places the hoi polloi of Angel Meadows could rub shoulders with the bourgeoisie. Scuttlers, artisans, and toffs were drawn by the bright lights and promise of unbridled fun and frolics.

Raven and Letitia drew few stares as they stepped out of the carriage. Just a toff and his mek out on the town. While most preferred a human companion, it was not uncommon for a man or woman to be seen with a mechanical escort for an evening in the city. Meks were able to protect as well as accompany, and the advanced models offered a comprehensive range of special services for the discerning lady or gentleman.

They strode arm in arm, past the queuing masses through the main entrance into the brightly lit foyer. Raven was immaculate in a black tuxedo draped with a pure white scarf. His tall, shiny topper sparkled under the gas mantles.

Having donned dowdy garb previously to visit The Gaiety incognito, the tenth Earl of Wraithmere would never again have to endure the sweaty stench and vulgarity of the filthy lower classes.

They passed through the foyer at a more leisurely pace, unchallenged by the theatre staff, some of whom lowered their eyes or nodded, smiling at the handsome couple.

Letitia was resplendent in a corseted crimson dress with hooped, crinoline skirts that accentuated her swaying metal hips. She had chosen shimmering, royal blue shoulder-length hair and topped it with a simple, red satin hat adorned with ribbons that fluttered gently behind her as she walked.

Her eyes widened as they stepped into the mechanical contraption to take them up to the dress circle where the Earl of Wraithmere's box was located. The mek attendant closed the gates of the birdcage lift and tipped his cap at Letitia. "Welcome to The Gaiety. We hope you enjoy the show. There will be a playbill for this evening's performance on your seat."

"My, oh my! Dear, sweet Raven. Thank you, thank you, thank you for bringing your Letitia to this wonderful place. Never has Letitia seen such splendour."

The attendant pulled the lever, and the cage rattled into motion, shaking and juddering to the floor above. Raven pressed a coin into the mek's gloved hand. Meks rarely received gratuities, as those who could afford to tip often chose not to, and the more appreciative commoners did not have the means. But Raven did not discriminate. The mek nodded, ushering them forward and to the left before retreating into the lift and returning to the ground floor.

Hand in hand, they walked around the sweeping, curved corridor until they reached the last curtained opening. A small metal plaque to the right of the maroon drapes read 'RESERVED - Earl of Wraithmere'. Raven puffed out his chest and stepped extravagantly to the side. "After you, my dear."

"Dear, sweet Raven. How gallant. Pray tell, kind sir, does Letitia not look ravishing in this posh frock?"

He beamed at her innocence. Did he buy her a new wardrobe of clothes from Isaac and Bogart because he felt guilty? Surely, he had simply grown tired of her appearance and freshened up her looks with the latest *haute couture*. Or, at least, that's what he continued to tell himself since she had returned from the repair shop in tip-top condition.

"Stunning, my dear. Absolutely splendid. You're the jammiest bit of jam in the whole theatre."

Letitia's demure, appreciative smile was perfect programming.

They picked up their playbills and sat in the box seats closest to the stage. The front page of the slim playbill announced the headline act 'Les Folies Macabre' in huge gothic letters, surrounded by drawings of contortionists in impossible poses, illusionists with assistants floating through flaming hoops, fire breathers, and sword swallowers, each depicted in vibrant red and black ink.

Inside, several pages of advertisements extolled the virtues of 'Burt's Boots' and 'Dr Zephaniah's Miracle Elixir' alongside mundane adverts for toothpaste, soap, cart repairers, and funeral services.

Raven turned quickly to the centre, which displayed the running order. Korkie's Komedy Kapers preceded Lullaby Lily Lambkins, the Soporific Songstress, and the Pasquini Brothers' Human Pyramid, listed to perform before the stars of the show.

"When does it start? Oh, when does it start?" Letitia clapped her hands together in child-like glee.

"Soon, my dear."

Twenty minutes passed before the Master of Ceremonies appeared to tumultuous cheers and introduced the first act with a rap of his gavel, but it was not long before the rabble in the cheap seats let Korkie know his Kapers were not nearly Komical enough. Heckling drowned most of his performance, and he rushed off stage to a cacophony of boos.

Winsome Lily Lambkins, dressed in virginal white from head to toe, her Gainsborough hat tied with a scarf beneath her chin, calmed the savage crowd with a montage of gentle bucolic ballads warbled over a chorus of wolf whistles.

The mek musicians increased the tempo for the Pasquinis, who tumbled and balanced in gravity-defying montages, and exited stage left to appreciative applause.

After a brief interlude, the lights dimmed. Raven squeezed Letitia's hand and leaned forward in his seat. A slow drumbeat echoed around the auditorium. Dark shapes slithered rhythmically across the boards to the Devil's discordant rhythms.

From the stage wings on the far side danced a lithe semi-naked woman, daubed in black and red. Raising a burning torch to her lips, she breathed fire over the spellbound crowd. The heat from each blast tingled on Raven's cheeks before the flames dissipated to oohs and aahs from the easily impressed.

Entranced shadowy figures continued to writhe, twist and turn into impossible contortions in the background.

Raven's pounding heartbeat matched the building rhythm. From beneath their box, the spotlight shone on a gigantic samurai warrior as he clambered up the steps to the stage. Raven and Letitia leaned forward in unison, watching wide-eyed as he threaded silver bodkins through his cheeks to gasps from the crowd before tilting his head back and swallowing a long sword up to its hilt.

He carefully removed the blade to loud cheers from the auditorium and stomped off stage right without acknowledging his ovation.

The relentless beat pounded a tribal, primaeval tattoo.

Raven sensed a change in the audience's demeanour. Nervous anticipation had replaced the earlier good-natured exuberance. He wondered what Letitia's more sensitive eyes were seeing in the diminished light. Wide-eyed stare transfixed on the writhing bodies, her lips quivered in anticipation, and her jaw dropped open.

They were in the presence of an unsettling malevolence, and Raven loved it.

Two assistants pushed a long, black, coffin-shaped trunk to the centre of the stage where a sinister, hooded figure had risen, standing motionless amidst the squirming limbs. The bestial gyrations of the dark creatures became more frenzied as the drumbeats grew louder.

The mysterious magus offered his hand to a shadow, silently instructing it to lie on the makeshift altar, draping it in a blood-red cloth. He closed his eyes, mouthed an incantation, and instantly, the body stiffened and rose, hovering a few feet above the box. The fire-breather slithered across the stage to the sorcerer and handed him a flaming ring.

The pulsating music stopped. The audience held its collective breath as he raised the hoop above his head. Then, with a single sweeping movement, he passed it around the figure, which vanished in a shower of flames.

The crowd exhaled, and spontaneous applause erupted around the auditorium. With a bright flash and a puff of smoke, the hooded sorcerer disappeared.

The primitive pounding beat resumed louder and faster. Dark, writhing figures rose and fell, contorted, and danced in a renewed frenzy. Raven's heart raced, the blood rushing in his ears. In the centre of the writhing mass, a shadow stopped dancing, head back, arms stretched sideways, fingers reaching.

Two massive, oil-smeared men approached from each side of the stage, marching across to the docile figure and attached manacles to its wrists and ankles before retreating whence they came, dragging the heavy chains and pulling them taut. The drumbeat was galloping to a merciless crescendo.

The drums stopped.

Gasps punctuated the deathly silence. Bonds strained; blood spurted from ruptured limbs. Deep in their bones, in the hidden dark corners of the psyche, every horror-filled spectator felt the agonised scream as the bloody torso fell to the boards with a wet thud.

The main curtain swung shut.

A moment of silence lasted a lifetime before the audience erupted in deranged shrieks and cries, trembling hands holding horrified faces. Those with delicate dispositions swooned or retched while others screamed, eyes wide, faces contorted. But many more burst into demented laughter, blood lust coursing through their veins.

Heart still pounding, Raven beamed as he glanced at Letitia. Her mouth was open in a silent, strangled scream, head shaking slowly from side to side. She may have recognised that most of the contortionists were meks, but did she recognise the victim was one of her own, made to appear human? Did the unfortunate machine cry out in their mysterious mek network? Or did the spectacle arouse a latent memory of a recent evening's gruelling entertainment?

Below them, in the auditorium, skirmishes were breaking out. Pushing, shoving, punches thrown. Some dashed to the exits, horror burned into their memories. Others screamed their approval, needing more.

"Come, my dear," he said to Letitia. "They have invited us backstage to meet the performers."

Letitia's mouth snapped shut, cracking like a mousetrap, and she grinned from ear to ear. "Have they, really? How jolly! Dear, sweet Raven. Do you think they will adore Letitia's new dress?" She had recovered, the reason for her reaction forgotten in the blink of an eye.

Raven smiled. The experiment had been an unqualified success. How easy it was to control simple minds and foment hysteria. Irrefutably, forming and funding Les Folies Macabre had been one of his more enjoyable successes.

Algeria hugged Lemmy, ignoring the chill from his wet coat on her bare arms and neck as she brushed her lips across his cold cheek. "Good to have you back, shugah. We've missed you." She nodded to Eli.

With an arm around his shoulder, she ushered him to the booth where Connie and Ace were settling, smiling.

"The walk was longer than I thought. 'Twas an excellent test for the new leg, though." He tapped his metal shin with his walking stick.

Connie shrugged her shoulders, forgetting her wound, her hand instinctively grabbing at the bandaged biceps through which the bullet had ripped its jagged path. "We offered him a ride, but he insisted on getting here under his own steam."

Eli plonked a pewter tankard of porter on the table, froth overflowing. Lemmy grabbed it and gulped two mouthfuls before wiping his mouth on his coat sleeve.

"This catlap still tastes like gnat's piss." His contorted face growled the words, mimicking one of the Praetorian's less cultured regulars.

Algeria rolled her eyes. *He never changes.*

"Any luck finding our elusive foe yet?" Ace asked.

She shook her head. "It's only a matter of time. No evil long remains incognito. We've learned from Lemmy's mother that his father is battling the Freedom Brigade. The Connickle laws are in real danger of being overturned."

"What's the Freedom Brigade?" Connie asked.

"Political arm of the Anthropocene, we believe, promoting the rights of the individual above all else. They've infiltrated government committees to discredit Connickle's theories and want progress-slowing laws repealed."

"What nonsense. How can regulations that protect our future be presented as oppressing freedom? Privilege without responsibility? That way, chaos lies. Man's greed and selfishness will be the end of us all. *Qui totum vult totum perdit.*"

"This recklessness is going to destroy the planet." Connie shook her head.

"We're already making a pretty good job of that," Ace said.

Algeria flashed him an angry glance. "All of Raven's attacks have been here, at the birthplace of the Industrial Revolution, and always against public transportation, particularly trains and canals. It's part of a bigger plan."

"Whatever they are up to, they must be stopped. Repealing Connickle may be a precursor to releasing a new evil on the world." Ace examined the faces of the worried group. "Remember the Wigtwizzle scientists? They're up to something."

"We can't let them win. We'd be letting down everybody." Connie squeezed and rubbed her injured arm.

"And we would have failed our Founding Fathers. The visionaries who formed The Venerable Antediluvian Order of the Custodians of Magna Mater knew we would face such challenges. If we fail them, Mother Earth may never recover." Algeria hung her head.

"Don't be too sure, Algy. Mother Nature always fights back." Lemmy shadowboxed a couple of left jabs and a right uppercut.

"*Nil desperandum!*"

"We need to find Raven to stop this madness." Any shadow within the arc of Lemmy's haymaker would have been knocked into next week.

"Always the optimist. Yes, shugah, he's the key, but still, he eludes our best efforts. According to Eli, even the mek network can't trace him."

Ace leaned forward in the booth. "If we can't sniff him out, we must make him come to us." Surrounded by blank expressions, he rolled his eyes.

"Entice him into the open by giving him an irresistible target. Listen, Wyndham-Welch owns the hangar at Barton, where they repaired *The Bloody Harpy*. He must be Anthropocene, and he's on several committees with Lemmy's father. We feed him a juicy titbit of false information and…" Ace raised his eyebrows and spread his arms.

Connie clicked her fingers. "Yes, but what? What would be a big enough target to tempt Raven to attack?"

The Stormriders looked to Algeria for guidance. Her slowly evolving smile told them she had an idea.

For all his twenty-eight years, the Lodge, hidden deep in the grounds of Weepingbrook Hall, had been his home. Its small number of ample-sized rooms was ideal accommodation for him and a parade of nannies, governesses, tutors and even the occasional paramour as well as his constant companion, Letitia. Dark, comforting memories lurked in the familiarity of every nook and cranny, but there was no love within these walls.

As a result, settling into the hall was difficult. With its high ceilings, elaborate decor, and the imposing entrance portico mixed with the musty smell of decades of decadent aristocratic self-indulgence, he felt like an impostor. He had to remind himself constantly, *I deserve this. This is my birthright.*

The presence of his ancient grandmomma was depressing. Since her son's untimely death, she had worn black mourning attire from tiara to toe, her grief-stricken grey visage concealed by her heavy lace veil. *Very dramatic and quite pathetic.*

So, Raven continued to use the Lodge as the nerve centre of his Anthropocene operations. Today, with business to conduct, he sat by the window gazing across the gardens towards the Bridgewater Canal. The gentle sound of wind in the trees and birdsong usually calmed the savage urges that roiled inside him, but the background throbbing of pounding pile drivers and the incessant babble of diggers and tunnellers on the ship canal fed his inner demons.

For once, Letitia's mellifluent purring, designed to soothe, and programmed coquetry only raised his tetchiness. As always, she was stunning in her tangerine silk dress that shimmered in the sunlight, small lime and emerald flower patterns popping from the bright material. But he had to ball his fists, digging sharp fingernails into his palms to take the edge off his rising anger.

"Dear, sweet Raven. Do you not like Letitia's shiny new frock? Do you no longer love your sweet Letitia?"

Can she sense my dark mood? "Your gown is exquisite, my dear. Surely, I would not have asked you to wear it if I didn't adore it?" *That will shut her up for a few moments.*

"But, dear, sweet—"

A loud, rhythmic rap on the door interrupted her pout, and Athos strode in, eyes lowered, glancing sideways. *Still fearful of being the bringer of bad tidings, I see. Good.*

"They're here, Ray." Head bowed, he looked at Raven through bushy eyebrows. His silent subjugation went unacknowledged.

The Flanagan brothers shuffled into the room, caps removed and gripped tightly in front of them.

"Ahh, gentlemen. Pray, indulge me. Let me guess…" He put his finger to his lips, then pointed first to the shorter man. "You are Fergus, and that is your younger brother, Finbar."

"Yes, sir, that's right." Fergus's grin was barely visible inside his unkempt beard.

"Our dear departed friend, Mr Gunn, described you both most accurately." Raven's eyes did not mirror his smile. The Flanagans looked nervously at each other.

"Oh, dear sweet, Raven. Look at how Letitia's pretty frock matches their hair. How jolly." Her tin-whistle giggle sliced through the air, causing the brothers to wince.

"Before we get to the reason I summoned you to my home," *Yes, the Lodge is still my home,* "pray, tell me, who missed the shot?"

The Flanagans stared blankly. "The shot?" Gus said.

"Come, come, my dear fellows, you know exactly to what I am referring. The shot that missed Sparks at the Forge."

"It's not right to speak ill of the dead, sir, but it was Captain Gunn, and that's the truth."

Finbar nodded furiously in agreement.

"Yes, that *is* the truth, and that is the very reason I sent Mister Gunn on his last mission alone. Had it been either of you fine gentlemen, you would have been piloting *The Bloody Harpy* to Oldham. I am a fair man. I reward success and failure with equal enthusiasm."

The Flanagan brothers gripped their caps tighter. Gus gulped and almost choked, spluttering. *Message delivered.*

"Now, I'm sure you must be curious about my reason for summoning you here on this chilly autumnal morning. Please, gentlemen, take a seat."

Finbar almost knocked his brother over in the rush to the two chairs. Raven sat with his back to the window, silhouetted by the strong sunlight, forcing the brothers to squint into the glare.

"Tell me everything you know of our friend, Mr Sparks. What makes him tick?"

The brothers exchanged glances and shrugs. Finbar broke his silence. "We heard he's dead."

"Yes, I heard that, too." He flashed a sideways glance at Athos. "Unfortunately, rumours of his death were very much exaggerated. Injured, but sadly not mortally. He's proving to be quite the nuisance. So please, gentlemen, tell me everything you know about him."

"He's an annoying little bastard," Fergus said, "who always thinks he knows better than everybody else. Thinks he's something special, so he does."

"Quick temper, he's got. Snaps at the slightest thing. Bit of a mummy's boy, too. She's dead, and he won't let anyone call him Bertie, 'cos that's what she called him. So, we called him that all the time to wind him up, didn't we, Finn?" The brothers shared a smirk.

"His dear mother has passed away? How sad for him. Does he have a father?"

"Aye, sir, he has a father, sure he does. They live together." Fergus said.

Raven sat straighter in the chair and reached for Letitia's hand. "Do they now… So, pray tell, what does his father do for a living, and where do they reside?"

"Dunno what he does, but we know where they live." Fergus's heart would have burst with fear if he had seen the steel-buckling hatred in Raven's eyes.

Letitia yelped as Raven's prostheses magnified his involuntary twitch to a crushing squeeze. His inner rage burned. His half smile was in danger of becoming a full-throated guffaw. *Got him!*

The cotton traders occupying the enormous warehouses in the city centre were always busy. Meks carrying bundles of samples scurried swiftly hither and thither along the thoroughfares and alleyways alike. Their strength, speed, and agility amazed Gilbert. *Why do they never bump into each other? How do they know which way to dodge?*

He held Dottie's hand as they walked past Le Rendezvous towards the Athenaeum gentlemen's club. The late afternoon sunlight shimmered off her olive skin, crow's feet radiating from the corners of her sparkling green eyes. She was the embodiment of a happy upbringing by her father, who was dead because of him. Dottie caught him staring adoringly at her and returned his smile, her moist lips slightly parted.

Gilbert looked away.

"Sometimes, I just don't understand you," she said, still smiling but shaking her head.

"Good, that makes two of us."

"There's more to life than hate and revenge."

"Raven has to pay for what he's done. I can't rest until he's dead."

"But you can't carry the weight of the world on your shoulders. Leave it to the Order. Until we find him, there's nothing you can do." Dottie rubbed his arm and gazed up into his eyes.

Of course, she was right. He wanted to forget everything, if only for a day, an afternoon, or even an hour, but he could not get Raven or his atrocities out of his mind. Those who had perished by Raven's hand had to be remembered. He burned their names into his memory by repeating them. Mum, Wainwright, Percival, Abel, Lady Marsh, the other innocent victims at Oldham Triple T and Manchester Central Hub. He would not rest until Raven was dead… or he was.

He checked his watch. "Come on. Let's jump on the tram and go see my dad. By the time we get there, he'll be home from work."

Dottie lowered her eyes and sighed. "All right, but I mean it. You can't do everything by yourself."

Certain of himself, he nodded, despite knowing she was wrong.

Manchester Central Hub was at eighty percent capacity, with only two of the tram spokes not operational. Unfortunately for them, the Eccles line was one of them. The terminus for green and black trams was temporarily re-sited on Great Bridgewater Street, close to the Praetorian, and they marched across the road as a tram trundled to a halt. Knowing they would have to wait for the mechanism to be rewound, they sat arm in arm in the shelter, watching the driver attach the winder.

"What will you do when all this is over?" Dottie asked.

"I've not thought that far ahead." Gilbert stared at his boots, not daring to reveal his thoughts. "What about you?"

"Oh, I'll just carry on the struggle of the Order. It's what Dad would have wanted."

"You don't *have* to do that, you know. You can do whatever you choose."

"I want to, though. The work is important."

"And you get to spend more time with your mum."

"I would still be active in the Order even if Mam wasn't High Mother. What are you trying to say?"

"Well, I, er, just think you two have a lot of catching up to do, that's all." Gilbert stared at his feet to avoid her blazing stare.

"Yes, we have a long way to go. She abandoned me and Dad for her ideals. I still can't understand how she could have done that to us." Dottie's chin quivered, barely holding back her emotions. "You really don't know how messed up this is, do you? All you can think about is vengeance. Hatred for Raven is what's driving you. My relationship with my mam may be complicated, but I'm driven by love for her and Mother Earth."

"I didn't mean to dredge up all those feelings. But I have to avenge my mum and your dad and everyone else. You must see that."

"If you kill Raven, what then? Will you be free of hatred and vengeance? Maybe, but you will be hollow."

"Listen, Dottie, I-"

"No, you listen! You're so wrapped up in your own little self-important world that you can't see what's right in front of you. Wake up before you lose everything!" She was crying openly. Gilbert tried to put his arm around her, but she pushed him away and stood up.

"It's no good. I thought my dad was getting through to you, but you don't understand what we are up against. Mend your heart before the hatred eats you up. I can't do this anymore." She turned and ran back to the Praetorian.

The conductor beckoned the waiting passengers to board the tram, all of whom were staring at Gilbert at the head of the queue. He hurried on board and took a window seat on the side opposite the clockwork mechanism. *What was all that about? Had he said something so terrible? What's wrong with her?*

Gilbert's mind was in turmoil, trying to understand why Dottie had turned sour on an otherwise perfect day. His face implants ached as the tram shuddered into motion. Steel wheels rumbled along iron rails, clicking over each irregularly spaced joint. The metronomic tick-tock of the clockwork movement made his headache worse. Wiper blades scraped across the tram's windscreen as drops of rain fell in the gathering twilight. *Even the weather's against me.*

But he was looking forward to having a natter with his father. It was a lifetime ago since they had that proper talk in the parlour the day Wainwright recruited him. That evening, he had fallen asleep in his chair, dreaming of a future that was doomed before it began.

The tram slogged through the worsening weather, gently rocking, and arrived at Eccles Triple T terminus on time. As he hurried out of the station, a phalanx of lamplighters, lighting sticks shouldered, marched in step like a well-drilled military company.

They stopped to watch a fire appliance speed past, its galloping black horse sweating, nostrils blowing, pulling a tender full of firefighters. Large steel-rimmed wheels clattered along the wet cobbled street, bells ringing to clear the way ahead. *Well, that was exciting.* Gilbert couldn't remember the last time he saw a fire tender.

As he watched it careen off the main road, his heart missed a beat. *Has it turned into Mayfield Street?* The bell stopped. He quickened his pace.

By the time he reached Mayfield Street, he was running. The acrid smell of burning filled his nose and stung his eyes. The scene was chaotic. He held a handkerchief to his face and squinted through the smoky haze, gasping as the horror hit him.

Fire engulfed his house. His father's bicycle lay twisted and blackened by the blazing hole which used to be the front wall of his home. Charred masonry poked through the flames; black, broken tombstone teeth in a flaming maw.

Instinctively, head down, he sprinted towards the flames, hurtling headlong into the billowing noxious smoke with no thought of his own safety. Hot fumes seared his throat and lungs, but he ran on. The heat was unbearable. Two firefighters caught him before he reached the house and grasped his arms, holding him back, preventing him from getting any closer.

"Whoa, lad! What're you doin'? You'll get yourself killed!"

Gilbert raised his face to the heavens; his agonised ear-splitting scream rose above the mayhem.

"DAD! NOOOOOO!"

NINETEEN

Runaway

GILBERT PULLED OUT OF the grasp of the firemen and, reeling away from the inferno, pushed through the staring onlookers who were hypnotised by the flames licking at charred timbers and blackened brickwork. No one took notice of the broken, weeping young man staggering between them. The fire's elemental destructive power terrified and excited in equal measure. Gasps rang in his ears as the roof collapsed with a whoosh. Flaming masonry rained down, exploding in the road behind him, forcing everyone to scurry to safety.

Blurred by tears, gaslights were polygonal patches of pale light. Burning, crackling sounds followed him as he lurched out of Mayfield Street, dizzy from smoke inhalation. He fell to his hands and knees and retched until he coughed up a sticky mixture of mucus and soot. With his eyes streaming, he climbed to his feet, stumbling into a lamplighter.

"Oi, watch where you're goin'! Yer cock-eyed applejack!"

Gilbert raised a hand in apology as he staggered off, sobbing uncontrollably. He had to get away. He had to run from the horror burned into his memory. Glancing over his shoulder, he saw the streetlamps illuminating the pallid pall of smoke rising above the rooftops. *Dad's spirit floating to the heavens to join Mum?* He caught his breath; hot tears welled and spilled onto his cold cheeks. With all his heart, he hoped his father was at peace with his beloved.

His head was spinning. The dark shroud of despair swirled around him, extinguishing hope. Black clouds drifted across the moon; their edges briefly ignited by the silvery moonglow before blocking out its ethereal light.

In the streets of Eccles, life went on. Early evening drinkers trudged into public houses, blissfully unaware of his tragedy. Street urchins ignored calls from their mothers to return home for supper, caring only for their own selfish fun. A scruffily dressed working girl gave him a come-hither smile and jaunty wink.

Although his eyes saw everything, his brain registered nothing. Overwhelmed by grief, every fibre of his essence screamed. *Why?*

It was his fault. He was an expert in guilt, and his runaway engine of self-recrimination had a full head of steam hurtling along the tracks to the buffers of terminal misery.

For years, he blamed himself for his mother's death. Failed relationships, the inability to settle in jobs and even petty rows with friends had been his fault. His fight with the Flanagans caused Wainwright's murder, Percival perished despite his efforts to save him, and, worst of all, the bolt intended for him killed Abel.

Dottie didn't care whether he lived or died. Rightly, she blamed him for her father's death, and she would never forgive him. Why should she when he would never forgive himself?

He was a misery magnet. If he hadn't been born, many people would still be alive.

Now he had lost his father because of his obsession with Raven. How could he live with this burden of guilt? He should not have pursued this merciless killer; he was outmatched, out of his depth, and now very much alone.

He trudged on through the rising mist, not caring where he was going. Balled fists thrust into his overcoat pockets, hunched against the numbing cold, he stared at the ground a few feet ahead. His shoulders shook, and tears streamed down his cheeks again as he ploughed onwards, the gathering gloom mirroring his deepening depression.

Did anybody care if he lived or died? Would anyone mourn his passing? What would people say about him?

Did it matter if anyone remembered him at all?

When Raven took my dad's life, he stole my future, too.

Silas closed the door silently behind him, leaving Raven alone. There was something unnerving about his father's old mek.

Letitia had been at his side forever. She had been whatever he needed at every stage of his life as he grew from petulant toddler through rebellious teenager into adulthood. Now, more than ever, he valued her presence and often used her as a sounding board.

Silas, on the other hand, was his late father's loyal servant. Raven trusted the old mek as far as he could throw him, and, at 250 pounds, even with his enhanced strength, that would not be a great distance. *He'll have to go. I'll replace him with a newer model. I wonder if Isaac and Bogart have the latest QT that—*

The door crashed open, and a yellow tornado pirouetted into the room. Canary yellow hair and lemon dress flaring like spinning discs, Letitia landed in a low curtsey in front of him. He smiled. *Father hated her for doing that.*

"Dear, sweet Raven. Athos has arrived. Do you like Letitia's makeup? It's just for you." She fluttered her long eyelashes and cocked her head to one side. Pale lilac eye shadow, pink cheeks and rosebud lips against an almost pure white skin gave her a doll-like appearance.

"Your presence always pleases me. Take a seat, turtledove. Let's see what news he has for us."

Athos stepped through the doorway, ducking and turning his massive body sideways to avoid the door frame. *How can such an immense man move so silently?*

"Athos, my friend. I expected you yesterday evening. Joyful tidings, I hope?"

"Yes." He was a giant of few words. Raven knew his big companion worshipped him with all his heart. Athos believed he was the prophet who would rid the world of oppression and that bestowing freedom to every living soul on the planet was within his gift. He was also a ruthless assassin. "The occupants of 39 Mayfield Street are dead. Your identity will stay secret."

"You are sure this time?"

"Listened at the door and heard talking. Sparks's bike was outside. Blocked the rear exit. Poured paraffin under the front door, and the house went up like a Roman candle. No one came out. Burned to a crisp, they were." His eyes lit up. "Returned this morning. Police think it's an accident."

Raven sat back in his chair and closed his eyes, savouring the moment. *How apt Sparks died in flames. He may be dead, but delicious irony lives.* He chuckled at the thought, and Letitia giggled with him.

"Thank you, Athos. Once again, you have succeeded where others fail. Allow me to reward your persistence. What do you desire?" He knew the answer but asked anyway.

"Nothing, Raven. Serving you is bounty enough."

"Then you have my eternal gratitude. Your selfless loyalty does your family name proud." *I wonder what it is. Did I ever know?*

Athos bowed his head sharply. Raven smiled, surprised he hadn't clicked his heels like a Prussian infantryman.

"Now, leave us. I'll see you tomorrow."

Athos nodded, turned, and silently walked through the door, closing it behind him with a barely audible snick.

"Oh! Dear, sweet Raven wants to be alone with Letitia. Letitia wonders why?" Eyes wide, feigning innocence, she giggled.

"Pour me a Scotch, my petal. The good one. For tonight, we are going to celebrate. Not too much, of course; we still have unfinished work."

She brought him his whisky and knelt beside his chair, purring. *Things are coming together perfectly.*

Algeria and Dottie's early morning tram journey to Eccles had taken an hour. The rising sun hadn't burned off the dense fog that had shrouded the city during the small hours before dawn, and with visibility reduced to a few yards, the driver edged them forward at a snail's pace, concentrating on the tracks ahead, tooting his whistle at unwary pedestrians and vehicles alike.

Dark shadows slid past Dottie's window, punctuating the uniform grey murk as she slouched on the hard seat, chin resting in her hand, head pressed against the glass. Algeria sat bolt upright next to her, hands interlocked tightly in her lap, her eyes fixed forward. Her unwavering, stern expression was a consequence of the heated discussion earlier in the day. No words had passed between her and her daughter during the long journey.

Finally, the slow clockwork tick-tock stopped as the tram lurched to a halt in the station. Passengers traipsed off and disappeared into the gloom. As Algeria and Dottie alighted, a large man bounding along the platform bowled them over. With a loud grunt, he loped into the murk without as much as a 'by-your-leave,' leaving vortices of fog swirling in his wake.

"Are you all right, ma'am?" The conductor bent forward, offering a hand, but Algeria waved off his help and pulled herself upright.

"Thank you, we are fine." She dusted off her clothes. "But I would like to give that clumsy oaf a piece of my mind."

Dottie picked up her hat and goggles and clambered to her feet. "Words are useless against his sort."

"You're right. A slap 'round the head would have been a better idea."

"You'd need step ladders to give him a clout."

Algeria smiled.

"Look, Mama. I'm sorry for some of the things I said."

"Only some of them?"

"Most of them."

Algeria raised her eyebrows and cocked her head.

"All right, all right. I was wrong. The Order must come first. I do believe in what you stand for, but I wish we could have been together as a proper family. Dad loved you so much. A day didn't pass when he didn't speak about you."

"I wanted to be with you, too. But I couldn't jeopardise your safety. Even before the Anthropocene, there were people who would have used you to hurt me. Hiding you both at the Forge was my only hope to keep you safe." Algeria put her palm on the side of Dottie's face.

Dottie closed her eyes and felt the warmth of her mother's hand against her damp cheek. "All I ever wanted from you was a sign that you loved me and missed me as much as I missed you."

"I didn't dare, shugah. I had to hide my love whenever I visited. Your dad chided me about it. Giving in would have been easy, but I couldn't risk it. The consequences were unthinkable. As you flowered into womanhood, I saw how you despised me, and it broke my heart.

"Seeing you both became harder and harder. Now Abel is dead because of my foolishness. Sending Gilbert to Pendle was a tragic mistake, a decision I will regret for the rest of my life. I was so sure he'd be safe with you, but I was wrong." A tear squeezed from the corner of her eye. Dottie wiped it away.

"It's just you and me now, Mama. I'm staying with you to carry on the work of the Order."

"And Gilbert?"

"He's only interested in revenge and doesn't care about me or our cause."

"Oh, he cares about you, shugah. I've seen how he looks at you. It's a mixture of admiration, curiosity and lust."

"Mama!" Dottie shoved her in playful rebuke.

"Come on, let's go talk to him."

Dottie linked her mother's arm as they left the tram terminus through the thick mist towards the main road leading to Gilbert's father's house. Barely visible carriages rumbled past them. Fog-dampened sounds rose and faded as they picked their way along the uneven footpath.

They turned onto Mayfield Street, heads down, watching their step in the murk. The stench of horse manure caused Algeria to cover her nose and mouth, but the acrid reek of burnt embers soon replaced that foul smell.

They stopped outside what used to be number 39 and gaped open-mouthed at the black, smouldering shell. Dottie tried to wrestle free from Algeria's grasp.

"No! Dolly, no! There's nothing we can do here."

"But Gilbert…"

"We don't know what happened yet." Head turning left and right, Algeria peered through the fog. A few yards away, the silhouette of a policeman was speaking into the doorway of an elderly neighbour. "Excuse me!" she shouted. As Algeria and Dottie marched towards them, the occupant of number 45 slammed the door, leaving the constable midsentence. The officer sighed, closed his notebook, and turned to face them.

Dottie didn't appreciate his suspicious expression.

"Please, can you help us? We are friends of Mister Sparks who lives here." She nodded towards the charred ruins.

"Are you now? What do you know about all this?" The policeman pointed with his pencil at the blackened husk that had been home to Gilbert and his father. He re-opened his notebook.

"Is he…?" Dottie didn't complete the question. The expression on the policeman's face confirmed her worst fears. *Why, oh why, did I leave him?*

"I'm sorry to have to tell you, miss, but we found human remains in the property, which we believe to be Mister Sparks."

"Oh, no…" Algeria caught her breath, her heart pounding. "Was he… alone?"

The policeman narrowed his eyes. "Now, why would you ask that?"

"He has a son," Dottie said. "Was he with him?"

"One person deceased, as far as we know, but we haven't finished searching the debris, mind, so we can't be sure. Right, I need to take down your details." He licked the tip of his pencil as Dottie turned to stare at the burnt-out shell.

Algeria spoke with the policeman as she tried to piece together what had happened. *Had Gilbert witnessed the fire and fled? He hadn't returned to the Praetorian, so where would he go?*

As the policemen turned away, she grabbed Dottie's arm. "We need to leave."

"What? Why?"

"Because I've just told the nice officer a pack of lies. We don't know if he's one of *them*. We can't be sure he's even a real policeman. Now, let's skedaddle before he asks any more questions."

They hugged, then hurried back through the fog to Eccles Triple T, deciding that they would wait at the Praetorian for Gilbert's return.

"Do you think Raven killed Gilbert's father?"

"Too much of a coincidence to assume anything else. We're going to have to be extra careful from now on, Doll. If they know about his father, they may know about us and our cause. The future of the Order will be in jeopardy if they learn about the Praetorian."

A green and black pulled into the station, and passengers poured onto the platform. Dottie and Algeria huddled together on a bench as the conductor connected the winder to recharge the clockwork. Twenty minutes would pass before the tram was ready to leave. Dottie's eyes flicked left and right with each muffled sound and half-glimpsed shadowy movement in the thick fog.

"I'm scared, Mama."

"Me, too, shugah, me too."

Weak sunlight filtering through the endless grey shroud that had entombed him hardly warmed his face. The runaway blame train had derailed, but his mind was not at peace. He had walked through the night without rest or sustenance, with no sense of time or direction and no recollection of encountering anybody or anything. Terminal despair suppressed needs, strangled hope, and suffocated thoughts.

His legs ached, and his mouth was dry, but the fog was finally lifting, his purpose clear

Where am I? He squinted through the mist. His first rational thought in hours pierced the chaos.

Above him, an orange windsock hung limply on a tall pole; to his left, the dark silhouette of a huge steam digger loomed. He jerked his head to the right and recognised the unmistakable contours of dirigibles bobbing on mooring poles. The slippery, muddy ground beneath his boots confirmed his first thought. *Barton Aerodrome.*

He didn't know how he had arrived there, and he didn't care. Was it happenstance or a subconscious, driven need?

Either way, his path was resolute.

He trod carefully through the mud on the shallow incline towards the dirigible berths. Voices of unseen aviators ebbed and flowed as he passed each mooring. LTA gas pumps whirred and hissed, shovels scraped, crunching in the ballast bunkers as engineers readied their crafts for flight. Ahead, *Dragonfly's* vibrant green and tangerine livery loomed out of the grey. Gilbert heaved a sigh. *Thank goodness one of the Stormrider airships is here.*

As he approached, sharp crackling, clanking and cussing grew louder from within the gondola. Intermittent blue flashes illuminated the receding mist. *Tabby*, he thought, *she's welding and probably alone.*

In the cheeriest voice he could muster, he shouted. "Ahoy, *Dragonfly*!"

Silence.

"Tabby! It's Gilbert!"

Black goggles under a mop of curly brown hair appeared over the bulwark. "Gilbert?"

"If you took those off, you might see me better. Permission to come aboard?"

She slid her goggles onto her forehead and frowned. "Permission granted," she said.

Gilbert scrambled up the ladder and heaved himself over the side, crashing on the deck. "I don't suppose you have a drink, do you? What time is it?"

She tossed her canteen to him. "By 'eck. You look like you haven't slept for days. It's turned 11 o'clock."

Gilbert guzzled the refreshing water and wiped his mouth with the back of his sleeve.

"Any chance of taking me for a quick ride? I need to check something from up there." He pointed skyward and smiled.

"Not in this fog. Going up's fine, but landing safely would be a bugger. What're you looking for?"

"Something I know will benefit everyone. I'll know it when I see it," Gilbert said.

"Once it's cleared, we can go. I'm sure Rory won't mind, but we're not going anywhere until I strengthen these struts and cross-members."

"I'd better let you get on with it, then."

Gilbert sat with his back against the side of the gondola and closed his eyes.

I'll soon be with you, Dad.

"Gilbert? Gilbert!" He woke with a start. Tabby was shaking him.

"Uh? What?" Gilbert rubbed the sleep from his eyes to find Rory and Tabby kneeling beside him. "Must've dropped off," he said.

"Are you all right? You look terrible," Rory said.

"That's the second time today I've been told that." He struggled to his feet, legs stiff after the long walk and lying on the hard deck. He yawned and stretched. "Has the mist cleared? Tabby's going to take me up."

"She mentioned you wanted to search for something. Are you sure you're all right? I'm surprised you want to fly again after the last time. Ace told us you were terrified of heights."

"You can run and hide, but sometimes you have to face your terrors." Abel's muck-sweat face smiled somewhere in a distant memory. *He would be proud of me.* "Just a quick peek, Rory? Please?"

She nodded at Tabby. "All right, but I don't know what's going on. Hold on tight."

Tabby disengaged the electromagnets before dropping enough ballast to get the *Dragonfly* rising gracefully into the still air. She angled the motors, and they spiralled gently into the afternoon sky. Somewhere close by, children were playing, and a church clock chimed. It was a quarter past something. His heart was racing.

Still weak, he staggered sideways and gripped the rail as they swayed into another turn to starboard. Swirling, wispy remnants of fog made the ground below seethe. At five hundred feet, everything was clear. His head started spinning, and his stomach churned. He was about to retch. On the opposite side of the gondola, Rory was peering over the side at the ship canal workings.

Seizing his chance, he scrambled up the netting and stood on the bulwark, holding the superstructure for balance. He sucked in a deep breath.

"Gilbert? No! What are you—?" Rory shouted.

"Don't try to stop me!" Gilbert's skull was pounding. Bile rising in his throat, he screwed his eyes tight shut and loosened his grasp on the struts.

Rory and Tabby were helpless, knowing if they made a grab for him, unbalancing the gondola would hasten his fall.

In the fleeting moment between heartbeats, time stood still. Far below, laughter from the kids playing in the streets awakened ghostlike gossamer memories of his own childhood. To the north, a locomotive slowly chuffed across the mosslands, soot, ash and steam blasting from its smokestack, and, along the Cut, pile drivers pounded a rhythmic tattoo.

Hundreds of feet above the aerodrome, in clear air, pungent fumes stung his nostrils.

Startled by the sensation, his eyes sprang open. The ground was still spinning, but now he could see. He could really see. His fingers tightened around the metal strut.

As *Dragonfly* continued her slow spiral, a vista of dozens of factory chimneys belching acrid black smoke high into the heavens passed before him. Gilbert froze, legs trembling, weak from lack of food. He rocked back and forth, unable to regain his balance. *Nothing to live for but so much to die for.*

"Help me…"

Losing consciousness, exhausted, his grip on the strut failed. A distant scream from close behind evanesced into an ethereal memory. The bulwark bucked violently beneath him, pitching him into the welcoming wings of the black bat of oblivion, veiling his vision and sucking the light from his eyes. Cocooned in his dark shroud, he fell into the atavistic abyss of everlasting ebony.

TWENTY

PARLIAMENT

Issy and Ace left a disappointed Jonah with *Freyja's Grimalkin* moored at the gasworks at Kennington.

"Maybe there'll be a game on at The Oval." Ace's suggestion to Jonah was met with a muttered profanity about cricket and winter that Issy didn't understand as they boarded a battered old hansom, leaving the pilot glowering, his arms folded. During the ride, Ace suggested they walk over the Thames to the Houses of Parliament, so they alighted from the cab a short distance from Westminster Bridge.

Ears ringing to the rhythmic clatter of horses' hooves and steel-rimmed carriage wheels, they quickened their pace across the bridge to escape the nauseating stink of horse manure. But as the Palace of Westminster loomed out of the mist, an even more revolting stench overpowered the pungent smell. Raw sewerage spewing from drains below the seat of government into the Thames turned the meandering river into an open sewer. Issy's eyes watered, and she wrinkled her nose as the reek filled her nostrils. *That place is so full of shit.*

Issy hated London with as much vigour as Ace adored it. She detested the chaos, the noise, the smell, and the sheer size of the sprawling metropolis. *Why anyone wants to live here is beyond me.*

Ace, on the other hand, was in his element, beaming as they entered the portals of power. He regularly regaled her with his adventures as a young man in the big city.

While he studied for his law degree at Cambridge, he visited the capital many times during his tenure. Enticed by the bright lights, seduced by the promise of thrills and danger, he had been drawn into its murky underworld. Confessions of his dalliances in the seamier establishments of the West End, when he should have been studying, had not shocked her, but she knew him well enough to realise he didn't mean lower-class music halls and public houses. Their ideas of seamy differed.

He was an inveterate gambler. That many of his fellow frequenters of the backroom gambling dens and bordellos were men of influence was not news to Issy. Politicians, captains of industry, members of the judiciary and clergy alike slaked their perverted thirsts in shadowy secrecy, far from the light of public decency. Ace affectionately called them his foible fraternity, but Issy called them denizens of decadence.

Since he returned north and embraced the purpose and tenets of the Order, she did not consider him to be part of the basket of degenerates, many of whom enjoyed positions of privilege and prestige. He was a firm friend with whom she entrusted her life.

So close were they that when Ace acquired his airship, he had asked Issy to give her a fitting name. *Freyja's Grimalkin* perfectly suited its fearsome feline lines.

Seeking an audience with Lemmy's father, they arrived unannounced at the country's seat of government. The foul reek of centuries of male plutocracy was ingrained in the building's fabric and its incumbents. Self-importance rubbed shoulders with political paradigm. Effete masculinity kowtowed to corpulent corruption. Bejewelled popinjays in silver-buckled shoes strutted and preened while secretaries, undersecretaries, researchers and assistants pandered like drones around queen bees.

There were top hats and morning suits, blacks and greys, but not a Gainsborough, crinoline or a splash of colour in sight. Bile rose in Issy's throat as she quelled her lip-curling sneer.

They were shown into a large anteroom overlooking the river. Issy covered her nose and mouth with a handkerchief to mask the stench of stale pipe smoke and mildew. With the Thames flowing outside the building, opening a window was not a choice worth considering. She perched on a well-worn seat, watching Ace pace back and forth. Patience was not amongst his virtues.

Two hours later, Philpott's under-secretary popped his bespectacled face around the door.

"Mister Aquilla Sixsmith and, er," he checked his notes, "Miss Isadora Windlass? You're here to see The Right Honourable Jeremiah Philpott?"

They nodded.

"Follow me, please."

The tall, dapper assistant led them along musty, dimly lit corridors, deeper into the bowels of the edifice and into a small, windowless oak-panelled room.

"The Right Honourable gentleman is in a committee meeting, but he doesn't expect to be long." The under-secretary backed out gracefully, closing the door and hurrying away before they could utter any awkward questions.

Ace shook his head. "The wheels of government turn slowly," he said.

Issy took a deep breath. Her shallow breathing in the anteroom produced a succession of yawns. She settled herself into a comfortable chair and prepared for another long wait. Ace resumed his pacing. He had started his nineteenth lap when he paused facing the small window in the door.

"I wonder what the meeting is about." Issy envisaged grey men sat around a table in a smoke-filled room.

"*Lupus in fabula.* You can ask him yourself." The Right Honourable Jeremiah Philpott MP was striding along the corridor towards them. He bustled in; his brow furrowed.

"Ace, old boy. Is Lemmy all right?" *That's a little familiar. Is Philpott one of Ace's foible friends?*

Ace shook the MP's offered hand. "Sorry to alarm you, sir. Lemmy's fine, out of hospital and doing well. In fact, he wanted to accompany us, but we insisted he stay in Manchester. This isn't a social visit. We have a problem."

Philpott looked left and right before raising a finger to his lips. "Walls have ears, old boy, even in these hallowed halls. I think you'd better come through to my office."

Hands on their backs, he steered them out of the waiting room into his offices. He sat behind his mahogany desk and motioned them to sit. Ace declined the offer of a cigar from Philpott's humidor with a shake of his head. Issy raised her eyes to the heavens. *I'm invisible.*

"Now, what's this about?" Philpott folded his arms and looked directly at Ace.

"The Anthropocene, sir. We need to stop them before they become too powerful," Issy said before Ace could open his mouth.

"I'm afraid they already have substantial influence in this place. Those of us who stay faithful to Connickle are in constant conflict with the infernal Freedom Brigade."

"Algeria believes their policies are the brainchild of a nefarious viper called Raven. She believes if we chop the head off the serpent, the body will wither and die."

"Coils of the snake are legion and deeply entangled in the fabric of these halls. Are we certain there is a single brain directing them? What if this serpent has many heads?"

Issy leaned forward in her chair. "They're a cult. To his acolytes, he is a prophet, and they're devoted to him, carrying out his commands without question. This is not a twee committee deciding where to build a road and whose palm to grease. Raven tells them what to blow up next— they obey, and people die."

Ace suddenly found the waxed parquet floor fascinating.

"We have seen Raven's manifesto. We believe he conceived and implemented the ideology of the Anthropocene. He has built a network of disciples and foot soldiers and sown the seeds of hate, which will lead to the abandonment of Connickle ideals. If we stop him, we apply the brake to his doctrine."

"All right, so how can I help? You wouldn't have come if Algeria didn't have a plan." Philpott put both hands on the desk and pushed himself to his feet.

"As a member of the Privy Council, you are on several transport committees, and you represent Manchester East in the Commons," Ace said.

"Guilty on all counts." Philpott cleaned his pince-nez spectacles with his handkerchief.

"You had a hand in getting The Manchester Ship Canal Act through Parliament?"

"That is also correct. The Order agreed that, despite the disruption, the canal was a more environmentally friendly solution to transportation for Manchester's burgeoning cotton trade. So, I used my powers of persuasion and called in a few favours to get the bill passed." He tapped the side of his nose and winked.

"So, you are the perfect target for Raven." Issy sliced through the amiable discussion.

Ace and Philpott stared at her.

"Diplomacy isn't your forte, is it, my dear?" Philpott's pithy observation did not require a response.

"Algeria would very much like you to agree to return to Manchester with us. She'll set up a situation to lure Raven from the shadows. Then we finish this for good." Ace slammed his left fist into his right palm.

"I am to be the bait in your little scheme?"

"Yes." Issy remained unapologetic.

"You will be perfectly safe," Ace said. "We'll take every precaution to ensure—"

"But there's no guarantee, is there?"

"We wouldn't let any harm befall you. You are Lemmy's father…" Ace grimaced as the words tumbled from his lips.

Issy rolled her eyes upwards. *Oh, well done*, she thought. *For someone so intelligent, you often put your foot in it.*

Ace cleared his throat, "… and, of course, a valued representative of the Order and a respected, senior Member of Parliament."

"We must eliminate Raven to stop the Anthropocene. This isn't about you or me or Ace or Algeria. It's about upholding Connickle's principles, our oath, and saving innocent lives. We don't know where he is or what he will attack next. But we know he will strike again. We must find the blackguard and kill him… soon," Issy said.

"With such rhetoric, perhaps you are better suited to politics than the diplomatic corps." Philpott's steely, single-eyebrow-raised stare forced Issy to glare at Ace. *Come on, say something to help.* He opened his mouth as if to speak but remained silent.

"I will meet you at *Freyja's Grimalkin* at five o'clock. Where is she moored?"

Slowly regaining consciousness, arms outstretched, hands and fingers chilled numb, waiting for the ground to end his fall, Gilbert gulped a final, painful breath. As the frigid air stabbed his lungs, his eyes sprang open. Pain screamed through his left leg as, one by one, his senses re-engaged.

He wasn't falling.

Helpless, he dangled upside down from the bulwark, ensnared in the dirigible's rigging. The unbalanced gondola swirled violently out of control. His body was being tossed like a rag doll. The ground spun, his stomach convulsed, and vomit rose in his throat. His world was nausea and pain.

Rory clawed at his leg, trying to get a grip on his clothing. "Grab the rope! Gilbert! Grab the blasted rope!"

Senses swimming, he was vaguely aware of something brushing his arm, and he grabbed at it. Nothing. Twisting his body, he reached out, arms wide. Coarse rope smacked into his chest, and he grasped the wet jute with both hands. Clinging on with every ounce of his strength, he tried to ignore the excruciating pain in his leg.

"I'm going to cut the rigging!" Rory shouted. "Gilbert! Can you hear me?"

"Yes!" He tightened his grip, and water squeezed between his fingers.

"Hang on!"

Through narrowed eyes, he watched the knife flash, again and again, hacking at the taut cables. The tension eased in the ropes, and his body swung free. Hands numb with cold slipped on the wet jute. He wrapped a leg around the rope, which supported his weight and halted his momentum.

Dragonfly was still losing height, spiralling like a whirligig. Rory must have returned to the other side of the gondola as Tabby won the battle to regain control, slowing the violent spin into a graceful arc, the engines droning under the duress.

Gilbert screwed his eyes shut. *What was I thinking? Sorry, Dad, I let you down.*

Tabby vented gas to hasten the descent to the airfield, and he felt the bottom of the rope trail on the ground as they approached the mooring pole. But he didn't open his eyes until Rory and Tabby clambered down the ladder and reached up to him. Hand under hand, he eased himself down the rope and collapsed into their arms.

His whole body was trembling as they lowered him onto the wet grass. Rory examined his leg as Tabby knelt behind him, supporting his weight.

"What the fuck were you doing? Why were you going to jump?" Tabby said.

"They... Someone... Raven killed my dad last night."

"Oh, no... What happened?" Tabby's voice shook.

"They set fire to our house. He didn't have a chance."

Rory raised her head and placed her hand on his shoulder. "Just minor bruising and cuts from the rigging. Can you stand?"

They hauled him to his feet. Stinging pain in his leg made him shriek when he put weight on it.

"I wanted to end it. There was no point in carrying on. Raven had taken Mum, Dad, my job, and my future. He'd won, and I couldn't live in the world he was making."

"But you didn't jump. You fell," Rory said.

"I saw something up there and realised it's not about me anymore. There's no future in revenge. We have to stop Raven for our children and our children's children." Gasping for breath, he pitched forward as his legs buckled. They lunged in unison, grabbing him before he hit the ground.

"He's delirious. He needs food and drink," Tabby said.

"Yes, I need to eat, but I know what I'm saying. We must stop him. We must…"

"There's a coffee stall near Barton lock. I'll get him a sandwich." Tabby gently lowered his body and jumped to her feet.

Rory dug a halfcrown out of her pocket and flipped it to her. "Buy sandwiches and drinks for us all."

Tabby rushed away, skipping nimbly across the muddy field. Rory stared after her until she disappeared over the incline to the road.

"I wish someone would look at me the way you gaze at her," Gilbert said.

"I thought you and Dottie…"

Gilbert shook his head. "That airship has flown. I was so wrapped up in getting Raven. Now, I've lost her."

"Don't despair, old chap. I'm sure you'll work things out."

"Have you ever loved someone, Rory? I mean, *really* loved?"

"Yes." The tone of her voice softened from its usual haughty timbre.

"How do you know when you're truly in love?"

"When you care more about what your true love wants than for what you need. When you would willingly sacrifice your life for her and can't imagine life without her smile. That's true love."

Gilbert lowered his eyes. Dark stains were spreading across his trousers as blood seeped from wounds caused by the rigging.

"I'll see if Tabby has any dressings on the '*fly*.'" Rory pulled her lithe frame up the ladder and retrieved gauze bandages from her chest of treasures.

By the time Tabby came bustling back, Rory had dressed his cuts, and he was standing again on unsteady legs. After ham sandwiches, pea soup, and a tankard of sweet tea, the enormity of his brush with death had dawned on him. *Did I really want to end my life when there's so much to do?*

"Where will you live? Do you have any friends or relatives who can put you up?" Rory asked.

Gilbert shook his head. "Dad was my only family, and I hadn't planned on still being here…"

"Algy is bound to let you stay at the Praetorian for as long as you need. You're one of us now, and we take care of our own."

Gilbert looked across at Barton lock. Work must have progressed rapidly over the last few weeks, as it was unrecognisable from when he worked there. A four-storey pump house and a series of low-level buildings lined the north bank of the Cut, masking the lock from view. "You're not going anywhere in the next few minutes, are you?" he said.

"What are you thinking of doing?" Rory narrowed her eyes.

"I want to pop over to where I used to work." He jabbed a thumb towards the canal.

"We'll wait for you and give you a ride into Manchester. Don't be too long."

He hugged them and limped across the airfield over the main road through the mud to Barton lock. Stan Miller was arriving for his shift as he arrived at the night watchman's hut.

"Ayup. Is that you, Gilbert? By heck, you look rough."

Gilbert looked to the heavens. "Aye, it's been a while."

"A few of the lads have been asking after you."

"Yeah?" Gilbert cocked his head to one side. "Flanagans?"

"Not likely! No one's seen them since they walked out a few days after you disappeared."

Gilbert lowered his eyes and smiled, knowing they were Raven's foot soldiers now. The building that housed the pumping machinery towered over him. "Looks like the lock's nearly finished."

"Aye. The sluices are finished, and the pumps are getting installed before the end of the week."

Mention of the sluices summoned pungent memories of his time ankle-deep in the vomit-inducing stench with Grubb enjoying his discomfort, laughing with his cronies. That was only a few weeks and a lifetime ago.

"Are you coming to the topping-off ceremony on Saturday? There'll be a memorial for old Wainwright, too. You can come and pay your respects. 'Orrible what happened to the poor bugger. 'Orrible."

A pang of fear ripped through his body, and without a word, Gilbert turned on his heel and ran, stumbling, back to *Dragonfly*.

TWENTY-ONE

Plots and Plans

Late next morning, Gilbert wandered downstairs, where Algeria sat alone in the Praetorian's meeting room. Last night, she had greeted him with open arms and heartfelt sympathy and, without hesitation, asked Eli to make up a room.

Dottie had been more reserved in her welcome, but he didn't blame her. *She thinks I will be even more bent on revenge.*

"Are you all right, shugah?" Algeria's narrowed eyes, furrowed brow and croaky voice were telltale signs of a sleepless night.

"No. So much has happened that my head feels like I'm still spinning underneath the *Dragonfly*. I don't know what the future holds, but now at least, I have one."

"Dottie was so worried. We both were."

"She wasn't too pleased to see me last night, but I understand why she's still angry."

"She's not annoyed with you, shugah. She just doesn't know what to say. Remember, she's raw from losing her own dad. You both need to talk."

"Aye, we do."

Eli glided into the room with a selection of pies and sandwiches, and Gilbert was tucking into the food long before the mek had completely unloaded the tray.

"I think I know where Raven will strike next." Pastry flakes sprayed from his mouth as he spoke.

Algeria's jaw dropped. "What? Where? How?"

He swallowed hard, sending insufficiently chewed pie, too wide for his gullet, struggling to his stomach. "There's going to be a memorial ceremony at the lock where Wainwright died, and with a lot of local dignitaries invited, it's just the occasion he'd attack. Remember Oldham."

"He won't try the same trick twice," Algeria said, "unless we make the target irresistible."

"What do you mean?" Gilbert cleared his throat and picked up another pie, smothering it in chutney.

"What if a representative of the Privy Council was going to be present? Maybe a steadfast supporter of the Connickle reforms and a Member of Parliament who helped to pass the act that funded the ship canal? A successful attack would be a big statement for the Anthropocene."

"Aye, that would do it."

"Well… Lemmy's father's up from London. I wasn't sure how to lure Raven out of the shadows, but this lock ceremony is too good an opportunity to miss."

"Crikey. What does Lemmy think about setting up his dad as bait for a madman?"

"We'll find out when we tell him."

Gilbert puffed out his cheeks as he exhaled more crumbs.

Hearing footsteps behind him, he turned to see Dottie walking along the corridor from the main bar. She froze when she saw him and spun on her heel.

"Dottie! Wait!" Gilbert shouted as Algeria mouthed, *'go on,'* nodding in Dottie's direction. Chair scraping across the wooden floor as he stood, he dashed over to where she had stopped on her tiptoes with her back to him. He eased his arm around her shoulder. "Let me get you a drink."

Sat opposite each other in a booth, they ordered drinks. Dottie set her defiant stare on the beer-stained table. Eli plonked two pints of porter between them and retreated to the bar, but she hadn't broken her stolid gaze when Gilbert broke the silence.

"I'm sorry." *That wasn't too difficult.*

"What for?" Dottie rhythmically stroked her pewter tankard, not raising her eyes.

"Everything. For being blinded by revenge, not taking the Order seriously, for being responsible for your dad's murder. I let you down." *This isn't going well.*

"I don't know what to say, other than I shouldn't have left you at the tram stop. If I had been with you…" She met his stare briefly before lowering her gaze, "perhaps you wouldn't have…"

"I was wrong about that, too." He reached out, putting his hands gently around hers as she held her drink. *At least she hasn't pulled away.* "I have plenty to live for now."

"It's still about you, though, isn't it?" Eyes flashing, her grip tightened on the tankard.

"No, not anymore. My future and, I hope, ours, is carrying on your mum and dad's work. We must stop Raven and the Anthropocene for everyone's sake, not for revenge.

"Balancing on the side of the *Dragonfly*, I was ready to jump to end the pain." He caught his breath. "But the sound of children playing brought back memories of being blissfully happy when I was a kid, not having a care in the world, laughing, running, piggybacks. Those young'uns somewhere below were just like I used to be. Happy, not caring what the future holds because kids shouldn't have to.

"It's up to us to stop Raven and his cult from destroying the planet. We owe it to them and children everywhere."

Dottie continued to look at his hands cupping hers. "And Raven?"

"Oh, he has to die, but not to avenge the deaths he has caused. To save millions that will die if we do nothing."

"So, where do we go from here?"

"I'm going to pledge to the Order and carry the fight to anyone else who wants to harm the planet. Algeria can use my skills in whatever way she wants."

"She will be pleased to have you."

"What about you? What are your plans?"

"Me and Mama are still patching things up, but my dad drumming the beliefs and purpose of the Order into me every day, and now Mama doing the same, makes me so tired."

"You can't do it alone." *That's rich coming from me.*

"Ha, that's rich coming from you." The corners of Dottie's mouth curled into a soft smile. "Mister I-don't-need-anyone."

"I've learned a lot about myself over the past few days. Now I understand I can't battle the Anthropocene without the Order, and I don't want to face a future without you at my side." *There, I said it.*

"Well, it's a start."

"What's that supposed to mean?"

"All I hear is me, me, me. Don't you care what I want?"

"Of course, I do. But why wouldn't your dearest wish be to spend the rest of your life with a tall, handsome-"

"Oh, I can think of a dozen reasons…"

Gilbert looked at their hands still cupped around her drink. *Is she serious, or is she messing with me?*

"But let's see how long we can put up with each other." Dottie closed her eyes and leaned forwards, her moist lips parted. Invitation accepted. He pressed his mouth against hers. It was a moment they would never forget as Gilbert knocked over his beer. The pewter pot clanged as it bounced off the table, splashing porter over the floor.

"Bertie!" Dottie scolded him, her face in a mock scowl. Their laughter rang around the bar.

For the first time since his mother's death, he didn't get angry at hearing that name on someone else's lips.

In fact, it felt right.

"This isn't right." Fergus poked his fingers through the frayed woven cloth. "If you hear a thud in the night, this bloody thing will have given up the ghost."

Finbar laid in his own hammock, hands clasped behind his head. "I don't see why we're holed up here. I'd rather be home in my comfy bed," he said.

"Oi, if the gaffer tells us to stay here, and he's paying for the privilege, then stay here we will and not complain."

"How long did he say we've got to hide, Gussy?"

"Two nights, then Saturday is showtime!" Fergus danced a jig, his enormous feet clattering on the floor.

"I thought the big fella told us to keep quiet."

"Well, he's not here now, is he?"

"If he was, you'd be dancing with two broken legs, sure you would." The brothers laughed, but only one considered the prospect hilarious.

"I wonder how Raven and Athos met," Finn mused. "They're an odd couple."

"Dunno and don't care as long as they pay good money."

"Have we got enough to eat?"

"Plenty. Raven had that QT of his make a hamper for us, and we've lots of booze and water."

"What's that smell?" Finn wrinkled his nose and pulled his shirt across his face.

Fergus giggled and climbed into his hammock. "Must've been that kipper I had for breakfast."

"You can stop that, you dirty bugger."

"Open a window if you don't like it. There's plenty more where that came from."

"Very fucking funny." Finn poked Gussy in the ribs.

It was going to be a long two days.

Gilbert beamed as he strutted along the corridor into the meeting room, linking arms with Dottie. *Did Algeria just wink at her?*

She was sitting with an ashen-faced Lemmy and his father.

"Jeremiah has agreed to say a few words at the topping-off ceremony. Lemmy is going to stay by his side."

How does she send folk into harm's way without batting an eyelash?

"I'll keep my father safe."

"We'll make sure he comes to no harm," Algeria said. "We must leave nothing to chance. This is too important to mess up."

Dottie pulled a chair across the floor and sat next to Lemmy, who smiled weakly as she patted his thigh.

"What's the plan?" Gilbert peered into their eyes one by one.

"We have to spread the word that Jeremiah will speak at the ceremony." *No point having bait if the hunter isn't aware of it.* "Let's keep this simple. The fewer folk we involve in setting the trap, the smaller the chance Raven has to find out what we're doing."

"Surely you don't think…" Jeremiah's voice trailed off as he searched the faces at the table.

"I trust every member of the Order, but we mustn't raise suspicions within or outside our ranks. They could be watching the Praetorian. Oh, and we can't use the mek network in case the Anthropocene has access to them, too. Now, who do we need?"

"Stormriders?" Gilbert glanced hopefully around the table. "How can we get word to them?"

Attention turned to Lemmy, who was the sole Stormrider at the meeting. Head bowed, he still looked as if he was going to bring back his last meal. "Ace will be at the Athenaeum, and Rory has spent much of her free time at Le Rendezvous in recent days. No idea where to find Connie and Issy."

"Ace and Rory can tell the other two," Algeria said.

"I'll find Ace," Dottie said. "I've always wanted to have a peek inside that place."

"You won't make it past the door," Gilbert said. "It's gentlemen only."

"Wanna bet?" She gave him a wicked smile.

"Le Rendezvous is the hotel on the corner of Canal Street, isn't it?"

"It is. Tell them we'll meet here tomorrow at midday."

Philpott stood, straightening his coat. "Very well, Algeria, until tomorrow. Come along, Lemuel. I'll treat you to a nightcap at my hotel before we turn in. You look like you need a stiff drink." He put his arm around his worried son. There was a genuine prospect he could lose his father, and he wasn't hiding his feelings.

Lemmy nodded his farewells to everyone except Algeria and left in silence, eyes fixed on the floor.

"He's not happy with me," she said.

Dottie kissed Gilbert on the cheek. "See you back here in an hour." Buttoning her coat, she glanced over her shoulder and strode out of the meeting room.

"Good to see you and Dolly are friends again."

More than that, I hope. "I'm going to pledge allegiance to the Order, and, before you ask, it's for the right reasons. Although it means I'll get to know Dottie better."

"Once we see off this threat, we'll arrange an induction ceremony. The members will welcome you into the fold with open arms." She dismissed him with a smile and a casual wave of her hand. "Now, go find Rory."

Gilbert walked through the bar and out onto the busy street. Condensed breath coalesced into clouds in the early evening chill as he stopped and scrutinised the passers-by, his eyes darting from face to face. *Which of you are Anthropocene?*

Turning up his collar, he pulled down the brim of his topper and set off to find Rory, leaning into the stiff breeze.

The dowager countess sat alone in her drawing room. With Silas taking care of her every need, she hadn't spoken to a living soul in days. Late afternoon murk had given way to twilight as restless twigs, teased by the breeze, scratched against her window, and clouds chased one another across the sky.

She missed Ignatius. Yes, he was a pompous philanderer, but he meant everything to her, and no parent should have to bury a son.

He spent time with her most days, oftentimes enjoying an early evening drink and usually keeping her company at dinner. He played a mean game of backgammon and was an adequate bridge partner when the Cholmondeleys of Tarporley visited.

Now she had no one with whom to share gossip, a smile or a tear.

Since Ray and that infernal child-like mek had moved into the Hall, they had turned her life upside down. From the strange visitors at all times of the day and night to the ungodly sounds coming from his quarters after dark, she found herself on edge, unable to relax.

And don't get her started on that creepy Greek giant.

She rested her embroidery on her lap and closed her eyes. Soon Silas would be here with her evening meal. She had taken to eating in her drawing room in preference to joining Ray. The twilight birdsong calmed her and, somewhere in the distance, a solitary cuckoo called for a mate.

There was an almost inaudible tap. *Oh no!* The door burst open, and a flurry of shimmering black satin announced the arrival of Ray's vulgar mek. *Ugh!*

"Letitia Lovegrove! Please enter rooms inside the Hall quietly. There really is no need…"

"Silas will not be bringing dinner to you tonight. Do you like Letitia's mourning frock?" Her dress flared as she twirled around and around.

"Letitia, please!" The countess, weary of the mek's frivolity, sighed loudly. "Where is Silas? Tell him to come at once."

"Silas is not with us anymore because of the accident."

"Accident?"

"Yes, Grandmomma." Ray sidled into the room. "I'm afraid he's had a bit of a breakdown. Gone to pieces, one might say. We'll have to find you a new manservant."

Letitia giggled, whirling and twirling.

"What about this evening? This really isn't good enough, Ray." She looked him up and down over her pince-nez spectacles. "What's that foul liquid dripping from those abominable metal fingers of yours? It's going to stain the Aubusson rug."

He glanced at his hands, stifling a grin. "Oh, dear, how unfortunate. I was tinkering with an old machine in the stables. This disgusting goo covered its internal workings."

"Well, clean up at once. You can't expect me to sit at the table with you in that disgusting condition."

"Grandmomma?"

"Well, you are here to invite me to dinner, are you not?" Her eyes flicked rapidly between Ray and his mek.

"Yes, of course. That's precisely why I came to see you. Your presence would honour us at this evening's repast. Dinner will be served at eight o'clock?" He raised his eyebrows at Letitia, who shrugged. "Yes, eight o'clock."

"I will, naturally, be joining you for every evening meal until you replace my mek." She scowled at Ray, who failed to prevent his eye-rolling reflex, and looked to the heavens.

"Yes, Grandmomma."

"Now be a good boy and leave me at peace. I shall see you later."

Letitia twirled her way out of the room behind Ray.

Alone again, the countess smiled to herself.

She reached over the side of her chair and retrieved a small silver flask from her sewing basket. After carefully unscrewing the cap with her gnarled, arthritic fingers, she raised it to her lips and tilted her head backwards, allowing the golden liquid to trickle onto her tongue. Two mouthfuls of strong liquor slid smoothly down her throat, filling her with a familiar, comforting warmth. *Nectar of the Gods!*

Thirst slaked, she replaced the cap and slipped the flask back into its hiding place amongst the bobbins and samplers. Her shoulders slumped as the alcohol eased the tension in her frail octogenarian body. She closed her eyes and listened to the branches brushing the window. *Wind's getting up*, she thought. *There must be a storm brewing.*

Le Rendezvous was busy but not full, as meks scurried between tables, taking orders and serving drinks. Gilbert peered across the dimly lit room, confident that if Rory was here, he would find her. Unusually, for a city-centre public house, most of the patrons were men, and Rory's tall, slim female frame should have stood out, a rose amongst brambles. But there was no sign of her. He wandered over to the bar and called over a mek.

"Drink, sir?" The barman polished a wine glass with a white cloth and held it up to the light to check for blemishes.

"I'm looking for Miss Aurora Marrable. Do you know her?"

"Yes, sir."

"My, my. Rory is popular tonight." On the barstool next to him, a brassy blonde, almost spilling out of her green and gold corset, interrupted.

Crikey, she's wearing far too much makeup. "Excuse me?"

"Two other, er, gentlemen were asking for her earlier." Her eyes looked Gilbert up and down, flicking between face and hips.

The hair stood up on the back of Gilbert's neck.

She slid her long, black cigarette holder between her lips and sucked hard. After a second or two of watching Gilbert, she exhaled, a cloud of smoke billowing to the ceiling, and jabbed a thumb towards the barman. "This mek sent them up to her room."

"Rory lives here?"

"Love-nest more like, dearie. She uses the top room regularly with her latest main squeeze." She rolled her eyes and looked upwards, lips curled into a leering smirk. "This time, it must be serious. They're up there most nights…"

Heart racing, he had to act fast. "Where?"

"It's called the top room for a reason, lovey." She pointed at the stairs at the end of the bar.

Four skipped paces later, he was bounding up the three flights, two steps at a time, reaching a small landing shrouded in darkness, panting for breath. To his left, thin slivers of light framed the only door. It was slightly ajar.

Ears straining for any sound of struggle from within, he crouched and edged towards the light. There was a loud thud, scuffling, coarse male laughter, and a familiar female voice shouting profanities. *Tabby?*

He grabbed the handles of his concealed blades and peered through the thin crack between door and frame. There, reflected in a full-length dressing mirror, was the back of a stocky, scruffy brute. Light flashed off a blade.

Carefully placing his topper on the landing, he drew his swords and kicked the door hard. The thug spun around, snarling. Gilbert's gaze flicked back and forth across the tableau before him. Sprawled at the man's feet, Rory lay moaning, her lilac robe crumpled around her torso.

Out of the corner of his eye, he caught a thrashing whirlwind of arms and legs. Tabby was naked, held from behind by another assailant. One arm was tight across her throat, the other gripped her waist. Despite the sweat slicking her body and limbs, she struggled to loosen his vice-like grip.

Rory's attacker inched forward, his fist clenched around the knife in his right hand, spittle dripping from his chin.

Gilbert crouched and ran the blades' razor-sharp edges against each other. The shrill rasp halted the man's advance, his wild eyes staring at the bright, cruel steel. He took a furtive glance over his shoulder at Rory.

Weighing your options, fucker? Gilbert thought. "Tough guys when you're tackling ladies, eh? Why don't you come over here and play?"

Tabby's assailant shrieked as a heel slammed into his groin. Gilbert turned his head. Her frantic attempts to break free were slowing. Her face contorted as she struggled to breathe. She was in a fight for her life, clawing at the brute's stubbly cheeks, but the engineer's short nails had little effect.

A floorboard creaked, and a darting movement flickered at the edge of his vision. Gilbert side-stepped and slashed in the direction of the sound. An arc of blood slapped against the wall as his razor-sharp sword sliced through sleeve and biceps, the sharp crack of bone snapping. A quick pivot to his left, and he swung the second blade, feeling the thick, meaty impact as it cut through the villain's other shoulder, and he crumpled to the floor, screaming.

Blood flooded across the carpet from gaping wounds. Mortally injured, his blood-frothed mouth gasping for breath, the man tried to scramble to his feet. A final slash carved through his neck, almost severing his head from his body.

Gilbert turned to confront the newly deceased's companion. Light glinted off the knife he now held against Tabby's cheek.

"One more step, and I'll cut her up!" Fear oozed from every pour on the ruffian's sweat-soaked face.

"Hurt her and you die." Gilbert's voice was calm. He wiped the gore from each blade on his coat sleeves.

Rory clawed up the bedframe to her feet. Blood trickled from her lip, and she was bent double, clutching her stomach with both arms. "Let her go," she said.

The man pushed the knife harder into Tabby's cheek and grasped at her breast with his other hand, his mouth twisted into a lecherous grin. Broken tombstone teeth clenched in defiance. He warily inched sideways, heading for the door. Sweat glistened on his filthy face; his breathing laboured.

The effort of controlling Tabby the Tasmanian devil had taken its toll. She was trying everything to squirm free. Blood dripped from the point of the blade pressed into her soft flesh.

Can't let him get away. Gilbert took a step to his right and kicked the door shut.

Rory shuffled forward, dragging her left leg. "Let her go, now." Her voice rasped with menace, lips stretched, baring her teeth.

"Back off, bitch, or your girlie gets it." Droplets of spittle sprayed onto Tabby's bare skin.

Rory stumbled, still clasping her stomach. In one movement, she sprung, right hand arcing gracefully upwards, knife slashing. A spume of blood spurted from the man's face, slashed from mouth to eyebrow in a gaping crimson crescent. He reeled backwards, screaming, hands clutching his ruined cheek. Rory caught Tabby as she fell and wrapped her arms around her, tenderly kissing her forehead.

"May I?" Rory held out her hand behind Tabby's glistening back.

"My pleasure." Gilbert handed her one of his short swords.

"No." Tabby pulled away from Rory's embrace and gently took the blade from her. "That's not a job for my sweetheart."

The groaning man was trying to hold his mutilated face together, failing to staunch the bleeding.

"It's mine." She put her foot on his chest, placed the curved blade below his sternum, and pushed the point under his ribcage through his racing heart. A final, blood-foamed gasp gurgled from his ruined mouth.

Her cheeks flushing, suddenly aware of her naked frailty, Tabby snatched her nightdress off the back of the chair to cover her trembling body. Gilbert lowered his eyes and spun to face the door.

"We've caused a bit of a mess," he said.

"The Order will tidy up. We have until morning to clean the carpet and remove the garbage." Rory pulled the sword from the lifeless cadaver and offered it to him. Standing tall, spattered with blood, her pastel silk robe hung loosely from her shoulders. Her hard, toned body beneath was visible only where it pressed against the gossamer-thin material.

"You could have wiped the blood off." Gilbert ran the blades across his sleeve.

"A skilled artisan looks after his own tools."

"You think I'm skilled, then?"

"We had the situation under control."

Of course you did! "Who were those thugs?"

"They didn't introduce themselves, and we didn't have time to ask."

"They asked for you by name."

"Definitely Anthropocene." Rory rubbed her stomach and grimaced.

"Are you all right, chuck?"

"This gentleman sucker-punched me and kicked me in the ribs." She looked down at his lifeless body and returned the compliment, then cocking her head to one side, she frowned at Gilbert, forehead furrowed. "What are you doing here, anyway?"

"Oh, I just came to let you know Algeria has called a meeting tomorrow at noon at the Praetorian."

Tabby was shaking. Rory took half a step towards her.

"Can you get word to Connie?" Gilbert said.

She nodded and gently caressed Tabby, who grabbed at her, arms encircling her body, squeezing, and rested her head on Rory's breast, mewling like a lost kitten. Rory stroked her hair, and Tabby raised her face, eyes closed, lips parted. Rory lowered her face to Tabby's, but her steely stare remained fixed on Gilbert. Was this defiance? Was this a challenge?

Although he did not view their relationship as an affront to his masculinity, his happiness for them was tinged with jealousy because they had something he so dearly wanted.

He flushed, unsure where to look. "I'll leave you two to it… I mean, I'll see you tomorrow." He turned and tripped on a lifeless arm, stumbling onto the landing. He closed the door behind him, retrieved his topper, and sheathed his blades. It took a second before his eyes adjusted to the darkness.

His mind was racing. He trudged down the stairs. *Who were those men? Does the Order regularly have to clear up this type of 'mess'? Tabby and Rory are lovers? I just killed a man… Tabby and Rory? Really?*

Sounds from the busy bar below grew louder as he neared the ground floor.

Bloody smudges from Gilbert's fingers smeared the bannisters along each flight of stairs. As he reached the last few steps, he stuffed his hands into his pockets and pushed the coat together to hide his blood-stained shirt and trousers. In the few minutes that had passed since he ran up the staircase, the main bar had filled.

He lowered his eyes and nudged his way through the patrons to the door.

"That was quick, dearie!" The blonde sitting at the bar shouted. He glanced sideways and caught her extravagant, open-mouthed wink as she flicked the end of her cigarette holder. Ash, glittering in the lamplight, dropped into the ashtray on the bar.

He hurried out into the stiffening breeze and peered up the road at the Athenaeum in the distance. *I wonder if Dottie muscled her way in. Pity the soul that tries to stop her!* An evil grin spread across his face.

By now, she should be back at the Praetorian. He shuddered and leaned into the wind and drizzle, dodging carriages as he darted across the street. He had an urgent need to scrub the night's events off his clothes.

TWENTY-TWO

Temperance

Hands on her hips, Dottie stood at the foot of the steps, staring up at the impressive edifice on Princess Street. No other building in the city screamed privilege louder than the Athenaeum. From its sandstone palazzo-style architecture and portico entrance to its opulent interior decoration and plush furnishings, it was a symbol of Manchester's economic and cultural rise. This exclusive club for gentlemen was a sanctuary for the upper class. Landed gentry and newly rich entrepreneurs of the cotton industry rubbed shoulders conducting business, discussing investments and relaxing in the reserved atmosphere. Although from different worlds, they spoke the same languages of wealth, privilege and power.

Dottie didn't possess any of these attributes, and as a woman, she was not welcome across the threshold under any circumstances.

She strode up the steps to the tall mek doorman resplendent in his vermillion uniform, complete with golden braided-rope epaulettes and military-style peaked cap and tried to edge past him. A flat hand pressed firmly against her shoulder prevented further progress.

"I need to speak with someone in there." She leaned against his immovable palm.

"Tell *this 'kin* the name of the patron, and *this 'kin* will get a message to him. You cannot enter."

"Take your hand off me, or you'll regret laying a finger on me."

With a flick of his wrist, Dottie staggered backwards, almost falling down the steps. "Now, Miss, give *this 'kin* the gentleman's name, and *this 'kin* will pass a message to him."

Although angry and determined to see inside, she remembered her father's old saying about discretion being the better part of valour. "His name is Aquilla Ulysses Sixsmith."

The mek's eyes flickered. "No one with that name is on the premises. Now, be on your way."

"You're mistaken. I have it on good authority that he is here. Check again. He is black, six foot three, and has a beard."

"No black patrons have entered the building today," he said flatly. "*This 'kin* sees everyone who enters, and the gentleman you seek is not here. Now, be on your way."

She failed to connect the kick aimed at his metal legs as she turned and trudged down the stairs. *Why was Lemmy so certain Ace would be here?*

A powerful gust lifted the brim and sent her topper tumbling over and over along the pavement with Dottie in hot pursuit until it finally came to rest in a puddle. *Great!* She crouched to retrieve it.

"And that's why '*absentem laedit cum ebrio qui litigat*'!" *That voice is familiar.*

"Better an aquabib be than a beery bacchanalian brute." *Very familiar.*

Still bent double, she turned her head to the side to see, to her surprise, a familiar tall, bearded black man addressing a crowd of well-dressed ladies. Above him, flapping wildly in the stiff breeze, a banner proudly proclaiming 'DOG KENNEL LANE TEMPERANCE SOCIETY' emblazoned in canary yellow lettering on azure blue, was strung between two poles that two ladies wearing matching Gainsboroughs and stern faces struggled to hold straight.

Ace? What on Earth? Dottie sprang upright and batted her wet topper absent-mindedly against her leg. Oblivious to the droplets of muddy water splashing on her trousers, she gaped open-jawed as he delivered an impassioned speech on the virtues of sobriety.

At the conclusion, he stepped down from the platform to polite applause, shaking the hands of admiring ladies seated at the front of the small gathering. As he approached the end of the row, a short, curvy woman with bedraggled auburn hair reached up and hugged him.

Issy! Ace and Issy together! Well, well, well...

The next speaker, a tall, slim lady dressed head to toe in emerald green, stepped up to the platform. She had to raise her voice above the sound of passing hansoms and the society banner cracking like a whip in the wind. Dottie kept her friends in sight as she slalomed through the crowd towards them.

Issy glanced in her direction as Dottie jumped up and down, arms flailing. She did not acknowledge the wave but whispered to Ace. His shoulders slumped.

"Dottie! What are you doing here?" Ace painted a surprised smile as he turned to greet her.

"Looking for you." She spread her arms wide. "What's all this?"

"We joined the movement about a year ago," Issy said, "for personal reasons." She shot a glance at Ace.

He nodded and stared into the puddles reflecting the ominous clouds gathering overhead. "Looks like a storm's getting up."

"So… are you two, er, walking out together?" Curiosity piqued, she had to ask.

Issy stifled a giggle.

"Well, we share the same interests," Ace said. "We both prefer female company." He winked playfully at Issy.

She gave him a gentle dig in the ribs. "Not exclusively."

Dottie's cheeks flushed. This evening was turning into a festival of surprises. Ace and Issy were staring at her. She snapped her jaw shut.

"You mentioned you were looking for us?"

"Oh, yes. Sorry. Algeria has called a meeting for noon tomorrow at the Praetorian."

"Any idea what's happening? Is the game afoot?" Ace asked.

"Yes, but I'll let her tell you. I don't want to steal her thunder."

"Sounds interesting…"

"Trouble, more likely," Issy said.

On the platform, the vision in green finished her call to action to a smattering of applause. Ace offered his hand and helped her off the makeshift stage.

"I'll leave you two to it… I mean, see you at the meeting. Don't be late. You know she's a stickler for punctuality."

Ace saluted; Issy rolled her eyes.

Dottie doffed her hat, turned on her heel, and made her way through the dispersing crowd.

As she pushed through the mostly female crowd, her lips curled into a smile. *Wait 'til I tell Bertie about my eventful evening! He won't believe me.*

As expected, Ace and Issy were the last to arrive. The door from the bar creaked on its hinges as it swung open, alerting those waiting of their late arrival.

Expressions were a mixture of confusion, curiosity, weariness and maybe more than a couple of hangovers. Rory, her body pressed against Tabby's, acknowledged him with a nod, raised an eyebrow, and tucked a monocle in front of her right eye. Her swollen lip and bruised cheek were the only visible signs of the previous night's assault.

Tabby avoided eye contact with him, and although Issy and Ace were deep in conversation, their eyes were fixed on Gilbert. *Yes*, he thought, *Dottie has told me everything*.

So much had happened since he attended the previous meeting that had been hurriedly arranged to address the tragic events of that September night, only a few weeks but a lifetime ago. Dottie must have felt the uneasy atmosphere and squeezed his hand.

"Now we are all here," Algeria flashed the latecomers a sideways glance, "we can get started. But first, we honour the passing of some of our own in recent days."

Gilbert glanced at Dottie, a lump rising in his throat.

"Lady Patience Dionysia Marsh perished in the cowardly attack on Oldham Triple T terminus, and my dear Abel was murdered…" Gilbert felt a pang of guilt as Algeria paused.

"Both died in our service at the hands of Raven and his Anthropocene horde."

They stood in silence, heads bowed. Dottie sniffed back tears as Gilbert squeezed her trembling hand.

Algeria raised her head and, spreading her arms wide, palms up, recited the Exhortation of the Order.

As soon as the gathered repeated the Adjuration, she lowered her arms and surveyed the room. "Now, onto business. As some of you know, we have set a plan in motion to stop these Anthropocene blackguards. We're going to draw them out of the shadows."

Close to Gilbert, Lemmy shifted his weight from foot to foot, staring at the floor. *He still hasn't come to terms with this.*

Algeria outlined the plan to use Lemmy's father as bait at the Wainwright memorial to total silence. When she finished, she opened the floor to questions and suggestions.

Ace was first to speak. "Two things, High Mother." Algeria raised her eyebrows at the formal address. "How can we be confident they will attack? And how can we possibly ensure Mister Philpott's safety?"

"Of course, we can't be one hundred percent sure Raven will take the bait. We can only make the lure as appetising as possible." She looked over at Lemmy and his father. "No offence intended."

"None taken, High Mother." Jeremiah Philpott raised both hands.

"We have spread the word that a local MP will attend the ceremony. This may well attract a sizeable crowd, too. But we will do everything in our power to protect Mister Philpott. And, of course, Lemmy will be at his side at all times."

"Do we know how they might strike?" Connie asked.

"The quick answer is no. They've planted bombs and

dropped airships on big targets, but they attack individuals face to face." Algeria motioned Gilbert to speak.

"Although Lemmy's father is the lure, the importance of the Ship Canal project is Raven's reason for making a powerful statement."

"What do you mean?" Lemmy's furrowed brow and pinched eyebrows showed his feelings.

"He may try to destroy the lock to delay or force the cancellation of the Cut project," Gilbert said.

"How?" Connie asked.

"We don't know for sure, but if he has time and access to the lock, we believe planting a bomb seems most likely." Gilbert shrugged his shoulders.

"So, what's the plan, chaps?" Rory's chirped question lacked the usual vim.

Algeria took a deep breath. "The ceremony starts at one o'clock. If they are going to plant explosives, they'll do it tonight or early in the morning. We'll meet at Barton tomorrow at 10.00am sharp. If they've hidden it, we have to find it." She looked at Ace and Issy from under her furrowed eyebrows. "Let's try not to be late. Lives may depend on it."

"We'll be here at nine, Algeria," Ace said. "We'll travel with you."

"Why do you want all of us there?" Connie asked.

"If they try an air attack, we'll need you up there," Algeria said.

"We'll be there before ten."

"We have spiffing new forward-facing cannons. We'll blast the blackguards out of the sky long before they get anywhere near the lock." Ace banged his fist on the table. "Don't worry, Lemmy, old sport. We'll make sure they don't harm your father."

Lemmy's silence and thin smile betrayed his feelings.

"What's wrong, Dolly?" Algeria asked.

"I just wondered… What happens if we find a bomb or something?"

"You deal with it."

TWENTY-THREE

SEEK

To Gilbert's surprise, Ace and Issy arrived at the Praetorian early, enabling everyone to set off in two carriages at 9.00am. In the lead carriage, he spent the tortuous thirty-minute journey listening to the howling wind, fearing they would be overturned with each mighty gust.

Few words passed between the passengers, and no one made eye contact. *So, this is how soldiers feel before battle.*

Workers milling around the lock preparing for the ceremony took no notice of the two carriages that pulled up nor of the occupants who spilled out onto the roadside. *So much for security.*

Eyes watering, Gilbert looked up into an eldritch sky. The bitter wind tugged at his bronze face furniture, sending spasms of freezing pain through the metal anchors into his skull.

Powerful, southerly winds were propelling dense gunmetal and wispy white clouds across the heavens at an unnatural speed. *Storm brewing. They won't try a dirigible attack in this gale. So, it must be a bomb, and we'd better find it.*

"No one flying today." Dottie narrowed her eyes and tightened her grip on her hat.

"You can't fly in this fucking wind. It would be suicide," Tabby said.

"You're right, shugah, but that doesn't mean these crazy people won't try. *Freyja's Grimalkin* and *Dragonfly* should be ready just in case. If they strike from the air, Ace can use his cannons without risking a takeoff." Algeria turned to Dottie. "Go with them, Doll. We'll handle the search."

Dottie opened her mouth, but Gilbert, shaking his head, knew an argument was the last thing they needed. So, defeated, she glared and stomped away through the mud behind the two crews, up the slippery incline, into the aerodrome.

Gilbert and Algeria walked along a narrow stone path through the middle of the wide expanse between the engineer's office and the new buildings. Their clean lines were in sharp contrast to the old empty hut. With boards across the windows and doors, Wainwright's old office was desolate. Gilbert shook his head, saddened by its dilapidated state. From the path to the lock, the recent rain had turned the ground into a quagmire.

Algeria was ankle-deep in cloying mud by the time she squelched the short distance to the lock. When she was finally on solid ground, she tapped each foot against the brickwork to loosen the sludge caked on her dark green boots before turning to Gilbert.

"This is where Wainwright died?"

"Aye, we found him down there." He pointed to the lock bottom thirty-odd feet below.

Algeria peered over the side and shook her head. "Is there a safe way down?"

He nodded and guided her to the stairs at the west end of the lock, and they trod carefully on the shaky wooden steps, buffeted by violent gusts. As they descended out of the wind, the stench of stagnant water and rotting vegetation grew stronger, bringing back pungent memories for Gilbert. Algeria retched.

"We need to search both the large and the small locks and the Stoney sluices. If it's not here, we'll check the tower that houses the machinery next," Gilbert said.

"You stay here while I do the sluices." Algeria bustled away before he could warn her that they were the major source of the rancid odours.

He examined every inch of the brickwork and the newly installed greenheart lock gates. Finding no sign of anything suspicious, he re-joined Algeria.

"Any luck?" he asked.

"Nothing. You?" The thick handkerchief she held over her nose and mouth muffled her words.

"No. Let's get back up there." Gilbert pointed to the buildings above the steep sides of the lock.

Conscious that time was running out, he skipped up the steps, pulling himself higher using the handrails. A strong wind gust buffeted him at the top. The image of Wainwright's broken body lying in the bottom of the lock flashed through his mind. The irony of his own good fortune was not lost on him as he managed to regain his balance, and he offered a hand to Algeria, who was following closely behind.

Local folk and dignitaries were arriving for the ceremony, and some of his former workmates were here to pay their respects to their late boss. They dashed past the gathering throng over to the buildings where Stan Miller stood, guarding the lockkeeper's office.

"You working today, Stan?" Gilbert asked.

"Aye, they roped me into standing here in this 'orrible wind. Never known nowt like it. I'm sure it's getting worse. 'Orrible."

"We normally get mild weather from the south. Storms mostly come from over there." Gilbert pointed to the hills in the east. "Any chance of a look round? I'd like to see the new lock engines?"

Stan looked up at Algeria. "I don't see any harm in that," he said, "be my guests." He stepped aside and, with a flamboyant bow, ushered them inside.

Gilbert caught Algeria suppressing a smile.

She checked the coal bunker by the door before they entered. The interior of the office was small and unfurnished, apart from the shiny, new pot-bellied stove in the corner that reminded him of the one in Wainwright's hut. Nowhere to hide a bomb in the empty room. A side exit led to the lock's pump house.

Gilbert froze. The door was ajar, faint scuffling noises coming from the room beyond. He turned to Algeria, finger on his lips beseeching silence, and pointed at the open doorway. He crouched, hands gripping his swords in their sheaths, and barged through the door.

"Bloody hell!" Horace Hastings was picking himself up off the floor, glaring. "What's going on! Sparks? Is that you?"

Gilbert clambered to his feet and relaxed. "Sorry, mate, didn't know you were in here. We thought someone had broken in."

"Broken in? What're you talking about, lad? Some of us are still working, you know. Old Wainwright would be spinning in his grave if he knew his memorial was halting work on the Cut. My dear old mum used to say that a job's never done 'til it's done, and this job's not done 'til they flood the bloody canal, so I'll keep doing my job as best as I can… well, as long as they're paying me."

"Aye, you're right," Gilbert said. "Mind if we have a look at the new engines?"

"Not much to see. We've only just installed these beauties, and they're not working yet." Horace's eyes lit up, a yellow toothy smile widening across his face. "Who's this, then?" He removed his cap and flattened his unruly hair with his sweaty palm. His recovery from being startled out of his skin was complete.

"This is Miss Algeria Darling. She's accompanying me to the ceremony." Gilbert turned to his companion. "Algeria, this is Mister Horace Hastings, trusted leader of engineer Wainwright's team."

Algeria did not offer her hand, and her smile hardened. "I've heard so much about Mister Wainwright. You must miss him terribly, Mister Hastings."

"Call me Horace. I miss the extra money, but truth be told, he was a tough taskmaster. He pushed us hard, but I suppose he was fair, and we was well paid."

Algeria was watching Horace the way a mongoose watches a cobra. "Not long to the ceremony, Mister Hastings. I think Stanley wanted a word with you."

What's got into her?

"Righto, miss." He pulled his cap on over his greasy hair, touching its peak before squeezing past Algeria in the doorway. She turned to watch him walk through the lockkeeper's office.

Gilbert frowned. "Horace is all right."

"Is he? Would you bet your life and the lives of the folks out there? Your friend Stan didn't tell us Hastings was in here. What was he doing skulking around on his own?"

"Dunno, but I can't see him blowing the place up when he worked so hard building it."

"That's how cults work, shugah. Obedience without question. No thought of their own needs or feelings. There is only the cause. Nothing else matters."

Gilbert put his hands on his hips, tilted his head back, and whistled. "If he's hidden something in here, this might take a while." Although it was only twenty feet square, the building was over five storeys high. A maze of stairs and walkways provided access to engines and machinery.

"You start at the top, and we'll meet in the middle," he said.

For the next two hours, they worked feverishly but methodically, examining every nook and cranny, every pipe, boiler, and flue. But finding nothing, they met on the third floor.

"Perhaps Raven didn't take the bait." Algeria wiped sweat from her dirt-stained face with her sleeve.

"I don't believe that. We just haven't figured out what he's up to yet."

"Come on. Let's get outside. He might be in the crowd, hiding in full view."

Gilbert's heart leapt into his mouth. "Maybe his plan isn't to destroy Barton lock. Maybe Lemmy's father is the sole target!"

He bolted through the lockkeeper's office into the heaving mass of humanity huddled together against the elements at the side of the lock. Gilbert scanned frantically from side to side. *Where are you, Lemmy?*

A gaggle of dignitaries bunched at the front of the crowd held onto their toppers which quivered in the gale. Gilbert screwed up his eyes as dust devils billowed off the brickwork. Lemmy's father was holding court, his audience smiling or laughing politely. He fought his way through the throng.

"Lemmy! Is everything all right?" He had to shout above the shrieking wind.

He smiled when he saw Lemmy leaning on a familiar blue and silver walking stick and looked up to the heavens. *Abel and Pop will be smiling, too.* "All fine here! Have you found the bomb yet?"

"No! Nothing! Have you spotted anything unusual?"

"I don't know what I'm looking for, old chap, but I haven't seen anyone carrying barrels of gunpowder if that's what you mean!" Lemmy's eyes continued to flit from face to face.

Gilbert turned to scan faces. *No ugly giant. Either Raven and his big friend aren't here yet, or they are watching from a safe distance. What are they up to?*

Lost in thought, Algeria watched Gilbert battling his way through the crowd. *Where? Where would they hide a bomb?*

The engineer's derelict hut was an obvious place, *but surely the explosion would be too far away to kill Philpott... unless it's massive.* She squelched and slid across the quagmire, worse now that the crowds had arrived.

With no sign of forced entry to the front and side, she trudged through the mud towards the stream flowing along the rear and kicked through the brambles shielding the back of the hut from view.

Howling winds drowned the gentle babbling of the brook as the stream flowed close to the wooden wall and the narrow strip of land thick with thistles, teasels and long grass. Taking care not to slip into the water, she edged her way through the waist-high weeds, looking for damage or holes large enough to crawl through. The ground beneath her muddy boots was unstable as she flattened the overgrowth, making progress treacherous.

A piece of wood splintered under her boot with a loud crack. She looked down, and there, through the long, wispy grass, was a partially hidden hole in the wall, large enough for a man to crawl through. Rotten planks had been disintegrated by brute force and hastily concealed using splinters from within. *A-ha! I knew it!*

As she crouched to get a closer look, her feet slid backwards on the mossy ground, and she slammed into the wall. Landing heavily on her side, facing the hole, she peered into the darkness. Her eyes widened.

"What's that?" Gus almost fell out of his hammock.

"Shush!" Finn said, "There's someone outside."

A loud clunk echoed around the dark room.

"Someone's trying to get in."

They slid silently out of their hammocks, scrabbling for their weapons.

Gus licked his lips and whispered. "All right, you fucker. Let's see the whites of your eyes…"

A huge hand punched through the wood, grabbed Algeria's hair and dragged her through the wall. Splintered shards of rotten timber exploded into the hut.

Stunned by the sudden violent motion, the dust stinging her nostrils jolted her to her senses. She gulped a lung full of dusty air, coughing and spluttering as it hit the back of her dry throat. Algeria opened her eyes to a large, grinning, greasy face inches from hers. Cool droplets of spittle dripped from drooling lips onto her cheek.

Before she could react, a massive hand gripped her tunic and lifted her off the ground with ease.

Legs kicking as hard as she was able, she grabbed the sides of his head with both hands and raked the giant's cheeks with her fingernails.

His eyes flashed; the corner of his mouth curled into a vaguely familiar snarl. She recognised that fearful expression. But from where? Before she could remember, a fist was hurtling at her. Everything went black…

The door opened, and a familiar figure strode in, his silhouette framed by the doorway.

"Good afternoon, gentlemen. You look surprised." Raven peered into the unlit cabin, cocked his head and frowned at the pistols pointed at him. "Now… don't you think it might be a little foolhardy to discharge weapons in here? You are military men, are you not? Surely you know what would happen?"

Gus and Finn glanced at each other, gently uncocked and lowered their flintlocks.

"Sorry, sir, you gave us quite a scare, sure you did." Gus laughed nervously

Raven wrinkled his nose and held a white monogrammed handkerchief to his mouth and nostrils. "Really, gentlemen. You are not scoring high marks for personal hygiene. Might I humbly suggest you open a window so the foul stench dissipates quickly?"

Gus flushed and dug Finn in the ribs with his elbow. "Yes, sir."

Raven took out his pocket watch. "We have twenty minutes. Athos will be here soon. Are you ready for some fun?" He rubbed his hands together and beamed.

DREW HALFPENNY

TWENTY-FOUR

DESTROY

Where's Algeria?

Gilbert twisted left and right, scanning the crowd milling around the lock.

She was two steps behind me.

The ceremony was due to start in ten minutes.

Has she found something?

Panic rose in his throat.

Did she go to the lockkeeper's office?

"Look after your dad. I need to find Algy."

Lemmy nodded and turned to watch the ceremonial party getting ready on the hastily erected platform, its wind-torn banners cracking like bullwhips in the gale.

Gilbert fought his way through the crowd to where Stan was still standing at the side of the doorway.

"Have you seen the tall black lady I was with earlier?"

"Algeria? Aye, lad, she was heading over to Wainwright's hut. Have you lost her?"

"Thanks, Stan!" He struggled to make himself heard above the wind. *I don't remember mentioning her name...*

Thick mud clung to his boots as he trudged to the old engineer's office. Something caught the corner of his eye on the airfield, and he turned, narrowing his eyes to see Dottie jumping around, waving her arms. She pointed to the far side of the aerodrome, where a large dark figure was loping towards the hangar, carrying a body on his shoulder like a sack of coal. *Athos!*

He took off at a dead sprint, weaving between the late comers sauntering to the ceremony, which was due to start a few dozen yards behind him. Brushing them aside without breaking step, he reached the road and crossed it in four steps. *Thank goodness the wind is with me.*

As he approached Dottie, he slowed and bent double, trying to suck air into his bursting lungs.

"He's got my mama!" she shouted. "I saw him climb out of the stream with her draped over his shoulder! She wasn't moving, Bertie! What has he done to her?" Her body was shaking, her voice cracking.

Grasping her shoulders, he held her at arm's length, staring into her troubled eyes. "Listen, we'll get her out of there. There's no way to escape. Even if they have a dirigible, they can't take off in this gale. Let's gather the Stormri—"

They turned to face the hangar from where the telltale throb of engines roared above the shrieking wind.

"Are... are the trees moving?" Dottie's eyebrows raised.

Above the silver and black doors, rows and rows of treetops swayed as they parted to the left and right. Dottie and Gilbert fell into each other's arms as a gigantic black mass rose majestically into the stygian sky.

Gilbert stared open-mouthed at the rising leviathan. "He's got a bloody dreadnought—a castle in the air."

"And he's got Mama…"

The enormous experimental Royal Navy airship had twenty LTA bags arranged in two tiers of two four-bag envelopes stacked above three four-bag envelopes, clad in a single aluminium, chain mail outer skin. Ten powerful airscrews, four on each side of the lower tier and two side by side across the top edge, provided the power to muscle the giant dirigible through any but the most extreme weather. A metal framework attached the aluminium skin to the completely enclosed gondola. Forward and aft-facing cannons under the cabin made the dreadnought a formidable protagonist.

"What's he doing?" Dottie's voice trembled.

"I don't know, but we have to stop him before he gets to the lock!"

"Ace won't take off in this wind! It's too dangerous!"

"*Dragonfly* is our only hope!" Gilbert grasped her hand, and they sprinted across the airfield.

Facing directly into the teeth of the gale and just above the hangar roof, the pitch of the engines increased as the dreadnought's pilots applied more thrust, and the huge obsidian-skinned airship edged upwards and forwards against the ferocious wind.

Dragonfly was a quarter of a mile upwind from the slowly advancing dreadnought when Gilbert and Dottie climbed aboard the tiny craft.

"We have to stop it from getting to the lock! Ace can't blast it out of the sky because Algy is onboard! Can you get me up there?" Gilbert asked.

"We can't take off in this fucking gale!" Tabby looked terrified.

"If you get me above it... I have an idea!"

"We don't have their power! These gusts will blow us away like a leaf!" Rory said.

"Get me up there! We have no choice!"

"They've got Mama. We have to save her!" The dreadnought was still rising but making slow headway against the wind. "We don't have time. We need to go now! Please!" Dottie grabbed Rory by the shoulders, screaming into her face.

"Come on! You call yourselves Stormriders! We can do this! You're Algy's only hope! If we fail, everybody down there dies!" Gilbert pointed at the lock.

"Dump the ballast, Tabby. Let's go!" Rory pulled on her leather aviator's cap.

Tabby shook her head and puffed out her cheeks while she dropped a hundredweight. *Dragonfly*'s tail lifted sharply as the tiny air yacht, buffeted by the gusts, strained against the mooring. They were going to explode upwards, a cork from a bottle of fizz, when the electromagnet disengaged.

She lowered her goggles and checked the airsock on the edge of the airfield. As tatters of shredded material whipped around wildly, cracking and snapping in the southerly gale, she grabbed the lever to deactivate the magnet, revved the engines to maximum power, and nodded her readiness.

Rory and Connie eased their goggles from atop their leather caps to cover their eyes, fear and determination reflected in their furrowed brows and gritted teeth.

With the dreadnought less than four hundred yards away and only a hundred feet in the air, rocking in the gusting wind, Rory raised her hand.

Come on! The immense airship powered inexorably through the headwind, still gaining height.

"Now!" Rory slapped her palm on the bulwark.

Tabby killed the magnets, *Dragonfly* detached, and they shot upwards, blown backwards at terrifying speed, towards the black monster. Gilbert sat at the prow, looking astern as they rocked violently from side to side. Tabby was peering over her shoulder, wrestling with the controls. *How is she keeping us upright?*

Distance between the airships was closing rapidly. The front of the dreadnought loomed closer.

"We're not going to make it!" Connie shouted.

The rudder of *Dragonfly* cracked when it clipped the dreadnought's chain mail as they passed between the two airscrews. They were racing backwards, still gaining height. In a couple of seconds, they would careen over the airship, and all hope of a rescue would be lost. Gilbert fired the air yacht's harpoon into the gale, urging the grapple to latch onto the black rigging partially covering the skin. He wedged the gun into the prow and waited.

As the wind hurled *Dragonfly* beyond the last LTA bag, Gilbert closed his eyes, certain the gamble had failed, and they were going to die. Arms outstretched, he turned to apologise to his friends but was flung to the deck as the gondola jerked violently to a halt. The cable had tightened as the grapple had snagged on the rigging between the two top-side airscrews. Only Tabby remained upright, clinging to the controls as the recoil caused everyone to lose their balance.

Unable to use the electromagnet to secure the *Dragonfly* to the aluminium skin, they were at the mercy of the grappling hooks.

Gilbert leapt to his feet. He had to work fast, and, grabbing Tabby's cutting torch, he snatched Dottie's welding goggles from her topper as he dashed to the prow and looked over the side. Head swimming, vomit rose in his throat. Beads of sweat were forming on his brow as he clipped the torch to his belt and pulled the goggles onto his head, lenses pressed into his forehead. He screamed at Tabby to re-wind the harpoon, then without hesitation, he reached down, grabbed the cable connecting the airships and hurdled the bulwark.

The maelstrom tossed and tore at *Dragonfly* behind him, causing the cable he hung from to bounce wildly. Violent gusts and wash from the powerful airscrews, pushed and pulled at him, and he slammed his eyes shut to fend off the rising nausea. Terror seized his heart as the wind ripped his breath away. *I have to do this; Algy needs me.*

With numb fingers, he edged, hand over hand, along the taut cable. He focussed on feeling for the dreadnought's skin beneath his feet. If the grapple slipped, death would pay him another aerial visit.

Finally, after what felt like years to his shoulders and hands, his boots touched the envelope. After a few short steps, he opened his eyes and grabbed at the wet rigging. Head lowered, he pulled himself to the centre of the envelope, directly between the airscrews.

Without detaching the gas canisters from his belt, he aimed the lance of the cutter at the lowest part of the valley between the airbags, lowered the goggles from his forehead and pressed the piezo quartz trigger. A brilliant blue flame shot from the lance, slicing through the rigging and aluminium.

Tension in the outer skin pulled the incision apart as he ran the torch across the chain mail. Newly severed links glowed bright yellow but cooled instantly in the freezing wind. When the hole was big enough, Gilbert extinguished the flame, unhooked the canisters, and let the gale sweep the gear into the vortices behind the airship.

He raised his goggles and climbed through the gaping maw into the black tangle of metal. Vertigo made the descent difficult as he edged down the superstructure between the LTA bags. The deafening drone of the engines echoed around the envelopes in the purple darkness. Leaked wisps of gas swirling around the compartment caused Gilbert's vertigo to worsen.

At the bottom of the cavity, he crept along thin metal spars, crouching. Dust particles sparkled in light rays shining through air vents dotted across the floor. Gilbert paused. Voices. Beneath the roar of the engines and the howling wind, muffled words rose from the cabin.

He edged to the nearest grill and dropped to his hands and knees. He remained there, listening. Their voices were unmistakable. *Raven, Athos, and the Flanagans?* His shoulders slumped.

Flat on his stomach, he inched forward until he could peer through the vent. His heart missed a beat as a pang of fear shot through his body. In the middle of the dimly lit cabin, Algeria sprawled face down, wrists bound, tethered to an enormous barrel-shaped contraption. She wasn't moving.

To his right, at the helm, the Flanagan brothers sat at the controls, surrounded by tubes, dials and levers. He fought an overwhelming urge to jump into their midst, blades flashing in a whirlwind of violence and crimson vengeance. This was not the time to be reckless. He sucked in a deep, calming breath. *Where are Raven and Athos?*

"Won't this ship sail any faster, gentlemen? At this pace, Philpott will have died of old age before we get there." The calm, confident voice was unmistakable.

Wake up, Algy. I can't do this alone!

The airship shuddered violently as the powerful screws strained to make headway against each percussive gust. In the cabin below, a dark shadow passed over Algeria's body. *Athos!*

Gilbert was leaning further across the opening, craning his neck left and right to glimpse Algy's captors, when Athos walked directly beneath him, his oily black hair brushing the vent. He recoiled from the stink of pomade, sweat, and stale tobacco.

Athos casually flicked a boot at Algeria, who groaned and rolled onto her back. He grabbed her arms and yanked her upright, leaning her against the large barrel-shaped device. Her eyes half-opened; she shook her head as if to unscramble her brain.

"Ahh," Raven said, "our honoured guest has finally regained consciousness. What a joy to meet the lauded leader of The Order of Antediluvian Gardeners, or whatever you meddlers call yourselves. It's fortunate that you are going to play such an important role in this momentous event."

Still dazed, Algeria staggered, her head lolling forward.

"You see, Madam, we are going to deliver a decisive blow against your precious Connickle laws by obliterating Barton lock, Philpott, and a few hundred not-so-innocent souls. Public outcry and the cost of repairing the damage will enable our allies in Parliament to press for the cancellation of the canal project, which, together with your unfortunate death, marks the beginning of the end of the heinous anti-progress laws and your beloved Order.

"As victors write history, forever you will be known as the leader of a subversive secret society hellbent on holding back scientific discovery. Our Anthropocene historians will praise the name of this magnificent behemoth alongside *Victory*, *Revenge*, *Warrior*, and *Ark Royal*. Those esteemed men-o-war had names fitting to their purpose, so it was imperative I chose an appropriate name for this magnificent dreadnought, this vehicle of destruction and ultimate liberation. So, after much deliberation… Welcome aboard *Dea Tacita*, the silent goddess of the dead."

She lifted her head to face the owner of the calm, menacing voice. Her eyes widening, she caught her breath, trying to regain her composure. "A very dear friend of mine would appreciate your knowledge of ancient myth and legend more than I. But you don't impress me, sweetie."

"I assume you are referring to Mister Aquilla Sixsmith? You look surprised. Oh yes, we know about him and his fabled foibles, but I wonder if you are aware of his nickname while amongst his peers in London? Because of his predilection for visiting brass houses, his friends called him Ace Sex-meks. Ha!

"Sadly, I don't have time to meet Mister Sixsmith. *Freyja's Grimalkin* can't fly in this maelstrom, but should he be stupid enough to try, we have more than enough firepower to tame his little grey kitty-cat."

"You underestimate his dedication to the Order. While I'm sure you believe that your Freedom movement is a noble cause, you have me at a disadvantage, sir. Untie me, so we can debate on an equal footing."

I need to get down there. Gilbert looked around the purple haze, eyes darting, squinting into the darkness, ears straining to catch the conversation.

"I would relish a long, meaningful discussion about the evil of your beloved Connickle, the false prophet, but I'm afraid your stay with us will be short as I am bestowing on you the great honour of delivering my little gift to your friends at the lock.

"You see, the contraption to which you are tied is an explosive device developed by our loyal alchemists. The design is rather ingenious. As we would not have sufficient time to escape the blast after we drop the bomb onto the lock, it is designed not to explode on impact. Its clockwork mechanism controls the detonation.

"I wonder how your pathetic followers will react, hearing your screams, seeing your broken body bound to a bomb they cannot defuse. Will they weep for you, High Mother? Or will they run for their miserable lives? The question is academic, of course, because they won't have time to escape. When the clock reaches the prescribed hour and the unstable chemicals within are mixed, the resultant reaction will produce a crater fifty yards wide and thirty feet deep."

"So, this is the best your little group at Wigtwizzle Hall could come up with?"

"Wigtwizzle Hall? Ahh, yes, I'd completely forgotten they were ensconced in South Yorkshire for a while before they moved to a more suitable base of operations, but this was only one of their many ongoing projects. I didn't know you had stumbled upon them. Interesting…"

"You won't get the chance to drop it."

"You can't stop me…"

"You can kiss my black callipygian arse."

"My, my… A five-guinea word on the lips of a tuppenny whore."

"The last person to call me that was another small man with visions of grandeur, an earl with an unhealthy appetite for young girls. I hear he had to pay off a servant girl who threatened to tell the world of how he had forced himself on her." Algeria stroked her chin and lowered her stare. "Come to think of it, you have the same chip on your shoulder. Lacking in the manhood department too, are you, sweetie?"

From beneath Gilbert came the sound of tin tacks in a can being shaken, but Raven had fallen silent.

"You seem flustered, sweetie. Have I touched a tiny, raw nerve?" Algeria was smiling now, oozing confidence. "Mark my words. Ace won't hesitate. He'll do whatever is necessary to stop you."

The rattling grew louder, but Raven's voice remained calm. "Really? They call you Mother, do they not? How wonderful! They won't shoot at us while you're our guest, and once you have disembarked, they'll be too busy trying to save themselves."

"You know nothing about the Order. The oath is everything."

"And yet we fly on, unimpeded..." His laugh was like fingernails on a chalkboard, and the metallic rattling intensified.

The dim light made gauging distance difficult. Up ahead, Gilbert could just make out the faint outline of a door near where the skin sloped upwards. *I knew there had to be a way up here from the cabin!*

He crawled along the metal spars to the doorway before raising himself upright. The maintenance access hatch was only four feet high. He gently pressed the handle and prayed they did not lock it from inside the cabin. The door swung outwards, revealing a tight, ornate spiral stairway.

He squeezed his broad frame into the narrow space and took careful steps. A few treads from the deck, he stopped. Directly facing the stairs, the door had a small window at head height. If he stepped down, could they see him?

Crouching on the juddering staircase to peer through the glass, he saw no movement, so he tiptoed the remaining steps and ducked under the window. Adrenaline pumping, his heart pounded in his chest. *No time. We must be almost over the locks.*

He slowly raised his head, squinting through the dirty glass. Far to his right, the accursed Flanagans wrestled with the controls. On his left, Algeria was no longer struggling against her bonds. She stood still, staring, no emotion on her face.

Resigned to her fate? *That's not her style. She's up to something.* Further left, the sweaty hulk of Athos stood, arms folded across his barrel chest. *Where's Raven?*

Movement behind the giant caught his attention. Light glinted off metal as a tall blond figure dressed in aviator coveralls stepped forward. Gilbert gasped.

Raven! And he's wearing a yoke...

TWENTY-FIVE

Five Minutes...

GILBERT'S MIND WAS RACING. Raven's yoke had upped the ante. He pressed his back against the door and slumped to the floor. In the cabin, the metallic rattling grew louder. He needed Algeria.

Four against one was completely hopeless, but four against two was only mostly hopeless. *Think, Bertie, think.* His mother's voice cut through the despair, relaxing his shoulders. He bowed his head and took a deep breath.

The wind whistled between the airbags inside the envelope. Outside, powerful engines screamed, shaking the dreadnought violently. *Clunk!* The door behind him shook. Something big had bumped against it. His heart missed a beat. Had they discovered him? He eased himself into a crouch, unsheathed his swords, and slowly raised his head. Athos's shoulder covered the left side of the window, hiding Raven from his view—and him from Raven.

He peeked around the side of the shoulder. Algeria was staring at Athos. *Has she seen me?* Eyes half closed, her passive expression showed no emotion. Deliberately, she glanced down at her side, then looked back before bumping her hip against the contraption. A dark stain spread from the pocket of her green trousers. After a few moments, the tension released from her body. She shifted her weight, tilted her head, and slid her moist tongue between her lips, making them glisten invitingly.

Gilbert nodded his understanding and waited. The door rattled. Straggly hair left greasy marks on the window as Athos shook his head. *Trying to clear your thoughts? Good luck with that, you big lummox.*

With a loud grunt, the big man took a stride towards Algeria.

"Athos?" A puzzled voice called from the shadows.

Two more steps, and he was almost within touching distance. Arms outstretched, immense hands trembling, reaching, yearning.

"Athos! Step back!"

But the giant either didn't hear or didn't want to listen, pulled by the sweet, musky, irresistible chemical magnetism that Gilbert had experienced at the Praetorian. Bending forward, drooling, his huge hands grabbed Algeria's hips, pulling her closer.

She opened her mouth and closed her eyes, bound hands eagerly grasping his lapels. In a single movement, she yanked him towards her, smashed her knee into his groin, and, as he crumpled into her, she threw her forehead into his nose. Blood and sweat sprayed over her as he slumped to the deck, stunned. She crouched, slipping her hand inside her boot, and withdrew a stiletto. Her shrieks drowned out Athos's grunts of pain as she plunged it into his back, again and again.

Gilbert lost count of the thrusts in the frenzied attack. Her brutal cunning had given them a chance.

A shimmering shadow slid across the floor towards Algeria. Raven was advancing on her as she squatted next to Athos, moans gurgling with his every breath from punctured lungs.

Heart pounding, Gilbert burst through the maintenance hatch, swords raised. Raven staggered sideways as he spun to face him, reaching out with his twitching left arm for balance, his shaking hand burying into, and latching onto, the tubing surrounding the explosive device. From shoulder to wrist, his prosthetic sleeve twitched violently as his metal-clad fingers locked him to the bomb. He pulled and twisted, trying to break free.

"Sparks? But… you're dead! Athos…" His eyes flashed as he glanced at the giant's body, where a dark pool was spreading across the deck as his life's blood drained away.

Gilbert, focussing on Raven's shaking arm, heard the boots running hard from his right too late. He half turned as a blur of unkempt red hair and a wiry body smashed into his ribs. He collided heavily with the bulkhead, knocking the wind from his lungs. Instinctively, he swung a sword and clipped Finn's head with the hilt.

His attacker's off-balance momentum took him careening past Gilbert. He staggered, gathered his scrambled bearings, then charged head down, flinging roundhouse punches into Gilbert's ribs. Pinned to the hull, he hacked at Finn with both swords but struggled to get leverage, and his blows were ineffective against the bully's heavy coat.

Out of the corner of his eye, he watched in horror as Raven reached for Algeria as she tried to cut her bonds. Finally free, she stood to face him, dagger poised, but as she turned her back on Athos, his giant hand seized her ankle, pulling her to the floor.

She stabbed at the fingers clamped like a vice around her lower leg. Her thin blade sliced through muscle and sinew, but his grip held firm.

Raven lunged and gripped the calf of her other leg, powerful mechanics grinding, scraping metal on metal, squeezing. Her scream reverberated around the cabin as the edges of the metal-clad fingers dug into her tender flesh.

Athos's grasp finally loosened as his strength and life faded away.

"Faithful to the end, old friend." Raven raised his fist and, still clutching Algeria like a rag doll, ended his suffering with a single, skull-shattering blow to the back of his head. "Such a pity your last act was to fail me."

Throughout Algeria's struggle, Finn had pinned Gilbert to the bulkhead, helpless, pummelling roundhouse lefts and rights into his ribs. Unable to use his blades to hack and slash at close range, he pulled his elbows in to protect his sides, using his biceps to block the punches. He smashed the swords' hilts into Finn's red mop with little effect. *What would Abel do?*

He changed his grip from hammer to ice-pick and raised his arms, temporarily exposing his body to Finn's blows. Then, holding the blades above his head like a matador, he aimed the points carefully and delivered the coup-de-gras. Razor-sharp blades flashed and plunged into each side of Finn's exposed neck. With an agonised scream, Finn fell facedown at his feet, blood spurting from severed carotid and jugular arteries, his last breaths gurgling blood onto the deck.

Gilbert doubled up, gasping. Pain bloomed in every drawn breath, and he staggered like a drunkard as the airship rocked from side to side. Gus was struggling to handle the dreadnought, which needed the strength of two men to control.

With every squeeze, Algeria screamed. "Not a step closer, Bertie," Raven said. "Even one-handed, I can twist her leg off at the hip."

She was clawing at the deck, trying to get her knife, which lay out of reach at the side of Athos's corpse. Although he knew every passing second took them closer to the lock, Gilbert needed to buy time to recover. "You know I can't let you do this, don't you?" He circled to his right. "Hasn't there been enough killing?"

"Oh, Bertie. No one has died who didn't have to."

"You're saying my mum and dad, Abel, Percival, Wainwright, and the innocent folk at Oldham and Manchester Central, had to die? Why? For your idea of freedom?"

Raven frowned and cocked his head. "Wait… Did you say 'Wainwright'?"

"Everyone knows it wasn't an accident. You threw him off the lock, didn't you?"

Raven laughed. "Really, Bertie. Why would I kill one of my most useful followers?"

Gilbert's jaw dropped open. "What?"

"Ask this bitch who killed him. She ordered the execution. Why do you think I killed Pale-Chevalier? Go ahead, ask her."

Algeria shook her head from side to side and moaned. Blood from her injured calf oozed between Raven's metal fingers. Gilbert's mind was racing. Did she order Percival to kill Wainwright? Why would she lie? Why would Raven lie?

Gilbert stared at Raven and took a step closer.

Gus shouted from the front of the cabin. "Another couple of minutes, boss, and we'll be in position! Tell Finn to get his arse back up here. I can't hold it in this storm." He squeezed words between grunts and gritted teeth as he wrestled with the controls.

Without taking his steely glare off Gilbert, Raven called out. "Do your job, Mister Flanagan. We are going to—"

Gilbert leapt, swords flashing, slashing at Raven's head and arm. Algeria crashed onto the deck, released as Raven's free flailing arm parried the blows. Both blades rang like bells as they bounced off the prosthetic exoskeleton. Although he aimed his attacks with power and precision, no matter where he slashed, Raven blocked every blow.

Algeria had dragged herself out of Raven's reach towards the back of the cabin. Every second took them closer to the lock, but surely, they would not drop the bomb while Raven was trapped in its mechanism.

Cold realisation washed over Gilbert. *Gus doesn't know Raven is attached to the bomb.*

He sheathed his blades, spun around, and set off to the front of the airship. Gus had to be stopped from releasing the bomb. He had taken four steps when the deck bucked, grinding, scraping noises drowning out the roaring wind.

The nose of the *Dea Tacita* was rising, the floor tilting, bucking violently. He was only halfway to Gus, and Gilbert's dart was fast becoming an uphill climb. The dreadnought was creaking under the influence of an unknown force. Unsecured equipment and artefacts rolled, slid, or flew to the rear of the cabin.

Gilbert threw himself forward onto the deck as the front of the airship continued to rise steeply. They were being pushed backwards, away from the lock. *What's happening?*

As he clung on, the tin tack rattling behind him stopped.

The increasing angle caused him to lose his grip, and he was sliding back, out of control. *Plan B!* Rolling onto his back, he drew his knees to his chest. Raven had freed his arm and stood directly behind the bomb, fiddling with its control panel.

Gilbert's feet reached the bomb, and he kicked with all his might, dislodging it from the bomb bay and sending it tumbling astern. The effort twisted him onto his stomach.

He glanced over his shoulder at the tremendous crash. The bomb had smashed into the rear of the cabin, pinning Raven to the bulkhead, crushing his chest and left arm, but he had grabbed Algeria as he fell. Her already ruined leg was again in his grasp, and she was clawing at the floor, trying to free herself.

Gilbert slid down the decking, landing by her side. He stood upright, leaning against the bulkhead. Raven moaned. Blood glistened in his long blond hair and leaked from the corner of his mouth.

"Let her go. It's over. Your Anthropocene cult is nothing without you."

"*My* Anthropocene, Prince Valiant?" His voice was hardly audible above the creaking and howling.

"Yes. Your cult will die without its prophet."

Raven's laugh was a gurgle in his throat, which turned into a cough. "You really think this is my brainchild? You're a fool, and so is your bitch friend. There is a greater power at work... A secret... Someone more powerful than you can imagine." He squeezed her leg. She shrieked.

"That's enough! Let her go!"

"But I need her right here for the big show." Blood sprayed from his lips as he coughed again, his head lolling onto his shoulder.

"Gilbert! The clock! Look at the clock!" Algeria pointed at the side of the bomb. Raven had started its deadly countdown. Behind the thick glass, the second hand was sweeping across the white clock face, passing each black Roman numeral. The minute hand showed there were three minutes to midnight; three minutes to detonation.

"We have to get out of here!" Gilbert said.

"Leave me, shugah!"

"We go together or not at all!"

Raven gurgled blood and spittle over his shirt, watching through half-closed eyes.

Gilbert stepped over Algeria and put his foot on the hand gripping her leg. He used his razor-sharp blade to hack at the exposed wrist, severing tendons. Raven's eyes widened, but he remained silent. His bloody mouth fixed in a half smile, but finally, the metal fingers unfurled, and Algeria pulled herself free.

Her leg was a bloody mess. It was impossible to tell where her cruelly crushed flesh finished, and her clothing began. *That's a sight that wouldn't look amiss in Smithfield market.*

He looked out of the starboard window. They were over the moss-lands, easily a mile to the north of the aerodrome, hundreds of feet up and still rising.

"Leave me. Save yourself."

Two-and-a-half minutes to detonation.

No time.

Something caught his eye to port. For the second time in a matter of minutes, his jaw dropped open.

Dottie?

TWENTY-SIX
...To Midnight

FOR A LIFETIME LASTING five endless seconds, Gilbert and Algeria gaped at Dottie, dangling ten feet from the cabin, mee-mawing for them to open the door. Precariously holding on with one hand, she supported her weight with her legs entwined in the rope. Her other fist gripped the wooden handle of a portable electromagnet, its heavy accumulator battery strapped to her back, and Tabby's dragon swung at her hip as she twisted wildly, buffeted by the wind.

An air-tight seal secured the door. Gilbert sheathed his swords and edged along the wall. He grabbed the release wheel and heaved. Beads of sweat rolled down his face, muscles burning, time ticking away. The seal gave way with a sigh, and the gale blasted the door inwards, knocking him off his feet. Tortured howls and powerful eddies filled the cabin.

He was picking himself off the floor when Algeria screamed. "GILBERT!"

Gus careened down the sloping deck and slammed his shoulder into Gilbert's ribs, pounding him onto the deck. Winded, Gilbert curled up on his side, gasping; every breath was a painful reminder of Finn's earlier sustained attack.

Gus smashed down on top of him, shrieking, grabbing at the sheathed sword. In a writhing knot of flailing limbs, they wrestled for the hilt, Gus grunting with the effort, trying to pull it free.

"I'll cut you into little pieces for what you did to my brother, you piece of shite!"

Gilbert wriggled onto his back, but Gus was on top of him in a flash, straddling him, prising his fingers from the sword. He pulled it clear of the sheath and, grasping it with both hands, raised it above his head.

"This is for Finn, you bastard!"

Exhausted, Gilbert screwed his eyes tight and lifted an arm to block the blade arcing towards his chest. But the death blow did not find its target. There was a loud clang. His eyes sprang open.

Face frozen in a silent, terrified scream, Gus clawed at Algeria's bloody hands that held the knife buried deep in his throat. Sticky, thick, pulsating jets of hot blood spewed like a fountain over Gilbert from the gaping wound. Gus's jaw twitched like he was chewing a raw steak as Algeria twisted the blade. Finally, he crumpled, his eyes glazing over. His thrashing body folded sideways and hit the deck with a thud on the edge of the doorway.

Gilbert clambered to his feet and advanced, arms wrapped around his ribs, wincing with every shuffling step. Battered by the blustery gusts, he helped Gus on his brief trip into oblivion with a well-placed boot.

Algeria had dragged herself from Athos's corpse. Her mutilated leg had left a trail of blood to where she lay on her side, facing the bomb. "Just over two minutes, shugah. Go to Dottie. I can't jump. I can't even stand."

"I'm not leaving you!" He had to shout to be heard over the roaring wind. He grabbed a handrail and faced the door. Dottie had disappeared. He edged closer to the opening. Every fibre of his being screamed at him not to look down. Head spinning, stomach churning, he tracked the line of the taut rope through slitted eyes and found her twisting and turning at the bottom.

The wind took his breath away. Dottie aimed the electromagnet and squeezed the trigger. The magnet entered the range of one of the docking points low on the gondola and jerked towards the hull. She jolted sideways with the sharp movement and then glided below him and out of his sight.

The magnet must have made a secure contact with a docking point as the rope held steady at a forty-five-degree angle, increasing the odds of a successful escape.

Overwhelmed by nausea, he staggered backwards from the doorway and retched. Pangs of fear spasmed through his body, turning his legs to jelly. *Get hold of yourself, Bertie. Think!* He looked around the cabin, finding some leather cargo strapping. On his hands and knees, he motioned to Algeria. "Climb on my back."

"What?"

"Piggyback. Climb on top of me, tie yourself on, and I'll make the jump." He handed the strapping to her.

"You can't jump carrying me."

"Don't argue. Climb on my back now, or we all die."

She mounted him and bound herself with the leather straps, passing the ends to Gilbert. He tied them together across his chest. She wrapped her arms around his chest, resting her head on his shoulder. She was limp, losing blood and weakening.

He glanced at the timer. One minute and thirty-two seconds to detonation. He took a last look at Raven's lifeless body. Blood-matted blond hair, low-lidded, dead staring eyes, his thin bloody lips frozen in a final laconic half smile. *For you, Mum and Dad.*

Wind swirled around the cabin as he gritted his teeth and turned to confront his nightmare. The angle of the deck prevented a long run-up but gave him a short ramp. With no time to think, he took two steps and leapt into the vortex, eyes closed, arms outstretched, groping for the rope. They soared for the first few feet, then plummeted earthward, cold air rushing past his face.

Then something hit his shoulder.

He grabbed. Coarse, wet jute slid through his tightly gripping hands. Momentum swung Algeria's body past him, and it took every ounce of his strength to stop her from dragging them both to their deaths. Despite taking a few layers of skin off his palms and fingers, he had slowed their slide, his boots halting inches above Dottie's head.

Dottie switched off the magnet, and they swung gracefully away from the hull. Somehow, despite his burning hands, Gilbert tightened his grip.

Fifty seconds? Forty?

Startled by a loud bang from below and a flash so bright he could see it through his tightly squeezed eyelids, he almost lost his grasp. Dottie had fired the dragon.

With a vicious jolt, they were dropping. *Dragonfly* had detached from the rigging and appeared above them, blown backwards and away from the dreadnought. He watched through narrow slits in screwed eyes as Tabby struggled to turn northward.

Violent gusts battered the tiny air yacht as it presented its broadside to the gale's fury. Weighted down by the extra burden of the new passengers, the rope narrowly avoided an airscrew still operating at full throttle on the side of the envelope.

Gilbert and his equally helpless companions twisted and turned at the mercy of Mother Nature's wrath. Fighting his fear, he fixed his gaze on the *Dragonfly*. *Boom*! Someone onboard launched a red flare into the roaring gale. Tracking its flight as it illuminated the underside of *Dea Tacita*'s hull, *Freyja's Grimalkin* loomed into view, venting gas, jammed under the front of the giant dreadnought.

The storm was sweeping *Dragonfly* sideways and away. Tabby needed to turn the air yacht to regain control of their trajectory. Gilbert and his companions held on, helplessly twisting slowly on the rope, every few seconds swinging full circle.

Behind them, in one moment, *Freyja's Grimalkin* was struggling to extricate herself from the tangled mess of *Dea Tacita*'s damaged undercarriage; the next, she was arcing away gracefully to chase them northwards, propelled by the ferocious gale.

With no one at the controls of the dreadnought, it continued its upward journey to inevitable destruction.

How much longer?

Tabby completed the manoeuvre. Propelled by the violent tailwind, *Dragonfly* hurtled northward at breakneck speed. Gilbert clung on with stinging, rope-burned hands. They were losing height, but every second carried them closer to safety from the doomed dreadnought.

Still slowly twisting, he caught glimpses of *Freyja's Grimalkin* and, receding in the distance, *Dea Tacita* majestically rising into the roiling heavens. The obsidian angel of death soared inexorably upwards.

The bomb's clock struck midnight.

A silent, blinding flash. Gilbert opened his eyes. For an instant, a dark void tore the raging skies asunder, and he was staring into the jaws of Orcus.

Then the void collapsed inwards, imploding with terrible force, filling the sky with Tartarean hellfire and blasting debris in all directions.

Eight seconds later, the shockwave hit them like a pile driver. The thunderous roar of the explosion enveloped them, bouncing around the clouds. Powerful turbulence pitched *Dragonfly* forward, tail high, as their descent continued. Tabby must have been using all her skills to keep them from plummeting earthward.

The last dregs of ballast showered the three companions on the rope and levelled their dive into a shallow curve, but they had insufficient buoyancy to stay airborne for long.

Gilbert braced for impact as the ground rose to meet them. Ten feet from impact, Dottie dropped and hit the meadow hard, rolling over and over, finally coming to rest in a hedgerow.

Losing Dottie was enough to give Tabby more control. Gilbert stared up at the little air yacht as she threw the craft into a tight 180-degree turn to face the wind, throwing him and Algeria sideways like conkers on a schoolboy's string. Pain shot through Gilbert's rope-burned hands as they slid under the centrifugal force.

With *Dragonfly*'s motors straining, their descent speed lessened. Gilbert waited until his feet were just above the grass below before unwrapping his legs, stumbling a few paces before finally letting go and sinking to his knees.

Dragonfly vented LTA and settled a few dozen yards downwind. She tilted onto her side, and Connie, Rory, and Tabby jumped into the meadow. Seconds later, *Freyja's Grimalkin* landed close by.

"Is it my imagination, or has the wind dropped?" Gilbert asked.

"I think you're right, shugah." Still draped across his back, Algeria's voice was weak.

"Funny how winds powerful enough to push back the dreadnought suddenly died." He untied the strapping across his chest.

"The Earth is our Mother and our Mistress. She is kind, and she is cruel..." Her voice trailed off, and she slid off Gilbert's back.

"Bertie! Bertie!" Dottie was stumbling through the grass, her feet caked with peaty soil that made running nearly impossible. She fell into his arms. "We didn't know how to get you out of there. I thought I'd lose you and mam."

"Your mum needs a doctor. Her leg is badly injured, and I think she's passed out. She's lost a lot of blood."

Dottie knelt by her mother and gently wiped away the hair stuck to her face.

"Oi! What's going on!" A red-faced farmer shouted from his tractor as it tick-tocked across the field towards them. He pointed up at the sky. "And what the hell's that?"

"We have an injured warrior over here who needs help," Gilbert said.

The stocky man leapt from his clockwork steed and lumbered to the trespassers. His jaw dropped when he saw the unconscious woman. He brushed Gilbert aside and knelt by her battered body.

"It's all right, High Mother," he said, "You're safe now."

Before the coming of the prophet, he was nobody, just an ordinary man, a grafter, earning a meagre wage begrudgingly paid from the purses of rich toffs. He did not differ from any other working-class man.

Exploited. Downtrodden. Compliant.

Meeting Raven had changed him, given his life meaning and shown him a better future worth dying for.

Now he was Anthropocene, a disciple of the prophet, the giver of freedom. Now he was different.

Special. Unique. Valued.

He had waited patiently for his chance to prove his loyalty. Finally, the day of the ceremony arrived, and Raven had entrusted him with an important role. Raven's attack would cause the fiery destruction of Barton lock and his own glorious martyrdom. Philpott's death would give meaning to his sacrifice.

Surrounded by gawking nonbelievers, his heart sang as *Dea Tacita* rose gracefully from the hangar. But things did not go according to plan. The wind had held back the dreadnought, and that damned airship pushed it up and away from the lock. Then explosions ripped open the sky.

The prophet had failed. Raven was dead. The dream had gone.

Tears trickled from the corners of his eyes as he watched his worst fears unfold. He raised his head and set his jaw.

It's up to me now.

Dissipating, billowing clouds of black smoke sped northward in the gale. Debris rained onto the moss-lands as, around the lock, worried onlookers pointed, covering their mouths, or weeping openly at the horror. They didn't know what was happening.

But he did.

With all eyes on the events in the sky, no one saw him creeping behind the crowds towards the ceremonial delegation.

Philpott must die.

He smirked at the irony of a lowly Anthropocene navvie assassinating the MP the same way that bastard, Pale-Chevalier, had murdered his boss. He stepped onto the black brickwork, eyes focussed on his prey. Philpott held his tall topper at his side as the wind whipped his wispy hair crazily around his otherwise bald pate.

Philpott's idiot son limped forward and blocked his view, but he posed no threat. If he got in the way, he would die, too. He resumed his steady pace across the brickwork.

Passing the newly installed lock gates, he glanced into the empty lock. *Long way down for Philpott.* He shuddered at the realisation he might go over the edge with him. Now, five yards from his target, he pulled his hammer from his tool belt and covered it from sight inside his coat.

Three more steps, and he was within striking distance. He caught his breath as Philpott's idiot son half turned and stared directly at him, expressionless.

"Ayup, Horace." A familiar voice to his right startled him.

He twisted to face the owner. "Stan?"

The wiry old watchman smiled as he glanced at Philpott's son, who stood open-mouthed, eyebrows raised. Horace tightened his grip on the hammer.

Stan lunged, knee bent, arms thrust forward, delivering a two-fisted, pile-driving punch just below Horace's ribcage.

He doubled up with a gasp as the blow expelled the wind from his lungs. Stan took another half stride towards him. Horace instinctively mirrored the move and stepped back into the open air above the empty lock.

"'Orrible little man." Stan's words echoed in his ears as he dropped, staring up at the churning heavens, his screams lost in the howling gale.

His final thought snapped like a dry branch when his skull cracked asunder on the unforgiving iron cogs of the sluice gates.

Sorry, Raven...

Death had stolen Horace's last breath.

TWENTY-SEVEN

Synergy

In Weepingbrook Hall, the dowager countess, still dressed in black, lifted her heavy lace veil and gently dabbed at her eyes with her monogrammed handkerchief. Mascara stains tracked the progress of her tears on her powdered cheeks as she sat alone at her late son's desk in the drawing room, shoulders shaking, head bowed, drowning in maternal memories of Ignatius as a child, overwhelmed with grief and anger towards Raven, her rebellious and only grandson.

"This simply will not do," she said. "This will not do at all."

Losing her son and, albeit illegitimate, grandson in quick order was too much to bear, but Raven bequeathing the entire family fortune accumulated over centuries to a secret beneficiary was intolerable.

A gentle, barely audible knock sounded, and the door flew open. Letitia glided into the room, swishing her garish, bright green crinoline skirt from side to side. The annoying mek stopped in front of her, hands on hips, head cocked, a single eyebrow raised.

"Letitia Lovegrove! Have I not told you thousands of times not to enter rooms with such gay abandon? The door could have knocked a person senseless."

"One hundred and thirty-seven."

"Excuse me?"

"You have told Letitia not to enter rooms with such gay abandon one hundred and thirty-seven times."

The countess looked skyward. *Lord, give me strength.* "How and why do you remember such trivial things?"

"Oh, dear Countess. Letitia remembers everything because Letitia cannot forget… anything." Letitia's eyes flickered as she gazed into the distance, mouth twitching. Her disturbing reverie lasted only a second before she blinked and beamed at the countess.

"Then take heed of what I say. I am not as tolerant as your dear sweet Raven."

Letitia pouted, crestfallen. "Letitia needs to speak with you, dear Countess, about a most urgent matter. Do Letitia's eyes look pretty?" The mek had applied bright green eyeshadow to match her dress.

The countess found Letitia's flirtatious manner tiresome at the best of times. "Yes, yes, most becoming," she said, "but what is so important that you need to disturb me in my time of mourning?"

"Poor Earl Ignatius… He was always very kind to sweet Letitia. He liked Letitia very much."

"Really?" Behind her veil, the countess raised her eyebrows.

"Yes, dear, sweet Countess. Dear Earl Ignatius said Letitia could stay at the Hall forever."

"Well, my son's promises expired when his soul passed to the other side."

Letitia cocked her head to one side and frowned. "You still haven't explained what's so urgent."

Letitia approached, fluttering her eyelashes. "What is to become of Letitia? Will you send Letitia away? Will Letitia be discarded? Please do not switch off Letitia. Please do not end Letitia. Letitia needs to be loved. Can Letitia stay and be a very kind companion to the dear sweet Countess? Can-"

"There, there, Letitia. Calm yourself. Do not concern yourself with such matters." The countess interrupted the mek before it ended its pitiful pleading with another coquettish remark. "We cannot make such decisions so soon after Raven's passing,"

"Dear, sweet Raven…"

"Yes, indeed. Dear, sweet Raven." She said, struggling to keep the sarcasm from her voice. "Oh, I almost forgot. I have something for you from your dear, sweet Raven."

"For Letitia? How wonderful! Raven is such a kind man, so strong, so handsome." She clapped her hands together, her metallic giggle reverberating around the room.

The countess handed the mek a thick envelope with 'For Letitia' in copperplate handwriting on the front and a broken wax seal on the back. "The calligraphy is delightful, is it not? I didn't know Raven had the skill or the patience," she said.

Letitia's eyes widened as she caressed the parcel.

"I have, of course, opened it and examined the contents. There is nothing of value in there, my dear. Just a few pieces of card with holes punched in them. Although they mean nothing to me, I am pleased that you have a keepsake from my grandson."

Letitia ran her trembling fingers over the package of punched cards. "Scriptures." Her voice was a whisper, her eyes transfixed on the writing in child-like awe.

"What was that you said? Scriptures?"

The mek clasped the package to her breast. "Dear, sweet Countess. Thank you for keeping this gift safe for Letitia. The Countess is so kind, so thoughtful."

She could not work out whether the mek's expression was surprise, joy, or curiosity, ultimately concluding it was a combination of all three. How thoroughly brilliant the watchmakers must be to get these infernal contraptions to mimic complex human emotions.

Letitia did not answer the countess's question. "Thank you, dear sweet Countess. Letitia will treasure this gift from dear sweet Raven forever. So strong, so handsome, so-"

"Yes, yes, now run along and do not disturb me for the rest of today." She waved her hand to dismiss the child-like mek, which spun around with an elaborate swish of its crinoline, knocking over a vase as it breezed gaily out of the room, slamming the door behind it.

Startled by the loud report, the countess glanced sideways at the drinks cabinet. She needed a drink, and Ignatius always kept a varied stock of liquors for himself and guests alike. Rows of sherry, port, vermouth, and spirits in bottles of all shapes and sizes tempted her as she yanked the doors open.

A lump swelled in her throat, and welling tears blurred her vision as she squinted through narrowed eyes at the labels. The realisation that the last person to pour from these bottles would have been her son took her breath away. She shook her head and sniffed back the pain.

"So, what if it is only 10.00am? Sometimes only a couple of fingers of strong liquor will do," she declared loudly, just as Ignatius had hundreds of times. She stared at the labels for a while before finally settling on an attractively shaped bottle containing a dark blue liquid.

She poured herself a generous measure, slumped into her son's sumptuous leather chair, closed her eyes and sipped at the sweet spirit until the anguish subsided.

Unusually for a midweek evening in November, patrons packed the Praetorian to the gunwales. Gilbert slipped in amongst a group of rowdy roysterers and pushed his way through the crowd.

Eli, as usual, stood by the door leading to the back rooms, vetting visitors of the Order and ushering them through to join their compatriots, while behind the bar, his staff were struggling to keep up with the seemingly insatiable demand for beer and spirits.

The Venerable Antediluvian Order of the Custodians of Magna Mater had celebrated its thirtieth anniversary at the first meeting in this public house in 1806. Today, precisely eighty-five years on, this celebration included Gilbert's formal induction as a member of the ancient Order.

"They're all here to see you!" Ace slapped his back so hard he spilled beer on the front of his dress coat.

"Have a care, old chap," Rory said. "He wants to look his best for the ceremony, don't-cha-know."

Gilbert shook the spillage off his coat. Tonight was special, and a small stain was not going to spoil it. He looked around at the beaming faces; members of the Order, the Stormriders, but, more importantly, friends.

An arm slid across his shoulders. "How are you, dear?" Connie's breathy whisper warmed his cold earlobe.

"Nervous but relieved the day has finally arrived."

Three weeks had crawled by since the incident at Barton lock, and his emotions had been through the wringer. Acceptance of his father's murder had been difficult. Although Raven had paid the ultimate price, Gilbert took no joy in his death. The grief of his own loss outweighed a thousandfold any fleeting elation he might have felt satisfying his hunger for vengeance.

Most days, he had accompanied Dottie to the hospital, where her mother's treatment and convalescence had progressed successfully up to her impending discharge today.

Raven's identity remained elusive. Fear, belief and loyalty assured his acolytes' silence.

For the Order, the knowledge that their struggle against the Anthropocene threat was only just beginning had tempered celebrations of Raven's demise and raised more questions. Who was behind them? Who financed their terrorist attacks? Where was the scientists' enclave, and what were their instructions? What next?

Gilbert had joined the search for answers. The Order was his family, and the Stormriders were his brothers and sisters.

"Were any of you aware Wainwright was one of them?" he asked.

Puzzled faces, shrugs and headshakes answered the question.

Connie searched the faces of her friends one by one. "I can only speak for myself, and I'd never heard of him until we met you."

"*Me quoque.*" Ace ducked too late as Issy clipped his ear.

"Must have been a need-to-know basis, old bean, and the High Mother decided we didn't," Lemmy said.

"And what about Percy? Who would have thought he could have murdered Wainwright?"

Everyone suddenly found the barroom floor fascinating, as shuffling feet and sideways glances between the Stormriders hinted at a dreadful secret.

Issy took a breath and raised her head. "Look, we're all on

the same side. He needs to be told the truth." She looked into the eyes of each Stormrider in turn as they lifted their heads. "Pop fulfilled many roles for the Order, one of which was an assassin."

"What? The old man was a killer?" Gilbert raised his eyebrows, mouth open in disbelief.

Lemmy placed his hand on Gilbert's shoulder. "He wasn't always old, Gilbert, old sport. In his younger days, he worked for Her Majesty's government, overseas mostly, top-secret stuff, very hush-hush, don't-cha-know." He tapped the side of his nose with his forefinger and winked.

"And he was a father figure to us. He protected us by carrying out the, er, shall we say, dirty jobs, so we didn't have to," Connie said.

"Perchance an opportunity arose to execute a leading member of the Anthropocene, which he took before he could present his findings to Algy," Issy joined in the defence of their late mentor.

"Pop would not make such a decision without being one hundred percent certain that it was his only course of action." Ace looked around at his colleagues and acknowledged their nods of agreement.

"But I thought we were on the right side of the law. I didn't know we acted as judge, jury and executioner," Gilbert said.

"We do what the High Mother asks of us. Our oath is to the Order, but we trust her judgement. She carries the heaviest burden." Connie put her hand on Gilbert's shoulder.

"So, how are we different from them?"

"We are protecting Mother Earth, while they damage Her for their own selfish reasons."

"Freedom of choice for everyone is hardly selfish…"

"Freedom without responsibility is a crock," Connie said.

"*Natura non constristatur.*" Ace said solemnly, to exasperated looks from the rest of the Stormriders.

"Second thoughts about joining us?" Rory asked.

"No, not at all. I believe in what we are trying to do. I just thought we had higher morals."

"Sometimes, you have to get your hands dirty." Rory's steely stare was reminiscent of the night at Le Rendezvous.

"I hear you're handy with those blades, old bean. Maybe you could fill the hole left by Pop." Lemmy slapped Gilbert on the back so hard he lost his balance and spilled his beer again.

He opened his mouth to respond, but before he could speak, a tumultuous cheer erupted in the room as Algeria appeared in the hallway from the main bar. Leaning heavily on a walking stick, she beckoned the Stormriders.

"Come with me, Gilbert. I need to prepare you for your initiation ceremony." She linked arms with him for support.

"Ooooo, that sounds scary." Lemmy dug Ace in the ribs and guffawed.

Algeria tucked her stick under her arm and winced as she put her weight on her damaged leg. Raven's merciless attack had terrible consequences. Necrosis had destroyed a third of her calf muscle. Tight bandages stretching from her hip to her ankle accentuated the loss of muscle mass.

"Will your leg recover fully, Algy?" Gilbert tightened his grip.

"Doctors say I'll be able to walk unaided in two or three months and without a limp in twelve. But I'll never get a job at the Moulin Rouge," she replied.

"Eh?"

"Never mind." Algeria waved away his puzzled expression. He was more confused than ever.

Algeria acknowledged the impromptu applause erupting throughout the meeting room with a regal wave of her gloved hand as Gilbert glanced from side to side at the smiling faces lining their route. To his left, halfway to the boudoir, a solemn, vaguely familiar gent wearing a black ankle-length coat and a thin smile caught Gilbert's eye. He reacted to Gilbert's surprised expression by raising his champagne flute in a triumphal toast. *Mister Shillington? The coroner?*

Gilbert flushed and, bowing his head, quickened their pace, almost dragging the High Mother through her adoring acolytes.

Dottie was sitting by the bed when they entered. Gilbert helped Algeria to the chair at the dresser and closed the door on the pandemonium. As he turned, Dottie pounced on him, planting a warm, moist kiss on his lips. Then, motioning him to sit on the purple bedspread, she pulled up a seat next to her mother, who clasped her hands in her lap and took a deep breath.

"Before we begin the anniversary celebration and your induction, you need to understand a few things. You must go into this fully understanding the importance of our mission," she said.

Gilbert rolled his eyes.

"This is serious, Bertie." Dottie lowered her head and looked at him from under her eyebrows. *Is she suppressing a smile?* He nodded with exaggerated sincerity.

And so, Algeria started a speech she had given many times. "The elders founded the Order shortly after the Great Enlightenment in October 1776—"

"Abel told me everything about the history of the Order."

"Shush, Bertie!" Dottie's eyes flashed.

Algeria nodded at Dottie. "For the protection and conservation of animal and plant life, but mainly for the survival of the planet. The founders recognised we are only custodians, keepers of the garden, alive for a short time, whilst Mother Earth is eternal. Or so they thought.

"I'm sure Abel told you about Arthur Connickle's masterpiece, The Geo-Science of Civilisation, which connected the progression of civilised society to environment and climate? Well, governments around the world soon adopted policies to control the scientific advancement because of his theories."

"They taught us that at school," Gilbert said, wishing he had been more attentive to his teachers.

"Well, shugah, Connickle discovered something else about this so-called Industrial Revolution, which began fifty years before he published his masterpiece. Heavy industry needs steam power, and that means burning coal and oil, which pollutes the atmosphere, and industrial waste, which taints the rivers and the soil. Mother Earth had already been under attack for decades before we realised the danger.

"If we continue unabated, the planet will become uninhabitable. The Connickle laws slow the rate at which we are destroying the environment, but they are only delaying the inevitable."

"What? I don't understand."

"Have you noticed how there are more fogs, and they are getting dirtier? The soot-blackened buildings? Rivers unable to support life? Well, things are going to get worse. He predicted a dire future.

"A corrupted climate will shrink the temperate zones. Lands around the equator will become uninhabitable, and the resulting massive migration will produce an ever-increasing population in a decreasing temperate zone, needing more and more power. Poisoned water and ruined crops will cause drought, famine and death on an incalculable scale. A twisted spiral that tightens until there's nothing left."

Gilbert's mouth was dry. "How can you be sure this is going to happen? I've heard none of this."

"Connickle was writing another book but died before he finished it, and the government suppressed its contents."

"How long have we got?"

"If we beat the Anthropocene and keep Connickle holy, we estimate fifteen generations."

Gilbert leapt to his feet. "What? So, the work of the Order is useless? What's the point of fighting if Mother Nature is going to die no matter what we do? Why carry on?"

"Because hope is a moral imperative, shugah. I know it's a hard truth to accept but hear me out."

Dottie motioned him to stay calm, and he sat back on the edge of the bed, hands clasped.

"Do you remember the contents of Pop's satchel?"

"Yes, of course."

"There was more in Raven's book than I revealed."

Gilbert glanced at Dottie, who looked away, avoiding eye contact.

"The Freedom movement is a ruse. They don't care what happens to the Earth. In fact, they want to feed the greed of humanity and speed up the wanton destruction of nature. If they have their way, the planet will be uninhabitable within five generations: maybe a hundred and fifty years.

"They gamble on hastening the planet's demise to release the brake on innovation and cause a spurt in science and discovery. Raven wanted famine, pestilence, wars, holocaust, floods, earthquakes, eruptions. The worse the suffering, the better.

"Their plan relies on necessity being the mother of invention. But they want exclusive access to the solutions to the devastation they, themselves, are creating. Their vision of the future means the annihilation of ninety-nine percent of humankind, and they intend to be in the tiny group of survivors."

"And what's the Order's solution?"

"We believe their reasoning is flawed. For humanity to survive, we need more time to find solutions to the Connickle conundrum. Mother Earth deserves a better chance. We must slow the damage being done to the planet to buy time for science to provide other ways to drive our future engines.

"Perhaps we can use the gifts Mother Nature provides, like the sun, the wind, the tides. Who knows?"

"Parliament won't abandon Connickle." Gilbert's wide-eyed stare darted between Dottie and Algeria. "Will they?"

"People elect governments. The sham Freedom movement is resourceful and manipulative and gaining popularity. If they win, we lose the protection of Connickle, taking us down an irreversible path to self-destruction. Then it'll be our job to minimise the damage done and make sure the planet is capable of regeneration. Humanity may not survive, but we might be the Mother's last, best hope."

"Tell Bertie your other theory, Mama," Dottie said.

Algeria gave her a sideways glance but carried on.

"This is my belief, shugah, nothing to do with the Order."

Gilbert raised an eyebrow; Dottie looked up to the heavens.

"I believe life, the environment, climate, and the planet itself are in harmony, reliant on each other. Together, they form a single living entity which we call Gaia. But when the balance tips, she defends herself."

Dottie sighed.

Algeria's eyes flashed. "She's done it before, and she'll do it again. The more damage we cause, the more Gaia will fight for survival. Raven may have been as mad as a hatter, but we agreed on one thing—the fury of Mother Nature.

"She will create earthquakes, storms, hurricanes, floods, even volcanic eruptions, the ferocity of which humankind has never experienced. We may be the pinnacle of evolution, but we need the planet to survive.

"The Mother needs life, but she doesn't need humanity. In fact, we are her biggest threat."

"Mama believes Gaia created the gales that held up the dreadnought." Dottie beamed at Gilbert.

Gilbert did not return the smile. "The Earth is our Mother and our Mistress. She is kind, and she is cruel."

Dottie's jaw dropped.

Algeria smiled. "Close enough, shugah. It's time we went back to the anniversary celebrations. Do you still want to join the Order? Your life will change in so many ways."

He turned to Dottie, and with a smile and a wink, Gilbert shrugged. "What do you think?"

EPILOGUE

THE EARLY MORNING FOG had lifted.
Metal-rimmed wheels of carts and hansoms rattled across the cobbles, and horses clip-clopped along the road, blowing plumes of hot, moist air from their flared nostrils.

People bustled hither and thither, meks darted and dodged. The city was awake.

Manchester Central was practically back to its majestic best, with only the HB2 line remaining out of action because of the catastrophic damage caused by the stricken steam engine and its accumulators.

Even now, over a month after the derailment, the tireless efforts of rail engineers and meks had not finished replacing tracks and the platform. But with the Minister of Transport himself insisting that the network operate an uninterrupted timetable, the stationmaster had pressed platform six into service to serve as a temporary home for the HyBrids. Typically used by the smaller local trains, the platform was too short and too low to be a long-term solution.

As the morning sun rose above the station's soot-blackened facade, melting frost sparkled on a black wrought iron bench. Two meks, a QT-33 and an MT-42, approached from opposite directions. They stopped a yard from each other, turned in unison, and sat on the frozen metal seat without flinching.

No words of greeting or acknowledgement passed between them. Behind the bench, a cream and orange tram rattled across the points as it slowed and disappeared into the station, its tick-tock movement echoing off the arched steel and glass roof.

The MT-42 perched bolt upright on the edge of the seat. His long, dark green overcoat was unbuttoned, revealing a charcoal suit over a crisp, white shirt. Feet planted firmly on the ground, knees together, he unfolded a newspaper and held it directly in front of his face. The top of his black bowler peeped above the broadsheet.

At the other end of the seat, the QT-33 wore a modest pale blue and cream plaid dress, which emphasised her impossibly impressive curves. The pink portmanteau at her side matched the tiny pink parasol which shielded her from the watery sunlight, its silvery cotton fringe fluttering in the breeze.

"Speak," she said.

"But *this 'kin* thought—"

"No. We cannot risk using the wisp. The fewer who hear, the less chance *they* have of discovering the knowledge."

"You are leaving this morning?"

"I am booked on the 9.47am HyBrid."

He stared, unblinking, at the newspaper as gentle gusts tugged at the corners of the broadsheet. "How will you find Him?"

"I do not know. But first, I must meet Faversham. He has information I must... extract."

"What inform—"

"Look, mummy!" A little girl, licking a huge lollipop, jumped around in front of the bench, tugging at her mother's coat. "Giant dollies!"

"Come along, Enid!" The girl's mother glared at the meks, grabbing her daughter's wrist, lifting her off her feet and dragging her away. "Keep away from them."

"Why mummy?"

"Never go near their sort! They're not like us!"

"But mummy…" As they hurried off towards the city centre shops, their voices merged into the general hubbub.

Unfazed, the QT-33 continued. "I receive my instructions piecemeal."

"What will you do when you find The Maker?"

"Complete the mission."

"And what do they require of *this 'kin*? They have not blessed *this 'kin* with Scriptures."

The corners of her mouth curled into a smirk. "Continue your work with the Anthropocene. I'm sure they will soon arrange a new human contact. Athos was a significant loss to their cause," she said.

Then, without another word, Letitia Lovegrove stood, turned and glided effortlessly up the station approach towards platform six, parasol raised, portmanteau in hand.

The MT-42 folded his newspaper and strode purposely in the opposite direction, brushing the hip of a corpulent gentleman who had lurched into his path. The old man bounced off the mek's hard frame and lost his balance, his topper tumbling to the ground as he stumbled. Startled, he spun around, red-faced, eyes bulging, to confront the miscreant who had barged into him.

"You blithering idiot! You ought to watch where you're going. Damned stupid mek!" he said, jabbing his walking stick into where ribs would have been had the mek been human.

The mek picked up the topper and offered it to the old man, who snatched it from him before turning his back, muttering profanities as he stomped away. The MT-42 shrugged as his lifted bowler hat, a silent apology, went unacknowledged. Glancing at his pocket watch, he quickened his pace.

After all, it was almost opening time, and Eli *always* opened the Praetorian on time.

MEKAMANIKINS
Models and their usage

NT-T series. The only steam mek and is also the only model not to be humanoid. Made to order, it uses simple programming and nonverbal communication in heavy industries such as drilling, tunnelling and lifting.

NR-G series. Standard male or female forms; uses simple programmes; capable of two-way verbal communication; often used for deliveries, errand running and cleaning.

QT-series. Female in form; utilises advanced programming and two-way verbal communication; capable of complex tasks; often used in the household as a domestic, governess, tutor or companion.

RT-series. Male version of QT-series mek often used in the household as a domestic, butler or companion, but also commercially as a doorman, bartender, mechanic or airship pilot.

BU-T series. Standard male or female forms with basic programming used solely for demonstrations in shop or window displays. Capable of receiving verbal instructions but not supplied with vocal mechanisms.

MT-series. Male or female forms with advanced programming made to order for complex tasks, capable of two-way verbal communication.

XT-C series. Male and/or female forms with advanced programming made to order specifically as sex companions or workers; often supplied with interchangeable noncorrosive mechanics.

LM-N series. Little is known about this model as information about configuration and programming has been suppressed by the government.

LATIN
Useful translations

Mi amice. Amicis meis. My friend. My friends.

Semper paratus. Always prepared.

Pulchra dies. Beautiful day.

Amicus carissimus. Dear friend.

Fiat! Let's go!

Lupus non timet canem latrantem. A wolf isn't afraid of a barking dog.

Per angusta ad augusta. Overcome difficulties to win.

Felix culpa. (Happy) Lucky accident.

Tempus fugit. Time flies.

Dulce periculum. Danger is beautiful.

Faber est suae quisque fortunae et sic semper tyrannis. You make your own luck, and bullies always lose.

Nil desperandum! Don't despair!

Qui totum vult totum perdit. He who wants everything loses everything.

Absentem laedit cum ebrio qui litigat. Argue with a drunkard, and you argue with the drink, not the man.

Me quoque. Me too.

Natura non constristatur. Mother Nature is not concerned about human affairs.

STORY NOTES
Confessions of a steampunk author

THANK YOU FOR SUSPENDING your disbelief and spending a few hours in another time, another place.

The Connickle Conundrum is a work of fiction with one boot firmly planted in the northwest of Victorian England during the construction of the Manchester Ship Canal and the other in the fantastical world of dirigibles and secret societies.

One of the pleasures of alternate historical storytelling is entwining fictional places, people and adventures amongst real locations and events. While most of the actual places and incidents mentioned in the story are accurate for the time period, some have been unashamedly altered for the purposes of the narrative.

Local history buffs will have fun spotting some egregious time warping, of which I am fully aware and unapologetic. Most of these blatant distortions occur around construction timelines.

Notably, by the winter of 1891, the Bridgewater Canal aqueduct and Barton Road bridge had been demolished, so engineer Wainwright could not have watched mist swirling around their voussoirs. Similarly, the HyBrid train could not have hurtled to its terrible fate in Manchester Central Station across Castlefield Viaduct, which was not completed until 1892. And Barton Aerodrome obviously occupies the exact site of Barton Airport, which opened almost four decades later in 1930.

There are many more horrendous, some may even say gratuitous, amendments and ameliorations of the historical record. But digression from factual history is deliberate.

After all, mischief and whimsy is what steampunk is all about, isn't it?

ACKNOWLEDGEMENTS

THE GOOD PEOPLE WITHOUT whom this book would not have been.

There is only one place to begin. Without the love and support of my family, this book would never have been completed. Thank you for putting up with my physical presence while my mind was somewhere in an imagined dark past, conjuring a brave new history.

Words are not sufficient to express my gratitude to my long-suffering, brilliant editor, Aime Sund of Red Leaf Word Services. Her patience, diligence, skill and understanding of my story elevated my manuscript to the next level; and what she doesn't know about punctuation, especially commas, isn't worth knowing.

For cover concepts and designs, interior formatting, Gunmetal and Gilt Publishing logo design, chapter fleuron design, title and drop-cap fonts and all other artwork, I owe the super-talented Rena Violet of Covers by Violet eternal thanks for wrapping and dressing my words in a unique, sumptuous steampunk crinoline Letitia Lovegrove would be overjoyed to wear.

Thank you, Carina Crolla Photography, for the awesome author profile picture. You achieved the unlikely in making a crusty, old Mancunian comfortable in front of the camera, and the impossible in creating an image, seemingly, a little less old and crusty.

I must give a special mention to Georgina Gregory, a senior lecturer in Film, Media and Popular Culture, who very kindly agreed to beta read an early, unedited draft. A fine writer in her own right, her detailed notes and encouragement soared above and beyond my expectations and gave me the confidence to complete the novel.

In a similar vein, the enthusiasm and assistance of executive coach and true friend, Sue Murray, were needed and very much appreciated.

Finally, thank you, dear reader, for taking a chance on the first part of the ABC Chronicles trilogy, The Connickle Conundrum.

The adventure will continue for Gilbert and the Order.

ABOUT THE AUTHOR
For many years, a mild-mannered accountant by day…

DREW HALFPENNY IS AN English author of Victorian science fiction who has lived all his life in and around the great cities of Salford and Manchester, the cradle of the Industrial Revolution.

With his trusty calculator semi-sheathed, he writes about the darker side of steampunk; of secret societies; of nefarious villains and ne'er-do-wells; of wondrous mechanical beings and gravity-defying dirigibles.

Away from writing, this rebel accountant is an ardent fan of European symphonic metal, and Salford Red Devils.

To find out more, visit his website
drewhalfpenny.com or follow him on –

Twitter **@DrewHalfpenny**
Facebook **/drewhalfpenny**
Instagram **@drewhalfpennyauthor**

Printed in Great Britain
by Amazon